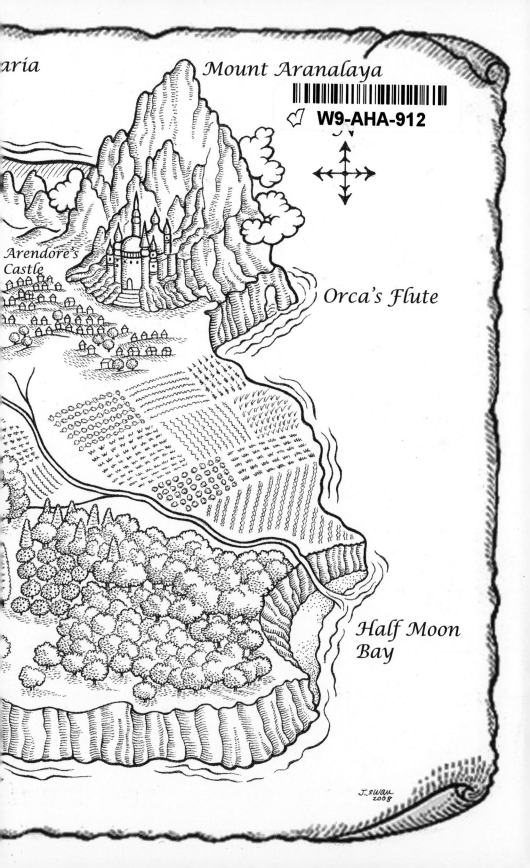

Mount Aranalaya

...aria

W9-AHA-912

Arendore's Castle

Orca's Flute

Half Moon Bay

J. Swan
2008

The Hole in the Sky

The Hole in the Sky

Barbara A. Mahler

Sea Turtle Publishing
Boulder, Colorado USA

THE HOLE IN THE SKY

www.theholeinthesky.net

Text copyright © 2009 by Barbara A. Mahler
Artwork and illustrations copyright © 2009 by Sea Turtle Publishing
All rights reserved. Published in the United States by Sea Turtle Publishing
Sky photo in title © 2007 Kent Judkins Photography
For information, contact
Sea Turtle Publishing
2525 Arapahoe Ave., Suite E4, PMB #145
Boulder, Colorado 80302, USA.
www.seaturtlepublishing.com

Publisher's Cataloging-in-Publication Data
Mahler, Barbara A.
The hole in the sky / Barbara A. Mahler.
p. cm.
ISBN: 978-0-9816764-0-1
1. Loss (Psychology)– Juvenile fiction. 2. Magic– Fiction.
I. Navarrette, Katherine. II. Swan, Joan.
PZ7 .M2765 Ho 2009
813–dc22   2008924912

10 9 8 7 6 5 4 3 2 1
Printed in Hong Kong
First Edition

Publisher's notes:
No part of this book may be used or reproduced in any manner whatsoever without prior written permission, except in the case of brief quotations embodied in critical articles and reviews without written permission from the publisher.

This book is a work of fiction. Names, characters, places, and incidents are either a product of the author's imagination or are used fictitiously, and any resemblance to actual persons, living or dead, business establishments, events, or locales is entirely coincidental.

We are concerned about the impact that the manufacture of this book has on the forests of the world and the environment. All the wood products used in this book are certified to be from managed forests or are recycled post-consumer waste, to insure the protection of the environment.

FSC
Mixed Sources
Product group from well-managed
forests and other controlled sources
Cert no. BV-COC-874701
www.fsc.org
© 1996 Forest Stewardship Council

To all lovers of peace

Table of Contents

Illustrations

The Artists

KN   Katherine Navarette
JS   Joan Swan

"It takes great courage to dream when you think you have lost everything."

Netri

Prologue • Long Long Ago

Morning mist swirled around Queen Rhiana as she rode her mare through the ancient limba forest. She stopped for a moment, losing herself in the harmonies of their tree-songs, but the ache in her heart drove her on. She urged her horse forward, deeper and deeper into the forest, until the trail abruptly ended in a mass of prickly bushes beneath the towering trees. She dismounted her horse and circled the trees, looking for the cottage, but found nothing. She searched again and again until, dizzy with despair, she crumpled to her knees, too spent even to cry.

Minutes passed as dampness seeped into Rhiana's clothes. She shivered, chilled to the bone, but was unable to turn back and face the emptiness in her heart.

Cre-e-e-ak

"Greetings, my queen." A woman's voice spoke, muffled.

Startled, Queen Rhiana bolted upright and turned in a tight circle, searching for the woman. "Who speaks to me?"

A thick wall of vines parted and a cloaked figure stepped forward out of the shadows.

"Please allow me to introduce myself," the woman continued. "I am Zella, from the ancient tribe of Zaren."

A crow cawed three times in the dense branches above.

"But – how? Forgive me. I am Queen Rhiana, wife of King Muraten."

"It is a great honor, Queen Rhiana, for you to grace my home with your presence." Zella bowed and continued, "Last night I foresaw that you would be visiting."

A voice deep inside Rhiana cried, "Turn! Run away, run away!" But the queen had heard rumors of the seer's power. Surely finding her was a sign that she had been right to come.

"Thank you, Zella," the queen said softly. "Please, I..." she hesitated and then, with tears bursting from her eyes, implored, "I need your help."

"Yes, my queen. I have seen your river of tears. I will try to help," Zella answered, almost kindly. "But you must pay," she added, "and there are no guarantees."

"I understand," Rhiana sighed, lifting the basket she carried over her arm. "I brought gifts for you."

"Then, please, come inside."

Zella held the vines to one side revealing an open door. Dim lamplight flickered from two windows within a wall of ivy. It took Rhiana a moment to make out the roof and sides of the small cottage built close to a massive tree. Vines hung like curtains from overhanging branches. They crept and clung to the trunk and the entire building.

Queen Rhiana entered and breathed deeply, willing her tears to stop. Inside, lush carpets covered the floor and velvet cushions surrounded a low table, where light from a silver lamp danced and swayed, its every motion reflected on the surface of a crystal ball. Zella pulled back her cloak and her golden hair shimmered in the light. Rhiana had expected to find a shriveled old woman, but to her surprise the seer was beautiful, with dark glimmering eyes and high cheekbones, full lips and ivory skin.

Eager now for the seer's help, Queen Rhiana reached into her basket.

"I brought these for you in payment," she said hurriedly, pulling items from the basket in handfuls, "The finest silks, sweet treats and a beautiful diamond." Rhiana carefully handed the jewel to Zella. The seer held the jewel to the light and admired its fiery sparkle. After a moment, the hint of a smile passed across her face.

"Thank you, Rhiana," she said. "It is beautiful. We will see if it is enough."

Zella placed the diamond on a table laden with offerings. Rhiana dared hope that Zella would help, but she had heard that the seer expected a surprisingly large bag of wheat from a farmer. What would she require from a queen? Rhiana's hand trembled as she pushed the red curls of her hair from her face.

"Please, my queen, sit – sit. I will look into my ball and see if there is anything I can do for you."

Sitting in a cross-legged position, Rhiana glanced down and noticed her white silk nightdress, spattered brown and green from riding through the forest, and she flushed with embarrassment. What had she been thinking, leaving the castle barefoot, still dressed in her nightclothes? She desperately hoped that she hadn't brought shame on her husband, the King. Lost in grief since her baby's stillborn birth, Rhiana often forgot to dress or eat, and sometimes found herself wandering from place to place without really knowing where she was going or how she had arrived. Rhiana searched for some sign of judgment from Zella – a smirk or a look of pity – but the seer simply stared deep into the violet crystal ball that seemed to float before her.

Zella released her thoughts, allowing them to drift like a rudderless sailboat. Gazing inside the crystal, she saw a translucent sack hanging from the branch of a tall tree. Mystified by the vision, she frowned.

"What is it? What do you see?" Rhiana asked overcome with anxiety.

Zella raised her hand, motioning for silence, and continued to float through her vision. Time contracted inside the crystal ball. Months became fleeting seconds. One moment, the sack wafted weightless in the breeze and the next the contents blossomed, causing the sack to expand and jiggle like a balloon full of water. Breath by breath the sack swelled larger and heavier, until the branch from which it hung bent close to the stream below. Finally, the cocoon dipped into the moving waters and melted away, leaving behind a baby cradled on a large leaf. An infant girl with hair the color of persimmons opened her bright blue eyes and smiled. One eye filled the crystal ball, blinked, and then, like a popping bubble, the vision disappeared. Zella looked up at Rhiana's hair and blue eyes – the same eyes she had just seen in the crystal ball – and realized the baby now sat before her as a grown woman. It was Queen Rhiana.

After remaining silent for a few moments, slowly waking back into the realm where Queen Rhiana sat before her, Zella shook her head.

"You are a stranger here. I am afraid that what you want is impossible. You were not born from a human. You are not human. You cannot give birth to a human."

Rhiana's hands gripped the table. She shook her head. "I am human *now*. You simply must help me." Accustomed to being treasured by her husband, the king of the land, and to being obeyed, words tumbled from Rhiana's mouth. "You must look again. I was once a Butterfly Woman, but I made my choice when I married the king. My midwife has told me my body is now human and I have everything I need to carry a human child. You must find a solution."

The seer looked down, shrouding her irritation in a mask of humility. Queen Rhiana's tone had burned away the sympathy Zella felt only moments before. Zella took orders from no one, not even the queen. Still, she bowed her head. "As you wish – I will look again. Still, there is no guarantee."

A familiar image recurred – Zella's own future daughter, a girl with light blonde hair, stood to marry a handsome prince, the beloved son of the Rugu king. He was destined to be a cruel and violent man. Zella ached for the girl, the daughter that she would one day carry in her belly. Then a new image appeared in the ball – two girls giggled, holding hands. One was older, with brilliant red hair, while the other was younger and blonde. The seer recognized the blonde child as her own. In the vision, Queen Rhiana called out for her daughter, and the red-haired child turned. Zella's eyes darted from the crystal ball, and for a brief moment she stared hard into Rhiana's. *Could it be?* She paused. *Yes, of course. This was perfect.*

Feeling naked, as if Zella knew all of her darkest secrets, Rhiana pleaded.

"Please, Zella, what do you see?"

"If I am to help you, it will cost you no less than everything."

"I, I can bring more jewels – or..."

A note of humility returned to Queen Rhiana's voice, but Zella felt no empathy for the queen. It was Zella's daughter who, more than anyone, truly needed her compassion and protection.

"Thank you, Your Highness," she said coldly. "Your diamond is indeed beautiful, but I am afraid there is something else that I require – something far more precious."

"I ... I," the queen stammered, "What is it?"

"In one year I will carry a baby girl in my womb. I see that her destiny is to marry the prince of the Rugu tribe. If you offer your first-born to wed him in my daughter's place, then and only then can I change your future and the future of the House of Muraten."

Although dizzy from the stifling heat and the smoke of incense wafting through the air, Queen Rhiana lost none of her wit. Her throat tightened as she whispered, "Why is it you do not want your daughter to marry this man?"

"Please do not be afraid for your daughter," Zella smiled. "A different boy is better for my child. We are commoners and do not know the ways of royalty. I have seen again and again the Rugu king building an army and defeating your husband in battle. If you marry your first-born to the Rugu prince, your world could have peace, and you will have time for many babies. Do you understand?"

"But how could I promise my daughter to the Rugu prince? The Rugus are my husband's mortal enemies — How could I begin to convince Muraten?"

"My queen, just think of the opportunity before you. You can have a child and you can bring peace to your people with this promise. If you accept my offer, I will help you. Otherwise, there is nothing I can do for you."

"Can you show me the man whom my daughter would marry?"

"Yes." Zella lifted the crystal and placed it on the flat of her palm. "Look inside the ball."

Within the violet crystal, a smiling young boy with raven hair and pale green eyes threw an apple up and down in the air.

"Is that the Rugu prince?" Rhiana asked, charmed.

"Yes."

Zella covered the crystal with her other hand and placed it on its wooden stand before Queen Rhiana looked farther – before she had time to witness the cruel images of the future filling the ball.

Rhiana watched the shadow of a frown cross the seer's face. "What ... what is it that you see now, Zella?"

"Nothing that concerns you. Many images dance through my ball. The dear boy is the one who would marry your daughter."

"You can see my daughter?" Rhiana grew excited, wanting a glimpse for herself.

"Not now, but yes – she has appeared in my ball. She is a beautiful red-haired girl, like you."

"Oh, please let me see her!" Rhiana implored, excitement bursting in her heart. "Let me see my baby."

Zella peered inside the ball and shook her head. "I am afraid she is not to be seen at this time, but I have seen her and she is beautiful. Have you a name for your child?"

Rhiana imagined the laughing face of her future child. "Yes," she said without hesitating. "Her name will be Gwenilda, like my mother. What about your child, Zella?" she asked a little shyly.

"My girl will be named after my grandmamma. Her name will be Zarenda." Both women smiled at each other in a moment of shared anticipation.

Aching to hold her baby, Rhiana had but one choice. She agreed to Zella's conditions.

"It shall be done," Rhiana said, bowing her head.

"Very well, then," Zella said brusquely. "I have medicine to help you conceive. You must cook these herbs and, on the night the moon is full, you will make an offering. Plant a sapling under the light of the moon. Drink one cup for yourself and pour the remainder on the tree."

Zella walked to a corner of the room lined with jars of herbs and spices. Opening jar after jar, she selected certain herbs and dried insects, piling them on a sheet of light blue paper. Folding it with practiced hands, Zella fashioned a small envelope and tied it tightly closed with a red silk ribbon.

Rhiana stood and bowed. Accepting the package, she held it to her breast.

"Please, please let me have a healthy baby," she whispered. The musty smell of dried herbs suddenly made her feel ill.

"Does the king know you are here?" Zella asked abruptly.

"No, no, he must not know," Rhiana implored.

"You are correct." The seer's voice was suddenly cold. "This matter is private, my queen. Remember our sacred agreement – you are bound by your word. Do you promise?"

Rhiana looked down. Inside, her heart was tormented with doubt and worry but, more than anything, she wanted a baby. "I promise," she whispered.

"Understand this, then. If your girl does not marry the Rugu prince, you will bring a curse on the King's family. It will be the beginning of the end. The curse will not be broken until King Grule's descendants secure a red-haired girl from the House of Muraten."

Clutching the blue envelope in her hand, Queen Rhiana nodded and hurried from Zella's cottage.

Zella watched Queen Rhiana's back disappear into the forest.

"Krakaw, Krakaw!" She cried, deep in her throat.

A huge crow flew into her home.

"Write a letter to the Rugu king," she commanded. Zella, who was unable to read or write, lay out parchment and a bottle of ink for the bird.

Krakaw took great pride in his penmanship. He dipped his claw into the ink and formed each letter into a work of art.

> *Dear King Grule,*
> *I have some information that could greatly increase your power*
> *in this land. It concerns King Muraten's Queen, Rhiana. If you*
> *would like to learn more, please send a bag of gold.*
> *To a prosperous future,*
> *Zella*

Krakaw added his own postscript.

> *P.S. Make sure no harm comes to my crow.*

"I promise much gold, Krakaw, and..." the seer hesitated, then held up Rhiana's diamond in the lamplight, watching it sparkle. "When Rhiana's daughter marries the Rugu prince, this diamond will be yours."

Excitement filled Krakaw's breast. He puffed up his feathers, crowing "*Caw!* I promise to help you."

"This is the most important job of all. It will make us rich, and it will protect my daughter. I am tying the letter to your leg. Will you still be able to fly like this?" Zella asked.

"*Caw, caw,*" Krakaw replied affirmatively.

She opened the door and motioned with her hand.

Krakaw pumped his wings, exiting and then flying higher. His black feathers flashed blue in the sunlight high above the trees. A strong offshore wind and the motion of Krakaw's wings carried him swiftly toward King Grule's castle to the northwest. Almost weightless in the strong breeze, Krakaw drew his limbs close to his body, careful not to drop the letter into the blue-green forest far below.

PART ONE
Promises

Chapter One · Kaela

"Come on, Shawn. You can do it!" Kaela Neuleaf cheered under her breath as her cousin approached the rope climb.

Shawn squinted towards the ceiling, pushed his glasses up his nose, jumped high and clutched the heavy rope between his hands. He swayed, struggling to secure a grip with his legs, but lost his hold and dropped back to the ground.

"You can do it, Shawn!" Kaela yelled.

He tried again, and successfully clenched the rope between his skinny legs and hands, and slowly began to inch his way up, hand-over-hand.

"What a loser!" Just behind Kaela, Stephanie Rickenbacker, the ultimate popular girl, snickered to her friends. "Just look at him! He'll never make it."

Kaela pretended not to hear, and kept her eyes glued on her cousin. She knew he'd been practicing for days and clung to the possibility that this time he'd make it all the way to the ceiling. This time, they would show the other kids they weren't losers. This time, maybe their luck would change for good. Shawn continued climbing higher, but then stopped halfway up and closed his eyes. His face, pink from the exertion, alarmingly paled to a light shade of green.

"Hey, nerd, what'cha doin'?" Stephanie yelled.

"Nerd, nerd, nerd!" Her followers chorused.

Kaela bit her lip and ignored the irritation churning inside her. She refused to give in to her anger – Shawn needed her. She focused in on her cousin's closed eyes, willing him to move up higher again.

But instead, Shawn looked down at Kaela, shaking his head.

"Shawn, you're doing great!" Kaela yelled, giving him the thumbs-up sign. "Come on, just a little farther."

He glanced up toward the ceiling and, once again, shook his head.

"Come on, Shawn!" Kaela shouted, desperate.

Shawn refused a final time, and then slowly made his way down the rope to the safety of the ground.

"You did great, Shawn!" Kaela cheered again, trying to reassure her cousin.

Stephanie giggled. "Loser," she hissed, right into Kaela's ear, and then turned and high-fived the boy next to her.

Flushed with anger, Kaela whirled toward Stephanie. "Just leave him alone," she demanded, gritting her teeth.

"Just leave him alone," Stephanie mocked.

"Drop it, Stephanie!" Kaela spun around to face Stephanie, clenching and unclenching her fists.

"Oh, does the poor baby need his mama to protect him?" Stephanie sneered.

A chorus of jeers rose at Kaela's expense.

"Stop it!" Kaela yelled.

"Oh, poor red-haired mamma. Look, here comes your baby *loser*." Stephanie said, loud enough for Shawn to hear. A pained look flashed across his brown eyes.

It was one thing for Stephanie to torture Kaela, but it drove Kaela over the edge when they tormented her cousin. Before Kaela could stop, her hands flew up and she pushed Stephanie. Stephanie shrieked and the gym teacher turned from across the gymnasium just as Stephanie fell. Ms. Halsey, the gym teacher, ran over to them, scowling.

"What is going on with you two? You know we absolutely do not tolerate that kind of behavior in this school. What happened here?" Ms. Halsey asked sharply.

"It's like, we were just joking around when Kaela, like, comes over and just pushes me for no reason." Stephanie simpered, forcing a tear down her flawless face. "That hurt."

"Liar!" Kaela said loudly, trying to speak over Stephanie. "They were teasing Shawn."

In the background, Kaela heard the din of other kids' voices, including Shawn, yelling out what they thought had just taken place.

"Stop. Everyone stop." Ms. Halsey said, putting up her hand. She looked back and forth between Kaela and Stephanie in the sudden quiet. "That's enough. Stephanie, go stand by the bleachers, and Kaela, I want you to go to my office. I'll be with you in a minute."

"But Ms. Halsey..." Kaela tried to explain.

"Kaela – go. Now." Everyone in the gymnasium stood, gaping at the commotion, until Ms. Halsey spoke again. "Carry on," she said, firmly. "Get back to your rotations."

Red-faced and fuming, Kaela turned on her heels and walked away. Certain everyone was still staring at her, Kaela glanced over her shoulder and saw the teacher nodding sympathetically as Stephanie sobbed.

"Why is Stephanie such a monster?" Kaela scowled, retreating to the teacher's office.

Kaela gazed out the window and, bit-by-bit, her outrage ebbed. Across the soccer field a row of trees dressed in oranges and reds danced in the wind, waving their arms as if beckoning to her. She imagined climbing to the highest branch of the tallest tree, just above the clouds. Maybe if she could poke her finger through the sky...

"So, Kaela..." Ms. Halsey began as she entered the small room.

"Yes, Ms. Halsey?"

"You know I think highly of you. You have so much potential, and I don't want you to throw it away by losing your temper."

"But, Ms. Halsey..."

"Please let me finish. I'm only looking out for your own good. I know that you've had a hard time..."

Kaela half-listened to the lecture, but the clouds outside drew her attention. They gathered into a dark mass, blocking the sun, chased by the rumbling of thunder. She waited for the downpour to begin, but the clouds parted, and a golden sunray escaped instead.

"Have you heard anything I've just said?" Ms. Halsey said with a note of irritation.

"Um, yes," Kaela stammered. "Um, I think it might rain."

"I don't know what we're going to do with you. I'm afraid I have no choice – obviously I can't get through to you. I'm sending you to see the principal. Change your clothes and go to Mr. Jones' office."

"But—"

"Please don't argue. Just get ready and go."

Kaela searched Ms. Halsey's face for some sign of understanding or mercy. Instead, her teacher shook her head and pointed to the door.

After changing back into a t-shirt and jeans, Kaela peered at herself in the mirror. Even though she brushed her long red hair smooth just before class, it had returned to its wild nature, tangling and curling into unruly knots. The mascara she put on earlier no longer accented her blue eyes. Instead, it settled into a black smudge on her lower eyelids.

Kaela pouted her lips, swept her hair back and mocked the voice of an announcer. "And here we have the world famous star, who, like only a small handful before her, needs only one name. The one, the only – Kaela! Trend-setter extraordinaire." She smacked her lips together and blew an exaggerated kiss, then sighed and dabbed at her eyelids with the corner of her t-shirt.

"Dream on..." she muttered. "I wish something good ... something magical would happen in my life."

Suddenly something flashed behind her in the mirror. She spun around, certain she'd seen a small boy run across the room.

"Hey, hello?" Kaela called. "Is someone there?" But there was no response. Kaela combed the rows of lockers, but didn't see anyone. "Hello? I'm just trying to help." Still, no one appeared.

A whiff of a lovely aroma stopped Kaela in her path. It wasn't the usual locker-room odor of armpits and sweaty feet. Instead, it smelled moist and fresh, like ocean air. What could it be? She turned around, and just behind her something softly gleamed from the cement floor. Kaela knelt down and found a seashell resting on a pile of fine white sand.

Kaela tentatively touched the shell where it lay, then couldn't resist cradling the spiral which was no bigger than her thumb. With her index finger, she traced the winding ridges around and around the shell. In shape, it resembled a conch shell she once found by the seashore, but in other ways there was something unusual, even otherworldly about it. It sparkled gold, as if set with thousands of tiny jewels, and made the skin on her palm glow with reflected light. Where on earth had it come from? The ocean was at least a thousand miles away.

Kaela held the shell to her ear, closed her eyes, and listened to the sound of waves brushing the sand. Warmth caressed her face like a gentle breeze blowing against her cheek, and a man's voice whispered, "It is time. It is time."

"It's time for you to go to the office," Ms. Halsey said with her arms crossed, audibly tapping her foot.

Kaela's eyes popped open, and she jerked her hand away from her head, with the shell safely wrapped in her fist.

"Why are you sitting on the floor? Mr. Jones is waiting for you."

"I, um, I thought I saw a little kid running through here," Kayla replied lamely.

"Please, Kaela... Get going." Ms. Halsey sighed. "I have to get back to the gymnasium." She walked to the gym entrance and looked back at Kaela. "I better not find you in here..."

"I'm going, I'm going." Kaela stood to leave, but when her teacher was safely out of sight, she opened her hand again and admired the unusual shell. She carefully placed it in her pocket, grabbed her backpack, and shuffled in the direction of principal's office. She thought about the unexpected gift. Maybe it was a good omen. Maybe the principal would say, with a kind look in his eyes, "Oh Kaela, we're so sorry. We've been so wrong about you! You are actually the long lost great-granddaughter of the Queen of..."

The door marked 'Administration' loomed large in front of Kaela, puncturing her day-dream.

The gray-haired secretary stopped typing when Kaela walked through the door. Eyeing Kaela over her wire-rimmed glasses, she said, "I'll let Mr. Jones know you're here. Please have a seat." The secretary pointed. "He'll be a few minutes. He's calling your father."

Why did the stupid principal have to call her dad? Kaela remembered a recent conversation in which her father told her she needed to pull herself together. Well, once again she had blown it. She hated making her father even sadder.

Things turned out pretty much as expected in the principal's office. Kaela tried to pay attention by staring in his direction, but his features blurred and morphed into a creature with flaring nostrils and crossed eyes. When he briefly paused to breathe, Kaela opened her mouth to eke out a defense, but Mr. Jones cleared his throat.

"Ahem," he coughed. "Unfortunately, Kaela, we were unable to contact your father. However, I – er, have this letter that I want you to give him." His chair squeaked as he abruptly stood. Towering above Kaela, the principal passed her the dreaded envelope.

Mr. Jones opened his lips for a few parting blows just as the final bell blared, so that the alarm seemed to erupt from his open mouth. Kaela fled the office before the bell silenced, and folded the envelope over and over into a tiny rectangle as she went to her locker. Then she shoved it into her pocket.

Kaela joined the throngs of kids bolting out the front door and spotted Shawn, who sat on a bench with his hair blowing in the wind. The dark clouds were gone, banished by an unusually warm breeze that propelled her forward.

Weighed down with a heavy backpack, Shawn hurried to Kaela and apologized.

"I'm sorry," he began.

"It was that stupid Stephanie," Kaela interrupted him. "I don't know why she has to be such a jerk. What should I do now? The principal sent home a letter." Kaela walked in long strides, eager to get far away from school.

"I'm not sure." Shawn said, matching her pace. "Do you know what it says?"

"Oh you know, 'Your daughter is a total loser and should probably be sent away to...'"

"Come on, Kaela. It's not that bad." Shawn laughed and patted her half empty backpack, and then frowned. "Maybe you could bring some books home for a change, though."

"Detention. Military School. Juvenile Prison," Kaela spat out, imagining the worst. "Forget it. School is a waste of my time. I'm better off in bed, reading."

"You used to like school, before your mom died." Shawn pulled gently on Kaela's arm, slowing her down. "It's been two years."

"Shawn, don't..." She shrugged off his touch. Talking about her mother was off-limits, even with Shawn.

"I'm sorry, Kaela. I didn't mean... I just want to help." Shawn gestured, at a loss.

"I know. It's okay." Kaela kicked a small pebble along the sidewalk. "I just don't understand why some kids get everything and the rest of us get nothing."

"Everyone's got problems, Kaela."

"Not Stephanie. She's mean, but she's still popular, and her face is perfect and her clothes are perfect." Kaela imagined Stephanie swelling and puffing up like a Thanksgiving Day balloon and floating away until she was nothing but a dark speck in the sky.

"Kaela, why do you care? You're way nicer than her," Shawn said, trying to comfort his cousin.

"Then why aren't I popular? Why don't boys want to be with *me?*"

"I'm a boy. I like being with you."

"Not like that, Shawn. Geez. You know what I mean. The popular kids are like school royalty, and the rest of us just have to bow down and lick their toes, or get sent home with a letter."

"Well, there's good royalty and there's bad royalty."

The warm wind intensified and whistled through the trees. Orange and gold leaves fluttered to the ground around them.

"I suppose you're right." Kaela stomped on one dried leaf after another, and then looked at her cousin. "Shawn, you know you could have made it all the way. You were doing great."

"Please, Kaela, don't." Shawn's cheeks flushed. He looked straight ahead, unhappy that Kaela had turned the conversation around.

"I'm just trying to help. I've told you again and again, if you don't want the kids to pick on you, you have to try to fit in."

"Oh, yeah, and you're so good at that." Shawn scoffed, and then saw the look on her face. "Not everyone wants to fit in, you know."

"Shawn..." Kaela scolded, but it was true. Shawn had his own way of doing things. In fifth grade he decided to read the entire encyclopedia. He made no effort to be "cool". Instead, he dressed in flannel shirts softened from endless washings, and insisted on cutting his own brown hair in a chopped-up mess, covering the oddly-shaped birthmark on the back of his neck.

Silent for a few minutes, Kaela frowned as she struggled to understand the mishaps of the day. She turned to her cousin. "Maybe I'm cursed or something."

"Cursed?" Shawn's eyebrows knitted together, "Like someone put a spell on you?"

"Yes, yes – think about it. Nothing I do ever turns out right."

"That's not true. You help me, and other kids too. You stand up to bullies. That seems like a really right thing to do. It just gets you in trouble a lot."

Comforted by his words, Kaela gave Shawn a small smile. When they reached her house, an old repainted brick building, Shawn stood on the front porch while Kaela reached behind a thick growth of ivy for the key. A colony of crows cawed in the trees around them, sharing tales of their day.

After opening the door, Kaela and Shawn threw their backpacks on the floor by the stairs, kicked off their shoes and marched through the living room toward the kitchen.

When she was younger, Kaela loved to bring kids to her house and watch their eyes widen with wonder at the sight of the bright mural that covered the living room wall. Behind the threadbare velvet couch, her mother had painted a wide, gnarled tree that grew all the way to the upper edge of the wall. The leafy branches arched onto the adjoining walls and covered half of the ceiling. Families of squirrels and birds nestled in the tree's branches, and one lone white bird painted on the ceiling flew toward the windows that faced the front yard. But, embarrassed by the now shabby room, filled with mismatched furniture and the clutter and dust that were now always present in her home, Kaela preferred to ignore her surroundings.

Though the house had a large formal dining room with an elegant wood table and matching chairs, Kaela and her father always sat at the old pine table in the kitchen at the back of the house. Like the living room, the kitchen was still filled with her mother's touch. A huge painted sun with yellow and orange rays surrounded the simple ceiling fixture.

Kaela yanked open the refrigerator door and shuffled through box after box of Styrofoam "to-go" containers. "Hey, I'm supposed to throw out the old food. Maybe you can help me while I look for something to eat."

"Sure, I guess."

With her head still in the fridge, Kaela passed Shawn a box that exuded a frighteningly pungent odor. "Smell this and tell me if it's still good," she said.

"Smell it yourself!" Shawn relented, however, and unfastened the box of Chinese noodles. Instantly a rotten, garlicky odor filled the kitchen. Shawn dumped the box in the trash, wrapped his fingers around his neck and fell to his knees with his tongue dangling from his mouth.

"Ga-a-a!" He cried, "I-I-I'm pois-s-s-o-n-ned!"

Kaela turned around and glanced at her cousin.

"It wasn't *that* bad," she scoffed. She felt around inside the fridge. "Umm... I'm thirsty. Oo! Orange juice." She plucked the carton from the fridge and leaned her head back with her eyes closed. The sweet juice ran down her throat, all the way to her stomach, in big, satisfying gulps. Unable to resist, Shawn tickled her in the ribs. Orange juice mixed with spit shot from Kaela's nose and mouth. She coughed and wiped her mouth with a towel, then shoved her cousin. "Oh! Very funny, loser."

"You had it coming." Shawn teased.

"Whatever." Kaela returned to scavenging in the fridge and pulled out a large flat box. "I forgot about this. We can have pizza,"

"Does it have any meat on it?" Shawn asked.

"Jeez, don't you think I know you're a vegetarian by now? It's just cheese and tomato."

"Okay, okay. Give me a couple of slices, and I'll heat them up."

The front door creaked just as the microwave beeped. Kaela grabbed a piece of pizza.

"Who could that be?" She muttered. "Dad always works late on Thursdays." Kaela stretched the warm mozzarella cheese and tore off a large bite as she walked into the living room, mumbling as she chewed. "Mello? M'anyone home?"

The door stood wide open, but there was no one in the room. Puzzled, Kaela stuck her head outside to look for her father's car in the driveway. Dry leaves rustled in the breeze, but there was no car. She started to close the door, but then stuck her head back out and sniffed a few times. Moist air filled her nostrils, suffused with the aroma of a humid sea breeze. She shivered involuntarily. "It must have been the wind," she said to a large crow that perched nearby, watching her with beady eyes. This time, she slammed the door hard and made sure to lock it securely.

When she walked back into the kitchen, the neighbor's striped orange cat looked up from Shawn's lap. "Was that your dad?" Shawn asked.

"Nope, no one was there," Kaela said, looking toward the living room, "But there's something strange going on..."

"Tiger must have pushed the door open." Staring into the cat's eyes, Shawn asked, "Did you do it, Tiger?"

The cat mewed softly and stretched as Shawn stroked his thick fur.

Kaela absentmindedly patted the cat's head. "Tiger's not supposed to be in the house."

"He's not doing anything wrong." Shawn snuggled the cat against his chest.

"You know, my dad's allergies..." Kaela gestured vaguely.

"Tiger, you're not gonna shed or anything, are you?" Shawn asked the cat.

The cat rolled onto his back, baring his soft white belly, stretching his legs and opening his mouth in a huge yawn.

"Shawn, there's something weird going on," Kaela said, choosing to ignore the cat. "The air smelled strange, like when we go to the ocean."

"Come on," Shawn scoffed.

"I swear! It smelled just like the beach," she mused, staring into space as she realized that it was the same aroma that she had sniffed in the locker room. "Wait, I've got something to show you, something special." Excited now, Kaela dug in her pocket, past the letter from her principal. She pulled out the sparkling shell and handed it to her cousin.

"Look at this!" She said proudly.

"It's beautiful." Shawn examined the shell, holding it between his thumb and forefinger.

"I know! Hold it up to your ear. Tell me if you hear something."

"What am I listening for?" Shawn asked.

"Just try."

Shawn palmed the shell against his ear. "Maybe there is just the quietest whisper, like waves on the beach."

"And?"

With the shell pressed against his ear, Shawn closed his eyes for a few seconds, and smiled.

"Give it to me." Kaela listened again. "I hear the ocean, but I heard something else, before. Promise me you won't think I'm crazy."

"I promise, I guess," Shawn hesitated.

"When I first found it this afternoon, I'm sure I heard a voice in it."

"Come on, Kaela, that's just your crazy imagination." Shawn looked back at Tiger, rubbing under the cat's chin.

"No, really! It was a beautiful voice, a man's voice. He said 'It is time.'" Kaela paused for a moment, remembering.

"Also," she continued, "just before I found it I'm sure I saw a little kid running through the locker room. The kid disappeared, and then this shell appeared, lying on a pile of sand. I swear it wasn't there before. I think the kid left it for me. I know this sounds crazy, but I think it's magic," Kaela said, speaking quickly so that Shawn wouldn't interrupt her. "When I hold it to my ear, it's like I feel something special. Don't you?" She handed the shell to Shawn again.

"Well, yeah, I guess. I love the sound of the ocean."

"It's more than that. I don't know how to describe it. It's like..."

At that moment, Tiger stood up in Shawn's lap, and arched his back, hissing. The cat leapt across the table, and raced out of the room, chasing something only he could see.

Chapter Two · The Diary

The blur of orange fur shot out of the room with Shawn in pursuit.

"I thought you said he wasn't going to cause any trouble!" Kaela called as she ran after Shawn.

The golden shell twinkled, left behind on the kitchen table alongside the two half-eaten pieces of pizza.

Tiger leapt onto the couch in the front room and scrambled over the back pillows as Shawn ran across the seat cushions. When the cat paused, looking up at the mural's painted tree as if intending to climb into the high branches, Shawn grabbed for his tail. Tiger howled with indignation, then jumped onto the top shelf of a tall bookcase in the corner.

"I told you he wasn't supposed to be in here," Kaela said.

Shawn stepped onto the highest corner of the couch, reaching up towards Tiger, but the cat stood unmoving, except for his twitching whiskers.

"Come on down, Tiger," Shawn pleaded, "No one's going to hurt you."

Tiger stared back at Shawn until Kaela turned to get a stool. The cat took advantage of Kaela's distraction and leapt over their heads. He landed on all fours, running past the stairs, down the hall, and through a crack in a doorway.

Sliding along the slippery wood in her stocking feet, Kaela muttered to herself, "Stupid cat. That's just great. Now he's in Dad's office."

"Chill, Kaela. It's no big deal."

"What do you know about it? You're not allergic."

She pushed open the door, flipped on the overhead light, and looked around the familiar room, searching for the orange cat.

"Boy, this place is a wreck," Shawn said, walking in behind her.

"Yeah, I know. But my dad says he works better this way." Even when her mother was alive this room had the appearance of total chaos. Stacks of files covered the floor and dusty texts crammed the bookshelves that lined the walls of the small office. Tiger sat on a pile of paper strewn across her father's huge wooden desk, in front of a small grouping of framed photos. He licked his front paw, ignoring Kaela and Shawn.

"Okay, Tiger," Shawn cajoled, "you've had your fun. It's time to go, now."

The cat glanced up, cocked his head, and returned to his bath.

"What a weirdo," Kaela muttered.

"Come on, Tiger," Shawn eased forward, and moved the swivel chair out of the way. "That's it. You just stay there. You're not in trouble." When the cat was within arm's reach Shawn tried to grab him, but the quick movement alarmed the cat. Tiger squirmed away, ran across the desk, and knocked over a picture. After scrambling onto the top of a four-drawer file cabinet, he meowed at them loudly.

Kaela picked up the silver frame to set it back upright. She rarely came into her father's office, and when she did, she pointedly ignored the photos. They reminded her too much of how great her life used to be before her mother died.

In the photo, her young parents stood barefoot on a beach, gazing into each other's eyes. Her mother wore a white dress that blew in the breeze and her red hair curled around her face. Her father wore a tuxedo. In the bottom-right corner of the photo were written the words, "I love you. I love you. I love you," in her mother's round, child-like script. Kaela traced the letters slowly with her ring finger. It was her parents' wedding picture.

A familiar lump swelled in Kaela's throat. Her parents looked so young, so unaware of the difficulties they would face. Long ago, they were all happy. Why did everything have to go so wrong? She pulled her eyes away from the image and returned the photo to its exact spot, which was marked by dust and an empty spot on the otherwise cluttered desk.

"Okay, Tiger, that's enough," Kaela said softly.

"*Meo-o-ow.*" The cat yelled back at her, as though he could speak.

Shawn stood below the cat and looked deeply into his eyes.

"Kaela, he's trying to tell us something," Shawn said nervously.

"Oh? I thought I was the one with the crazy imagination." Kaela said sarcastically.

"Really, there's something he wants us to know."

"Come on, Shawn."

Tiger's tail swept back and forth across the top of the file cabinet and another small frame fell to the ground.

Shawn leaned over and picked up the picture. "Look, Kaela," he said, showing it to her. "I never saw this before. I think it's of our dads. They must have been around our age when this was taken."

The two boys in the picture stood with a large telescope between them. They wore glasses and half-closed smiles that couldn't hide the braces on their teeth. Kaela glanced back and forth between the photo and Shawn. "Boy, you really look like your dad," she said.

As Shawn replaced the photo, Kaela caught sight of two other small pictures on top of the file cabinet.

"She was so pretty," Kaela said, tracing the outline of her mother, young and dressed in a cheerleading uniform. Her red hair fell in soft waves, and her shining blue eyes made her joy palpable.

"Yeah," Shawn sighed wistfully.

Kaela rubbed the next framed picture with the edge of her t-shirt, removing a thick veil of dust. As the details of the dirty photo became clear, she noticed something that made her heart pound with excitement. The unusual events of the day gathered together in her mind, like pieces of a puzzle that unexpectedly fit. Could magic really be unfolding? The child, the shell ... maybe the cat really had purposefully led them to these pictures. Flushed with excitement, Kaela said, "I can't believe it. Look at this!"

"What? What do you see?"

"Wait, I need the magnifying glass to make sure. It's in my dad's desk." The drawer of her father's ancient wooden desk was always stuck, so Kaela pulled hard. Crammed inside were pencils, pens, calculators, old keys that didn't open anything, rubber bands, paper clips, and scraps of paper with unidentified phone numbers that all rolled and tumbled together as she yanked the drawer open. Kaela felt around until she located a small magnifying glass, and then held it over the photo.

"Look. Look what my mother's wearing in this one." Kaela and Shawn stood side-by-side with their heads bent over the photo. In the photo, a thin girl with inch-long red hair sat between two teenage boys on the porch swing in front of Kaela's house. Even though it was just a picture, the girl's clear blue eyes seemed to look into Kaela's, as if she had something to tell her daughter. Kaela stared back, wondering whether she might understand her mother's message if she looked hard enough.

"This must have been after she got sick – the first time." Shawn hesitated, careful not to upset Kaela, but continued when she didn't object. "You know, when she was fifteen. There's my dad and your dad on either side of her."

Kaela's mother, Marisa, and Shawn's father were brother and sister. In the picture, her mother leaned against Shawn's dad. On the right, her fingers gently rested on Kaela's father's forearm. Kaela's father gazed with obvious puppy love at his future wife, while she looked directly into the camera.

"Look what she's wearing, Shawn."

Shawn squinted and pointed at the picture. "Her pajamas?"

"No. Look at her neck."

"The necklace?" Shawn took the magnifying glass and examined the photo more carefully. "Is that a butterfly?"

"Yes. A long, long time ago, I tried that necklace on. She told me I could have it when I was old enough."

Kaela remembered the night when, as a small child, she had discovered the necklace. It was evening and her mother was dressing for a party. Her mother's jewelry box sat on her parents' big bed, unattended. While her mother sat in front of her dressing room table applying her makeup, Kaela accidentally pulled the drawer of the jewelry box all the way out, spilling its contents on the comforter. A tiny golden handle poked up from the base of the drawer. Intrigued, Kaela pulled on the handle and found the butterfly-shaped pendant resting in a second velvet-lined drawer.

Shawn touched his cousin's arm. "Kaela. Hello!"

"Huh?" She mumbled, still caught in the past.

"Where are you?"

"Remembering ... there's something about that pendant. Maybe something magic."

"What? I don't understand," Shawn said, trying to pull her back to reality.

"I tried it on when I was little. I pulled it over my head, just like I did with her other necklaces."

The memory was so clear it was as though it had just happened. As soon as the cool crystal was over her head, the wind blew through the trees louder and louder, and the curtains flapped in the breeze. The sound of the crystal drew her in and the room grew fuzzy, like it was fading into the distance.

"I heard singing. It was like the trees were singing. When my mom turned around and saw me wearing the necklace, she stood up and pulled it over my head saying, 'No, don't wear that.' She frightened me and I started to cry."

"Was she afraid you were going to lose it or something?"

"No, it wasn't like that. She pulled the chain over my head and hugged me. Then she said, 'I'm sorry. I'm so sorry for scaring you, but this necklace is magic. You're not old enough for this. When it's time, you will have it – I promise you'll get it when it's time.'"

"That's weird." Shawn said.

"More than weird," Kaela mused.

"Did you ever look for it afterwards?" Shawn asked.

"Yeah, of course. I tried the jewelry box, but it wasn't there anymore."

"Do you know where it is now?" Shawn asked.

"My dad keeps it locked up." A shadow of sadness passed across Kaela's face. "I don't think he'll ever give it to me."

"I don't understand. She said you could have it."

"Dad doesn't believe in magic," Kaela said abruptly. She grimaced and returned to the magnified image. "Shawn, my mother left behind so many mysteries, things I don't understand. I need your help. Maybe Tiger really is trying to show us something."

The cat sat unmoving, like a sphinx, his front legs folded under his body. The white tips of his paws stuck out primly in front of him. Only his tail flicked back and forth as he purred from the file cabinet.

"It must here in this cabinet," Kaela realized with a rush. "The one Tiger's sitting on. Look. The label says 'Marisa'. This drawer must have all my mom's stuff. I just need to get the key."

Kaela felt around under a tray in her dad's desk drawer until she pulled out a silver key.

"Are you sure this is okay?" Shawn asked uneasily. "There must be a reason your dad keeps it locked."

"I don't know – he won't be home for hours, yet. But I think my mom would want me to see this stuff, don't you?" Kaela thought about the voice she had heard in the shell – the man's voice that had told her, "It is time."

"It's not like we're going to hurt anything," Kaela said, unlocking the cabinet.

Kaela quickly rifled through a bunch of manila folders and mumbled, "Not here ... or here ..." She pulled the folders to the front of the drawer, then dug under a stack of papers. "Wait – this is it." She pulled out a red diary and stroked the soft leather, imagining her mother bent over the book, writing in it.

"How do you even know about this?" Shawn asked.

"I came in here once, a few months after Mom died. One day I tried and tried, but I couldn't remember what she looked like. I snuck in here to look at the pictures on Dad's desk." Her mental image of her mother had grown as clouded and vague as the sky outside. "Back then her stuff was sitting on my Dad's desk, but..."

"Kaela..."

"There are strange secrets here. This is the journal she kept when she got sick the first time. I read it before..." Kaela was about to open it when Shawn put his hand on top of hers.

"Kaela, are you sure? I mean, it could make you sad."

"I know, Shawn. But she left so many mysteries behind – big mysteries. I tried to solve it on my own, but I couldn't. And now, well, now it seems like there's something really weird going on, and I need your help." Kaela looked straight into Shawn's eyes, trying to show him how important this was.

"Okay." Shawn nodded. "I'll do what I can."

The book fell open to the final few pages, which were marked with a red ribbon. As a teenager, her mother drew a heart between each entry. Shawn looked over Kaela's shoulder as she read out loud:

May 10
Dear Diary,
    I spend a lot of time by myself these days, so I asked my mom to get my old teddy bear out of the closet, the one with all the fur rubbed off. I threw it in there when I started high school. Now I really miss it. She looked and looked, but she couldn't find it. Stuff has been disappearing from my closet. I don't know what to make of it, because who would steal a teddy bear?

Marisa

♡

May 12
Dear Diary,
    Weird things are definitely happening in my closet. Remember my teddy bear that disappeared? Well now the top of my favorite pajamas vanished and one of my furry slippers is missing.

Marisa

♡

May 17
Dear Diary,
    Last night I dreamed I saw a young girl with blonde curly hair and a billowing white dress standing next to my bed. I think maybe she was an angel. She reached out her hand to me, but I was afraid that if I took it she would take me away forever. It was so real that I actually woke up. When I opened my eyes, I saw a flash of white in my closet and my room smelled like the ocean. Every time I thought about that little girl today, my heart felt full and happy. Maybe I should have gone with her. Maybe she wanted to help me. If you dream something happens and it makes you happy, then does that make it real?

Kaela halted, trying to understand what had happened. Maybe the girl was an angel who had helped Kaela's mother heal when she was fifteen. But why didn't the angel come when Marisa was a grownup, when Kaela needed a mother? Kaela pushed away the thought, and the tide of unbearable sadness and injustice that washed over her. She knew too well that she had to avoid that kind of thinking – it was like entering an endless dark cave with no exit.

"Do you think it was really an angel?" Shawn held the magnifying glass over the word 'angel'.

"I don't know. I don't know. What do you think?" Kaela said quietly, and turned to the next page.

May 20
Dear Diary,
I just want to run away to some place where everything is okay. I know it sounds crazy, but I think maybe there is some kind of secret passageway in my closet. I am determined to find it. I just know there must be one. Stuff keeps disappearing and something really scared me the other day. It felt like my arm went though the floor when I was looking for my slipper.
Marisa
♡

May 21
Dear Diary,
My grandmother came to visit me today. She always told me such amazing stories when I was little that I decided to tell her about all the strange things that have been happening. I thought she would just laugh, but then I told her about the little girl in the dream.
She grew quiet and said, "Marisa, you must promise me when you go through the hole in the sky you will only stay as long as absolutely necessary – then you must come right back."
I told Nana that I didn't understand.

A chill shot through Kaela as she mouthed the words:

> *"It is time, Marisa. It is time. They will help you. I can't tell you any more. Do you promise to come right back?" Nana said.*
> *She looked so serious that I promised I would come right back, but I didn't really know what she was talking about.*
> *Marisa*
> ♡

On the final page, her mother wrote a single line:

> *It was the fire that saved me.*

Kaela closed the book, held it against her heart, and carefully returned it to the exact same place she had retrieved it from. She turned toward Shawn. "What do you think it all means? Why would her grandmother say that?"

"It was probably some kind of make-believe." Shawn sat down in the old wooden swivel chair and spun around a few times. "You know – something to make your mother feel better."

"I don't know." Kaela hopped up on the desk and sat cross-legged with her chin in one hand. She considered Shawn's idea and shook her head.

"That's kind of a dumb consolation. I mean, Mom didn't even understand what Nana was trying to tell her. Why bother telling her to come right back if it's just a story? That seems like a strange thing to say. It's kind of scary."

"Yeah. And what's all that about the fire?" Shawn asked, thinking.

"Shawn, do you remember the shell?"

"Sure, of course I do," he answered, turning again in the office chair.

"Well, ever since I found it strange things have been happening to me."

"Come on, Kaela. Your mom was really sick – she was confused."

"I swear! When I picked up the shell at school I heard a voice say, 'It is time. It is time.' It's the same thing that my mom's Nana said!"

"Okay, fine." Shawn said, shrugging. "What do you think it's time *for?*"

"I don't know, Shawn. I really don't know. What do you think the hole in the sky is?"

"I've never heard that before. But I do know the feeling," Shawn leaned forward in the chair and his face lit up. "You know, like there is something on the other side..."

"Yeah, like there's a world in the back of the closet or on the other side of the mirror?" Kaela dropped her legs and swung them back and forth. "My room now was Mom's then, and stuff disappears from my closet all the time."

"Well, Kaela, you're pretty messy."

"No, really, Shawn, stuff disappears."

"Did you ever try cleaning out your closet?"

"Yeah, of course! When I first read the diary." While she spoke Kaela picked up the magnifying glass and examined the lines in her palm. "I even used the magnifying glass to see if I could find a little crack or opening in the closet."

"And?" Shawn asked.

"Nothing. Just the wood floor," Kaela said, remembering her disappointment.

"Kaela, it's one thing to pretend ..." Shawn began, but was interrupted when Tiger perked up, stretched, and leapt off the cabinet into his lap. "Ooph, Tiger! Give me some warning," Shawn grunted.

"Think about it, Shawn," Kaela continued. "She was really sick, and then she got better. I never heard anything about a fire, did you? Then she got well. I wonder what happened?"

"Well – was her treatment kind of like going through a fire?"

"I don't know, maybe. But they never called it that." Kaela slid off the desk and turned back to the file cabinet. "Remember the necklace in the picture?"

"Sure."

As she reached into the back of the cabinet, Kaela's mind was filled with the sound of her mother's words, "I'm sorry. I'm so sorry for scaring you, but this necklace is magic. You're not old enough for this. When it's time, you will have it - I promise you'll get it when it's time." Kaela pulled out a small blue box with a gold elastic string wrapped around it.

"Is that..."

"Yes." Kaela rubbed her fingers on the soft velvet box. "I opened it the last time I was in here, but I was too afraid to put the necklace on. I didn't think I was old enough."

Kaela flipped open the lid and held it in front of her cousin. Inside lay a butterfly-shaped pendant, hung from a long silver chain. Cut crystal encased a portion of real butterfly wings, and when she held the pendant up to the light, the translucent wings glowed blue-green.

"It's so beautiful," Shawn said, touching the crystal with his fingertips.

"Kaela, I'm home!" Her dad yelled as the front door slammed.

"Shawn, get Tiger out of here. Quick!" Kaela whispered, staring at the necklace with longing.

Chapter Three · Magic

Kaela gazed at the butterfly, knowing that she had no choice. She shoved the box into the back of the cabinet and pushed the silver lock into the closed position, putting the key back into its hiding place. She slipped into the bathroom next door and flushed the toilet to hide the fact that she'd been in her father's office. Then she ran down the hall to greet her dad with one hand tightly closed behind her back.

"Hi," her father said to Shawn as he flipped through the mail. "How was school?"

"Hello, Uncle Jake. Uhm, Tiger got in somehow. I'm just letting him out." Shawn turned around, opened the door, and whispered in the cat's ear, "Thanks for your help." Tiger stuck his tail straight into the air and meowed softly, then ran home.

Flushed with excitement, Kaela tried to act calm.

"It was okay," she said. "I mean, school was fine." The tips of the butterfly wings dug into her palm, while the envelope with the letter from her principal dug into her jeans, reminding her of her not-so-great day. She wasn't trying to hide the letter from her father because she was afraid. He just looked so worn out from work. It would be better for him to read it later, after he rested.

Kaela loved her father more than anything, but since her mother's death he wore his sadness like a protective cloak, guarding him from anyone who might get too close – and that included Kaela. As a little girl, she thought he was the most handsome man in the world, but now gray hair covered his head and he always looked disheveled. When Kaela looked into his blue eyes, he seemed as though he were in another place entirely. These days he spent most of his time teaching astronomy at the university, grading papers, reading articles, and attending meetings.

Her father smiled, but the dark circles under his eyes exaggerated his weariness.

Kaela stuffed her fists in her pockets, unsure of what to say, while Shawn fiddled with his glasses.

"Shawn, you look a little strange," her father said. "I hope my daughter hasn't been feeding you any of those ancient Chinese noodles."

Shawn and Kaela laughed uncomfortably.

"No. I mean, well, she tried." Shawn's face paled and he held his stomach with both hands as he remembered. "They definitely smelled disgusting."

"I've noticed. It's like a science experiment gone wrong in there. I suppose she fed you the moldy pizza instead," her father said with a twinkle glimmering across his eyes.

"*Moldy* pizza?" Shawn's eyes widened.

"Da-a-a-d." Kaela laughed, relishing the rare moment of fun with her father.

But the moment was brief. Her father's eyes clouded over as though he was once again looking at something far away. He glanced down at the mail again and asked absentmindedly, "What about cleaning out the fridge?"

"I did," she answered quickly, eager for his attention. "I, I started," Kaela's voice faded seeing the glazed look return to her father's eyes. "I promise to finish it later. Well – we better get going." Kaela sighed and she clutched the pendant more tightly, hoping again for some kind of magic. "Come on, Shawn. We've got a lot of work to do." When Shawn didn't budge, Kaela discreetly pinched his arm. "You know, Shawn, the big test."

Shawn blushed. "Oh right, the test, yes sir, we're just here to study for our history test."

Kaela's father waved vaguely to both of them as he turned to the hall. "That's good, kids. Enjoy your studies. I still have papers to grade. I'm going to be in my office, if you need me."

"Well, we're just going to head upstairs." As Kaela and Shawn backed out of the room, Kaela realized that she wouldn't be able to return the pendant that night. She would have to wait until morning, after her dad left for work.

As they raced up the stairs, Shawn asked, "So, are you trying to poison me?"

"My dad was teasing."

"I'm not so sure. My stomach is queasy."

Relieved to enter the safe haven of her room, Kaela sat down on the unmade bed. She still remembered when she was a little girl and her father and mother painted the walls a deep pure blue, like the color of the sky on a clear night after sunset. Her father had pasted glow-in-the-dark stars glued into patterns of actual constellations on the ceiling, while her mother painted sea turtles and multi-colored fish swimming in an open sea along one wall.

"Quick, Shawn, close the door behind you."

"What was your problem down there?" Shawn frowned, rubbing his arm. "Why did you pinch me?" He pushed a pile of clothes off her desk chair, sat down, and examined his upper arm for marks.

"Look, Shawn. I didn't have time to put it back." Kaela unfolded her fingers to reveal the blue-green butterfly on its silver chain. Bright pink indentation marks tingled on Kaela's palm.

"What about your dad?" Shawn raised his eyebrows at her.

"He won't know," Kaela mumbled. "He's too busy working. Besides, I'll return it in the morning. He'll never even know."

"I don't know, Kaela. This is starting to weird me out."

Kaela tried to display a confidence that she did not feel. "What have we got to lose?" she asked. "Either it's magic or it's not."

"Well, then, why don't you put it on?" Shawn goaded.

"Yeah, well, maybe I will." Excited and nervous at the same time, Kaela hesitated. "I just wonder what it's for, you know?"

"Go on." Shawn smiled. "I dare you!"

Despite Shawn's dare, Kaela fiddled with the pendant, holding it up to the light, watching rainbow reflections dance across the wall. "I'm not afraid ... I'm just not sure...."

"Well, then put it on! I double dare you."

"Okay, okay." Kaela exhaled. She stood, closed her eyes, and swung her hand with a flourish to throw the necklace over her head; it settled, warm and heavy, against her breast.

Shawn eyed his cousin for some sign of change. "Well, do you see a hole anywhere? Do you hear singing or anything?"

"No, not really," she replied, plopping back on the bed. Disappointed, Kaela thought for a minute, and brightened with a new idea. She took off the pendant, dangled it in front of Shawn, and dropped it into his hands. "Here. I'll open the window and then you put it on."

Kaela rushed to the window and pushed on the wooden frame. "Okay – now!" She said excitedly as the window creaked open.

"Okay." Shawn pulled the pendant over his head. At that moment, a wind strong enough to blow papers across the floor gusted into the room. Shawn's face paled; he tore the chain from around his head. As he did so, the wind died.

Wide-eyed, Kaela asked, "Wh-a-at ... was that??"

"I heard it, Kaela. I heard the singing!"

"No way! Really? Here ... give it to me." Kaela slipped the chain over her head once more. She waited and tapped her foot, crossed, and uncrossed her arms. Nothing happened.

"Don't you hear singing?" Shawn asked curiously.

"No, I don't, Shawn. Be quiet for a minute," Kaela demanded.

"Maybe it's because I have magic powers. You know, I *can* understand animals," he joked.

"Stop it." Kaela walked up and down the wood floor of her small room, peering under her bed and along the bookshelf, frustrated.

"It was so-o-o cool." Shawn grinned and stepped in front of his cousin. "C'mon, Kaela. Let me try again."

"No, Shawn."

"Come on, Kaela," Shawn persisted.

"I said no. It's mine." Kaela raised her voice.

"Come on. Let me wear it again." Shawn grasped the butterfly, pulling the chain hard against Kaela's neck. "Can't you see that I'm the special one?"

"Ouch! Stop it." Kaela shoved her hand beneath his and pulled the pendant away, jealous that her cousin had heard something and she couldn't. "It was just some kind of fluke. This whole thing is stupid."

Shawn kept reaching for the pendant; Kaela interlocked her right leg around his left and pushed him. He tumbled to the ground, pulling her down with him as they wrestled for control of the pendant. Kaela gained the upper hand and sat on his stomach, clutching the pendant to her chest with one hand and pinning his arms down with her knees. She resisted the urge to punch him. His know-it-all attitude drove her crazy.

Knock ... Knock ... Knock. Kaela heard the sound of a fist tapping wood.

"Is that the door?" Shawn asked, trying to push Kaela off his stomach. "It must be your dad."

Shawn pointed to the door with his left hand and rapped his right knuckle against the floor.

"Oh, very funny." Kaela resisted the urge to punch him again.

"Get off!" Shawn said, kicking and twisting to free himself. "You're crushing me."

"Do you give up?" Kaela demanded.

Knock ... Knock ... Knock.

They both stopped as they heard it.

Knock ... Knock ... Knock.

"Maybe it really is your dad," Shawn whispered.

"Shusssh!" Kaela hissed.

Knock ... Knock ... Knock.

"It's coming from the closet." Kaela released Shawn and put her finger to her lips. She stood up, careful not to make a sound, and whipped open the closet door. Something small but heavy fell with a thump onto the floor in front of her.

Kaela's mouth dropped open. She stared, flabbergasted, at what looked like a little man sprawled on the floor.

The man rose to his feet, brushing his clothes smooth with his hands. A long white braid hung down his back, and his pointy ears stuck up through his hair. One second he seemed old with a deeply lined face and crinkly eyes. The next instant he looked young, with baby-smooth skin and wide brown eyes.

Kaela blinked hard as the little man's clothes changed from a dark gray to the clear blue color of her room. Even his toenails and fingernails turned blue.

"What do we do?" Kaela whispered, cupping her hand over her mouth so only Shawn could hear.

Shawn pointed to the pendant. "Take it off."

"T-take it off?" she stuttered, not moving.

"Take the pendant off. Seriously. Get rid of him."

"Get rid of him..." she echoed, still stunned.

"Yeah – duh. Get rid of him." Shawn spoke a little more loudly than he intended, and blushed.

The little man watched them with a half-smile on his face.

Kaela touched the pendant, hesitating. "But ... he's so small," she said.

"Kaela, ahem..." the little man said, loudly clearing his throat. "You should keep that on for now."

"What?" Kaela blurted. "How do you know my name? Wait a minute. Are you here to kidnap us?" She eyed the baseball bat propped against the bed.

"Certainly not!" the man said, frowning. "I'm here to guide you." His eyes softened. "Kaela, I've known you for a very long time."

"Why should we trust you?" Shawn said suspiciously.

Still not completely won over, Kaela scanned the man's face for some sign of threat, but instead he smiled warmly. Unable to unlock her eyes from his face, she found herself lost in the kindness of his warm brown eyes.

"Please let me introduce myself," the little man said. "My name is Netri."

"What? Who? Are you an elf?" Shawn blinked his eyes repeatedly to avoid being hypnotized by the little man's intense stare.

"I should think not!" the man huffed.

From his tone, Kaela thought that Shawn had insulted him. "Then you are a really, really tiny human?" she guessed.

"No, no. Both wrong! I am a wizzen, of course."

"A-a wizzen?" Shawn frowned. "What's that? There is no such thing."

"Says the boy who believes in elves!" the wizzen chuckled. "Let me explain," he continued. "A wizzen is similar to a human, but our bodies are not built the same as yours. Our ribs hide giant hearts. For every three breaths you take, we take one. We hold onto each breath like the kindest caress, savoring each one, for it is through our breath that we can reach the heavens. My people live for many, many generations, compared to humans. We watch them be born, grow, love, wither and die – it is like how you watch the blossoming and waning of flowers each summer."

"But how is that even possible?" Shawn frowned, trying to make sense of this information.

"You live for many generations ... you hold onto your breath? Whoa." Kaela lightly slapped herself and said, "You're like a real magic person. Did I bring you here, you know, with this pendant?"

"May I see that?" Netri asked.

Kaela bent down so the wizzen could get a closer look.

"Yes, I know that pendant. It does have great magic."

"What kind of magic?" Kaela asked eagerly, wondering if Netri knew how to make her hear the singing.

"Well, you will find out soon enough. But know this – when you are ready for the quest, the quest finds you." He smiled at Kaela.

Not wanting to be left out, Shawn offered his hand. "I'm..."

"Shawn, Kaela's cousin." The wizzen shook hands vigorously.

"You know me?" Shawn said, pushing his glasses further up his nose. "This is really too weird."

Kaela noticed that the wizzen was almost the exact height of Shawn kneeling. She stuck out her hand and the wizzen gripped her in return. Even though his hand was smaller than hers, his touch somehow made her feel safe and warm inside. When she withdrew her hand, something slimy and thick stuck to her index finger. She shook it onto the floor and saw it was a piece of brown seaweed. She breathed in the unmistakable aroma of ocean air that wafted from the wizzen's clothes.

"You know, you should clean up in here more often." Netri handed Kaela a wadded-up napkin from the floor.

A strange, sickly aroma filled the air as Kaela unfolded a rotten moldy orange. "That's what's been smelling!" Kaela exclaimed. "But where did you find it?"

"I was looking for the hole in the sky under your bed."

"I don't believe it," Shawn said, still trying to take it all in. "So there really is a hole in the sky?"

"Well, of course there is!" Netri said as Kaela tossed the moldy orange into her overfull trash basket. "Now, we need to get down to business," he continued. "Kaela, we have been waiting for the right moment for you to join us. I was sent here to bring you back to Muratenland. It is time."

Kaela tilted her head. "Me? Time for what?" She rubbed her index finger, which was damp and sticky from the orange, on her jeans.

"Hey, if the hole is in the sky, why were you looking for it under the bed?" Shawn asked.

Netri ignored the question and abruptly began to rush through the room, disturbing the messy piles of clothes, books, and papers. "I know the hole's in here somewhere," he muttered. "I'm just not sure where." He returned to the closet and heaved more of Kaela's laundry into the center of her room.

"Hey, what're you doing?" Kaela demanded. "You're the one who told me I should keep my room clean." She gathered the piles of clothes into her arms and tried to shove them back into the closet as the wizzen continued tossing them out. "I'm in enough trouble as it is without you messing up my room. My principal even sent a note home with me."

She pulled the envelope from her pocket and waved it in front of the wizzen.

"Here. Let me see that," Netri said kindly.

"I don't think you should read it," Kaela hesitated. "It's for my dad...."

"Allow me." Without hesitating, Netri ripped the envelope into tiny shreds. "You must forgive them, Kaela. They simply have no idea who you are."

"I can't believe you did that!" Kaela said.

"That's from the principal!" Shawn said, bug-eyed. "Kaela, you are going to be in so much trouble."

"Listen to me, Kaela," Netri said emphatically, locking Kaela's gaze with his own. "You *are* the chosen one."

"Yeah, the chosen *loser*," she scoffed. Despite the fact that Kaela had dreamed for so long of being recognized as someone special, she still found it difficult to embrace the idea in real life.

"Please, Kaela," Netri pleaded. "The time has arrived for you to fulfill your destiny. We are all counting on you."

"Who is counting on Kaela?" Shawn asked, raising his eyebrows. "Are you sure you have the right Kaela?" he snickered.

Netri scowled at Shawn as Kaela hit him in the arm. "Why not?" She demanded.

"You're not exactly the most…"

"I am too!" Kaela shoved Shawn for emphasis, and he fell back into a pile of jeans.

"Don't worry," Netri said, directing his comments to Kaela. "I am certain that you are the one, Kaela. My people have been awaiting the arrival of the red-haired girl for quite some time."

Kaela stared at Netri, trying to digest this information. "The arrival of the red-haired girl…" she muttered. A smile spread across her face. "You mean that I'm special, like, you know, have secret magic powers or something?" Kaela imagined herself disappearing at will and shooting into the air like a rocket.

Shawn crossed his arms over his chest. "Kaela…" he groaned, trying to reason with her.

Kaela's fantasy popped like a bubble. "Hold on a minute. Who's been waiting for me?"

"Why the people of Muratenland, of course," Netri explained. "The situation is desperate. King Arendore's and Queen Skyla's baby has been kidnapped, and Gulig will kill him. You are the only one who can rescue the child!"

"Uhm, okay – what?" Overwhelmed with Netri's sudden seriousness, Kaela realized that she could not fly, and had absolutely no idea what the wizzen was talking about. "I don't understand. I mean, who are these people? And um, and me, really?" Kaela trailed off in disbelief.

"Do not worry, Kaela. Arendore and Skyla are people who live on the other side of the hole in the sky. I will take you to them." Netri patted her knee. "I have already told you – you are the red-haired girl. There is no mistaking you." He turned his face towards Shawn and said firmly, "Shawn, if you are to accompany Kaela, you must put aside your doubts."

"But how do you know she's…" Shawn began warily.

"Shawn, you too carry great gifts." Netri looked directly into the boy's eyes. "Often you can hear that which others cannot."

"Me? Well, I did hear the singing." A smile spread slowly across

Shawn's face and his eyes brightened with intrigue at the possibility that he might have special powers. "Yeah, I was the one that heard the singing with the pendant," Shawn said proudly.

"Shawn, we should do this - you know - go with him." Kaela grinned.

"We have wasted enough time. Please, help me find the passageway," Netri insisted.

"Well, how did you get here?" Shawn asked. "Can't we go back the same way?"

"I used the hole in the sky, and found you in a building filled with human children. I could not find the right moment to take you with me, so I followed you home. There should be one here, though...." Netri began to search again, checking under Kaela's bookshelves.

"Wait a minute." Kaela finally began to understand the strange events in the locker room. "It was *you*. You were the little kid in the locker room. And the smell."

"Well, I'm certainly not a child, but I did leave a shell for you."

Kaela reached into her pocket for the shell, but came up empty-handed, "Oh no! What did I do with it?"

"I think I left it in the kitchen." Shawn's face reddened. "I could run down and get it."

"Do not worry," Netri said. "It was just a calling card. We don't need it, and there's no time. We must proceed. Now, where is the passageway?"

"Well, my mom seemed to think it was in the closet," Kaela said shaking her head. "But I've looked there many times before and found nothing but the floor."

"Well, of course!" Netri exclaimed, rolling his eyes and diving into the closet. "It is not always open, you know, and you need a guide if you've never used it before." Netri stood back up and squinted his eyes, examining the inside of Kaela's closet. A grin spread across his face and his eyes crinkled with delight. His hand quivered with excitement as he pointed at the closet floor. "Look - there it is."

Kaela peered past Netri. "I don't see anything."

"Look, Kaela." Netri hopped forward, and the lower half of his body disappeared through the floorboards. "Can you see it now?"

"No way!" Kaela's eyes widened and she blinked a few times, utterly shocked by the sight.

"Hey, how did you do that?" Shawn said, mystified. He kneeled down and patted the cold floor next to the wizzen. "That's just not possible."

"Quickly, now – you try it, Kaela." Netri pulled himself from the passageway by pressing his hands firmly against the floor. When his legs re-emerged, he urged her again. "Go on, Kaela. Jump in."

Only half believing what she had just witnessed with her own eyes, Kaela hesitated. She looked at Shawn, who was busy tapping the floorboards in the closet.

"Go on, Kaela. Jump," Netri said, smiling.

Shawn stepped to the side and Kaela gave a small jump, but nothing happened.

"Well, I tried!" she said, laughing nervously. "I guess I don't fit!"

Netri looked at her for a moment with a look that bordered on disappointment. "You must believe that it is there," he explained, as though talking to a child.

"Well, I'm trying!" Kaela huffed.

"I'll do it. I could hear the song, after all!" Shawn said with an arrogant tone.

"Shawn." Netri frowned. "First, help get Kaela through."

"Jump, Kaela!" Shawn and Netri said together.

Kaela closed her eyes and jumped hard. Like a warm knife through butter, one leg slipped through the floor and she felt a sudden breeze ruffle her pant leg.

"Whoa, this is scary!" Kaela hollered, kneeling with her other leg on the closet floor. "Get me out! I don't want to get stuck!"

Shawn offered Kaela his hand and she jerked her leg from the floorboards.

"You almost did it, Kaela," Netri urged her on. "I have an idea." Netri scooped up armfuls of clothes and threw them back into the closet. "I want you to remember a joyous time in your life, and then jump on this pile."

Kaela tried to overcome her fear of the hole and her momentary dislike of Netri for trying to make her jump into it. Instead, she thought of a fall day long ago, when her father had raked for hours to build a huge mound of colorful fallen leaves. Kaela could almost hear him laughing.

"Come on, Kaela," he had called. "Come on, jump in!" The evening light had danced against the leaves while her father stood on the other side, smiling, with his arms open wide. Her curls bounced against her neck and her corduroy overalls went *swish, swish, swish* as she ran with all her might and leapt into the soft pile. Filled with the warm memory, Kaela jumped into the heap of clothes as though she were still that little girl, and this time her whole body slid through the floor.

"Grab my foot!" Netri yelled behind her.

Kaela slid into another world.

Chapter Four • The Hole In The Sky

With her right arm stretched behind her, Kaela clung to Netri's big toe. They wound around and down and around a spiraling dark tube, until one particularly tight turn yanked Netri's foot from her grasp.

"He-e-e-el-l-l-l-p-p-p-p!!!!" Kaela screamed. Her heart pounded like a beating drum. A cold wind blasted across her body as she shot out into open air.

"Who-o-o-o-a-a-a-a-a!!!!" Shawn yelled behind her as she fell.

A spray of water surrounded Kaela, and she inhaled reflexively just before her momentum drove her deep into a huge body of water.

Kaela pointed her toes, reaching, hoping to find something solid – anything. But there was only water. She knew how to swim, but ever since she was caught in the undertow of an enormous wave, helpless to extract herself, Kaela sometimes panicked in water where she couldn't stand up. Now her arms and legs flailed in all directions.

Crosscurrents spun Kaela in a whirlwind of seaweed and churning water. Confused and frightened, she opened her eyes, hoping to discover some means of escape. Where were the bubbles? Kaela knew they always rose towards the surface, but her dizziness and the murky water made it impossible to see anything. She fought to break free of the long strands of vine-like seaweed that had twisted around her right hand. She reached in the direction she thought was up, hoping to break the surface of the water, but found only more water. Kaela's lungs ached, screaming for oxygen. Colored spots began to flash before her eyes and her arm suddenly seemed too heavy to move.

Then, like a miracle, something lifted her from below, supporting her limp body all the way to the surface. She gasped for breath as she broke through the waves, coughed and gagged, then coughed some more. She wiped her eyes with the back of her hand and blinked a few times. Where was she?

"Kaela, what happened to you?" Shawn asked, concern filling his voice.

Dazed by her ordeal, Kaela slowly sat up on hard rock, expecting to find herself on a beach, facing a stormy sea. Instead she found herself rocking gently on a vast still ocean. A huge round moon shone down, bathing them in silver light. "Where am I? Where's the storm?"

"Kaela, there was no storm," Netri said softly, treading water beside her. "The only storm was the one inside of you. Gulig thrives on others' fear, and I'm afraid his power is spreading across the land. His greatest weapon is to turn that which we fear against us."

"I don't understand," Shawn said with his arms and legs in motion to stay afloat. "Kaela, you're a great swimmer. This water is completely calm, warm and beautiful. Why were you afraid?"

"First it was the hole in the sky – I was out of control, but then ... when I landed in the water ... it happens sometimes; deep water makes me panic." Kaela's teeth chattered. "I thought I was going to die. A hand held me down. I thought I was dead – an angel came."

"You are blessed with many friends in this world," Netri said, smiling. "Kaela and Shawn, I want to introduce you to your newest friend - your angel, Kaela. This is Malana."

Eager to meet and thank her benefactor, Kaela sat up even straighter, craning her neck to see the angel, looking for a woman dressed in white. "Where is she? I don't see anyone."

Shawn swam towards Kaela, but spoke instead to the rock upon which she sat. "I am honored to meet you, Malana. Thank you for saving my cousin."

"Who are you talking to, Shawn?" Kaela asked, mystified.

"Here, Kaela," Netri said, gesturing. "You are sitting on Malana's back. She is a giant sea turtle."

Malana stroked the sea with her flippers and spun in a gentle circle while Kaela sat comfortably in the middle of Malana's shell. Then the turtle lifted up her head and turned her face towards Kaela.

Tears of gratitude rolled in large drops down Kaela's cheek. "Thank you," she whispered. Kaela stroked the skin of the turtle's soft leather-like head. "I can never thank you enough for what you did for me."

Nodding slowly, the turtle continued to gaze at Kaela with one of her soft, dark eyes while Netri climbed up just in front of Kaela.

"She says that it is her honor to serve the red-haired girl," Shawn translated. "Is that right, Netri?"

"Yes, very good, Shawn. Your skill with languages will serve you well on this journey." Netri replied.

"Wait. There's more, Kaela," Shawn said, proud of his ability. "Malana says, 'It would be my pleasure to escort you to shore.' She also says that someone named Leia is coming to take me." Another giant turtle popped her head above water just in front of Shawn, and then his body lifted halfway out of the water as the turtle rose beneath him. Shawn laughed.

Netri stood up on the turtle's back and gracefully dove back into the sea.

When he surfaced again a few feet away, Kaela asked, "Wait, Netri, aren't you going to ride with me?"

"Thank you, Kaela, but I have much to arrange. Do not worry – I will see you soon. Remember that one of your great strengths on this journey is the support you give one another. When one of you is afraid, the other can be a rock to help carry you. Or a turtle shell," Netri said, winking. "Do you understand?"

Kaela and Shawn nodded.

A dolphin burst from the waves with a great splash. Netri whooped as the dolphin dove under and rose once more, lifting the wizzen with its back. "I leave you in good hands!" Netri called back to them. "Trust the kindness of the turtles – they will be great friends to you. I will see you soon." The dolphin leapt, arching into the sky, and then dove deep, Netri clinging to its dorsal fin. Just like that, he was gone.

Kaela and Shawn sat motionless on Malana and Leia's shells for a moment not quite believing what they had just seen.

"Malana says that it is time to get going. She wants you to lie on her back," Shawn said, doing the same. "They are going to take us to shore, but first they want us to practice breathing."

Lying stomach down on her turtle's back, Kaela grasped the front of the shell in her hands. The shell was similar in shape to a huge heart. It was long enough to carry most of Kaela's body, although her feet hung off the end. The shell's roughness made it easy to grip.

"We're supposed to breathe out when they go under the water and breathe in when they come up," Shawn instructed.

"What if I run out of air?"

"Don't worry," Shawn continued. "Malana says to tell you, 'I will show you the friendly side of the sea.'"

They practiced a few times, and when Kaela first surfaced she sputtered, choking with water and the dreaded fear that gripped her belly. But after several more tries she relaxed, supported by the turtle's shell.

"They want to know if we feel ready," Shawn called.

"I think so, Shawn."

Kaela's turtle led the way. The slow breathing washed away her panic and filled her with new life. Up and down they swam through vistas of shimmering coral illuminated by the full moon; tiny pink, purple and peach-colored rock castles grew from the ocean floor. Kaela surfaced once again in water so calm it was like glass, rippled only by the peaceful undulations of the turtles. Captivated by the movement of her own breath, Kaela's mind came to rest and the ocean, once her greatest foe, held her in its warm arms.

The turtles dove down deep, where three women's bodies floated belly up, just above the sandy floor. Their hands folded over their chests, and their long hair drifted like fine strands of seaweed around the women's heads. As if in deep slumber, their faces were completely still, eyes closed. Three turtles rested beside the women's bodies.

When they surfaced again, Shawn and his turtle swam a few yards in front of Kaela.

"Shawn!" She yelled.

He turned his head towards her.

"Did you see? Sleeping mermaids!" Kaela said, wide-eyed.

"They didn't have tails," Shawn yelled back, shaking his head.

The turtles dove under again, but this time they saw that the women were already far behind them. When they rose again to the surface, white cliffs appeared just beyond a sparkling beach, and rolling waves pushed them forward. Surf crashed against the shore, and an anxious, excited feeling filled Kaela. If there were big waves, then there would also be a strong undertow.

"Kaela, we're coming to the shore now. They want you to know their shells will support us. They will stay on the surface and you can trust Malana to keep you up, even through waves."

"Are you sure?" Kaela yelled above the roar of the surf.

"Don't worry!" Shawn called, but he was interrupted by a huge wave cresting behind him. "Here I go-o-o-o-o-o!" He called, and rode to shore like he was on a boogey board. He jumped off into the knee-high water when the turtle stood on sand, punching his fists into the air.

When the next wave loomed large behind her, Kaela drew a breath and held tight to Malana's shell. Malana paddled just in front of the crest, gaining momentum, and then the pull of the wave lifted them both up to the peak. Kaela and Malana soared towards the beach as the wave broke. Whitewater crashed and swirled around them and Kaela slid off before the undertow could drag them back. She bent down, holding onto the turtle with both hands in the roiling water.

Kaela put her mouth close to Malana's head and said, "Thank you for all of your kindness. I owe you my life."

Shawn bent down and looked into Leia's eyes and said, "Good-bye. Thank you for everything." Shawn stood as the turtles turned in the water. "Malana says, 'Please tell the red-haired girl our hearts are with her, and bid her to remember our time together,'" he yelled.

The turtles dove under and were gone.

Kaela waded after Shawn through the strong undertow up to shore, water pouring in streams from her clothes. Kaela wrung out her long hair and squeezed handfuls of water from her t-shirt as she looked around her. The two stood on a long crescent shaped beach with white cliffs jutting into the sea at either end.

Buoyed from the journey through the sea and her ride on the wave, Kaela spread her arms wide, twirled in circles, then leapt in long strides down the beach, singing, "I can fly! I can fly!" The moon shone huge and bright just above the cliffs, casting long wing-like shadows of Kaela's waving arms. Shawn bounded after her, whooping and laughing until, giggling and completely out of breath, they both collapsed in a heap on the soft powdery sand.

Kaela lay on her back and swung her arms and legs in and out in an arc. "Look, Shawn, I'm an angel. Look at the sand – I'm an angel!"

"Actually, you're more like a wet, sandy mess." Shawn laughed and tossed a handful of sand in Kaela's direction. He paused and a peaceful look settled on his face as he scanned the waves rising under the setting moon. "Kaela, we did it – we went through the hole in the sky – we're actually in another world now."

"It's so beautiful," Kaela said softly. Despite the silver light of the moon, she looked up at a sky turning from black to dark blue. She sat up and brushed the sand from her wet clothes. Somewhere along the way her socks, and Shawn's as well, had been lost.

"It's magical here." Shawn closed his eyes and listened to the sound of the waves crashing against the shore. "Kaela, it's like the seashell, the sound in the shell."

"Yeah, like the shell carried this ocean to us." She rested her chin on her knees and wrapped her arms around her legs, relaxing in the balmy air.

A bank of clouds along the horizon grew pink with the approaching sun and Kaela's stomach audibly rumbled with hunger pangs.

"I'm starving." Kaela stretched and stood up. "Let's head towards the cliffs. There must be food around here somewhere."

Shawn joined her and squinted his eyes, gazing inland. "Look! I don't think we're alone. Is that a horse there?" He pointed towards the white cliff to their left.

"Where?" Kaela followed Shawn's pointing finger. "I don't see it. Oh, yeah, there it is!"

A horse trotted steadily down a path, which wound back and forth along the cliff.

Shawn took off. "I bet you can't beat me," he yelled.

"Yes, I ca-a-a-an!" Kaela flew after her cousin, eager to outrun him. Her hair flew around her face in the breeze, steadily drying into a thick mass of curls. She tagged Shawn and they chased and pushed one another while the horse continued his steady descent.

When the horse reached the beach, he trotted towards them, neighing his greeting. Seconds later, Kaela and Shawn stood before the brilliant white horse with kind eyes and the scruffy hair of an elderly animal. He lowered his head, and Shawn and Kaela patted his muzzle and neck.

"Hello," Kaela said. "Are you here to help us?"

The horse kissed their palms with his soft lips, and whinnied.

"His name is Blanco," Shawn translated. "Netri sent him. He says that there is spring water here to drink, and that it is special somehow. It comes from the sacred mountain. He says that, after we drink, he will carry us inland."

Kaela and Shawn knelt down and rinsed their sandy hands in the small stream that flowed past Blanco's hooves. Realizing a sudden thirst, they swiftly cupped handfuls of water to their mouths.

"This is the best water I've ever tasted," Kaela said between gulps. "It's delicious!"

When Blanco whinnied again, Shawn untied a white scarf knotted to his mane. "Blanco brought this for you to wear," Shawn translated. "He wants you to cover your hair so that no one can see that the red-haired girl has arrived."

"But I thought they were waiting for me," Kaela said, tossing the scarf over her head and tying it behind her neck.

Shawn touched Kaela's arm and they looked at each other. "Maybe the bad guys are also waiting for you."

"Oh yeah. I didn't think of that," Kaela said, giggling nervously. Then she stood up and stuck out her chin. "Well, they're not going to stop me."

Blanco shook his mane and neighed.

"Blanco agrees. He says, 'The red-haired girl has deep powers and many friends.'"

"Thank you, Blanco. Will you take us to our friends, now?" Kaela patted the horse and rubbed her cheek against his muzzle.

Shawn climbed up a rock to mount Blanco, and Kaela settled just behind him. As soon as they made themselves comfortable, the horse headed toward the cliffs with a steady gait. His hooves pounded through tough sea grasses, wild rosebushes with pink and red blossoms, and then ascended up the rocky path edged with a rainbow of colored flowers. Shawn leaned forward, gripping Blanco's neck, and Kaela clung to her cousin's waist to keep from sliding off.

When Kaela turned around for one more look at the ocean, the sun appeared over the distant swells like a crimson sliver, casting a path of pink shimmering light on the sea.

At the top of the cliff a dense mist surrounded them, cloaking their surroundings. They rode through gangly bushes that scratched at their legs then entered a tangled forest of trees rising from the fog, reaching for them with arm-like branches.

Kaela didn't notice when a twisted twig caught the scarf, partially uncovering her red hair.

As the sun rose higher in the sky, the warmth of the morning sun evaporated the mist into wisps and whirls. It was difficult to see through the trees, but a light breeze wafted through the air, bringing a deliciously sweet scent with it. Kaela's mouth watered. She was starving.

Then the forest opened into an apple orchard. Rotten apples littered the ground around a nearby tree, and two pieces of fat, ripe fruit still dangled from a branch.

"Look!" Kaela nudged Shawn and pointed. "It's a giant apple tree. I'll get us some breakfast." She slid off Blanco's back. "I'll be right back. Tell Blanco to wait for me." Kaela called over her shoulder.

A large crow startled into the air and flew around the tree, cawing loudly.

"The crow is saying, 'the red-haired girl is here'!" Shawn yelled, but Kaela didn't stop. Shawn jumped off Blanco, and yelled again, "The crow is telling people that you're here!"

Kaela pulled herself up to the first branch, and the shaking tree leaves drowned out the sound of Shawn's voice.

Shawn turned back to Blanco in fear as Kaela scrambled along the limb to the outer reaches of the tree. Eyeing two ripe apples at the end of the branch above her, Kaela's mouth watered with hunger. She imagined the juice of the apple tingling her taste buds as she bit into the crisp fruit. Even more determined, she stood up with her feet firm on the branch below, and strained to bend the upper branch.

Twigs snapped in the woods and an eerie silence filled the air. Kaela looked around from her perch, and her eyes opened wide as a ghostly apparition materialized out of the dark woods. It was an old woman with a long, pointed nose and filthy grey hair. Her ragged clothes hung on her skinny body. Extending a gnarled finger, the woman pointed at Kaela.

"*It's her! She came back! I told you she would come!!!!*"

The ancient woman dashed at the tree and strained to reach Kaela. Sharp pain seared through Kaela's leg as the woman dug in with her long, filthy nails.

"Let me go!" Kaela screamed, kicking to free herself from the haggard old woman. The tree's branches shook wildly, and Kaela almost lost her hold.

The crone stared at Kaela with hatred in her bloodshot eyes. "Go back where you came from!" The old woman screamed, "No one wants you here! Do you hear me! *The red-haired girl brings the beginning of the end!*"

"She's a witch, Shawn," Kaela screamed. "Get her off me. She's gonna kill me!"

"Let her go!" Shawn hollered.

The woman turned her enraged face towards Shawn and hissed, "How dare you help the red-haired girl?! You will suf-f-fer!"

"*Leave him alone!*" Kaela screamed, shaking her leg and trying to loosen the woman's vice-like grip.

The woman locked her eyes onto Kaela once again.

A boy with shaggy black hair and worn clothes appeared out of the dark trees and raced to the old woman's side. "Come on, Tazena. It's time to go," he pleaded, tugging on the old lady's arm. The hag's clasp loosened. She hunched over, mumbling to herself, her eyes glazed over. The boy coaxed her away from the path, guiding her as though she were blind.

The young boy looked back and locked eyes with Kaela. A cold fog descended over her, chilling her to the bone. She shuddered, certain it was a premonition – a warning of terrible things to come.

Kaela sighed with relief as the faint sounds of crunching leaves faded in the distance. Then, out of nowhere, the wind carried the woman's terrifying screech to Kaela's ears, "The red-head is back! It's the beginning of the end!!!" The witch's wails rose and died.

Completely spent, Kaela released her grip, falling to her hands and knees in thick grass mottled with rotting apples. Her hands and knees stung with the impact, but she quickly grabbed Shawn's extended hand and rose to her feet as he tugged her arm. The image of the woman's eyes propelled Kaela to bolt full-speed towards Blanco, who stood munching on grass a short distance from the tree.

Kaela dove onto the horse and grunted as her stomach folded over Blanco's back. She quickly sat up and offered her hands to help Shawn mount the horse.

"Let's go, Blanco!" Shawn and Kaela yelled in unison.

Chapter Five · The Tree Song

Once they were a safe distance from the apple tree, Shawn turned slightly. "Are you okay?" He asked. "Did she hurt your leg?"

Kaela tugged on her pants and examined her ankle as best she could while sitting on the horse. There were still dirty marks from the old woman's fingernails, but she hadn't pierced the flesh. "My ankle looks okay. But that woman was super creepy." Kaela shuddered. "Was she putting a curse on you?"

"Did you see her eyes?" Shawn asked as he stroked Blanco's neck.

"Yeah! Well at least we're both okay," Kaela said, trying to reassure them both, but she couldn't shake the memory of the deranged look on the woman's face.

Blanco continued on, following a narrow path through tall evergreens and dense bushes. Pine needles scratched their faces and arms, so Kaela was relieved when the path widened. Around them, massive roots twisted and turned, forming caves at the base of ancient trees that reached to the clouds. The trees swayed and danced with odd bouncy movements, as though they were made from rubber. Ferns taller than a grown man rose from the fertile mulch. Where sunlight burst through the foliage, bright green grass grew, straining to meet the sun.

"Whoa!" Kaela said, breaking the silence. "That tree trunk is bigger than a house. And look how tall it is! It's like it goes on forever."

"It looks like the bark forms a winding stairway." Shawn pointed. "See?"

"Hello there. Welcome," a soft, invisible voice greeted them.

"Did you hear that?" Shawn whispered.

Kaela leaned forward, whispering in Shawn's ear. "How do we know it's a good guy?"

Blanco whinnied, and stood still.

"Over here," a young girl's voice giggled.

They slid down Blanco's back and turned in the direction of the girl's voice, but no one was in sight.

"Here!" The girl called.

Kaela and Shawn twirled around until they saw the movement of the girl's arms, flapping up and down above the tall grass.

"You've nothing to fear from me," she said softly. "Netri told us 'bout you. We be on your side. We have wonderful surprises for you!"

The young girl suddenly materialized, turning and whirling in cartwheels. Even when she reached the place where they stood, she danced around like a hummingbird, constantly in motion.

The girl's unusual hair – red, gold, brown and orange locks shaped like long leaves – fell to her shoulders. Kaela reached over, unable to resist the temptation to touch the girl's hair, but caught herself and dropped her hands by her side. Instead she said, "My name is Kaela. And this is my cousin, Shawn."

"Pleased to meet you. Me name's Tressa. It's OK – go on if you like, touch me hair." Tressa skipped up to Kaela.

"It feels just like mine," Kaela said, rubbing a deep auburn strand between her fingers. "It just looks so different."

"It's 'cuz I'm one of the Tree People," Tressa explained, bouncing up and down on her toes. "Come on, then. You can clean yourselves and have a bite to eat. Then I'm taking you home for the surprise."

"Where's your house?" Shawn asked, turning around to look for it.

"Here, silly – in front of your face!" Laughing, Tressa grabbed both their hands and skipped to the trunk of the huge tree, which was bigger than the largest redwood. She placed their palms against the bark. "This is our Grandmother Tree, our limba tree," she said, twirling about. "This is our home."

"Do you live in these rooms in the roots?" Shawn wondered.

"Not right now! No – when it's warm we live up there," Tressa said, pointing straight up and jumping high. "The root rooms are for winter and when the wind is blowing so hard it could knock a man to the ground!"

Arching back, Kaela saw platforms scattered throughout the thick swaying tree branches.

Leaping into handsprings, Tressa said, "Come on then. Follow me."

The sounds of running water grew louder and louder as Shawn and Kaela trotted after Tressa.

Shawn looked back as he caught a glimpse of the river and grinned. "Last one in is a rotten egg!" He called.

Kaela chased Shawn a few yards through the thick grass, and then her foot slid from under her in the slick mud and she slid down the riverbank. Her breath caught as she landed with a *SPLASH* in ice-cold water that rose to her neck. Her skin tingled from the cold, but it felt so refreshing that she laughed out loud. She rubbed the sand and mud from her clothes and floated for a moment in the placid current, letting the river take her downstream. She looked up at rays of sunlight flitting through the green tree branches, forgetting all the terrifying things she'd had to face since she fell through the hole in the sky.

"Hey, don't go so far." Tressa yelled, "I've got food and dry clothes for you, just like mine. Hurry ... the surprise is waiting. It is!"

⟋ ⟍

The young boy stroked his grandmother's hair. Even when Tazena slept she tossed and turned, tormented by endless visions of the future.

Today, Zeke had no choice but to help her fall asleep with a brew of passionflower and hops tea. Tazena had resisted at first, pushing the mug away, spilling droplets of the hot fluid on Zeke's arm. He flinched as the tea sizzled his skin, gritted his teeth and sighed with frustration.

His grandmother stared at him.

"Who are you?" She demanded. "What're you doing here? Those Rugus sent you, didn't they?"

"No, Gramma, it's me. I'm here. It's Zeke."

After blinking a few times, Tazena's body noticeably relaxed, and her hunched shoulders dropped an inch. "Zeke, it's you. How'd you get away?"

"I didn't go anywhere, Gramma. I'm here. Just relax."

The day before, Zeke had gone to the market and purchased a stale loaf of bread from the baker with the single coin in his pocket, and when no one looked his way he swiped a block of moldy cheese from the dairy farmer. He tore off a third of the wheat loaf for his grandmother and scraped the mold from the cheese.

Although Tazena was so thin that every vein and wiry tendon showed through her parchment-like skin, she often refused to eat, insisting that all food and drink contained poison. This time, Zeke sighed with relief when his grandmother gulped the tea and wolfed down the food, stuffing her mouth with hunks of bread and cheese.

As she finished her simple meal, Tazena mumbled in satisfaction.

"You're here. Zeke. Promise you'll never leave me." Her eyelids fluttered closed as he helped her lie back down on the cot.

He pulled the covers over her shoulders. "Sleep, Gramma, sleep. You'll see - I'm gonna help us. You'll see." Zeke padded across the tiny room and closed the door behind him, clutching a wad of fabric that bound his meager rations. Though he had never been far from home before, the red-haired girl held the only hope for their future, and there wasn't much time.

He began the long walk toward town, and when a farmer in a horse-drawn carriage offered him a ride, Zeke eagerly accepted his help.

A large black crow leapt off a branch and, flying high into the sky, followed the boy.

<hr />

Tressa beamed and clapped her hands as Kaela emerged from behind some bushes. "You are looking like a Tree Girl now, wearing those clothes," she said, laughing.

Kaela twirled around, delighted with her new outfit. The shirt and pants were sewn from suede so soft that it felt like silk. She rubbed her hand along the sleeve. "Thank you, Tressa," she said. "These clothes are wonderful."

"What's that 'round your neck?" Tressa asked, reaching toward the pendant. "'Tis beautiful, it is."

Kaela looked down at her chest and touched the butterfly necklace. She had forgotten all about it. "It used to be my mom's. I think it's kind of magic."

"That's good," Tressa said. She looked carefully at Kaela and her tone became serious. "Seems like you may be needing magic." The young Tree Girl smiled kindly and pulled Kaela's hand as she stood, dispelling the somber mood. "Come on then," she called. "Come see the surprise."

"What should we do with our old clothes?" Shawn asked as he stepped out of a thicket of grasses.

"Just leave them under the tree. Someone will wash 'em for you."

Kaela eyed the wooden bark stairs that wound around the tree and groaned at the thought of climbing all the way up.

"Well, I guess we might as well get started," she sighed, walking towards the tree, where a brown curly-haired dog sat whining.

"Who's this?" Kaela asked, petting the mutt.

"Wollan's his name. He's a special guest," Tressa said, jumping over the dog. "Refuses to go up the tree, though. He'll have to wait. Not us, though! Come this away. The stairs are too long. I'll ask the tree to bring us up." Tressa dashed up to a large knot in the tree and blew air through her lips, making a sound like rustling leaves. She turned back to Kaela and Shawn. "Me tree says I'm too much of a chatter-box," Tressa explained. "If I need her to listen, she told me I best just speak into one of her knots – otherwise, she won't listen!"

Shawn frowned, "You can talk to trees?"

"Well, now, 'course, I can. Doesn't everyone?"

"No, I don't think so."

Tressa stared open-mouthed at Shawn. Her eyes moistened and she patted his arm. "Oh me, oh me, 'tis the saddest thing I ever did hear," she sighed.

"Do you talk to all of the trees?" Kaela asked.

Spinning in a quick circle, Tressa returned to her cheerful self. "No, no, silly, most trees be too busy talking to each other! Mostly ignore us. 'Tis the limba trees that loves us. Yes, our dear limba trees."

Shawn thought for a moment. "I don't understand. Why do the other trees ignore you?"

"'Tis like ants," Tressa exclaimed. "There's a bazillion-trillion of them all around, but we don't pay them any mind 'til they crawl on us." She danced around as if she really were covered in ants, and then laughed. "Even me own limba tree don't listen to me all the time!"

"Yeah, okay," Shawn said. "But what do the trees have to say to each other?"

Tressa put her index finger to her lips. Quiet and still for the first time since they met, she closed her eyes, smiled, and said, "Shhh, listen then. You can hear them. Right now they're singing about the wind stroking their leaves and the blue sky and the warm sun. At night they sing and you can feel the silver of the stars tickling your skin. Oh, 'tis the most marvelous thing, to hear the trees singing."

"Wait. Maybe I did hear, once before," Shawn said, remembering when he wore Kaela's pendant.

"I bet you did!" Tressa cried, and turned a somersault. "Let's try! Now, give the tree a hug and for sure she'll sing to you."

Kaela laughed and said, "I'm sorry, did you say that you want me to hug the tree?"

"Don't you hug the ones you love?" Tressa asked, wide-eyed.

"Yes, of course I do, Tressa, but this is a tree. I don't even know the tree very well," Kaela joked. Then, seeing the expression on Tressa face, she sobered up. "I mean, I guess I didn't know ... do trees have feelings?"

Tressa's hands covered her face and once again her eyes glistened with tears.

"Oh, don't you talk like that near me Grandmother Tree," she cried. "That would hurt her terrible."

"Oh, I'm sorry!" Kaela said. "I just never thought of it like that. Sure, I'll hug your tree. How do we do it?"

Tressa burst out laughing. "You live in a very strange world, very strange indeed. You just open your arms wide and hug." Spreading her arms she turned her head to one side and rested her body against the trunk of the tree, looking like someone trying to hug a giant's thick leg.

Shawn and Kaela imitated their young friend. The limba tree's bark, cool against the bare skin of Kaela's arms and face, softened as if there was a layer of foam rubber underneath it. Kaela stood against the tree with outstretched arms and the memory of the maple tree in her own backyard filled her. Hour after hour the tree had offered her shelter after her mother's death. She had found comfort in that old tree, climbing into the highest branches while the tree rocked Kaela in the wind.

The bark of the massive tree in Kaela's arms rubbed against her skin, reminding her of the present, and she awoke to the world. Kaela turned her head to Tressa, ready to get on with her adventure. Both the tree maiden and Shawn still had their eyes shut, and their lips formed gentle smiles. Kaela closed her eyes, and this time she sank even deeper into the tree. Warmth spread through her body, as though the tree actually hugged her back.

Kaela's thoughts slowed, and in her mind's eye she saw the bluest blue like the sky on a clear day after a rain or directly after sunset. She breathed the color blue in and out of her nose like she was soaking in it. Her tongue awakened to a delicious sweetness, like a drop of nectar from honeysuckle had exploded in her mouth. All the while the tree's song rippled through her body, the beautiful music making every cell tingle with joy.

The vision of blue changed until she saw a massive tree before her, starving and then dying. The once green leaves dried from red to brown until it stood bare and naked against the warm summer winds. Dry dust parched Kaela's mouth, and a hot wind blew against her face. The tree, too large to be cut down, was stripped bare, limb-by-limb. As the branches crashed to the ground, a mournful song, sung from the throats of a thousand weeping voices, evoked an aching sadness in Kaela's heart.

Then a baby with jet-black hair and bright brown eyes appeared in her vision. He broke out in a smile and lifted his arms to be embraced, while the lullaby her mother sang every night played softly. As clearly as the song began, it was silenced, and stillness beat in Kaela's heart as her mind's eye became blank. She was enfolded by the kindness and love of the great being she held in her arms. A voice whispered, "It is time. It is time."

Kaela, Shawn and Tressa stepped back from the tree with one accord and, after a few minutes of silence, Tressa whispered, "See, it isn't hard ... isn't hard at all."

"That was incredible," Shawn said, sniffling.

As she wiped the tears with her sleeve, Kaela asked, "Tressa, what did that mean? What happened to the tree? It was the saddest thing to see it die. Who was that baby?"

Tressa's hand flew to her mouth. "Oooh, almost forgot, I did. The surprise is still waiting for you. Best follow me." She sprang from her hands to her feet until she reached the edge of the tree's shadow. "Now, stand like this." She turned her back to the tree and spread her arms out wide. Kaela and Shawn imitated her. "Be ready and hold on tight."

A large branch bent down to the ground and swooped them up from behind as a little branch reached under their butts and two small branches formed armrests. The blood drained from Shawn's face as the branch sprang off the ground, high into the air.

"This is the coolest thing!" Kaela whooped. "This tree is amazing!"

Kaela and Tressa giggled as the tree branches bounced up and down at their proper height, but Shawn sat stiff and quiet.

"Shawn, are you okay?" Kaela asked.

"I - I don't know. If I fall, it's gonna be really bad!"

"Oh dear," Tressa said. "Shawn, are you gonna be sick?"

Shawn blushed, and Kaela explained. "He kind of has a fear of heights."

"Oh, for sure. Everyone's afeard of something. Just stay there for a minute. I'll ask the tree for help." Kneeling down on the branch, Tressa again spoke into a knothole. The tree raised a row of little branches and formed a hallway for the three of them to walk down. "Don't you be worrying about a thing. She watches out for all of us. If anyone starts to fall, she'll catch you. You'll see."

"But how does your tree do that? I mean it must be made of wood, not putty. How does it bend like that?" Shawn asked.

"Limba trees are unique," Tressa explained. "They can bend every which way until someone cuts them down. It takes three days for them to harden into regular wood. That's why there are so few. People cut them all down so they could make stuff with the wood before it hardens."

They walked down the wide branch. Kaela peered through an opening in the thick green leaves. Close by, other large trees stood with people scattered throughout the branches. To the right there was a village of little gray houses with orange roofs. In the distance there was a lush valley that looked like it was draped in shades of green velvet. Just beyond the valley, two large mountains rose into steep cliffs.

"Tressa, what's that white building in the distance, against the mountain to the right?" Kaela asked.

The building looked like a fairy castle. Unlike the castles in movies or books, this building appeared to grow right out of the mountainside. Curved towers rose above the structure, with turquoise rooftops crowning each level. It reminded Kaela of a castle she had once seen made from cake and spun sugar.

Standing next to Kaela, Tressa's eyes glittered. "Oh, 'tis so beautiful. 'Tis where the king and queen live. The queen be me auntie. She used to be Auntie Skyla and now she be Queen Skyla," Tressa giggled.

Kaela's eyes lingered for a moment more on the castle. There was a time when she'd dreamed of being a princess with beautiful silk gowns and servants to wait on her hand and foot. It would be wonderful to have a room high in a tower where you could watch the sunrise from one window and the sunset from another. She imagined room after room filled with sparkling treasures and smiling friends. Maybe she would have a chance to stay in this fairyland castle.

Behind them, someone jumped to the platform. Kaela startled as she, Shawn and Tressa turned to face a boy not much older than they, whom had shoulder-length black hair shaped like Tressa's, and green eyes the color of summer grass.

"So, these be the wee ones Netri brought to rescue Eiren?" he sneered.

Excited by his arrival, Tressa jumped up and down. "Look Mika, 'tis Shawn and Kaela. This is me brother, Mika."

Mika slouched in front of them with his hands in the pockets of his brown suede pants. "I'm not so sure I be happy to see you. I don't think you could rescue a squirrel from a tree. If you had half a brain, you'd take me with you."

Chapter Six · King Arendore and Queen Skyla

"Ooh, Mika. Don't be talkin' like that," Tressa said, covering her mouth with her hands. "Come see. Come see the surprise!" Tressa sang as she skipped ahead. "Follow me – follow me."

Kaela and Shawn followed Tressa up small branches that formed a ladder until they arrived at a wall of leaves. Mika's scowl burned into their backs.

Tressa parted the leaves, revealing a large room crowded with Tree People who had varying shades of leaf colored hair. As soon as Kaela and Shawn appeared, everyone turned in their direction. The people in the back craned their necks and discreetly pointed. Above the hum of the crowd could be heard, "It's the red-haired girl. The red-haired girl is here."

Kaela flushed with excitement and grinned. Then she waved while Shawn smiled shyly and pushed his glasses up his nose. The crowd parted and a man and woman dressed in white walked to the front of the group. Beams of sunlight shot through the leaves and illuminated the couple. The man's red hair and beard sparkled like burnished copper; he towered over the compact bodies of the Tree People. With a slight motion from his hand, everyone in the room became still.

"Welcome to Muratenland," he greeted them warmly.

The tone of his voice was somehow familiar and comforting, and Kaela was surprised to feel a sudden urge to run to him, like he was a long-lost friend.

"Kaela, we are honored to have you with us," the woman said. "And Shawn, too. We can never be thanking you enough for coming from such a great distance to help us. Oh!" She smiled, "Please, forgive me - we've not been introduced."

"Please allow me, Your Highnesses," Netri stepped forward. His clothes were colored in splashes of green, and his cheeks were pink and wrinkle-free.

"Oh, Netri!" Kaela cried. The wizzen winked at her. For a brief moment he looked young enough to be a baby.

"May I present Kaela and Shawn, who have traveled far and at great cost to come to our aid," Netri began, bowing. "Kaela and Shawn, before you stand King Arendore and Queen Skyla from the House of Muraten, the wise and fair rulers of all the tribes of Muratenland."

As Kaela looked into the Queen's deep emerald eyes, she knew she had never seen anyone more beautiful in her whole life. A crown of fragrant white flowers set off the Queen's amber skin and long black hair, which shimmered with olive green and brown leaf-like highlights. Her feet were bare, and she wore gold rings on two of her toes. Other than these, only the Queen's long pearl necklace revealed her status.

Even as Queen Skyla and King Arendore smiled their greetings, there was something so sad in their eyes that it broke Kaela's heart to look into them.

"Kaela and Shawn, I have no words to express the depth of my gratitude to you for coming here - coming to our aid," the King said, his voice cracking slightly in the silent room. His gaze rested for a long time on Kaela and his eyes brightened as though shining with tears.

Humbled by his words, Kaela said softly, "Thank you. Thank you for inviting us." Kaela didn't know whether she should curtsy, nor was she sure of the right way to do it. In the movies, women who curtsied always wore long fluffy skirts, and all she was wearing were the suede pants she got from Tressa. Instead of curtsying, she bowed forward from the waist.

Instantly, all of the Tree People bowed deeply to her in return and to Kaela's surprise both the King and Queen also bowed their heads.

Shawn mimicked Kaela, and the Tree People bowed again. Overwhelmed by the show of respect, Kaela blushed and bowed again, then stood awkwardly with a stiff smile on her face.

"Thank you – thank you everyone," Shawn squeaked.

Arendore turned to Netri and said with a trace of awe in his voice, "It is the red-haired girl! It is truly she!" he said softly.

"Yes sir, she's the one," Netri said. "And she has come."

Kaela and Shawn glanced at each other, surprised by the tone of admiration in the King's voice. The King clearly felt the red-haired girl was someone special – someone important.

"I would like to introduce you to Leland, Chief of the Tree Tribe, and his lovely wife, Clouda." Netri continued, "They are also Queen Skyla's mother and father." Netri gestured to two older Tree People, who stood proudly out from the crowd. "Of course, you have already met Tressa and Mika. I'm afraid there is not enough time to get acquainted with the rest of the family, but I am certain that I speak for everyone when I say how pleased we all are to have you here."

"Now please – we need time alone with our guests," King Arendore requested. "Clouda and Leland, I hope you will remain with us."

"Of course," Leland said, glancing towards his wife as she nodded.

The moment the King finished speaking, the room came to life. Instead of leaving the room in an orderly fashion, the Tree People used the occasion to show off their gymnastic abilities. Leafy walls suddenly shifted as branches stuck out from the ceiling above them. Some of the Tree People leapt onto each other's shoulders and grabbed limbs just above their heads. Hanging by their knees from the high branches, they reached down and grabbed their partners' wrists. Others swung around and around branches in faster and faster circles. After gaining momentum they leapt through the air onto distant limbs.

The limba tree dropped additional limbs to the remaining Tree People, who clambered higher and higher with ease, as though they were merely jogging down a paved road. When three of the Tree People reached branches high above the heads of the rest, they performed a trapeze act, swinging in giant arcs across the breadth of the tree.

"This is so-o-o-o cool!" Kaela exclaimed under her breath. Fascinated by the spectacle, she longed to join in the fun. Noticing a sudden weight around her shoulders, Kaela glanced to her side and found Clouda had wrapped her arms around both Kaela and Shawn and was smiling.

"'Tis a wonderful thing to be living in a limba tree," Clouda said.

"Can I stay here ... with you?" Kaela asked, flushed with excitement.

Clouda smiled as the tree gently rustled. "Yes, one day it would be a great blessing to be hosting you in our home." Turning to Shawn, Clouda said, "Shawn, our tree says she would be honored to show you how to dance in her branches."

"Thank you," Shawn smiled wanly. "Uhm – maybe ... I mean, sure – that would be nice."

Clouda patted Shawn's arm and returned to her husband's side.

Leland cleared his throat impatiently. Leland was Queen Skyla's father, Kaela remembered. The deep lines of his brown skin revealed his age, but his hair still shone jet-black with burnt orange leaf-like characteristics, and he and Skyla had the same green eyes. Although shorter than King Arendore, Leland still stood taller than most other Tree People.

"Arendore, I will not be resting until Gulig is stopped." Leland's bushy black eyebrows knitted together and he clenched his fists. "After all he's done to me family and now this horror." A spark of fury flashed across Leland's eyes, as if a fire simmered down inside him that at any moment could burst into a raging inferno.

Clouda set her hand on Leland's arm. Age had mixed the reds, oranges and golden tones of her hair with white, making peach, rose and the palest yellow locks. Kaela searched Clouda's eyes for some sign of the anger that burned in her husband's, but instead found softness, patience and hope in her deep brown gaze.

"Where are Gannon and Gavin? I thought they were meant to join us," King Arendore said.

Leland looked up, stuck his index fingers on either side of his mouth and whistled loudly. High in the uppermost branches, two men wrapped long slender branches around their waists and, without hesitation, dove towards the group below.

Kaela flinched and Shawn squeezed his eyelids closed as the two plummeted towards the room. They bounced up and down a few times when they reached the end of their branches, and then dropped in front of Kaela, giggling like small children. The two men, whose faces looked like mirror images, bowed and smiled at her and Shawn. They resembled Tressa, with their leaf-like fall-colored hair and twinkling brown eyes.

"This is no time for foolishness," Leland scolded.

"This is Gannon and Gavin," Clouda said with obvious pride, "two of our grandsons."

The young men grew solemn at their grandfather's reprimand, while Kaela's heart beat fast against her chest as she shook the calloused hands of the two handsome young men.

Clouda turned around and appeared to be talking to the tree.

"Thank you for caring for our dear guests."

Kaela and Shawn looked at each other in confusion.

"Best be taking your leave now, both of you," Leland interrupted his wife. "We have urgent business."

Tressa and Mika stepped out from their hiding spot behind a thick growth of leaves at the edge of the room.

Before anyone else could say something, Mika blurted, "I think I should go. I heard you talk about sending Gannon and Gavin with them as bodyguards."

Kaela tensed and discreetly poked Shawn. Frowns flitted across their faces at the thought of spending more time with the unpleasant teenager.

Leland's eyebrows jumped up. "Mika, you are only fifteen. Don't be a fool."

"I could help! I'm older than these two!"

King Arendore said kindly, "Mika, I am honored that you would like to assist us, but this is *not* a child's game. I am painfully aware of how young Kaela and Shawn are, but they have special gifts, and their age cannot be helped. I will do everything in my power to protect them, but Gannon and Gavin will have their hands full without adding you to the mix."

"I'm only three years younger than Gannon and Gavin!" Mika cried.

Skyla injected, "Arendore, he wants to help."

Buoyed by the support of his aunt, the Queen, Mika stood straighter and squared his shoulders. "I promise I won't be disappointing you. I can do way more than the two wee ones."

Kaela's stomach instantly knotted in irritation. She wasn't a baby, after all.

"Absolutely not," King Arendore replied, losing his patience with Mika's blatant disrespect.

Mika opened his mouth to protest, but Tressa, oblivious to the tension in the adults, twirled back into the room, ran into her grandmother's arms for a good-bye hug and then embraced her tall stern grandfather. Leland's face softened into a smile as he leaned over and hugged his granddaughter. He whispered something in her ear, and Tressa giggled. After released from his embrace, Tressa ran out of the room.

Frowning, Mika tipped at the waist and left without a word.

Clouda blew air between her lips, making a *shushh-ing* noise. Kaela watched, amazed to see the tree respond by drawing its branches tightly around the room, reinforcing the leafy walls and ceiling, enclosing them in a now still and stifling layer of foliage.

Kaela scanned the room from floor to ceiling taking in her surroundings. She dug her toes into a thick carpet, woven from grass and flowers, which lined the floor; it filled the room with a beautiful fragrance. Now that the crowd was gone, she could see that soft grass bundles draped with velvet cloth created inviting seats around the room.

Kaela continued to inspect the room until she noticed something odd in the leaves above her. She touched Shawn's arm and motioned above with her eyes. Two sets of eyes stared down at them. After squinting to be sure, Kaela observed Tressa and Mika lying flat on a tree branch. Tressa brought her finger to her mouth as if to say, "Please don't say a word." Mika stuck his tongue out. Kaela rolled her eyes at him, but let them both be. After all, she rather liked Tressa.

Once the King and Queen were seated, Netri directed everyone else to their places, and the group surrounded the royal couple in a semi-circle. Kaela and Shawn sat directly opposite the King and Queen. Gannon and Gavin stood, still and silent, behind Leland and just to the left of Shawn. Clouda handed Kaela and Shawn cups filled with fragrant jasmine tea, and then took her place with her husband, while Netri stood to Kaela's right.

"Are you comfortable?" King Arendore asked, leaning forward slightly. His eyes shone with genuine concern as he looked first at Kaela and then at Shawn. "Are you feeling well?"

Kaela stuttered, "Yes sir, I'm fine. But, I'm not sure – I mean ... I'm here to help, but what..." Her mouth dried to a croak and she wanted desperately to drink her tea, but was afraid that she'd do something stupid in front of the King and Queen.

Netri smiled and leaned closer to her.

"Kaela, we will answer your questions," he said, placing a small hand on her knee. "Relax," he whispered to her, "Drink the tea."

Kaela sipped the tea carefully, feeling Arendore's eyes upon her. She placed the cup on a small table next to her, trying not to spill, and took a deep breath. She instantly felt better.

Shawn smiled as the tea hit his stomach.

"Thank you, Clouda, this is delicious," Kaela said.

"Yes, thank you." Shawn nodded in agreement.

King Arendore said kindly, "I wish Queen Skyla and I had time to host you in our castle, but it is too far away and our situation is desperate. Time is short, too short, so Skyla and I decided it would be best to meet you here in her family home, the home of the Tree Tribe, which is far closer to your ultimate destination." He closed his eyes against a tear, which collected in his eyelashes and dropped. "Here we are closer to our son."

Though the breeze had long since died, the tree's leaves shifted, crackling.

With tears slowly rolling down her cheeks, Skyla looked deeply into the cousins' eyes and said, "Kaela and Shawn, our Grandmother Tree tells us that you met our son – in the song. Do you remember?"

Kaela and Shawn looked at each other, momentarily confused, but then the tree rustled gently and they remembered the vision of the baby in the tree-song.

Kaela said. "Yes, yes, I saw him – that beautiful baby." She stopped and looked from the King to the Queen, realizing the awful truth.

King Arendore's said, "That child, our precious baby son, Eiren, has been kidnapped along with Skyla's beloved aunt, Anya." Arendore's brow furrowed and his face flushed with anger. He hesitated, gathered his composure, and continued, "Gulig, the man who initiated this evil scheme has sent word, in no uncertain terms, that he will kill Eiren if we make any attempt to attack, even though Gulig is massing troops at our borders." Arendore's tone grew harsher. "Furthermore, Gulig swears on his blood that he will kill our child unless we surrender to him. I must come before him and bow at his feet in recognition of his power by midnight tomorrow – only then will he return our child in safety."

"But Eiren's just a baby!" Shawn said.

Queen Skyla nodded silently.

Kaela shook her head, horrified by the thought of so tiny a child being taken from its parents. Now Kaela understood the ache that pulsed in Skyla and Arendore's hearts – it was because they had been torn from their son. It must be like the ache Kaela had felt when her mother died.

"Yes, Kaela and Shawn." Netri said. "We brought you here to rescue that beautiful child."

"Sir, why would that man do such a thing?" Shawn asked with a shaky voice.

The lines on Arendore's face deepened and he paused a moment to control his rage. "Gulig is the leader of a tribe called the Rugus. He is a man with no conscience, who is bent on revenge against the House of Muraten."

Growing more and more outraged, Kaela said, "It's not right to take it out on a baby!"

Skyla's hands clenched into fists until the skin on her knuckles turned white. The anger in everyone's eyes intensified until the air felt charged with electricity.

Shawn asked, "Sir, but why?"

"Kaela and Shawn, this is a very large puzzle that goes back for generations." King Arendore sat back in his chair and sighed. "Long ago my ancestors, King Muraten and Queen Rhiana, negotiated a peace agreement with King Grule of the Rugu tribe. They agreed to marry their beloved daughter, Princess Gwenilda, to King Grule's son when Gwenilda turned eighteen. In exchange there was to be a power sharing agreement so that there could finally be everlasting peace between the tribes of this land.

"One day before the wedding, Gwenilda's life came to a tragic end. The wedding never took place. The contract was broken."

"Sir, what do you mean, a tragic end?" Shawn asked.

Arendore said with a sad faraway look in eyes. "Gwenilda would have been queen of this land, but she died at the age of eighteen. There are rumors she loved someone other than the Rugu prince and that she died of a broken heart. Some people say she took her own life so she would not have to marry the cruel Rugu prince. I cannot say for certain what happened to Gwenilda. Her story is shrouded in mystery."

"The fragile peace agreement was broken and there was a terrible war. After the loss of too many lives, King Muraten and his men finally chased the Rugus from this land. Since then, the Rugus have lusted after revenge."

Shawn listened intently, nodding now and then as he absorbed pieces of information. "And you said that Gulig is a Rugu?"

"Yes, Shawn. Gulig is the rightful heir of the Rugu Tribe. Now, through trickery and deceit, the Rugus have returned to Muratenland," King Arendore continued. "Gulig, their leader, has taken over the province where my twin brother Lorendale lives. Gulig has my brother imprisoned in his own castle – along with my son. We meant to attack soon to win back the lands that we'd lost, but that changed two nights ago, when Gulig's men poisoned Eiren's bodyguards and kidnapped my baby in the dead of night."

Anger, like a bolt of lightning, flashed in his eyes. "The man is a monster," he hissed.

Leland's forehead creased until his eyebrows gathered into one straight line. "He is a monster bent on revenge," he agreed, nodding. "Arendore, the men of the Tree Tribe are prepared to fight here and now. I don't trust that man even for a moment to keep me grandbaby safe. I know the red-haired girl is the vessel of great power, but I think it is time for us to fight. With her by our side, we can win this."

"All the men of Muratenland are prepared to fight, but we would just be playing into Gulig's hands." Arendore's jaw tightened as he shook his head. "You know as well as I do that he won't hesitate to harm Eiren. He will leap at any reason to start a war. War means sending hundreds of our people into battle and possibly to their deaths. As king, I must do everything in my power to find a peaceful solution."

"But Arendore, our baby, he has our baby..." Skyla's voice broke, and she sobbed once.

"Skyla, please," Arendore looked into his wife's eyes as though pleading for her to understand. "My heart is also breaking, but we must act carefully, or Gulig will do what we dread most."

Skyla dropped her head into her hands and sobbed.

"You think he'll actually hurt a little baby?" Kaela asked, unable to comprehend that kind of cruelty.

King Arendore nodded silently.

"Think on it, Arendore. We could sneak in through the trees," Leland said. "He wouldn't have time to hurt the child before we be on him."

"No, Leland." Arendore said firmly. "We would be seen."

"I want to help," Shawn began, "but how do we do this? There is so much at stake. What can we do?"

"Long ago, a seer foretold of the arrival of the red haired girl." Once again, King Arendore looked into Kaela's eyes. "Not just any red-haired girl, you understand – she predicted that you would come to us, Kaela."

"Me? But why?" Kaela questioned, wondering.

"What did the seer say Kaela would do?" Shawn asked.

"There is a prophecy," Skyla explained.

Clouda handed her daughter a handkerchief to wipe away the tears that ran steadily down her cheeks.

Skyla murmured, "Thank you." Then she continued, "It was written long before our time." She recited the prophecy slowly from memory:

"The Queen made a promise, and then gave birth,
But defied the seer and brought on the curse,
That left her offspring to keep the contract
With the Rugu warrior and his dreadful acts.
He schemes and plots, determined to destroy
By stealing away with the king's baby boy.
But all is not lost for this fractured land –
From near and far, help lends a hand
To free the prince from the frightening grasp,
Of the vengeful man who is stuck in the past.
But where is the wynd that blew far away,
Is it cocooned in a seed to return one day?
Is there someone with a heart strong and pure?
Yes! The key is inside the red-haired girl.
She must find butterfly breath within her heart,
Then lives will be saved and peace will start."

Kaela listened attentively to the poem, staring at Queen Skyla, hoping to somehow see into her mind and understand its meaning while King Arendore's eyes moved between his wife and Kaela.

"Netri," King Arendore said. "Please show our guests the painting of the red-haired girl."

Netri untied a red ribbon from the rolled parchment. He unfurled it and handed it to Kaela.

The parchment curled around Kaela's hand as she touched the painting of a girl with blue eyes and wild red hair painted to look so much like her own. Even the shape of the mouth, the nose and the sprinkling of freckles were the same. "It really does look like me, but how..." Kaela murmured to herself. Then she caught sight of something else in the painting. She stroked the image – the necklace that hung around the girl's neck. It was identical to Kaela's butterfly pendant!

Excitement rose inside of Kaela. She had always wanted to do something special – something important – and now the opportunity was in front of her. She turned to Shawn and said, "Look at this, Shawn." Then she whispered to him, "Do you have any idea what this poem means?"

Shawn followed the lines of the poem written just above the portrait. He loved to solve puzzles, so he was finally in his element. He said, "The first part seems like what has already happened. I think I understand the part about 'the man forever stuck in the past'. Would that be the evil man? The kidnapper?"

Netri nodded in agreement, "Gulig – yes. I believe that is correct, Shawn."

Shawn continued. "This does look like Kaela, and she does have a good heart. She's one of the only kids I know who stands up to bullies."

"Thank you, Shawn," Kaela said softly, with a shy smile on her face.

"Indeed, it's obvious that you both have beautiful hearts," Netri agreed.

"What is butterfly breath," Shawn wondered.

"I don't understand either. Butterfly breath? What is that?" Kaela asked.

"It already lives inside of you, Kaela," Netri said.

Kaela frowned as she read the prophecy again. "Butterfly breath. I don't think I've ever looked that closely at a butterfly."

"When it is time, the magic of your heart will know."

"The magic of my own heart?"

"Yes, Kaela. Your heart is filled with untapped beauty."

Netri's face was so kind as he looked at her that Kaela knew there was truth to his words. She couldn't stand the thought of the innocent baby in the arms of a cruel man, and knew she had to do what she could. "How can we help?" She asked.

"Yes, what can we do?" Shawn nodded quickly.

"Thank you, Kaela and Shawn. Thank you," the king said. His voice deepened as he continued, "Every minute is precious, so Gannon and Gavin have already been briefed on the details. They will share what they know with you on the way. They will guide you up Mount Sankaria, sacred home of the Butterfly Tribe, and they will act as both bodyguards through the caves..."

"Excuse me, Sire." Netri said, interrupting the King.

"What is it, Netri?"

"I have been contemplating this matter. I know it is your sincere wish to shield these children, but I am afraid Gannon and Gavin carry too much anger. It will draw the attention of Gulig's men."

"Of course Gannon and Gavin carry anger," Skyla snapped. "After all that Gulig's done."

"I will not send these children to the castle without protection," Arendore said firmly.

The wind whistled through the tree, and Leland interjected, "Netri, our tree is reminding us that these boys have kind hearts. They draw more from their gentle grandmother, Clouda, than from me."

"Yes, I can feel their kindness, Leland, but you know as well as I do that all of the Tree Tribe takes nourishment from the same soil."

Kaela thought of her own quick temper. What if it got in their way? Her hand shot up as though she was in a classroom, "Excuse me..."

All eyes turned towards Kaela.

Netri said warmly, "How can we help you, Kaela?"

"Well, I kind of have a problem with anger, I mean, I get mad sometimes. Like yesterday, I pushed a girl in gym."

Netri smiled. "We all have anger, Kaela. Anger is a normal response. But when it takes a hold of you and won't let go - like a taproot growing deeper and deeper into the ground – it is not good. That kind of anger can fester and swell until it leads you away from your heart. That kind of anger leads you away from your true destination. Do you understand?"

Kaela nodded slowly. "I think so – I get mad, but then it's over."

The tree fluttered the branches above their heads, shaking her leaves like hundreds of rattles. Skyla nodded her head and whispered something in her husband's ear.

Looking deeply into Kaela's and Shawn's eyes once again, King Arendore spoke. "Thank you for your advice, Netri, but – I have made my decision. These children are precious to me. Gannon and Gavin *will* accompany Kaela and Shawn."

Netri bowed slightly and blended into the background.

King Arendore continued. "Kaela and Shawn, your bodyguards will guide you to the caves of Mount Sankaria. There you will find a secret entrance into the bowels of the castle where Gulig holds my son. The castle was once nearly identical to the one where Skyla and I now reside, so we know the stone rooms very well. The entire castle was carved directly into the mountain, but Gulig has recently built an enormous wooden structure around it. Our spies tell us that Eiren and Auntie Anya are locked away in one of the old rooms. It will take great cleverness – and your own special magic – to find them and set them free."

"Kaela, you hold the map of the future in your hands," Netri added, pointing to the parchment. "Do not forget the purpose of your mission, and remember, all along this journey your heart is your best guide. Listen to the soft voice within you, and you will find the magic of your heart ... and then you will find Eiren. Remember that many friends and unseen forces support you, even in unexpected places."

Kaela lifted her right hand and covered her chest, feeling for her heart and hoping to discover the unseen magic. Instead, she felt the hard crystal of the butterfly pendant, hanging heavy from her neck. She palmed it and drew comfort from the shape. *What magic power does it have?*

Just then, one of the twins spoke up. "Sire, we best leave quickly while the sun is still fresh in the sky. Shall we go now to fetch the horses?"

King Arendore nodded. "Yes, that is an excellent idea. But first, please stand before me. I have something to ask you."

The twins did as instructed and asked in unison, "Yes, your

highness?"

"Do you promise to do everything in your power to keep these precious children safe?"

Both men knelt on one knee and bowed before the king. "Yes, sire. We promise to do so."

"Very well! May the blessings of the Great Spirit shine on you and illuminate your path."

The twins bowed their heads and rose once again while the tree created a doorway by parting a section of leaves. The two young men moved swiftly out of the room.

As soon as the tree gathered her leaves into a solid wall, Skyla said, "They need to be knowing about the ganba."

"Yes, yes they do," The King nodded solemnly. "You have been witness to the power of the ganba more than I, Skyla. Would you please share what you know?"

Skyla sighed, looking off into the distance as her eyes welled once again with tears. She shook her head, clearing her vision.

"Ganba is a terrible brew, which is concentrated from the root of the ganba plant. The entire Rugu Tribe is addicted to that elixir because of the strength and power it brings to them," she began. "Ganba makes the body strong, but at the same time it also clouds the mind, and closes the heart, and ... and not everyone can tolerate the drink." Skyla continued in a whisper as though she were sharing a secret, "I've been hearing that Lorendale, King Arendore's twin brother, is drinking the elixir."

"And he can't handle it?" Shawn asked.

"No, the ganba is a poison to Lorendale," Skyla said. "He thought it would make him strong like the Rugu, but no – now he is using it to forget ... some people use it to forget. They use it to shield themselves from the searing pain in their hearts." Skyla shook her head again, and her voice caught as she said, "I've been hearing that Lorendale may be dying from it."

King Arendore gently touched his wife's hand.

"All the more reason why we must defeat Gulig," Netri said, and the lines on his face deepened instantly until his skin looked as old as the bark of the ancient limba tree. "There is no more time to waste."

Chapter Seven · To The Rescue

"Shawn, Kaela," Netri continued, turning towards them, "We have prepared some supplies for you, warm clothes, food, and gifts from the King and Queen."

The King stood in front of the two children and said, "Kaela, the prophecy says you contain a treasure that is your birthright, the mysterious butterfly breath, the key that can set this land free." He looked from Kaela to Shawn. "It is not our intention to send you into battle. Rather, you are going to the land of our enemy to unlock the curse of ancient wounds that binds the tribes of Muratenland to conflict.

"These beloved sons of the Tree Tribe, Gannon and Gavin, will accompany you and protect you. Events can take unexpected twists and turns, so we also have weapons of great strength that will enable you to defend yourselves against the forces of evil."

King Arendore held up a small sword and said, "Before my father's death there was a terrible fire. My father's crown and many other royal treasures melted in the heat of the terrible blaze, and the molten metal ran into a crevice in the floor. After the fire, we found the cooled lump of metal, which we forged into the handle of this sword. This weapon has never been used. It must only serve freedom and must only be used defensively. Though it appears to be a simple weapon, it will guide you on your quest."

Filled with excitement, Kaela offered her open palms to the king. The golden hilt fit her hand perfectly and the blade's edge was razor sharp. It was polished to such a fine sheen that she could see her own eyes in the mirror-like surface of the shining metal.

"This is amazing! Thank you – I promise I will use it wisely," Kaela said. She bowed low to the king and the queen.

Clouda wrapped a leather sheath around Kaela's waist and, after feeling the weight of the sword in her hand a moment more, Kaela stowed the sword in its holder.

"Remember, Kaela," Netri said. "It is as important to know when to put down the sword as when to use it."

Queen Skyla pulled a weapon from under her pant leg and a beam of sunlight reflected off the bright red of a ruby-handled dagger. "Shawn ..." she began.

"Skyla," King Arendore interrupted his wife. "I am not sure that weapon is right for this journey."

In an instant, the Queen's voice took on her father's fierceness and the staccato sound of a rock striking another stone. "I mean no disrespect, Arendore, but this is the very dagger that me grandfather used to remove the Rugus from this land generations ago. This will serve them well on their journey."

Leland crossed his arms and said, "Arendore, please – that weapon holds great power. I think the boy should have it."

The Grandmother Tree rustled.

King Arendore looked at his wife, then at Leland, and nodded his head in agreement.

"Shawn, this is a special weapon with great powers. It has been in my family for generations," Skyla said, handing it to Shawn handle first, and then removed the sheath from around her calf as Shawn examined the blade.

The handle shimmered in Shawn's hand. Running his thumb along the blade, he examined the dagger's strength, its balance, and its sharpness. This was a real weapon, not some mere toy for show.

Kaela suddenly recalled playing swords with Shawn using sticks. Somehow she always ended up bruising his thumb or poking him in the stomach. More often than not, their games ended with him throwing down his stick, saying, "This is stupid. I don't want to hurt you. Let's do something else." What damage could he possibly do with a real weapon? Kaela thought he was less likely to get hurt without it.

"Thank you, Queen Skyla," Shawn said. "But – excuse me – why is King Arendore worried about me having it? Is it dangerous?"

"Shawn, this dagger was with me from the time I first left me parent's home. My father gave it to me." A glance of tenderness passed between Leland and Skyla, and then she continued. "It served me well, but the weapon carries a history. It was drawn when anger rose like a volcano erupting from the bowels of the earth, but my father's father used it long ago with great courage to defeat the Rugus. This weapon holds a mighty strength, but it takes a powerful heart to use it well."

"Both these weapons are powerful," Netri warned. "Please do not use either one in haste – understand that every action has consequences."

Kaela hesitated. "How will I know when to use the sword, then?"

"These gifts are not meant to be a burden," King Arendore said, looking from Shawn to Kaela to be sure they understood his words. "I trust you will use your best judgment."

"I promise to use it honorably," Kaela said solemnly.

"I will take great care with this weapon," Shawn said, bowing.

Clouda stepped forward, holding two suede drawstring bags in her hand. "These are nuts from the Grandmother Tree. A single nut holds the strength and wisdom of an entire tree. Tie these onto your belts. When you are needing it most, the Grandmother Tree will be with you." She handed over the bags and bowed. "The clothes from our people will offer you some camouflage as you move up the mountain."

Netri presented two pairs of brown suede boots. "The finest cobblers in our village labored all night to make these for you," he said.

Kaela and Shawn took the soft boots in hand and sat down to pull them on. Kaela brushed away sand that was still lodged between her toes from their romp on the beach. Reminded of her ride on the back of the sea turtles, and the way her breath quietly filled her on that peaceful journey, Kaela took a deep breath, and pulled on the beautiful boots. They were a perfect fit.

"Thank you," Shawn said, standing. "All of you have been so kind. I promise I will do my best to serve you well."

"Thank you for trusting me," Kaela said, joining her cousin. "We will rescue Eiren. We'll find a way."

"We must say our goodbyes here," King Arendore said. He clasped

Kaela's hands and then Shawn's. "Thank you, thank you, thank you. More than anything I wish I could be by your side, but know that I am with you in my heart. The Great Spirit is with you."

Queen Skyla hugged each of them. "Thank you," she said. "Even if I said a thank you for every star in the sky, I could never be thanking you enough for your help."

Moved by the Queen's words of gratitude, Kaela and Shawn bowed low. Then they joined Netri and walked to the end of a large branch, which gently lowered them to the ground. Kaela hoped Tressa would be waiting for them at the base of the tree, but she was nowhere to be found. The twins sat atop two large horses a few yards to their right. The only friends waiting to say goodbye were Blanco and Wollan. The large brown dog sat before them, wagging his tail.

"Great forces support you in this journey," Netri reminded them. "Remember to look into your heart to know whom you can trust. Gulig's power is immense, but you are in the care of something much greater."

Shawn stroked Blanco while Kaela dug her fingers into the curly hair of the dog.

"This journey is your destiny," Netri continued. "Here is a lantern for each of you. Tuck this tin of matches in your pockets for safekeeping. Where you are going, you will need light to guide you. Kaela, here is another scarf for you. It is still best to hide your red hair," he smiled inexplicably. "The next time I see you, I trust it will be in happier circumstances." Shawn and Kaela each gave Netri a hug before turning to leave.

"Aren't you going to say goodbye?" One of the twins asked.

The other twin said, "Someone is waiting to say goodbye to you."

Kaela spun around, certain this time she would find Tressa emerging from a hiding place, but there was still no sign of their friend.

"Grandmother wants to say goodbye," the twins said in unison.

Kaela and Shawn approached the massive tree, closed their eyes, and leaned into the trunk. The familiar lullaby rang in Kaela's ears, and a vision of the baby boy with deep brown eyes once again filled her thoughts. The leaves on the tree rustled, *Shhweeeshannasha, shhweeeshannasha.*

"Kaela and Shawn," Netri urged, "it is time. It is time."

The twins each rode a large stallion with supplies strapped behind the saddle. They guided the horses over to Kaela and Shawn.

"We best be leaving to reach the caves before darkness falls," one spoke. "I be Gavin – my red headband sets me apart from Gannon in the green. I'd be honored to carry the red-haired girl."

Once again, shyness overcame Kaela. She looked down even as she smiled at the handsome twins.

"Oh, don't be all bashful around me. We practically are family. Put your foot in the stirrup and give me your hands and I'll help you up."

Kaela did as instructed and Gavin easily lifted her into the saddle behind him, while Gannon did the same for Shawn. Then they were off.

Kaela bounced up and down, clutching the saddle behind her until Gavin said, "Hey, Love, you best hold me around the waist. I can't be responsible for you falling off this horse." Still feeling awkward, Kaela tentatively wrapped her hands around the handsome young man. He gripped one of her hands, saying, "There now, that be better. You ready for some fun?"

"Ok ... I guess."

Gavin urged the horse forward into a gallop before Kaela could say another word.

The sun was high in the sky and warmed their backs as the horses flew toward the distant mountain. Kaela looked over Gavin's shoulder, trying to get a sense of what lay ahead, but most of Mount Sankaria was cloaked in a low-lying cloud. On either side, a blur of trees and expansive fields swept past them. The twins raced each other along the broad path, at times riding neck-on-neck until one or the other of the twin's horses would take the lead. The horses neighed joyfully as Shawn and Kaela laughed out loud, enjoying the sensation of speed. Although Kaela had seen a village from high in the tree, the twins guided the horses on the other side of the valley far from prying eyes. Kaela sighed, wishing she had been given a chance to see the fairyland castle up close.

Chapter Eight · Poisoned

Their pace slowed to a walk as the horses ascended a narrow path through the forest of towering evergreen trees that coated the base of Mount Sankaria. The horses walked slowly upwards, through low-lying branches and roots, and Kaela clung tightly to Gavin, afraid that she might slide off the back of the horse. Her butt and legs grew increasingly sore with every plodding step. Finally, the mountain trail became so steep that the horses began to lose their footing on slippery shale rocks. Gavin and Gannon reined their horses to a halt after a slide that made Kaela squeak with fear.

"This is as far as we're taking the horses," Gannon said. "Best to hike the rest of the way."

The twins dismounted and Shawn and Kaela jumped down. Kaela stretched her arms and legs, relieved to be on solid ground once again, while Gavin unpacked the supplies from the back of the horse and handed out leather backpacks to each of them. Then Gannon slapped the horses on their rumps and sent them home.

As Shawn and Kaela adjusted their packs, Gavin motioned for them to come near. "Okay you two, listen carefully," he began. "If anything happens to us, you'll need to find your own way. If you keep your ear on the sounds of the stream, she'll lead you up the mountain to the entrance of the cave. Follow the cave until you reach a huge cavernous room filled with the most marvelous mineral formations. When you hold up your lamp, the cave will sparkle like millions of precious jewels. It's called the Crystal Cave." Gavin looked back and forth between Shawn and Kaela to be sure they understood. When they nodded he continued, "Just beyond that there is a semicircular cavern. Netri says that, in the middle of the cavern wall, behind a large boulder, there is a small opening into Gulig's castle. It hasn't been used for generations and leads to an alcove in a bedroom in the old part of the castle. If we are very lucky, it will lead us straight to Eiren. Do you understand?"

"Wait a minute," Shawn frowned. "The castle is on the other side of the cave wall?"

"Yes. There are lots of winding caves that make their way through the mountains in these lands, and the castle is built right into the mountain. In times of peace, the caves are wonderful short cuts. But now we will be using a cave to sneak our way inside Gulig's castle."

"Okay, I understand. But you'll lead us, right?" Kaela said, grateful to have the twins as bodyguards to guide them.

Gannon nodded, "Yes – we'll be here for you."

The foursome hiked single file through the dense forest. With each step, they rose steadily higher and higher up the mountain. They walked in silence, lost in their own thoughts as they panted with exertion. It was cool and dark under the canopy, but every few minutes a shaft of sunlight burst through the foliage, bringing comfort and warmth. After awhile, the path widened into open terrain covered in tough grass and scrawny trees that were bent from the mountain's fierce winds and shallow soil.

As they approached a flat moss-covered rock, Gavin said, "I think we best stop for a few minutes to catch our breath and eat a bite." He pointed to the stream by their side. "We all should drink from these waters – they'll fill us with new energy. The waters from Mount Sankaria are blessed, despite Gulig's wretchedness."

"How much further do we have to go?" Shawn asked, shading his eyes. "The sun looks like it may set soon."

Gavin said, "It will be early evening 'fore we reach the caves."

They perched on flat rocks and dug around in their packs for food. Inside were leaf-covered packets containing a mixture of dried apricots, nuts and seeds soaked in honey. They all wolfed down the mix and knelt by the stream, gulping handfuls of ice-cold water.

Kaela was surprised to feel renewed energy coursing through her veins as she refreshed herself. When she had drunk her fill, she sat back, and the twins sat on either side of her. She relaxed for a moment and thought again of the fairy castle they had left far behind.

"Have you ever been to Arendore's and Skyla's castle? I was hoping one day I could go there. It looks like such a magical place," she mused dreamily.

"Oh yes, we were there," Gannon said. "All the Tree People were invited for the wedding. What a grand day that was!"

"What is it like – the castle?"

"Oh 'tis a beautiful place. It was carved long ago from limestone, right out of the mountain. There are hundreds of mosaics of animals, of forests and birds, made of bright tiny tiles. Now it must be the saddest, emptiest place, with Eiren gone and all."

Shawn sat down across from the group to listen in.

Gavin added, "No sadder than when we first be arrived here..." But a sudden movement from Gannon prevented him from speaking anything further.

Kaela looked from one profile to the other, each absolutely alike. For the first time, the twins displayed a hard edge similar to that of their grandfather's. Their jaws were clenched tightly, and the smiles that had passed so easily across their lips tightened into a straight line. "What do you mean? Arriving where?" Kaela asked timidly, her curiosity overcoming her sudden nervousness.

"That's a subject for another time," Gannon said.

Confused by the unexpected change in the easy-going twins, Kaela asked, "But ... why?"

"It be best to drop this questioning, Kaela," Gannon said.

Gavin looked at his twin. "I disagree. These two deserve to know the truth."

"King Arendore didn't want to be dragging them into our old problems...."

"What, what aren't you telling us?" Shawn interrupted, disturbed by the change in the bodyguards.

"It's best they know." Gavin looked hard at his brother, who finally nodded in agreement. "Years ago, Gulig sent his henchman in the middle of the night and cut a deep ring around the base of our Grandmother Tree," he explained. "He killed her without a second thought."

"But you live in a Grandmother Tree..." Kaela trailed off.

"We didn't want to be airing our problems," Gannon said. "It happened a long time ago. We used to live in a Grandmother Tree not far from Lorendale's castle, but Gulig murdered her. When a tree be ringed, it be like cutting off your life blood. We lost our home ... our history ... our dearest friend the night our Grandmother Tree died."

The vision of the dying tree and the mournful melody in the tree song flashed through Kaela's memory. "Oh, I'm so sorry." Kaela touched each twin gently on the arm. She felt a greater kinship with the twins, understanding well the pain of losing someone you love. "We won't let Gulig hurt Eiren," she said softly. "I promise."

"Gulig must be stopped," Gannon said with an abrupt urgency in his voice. "There's no bringing back our Grandmother Tree, but from this day forward I'll be doing everything in my power to stop him from harming another soul." The dark mood that had loomed over the group like a giant wave crashed and receded.

"Are you with me?" Gannon reached out his hand.

"I am!" Shawn exclaimed, placing his hand on top of Gannon's.

"Me, too!" Gavin and Kaela chorused, joining their hands to the pile.

They all smiled at one another. There was a moment of quiet and then they all settled back, bringing their hands to their sides.

"Can I ask you something?" Kaela asked softly.

"Of course, Kaela," the twins said in unison.

"The tree kept playing a lullaby for me, like a song my mother used to sing. I haven't heard it for years." Kaela looked at the ground, overcome with shyness. "Do you think your tree might have met my mother?"

"I don't know, Kaela," Gavin said. "When was she here?"

"It would have been long ago, before I was born."

"Everything about a tree is recorded in her yearly rings. And her memory is long," Gavin said.

"Even more, the tree also is in touch with the roots of the entire forest, so her information is almost limitless," Gannon concluded. "Our tree's roots are drawing on such a wealth of information, it is impossible for me to say whether she is the one that met your mother."

"Lullabies are so lovely," Gavin said, a far-off look in his eyes. "Every night our tree wraps us in her branches, pillowing our bodies in her leaves, and sings us to sleep. It's a lovely thing to be rocked in the wind to a soothing song. Doesn't your mother sing that song for you anymore?"

"Her mother died two years ago," Shawn quickly interjected, saving Kaela the agony of having to say the words aloud.

Gavin placed his arm around Kaela's shoulders while Gannon touched her face.

"Oh, I be so sorry," Gannon said. "No one told us, you see."

"It's okay." Kaela said, her sadness for once overcome with a fierce blush.

Gavin gave her a gentle smile, then shaded his eyes and looked at the sun dropping lower in the sky. "We best be moving on. Darkness is coming on soon."

They gathered their things together and resumed hiking up the mountain. They walked for some time in sunshine, and then the mist, which hung like a giant cloud over the top of the mountain, enveloped them in a dense fog. The burbling of the stream was like an unseen companion that guided them ever upwards towards the caves. Inspired by the chilly air, they pulled their warm sweaters out of their packs. They walked in single file, with Gavin leading the way, then Shawn, Kaela and Gannon bringing up the rear.

Cheep, cheep, a small bird cried a short distance away.

Shawn slowed until he was even with Kaela, and then he shook her shoulder.

"Kaela, did you hear that?" Shawn whispered.

Still thinking about the conversation with the twins and the dying tree, Kaela startled back to the present. "Huh?"

"A bird – do you hear that bird?" Shawn squeezed her shoulders until she stood still.

"Umm ... no," Kaela said.

Che-e-ep! The bird screeched frantically.

"Oh!" Kaela exclaimed.

"That bird's in trouble. Let's help him." Shawn urged.

Che-e-ep!

"I think he's over there," Kaela pointed.

"I'll stand watch," Gavin offered. "Gannon, why don't you keep an eye on Kaela and Shawn?"

Tall dry grass bent under their feet as Kaela and Shawn slowly walked toward the cheeping bird. The sound grew near, so they carefully parted the grass searching for the bird. Then they knelt and crawled through the damp undergrowth until they reached a depression behind a large rock. Gannon followed at a greater distance, taking his time. Hidden in a tuft of grass, a small bird with feathers of the brightest green stood, holding its wing in an awkward position. Its creamsicle-orange head drew back upon seeing the two pairs of eyes peering down at him. The bird scurried a few steps and fell over, cheeping in pain and fear.

"It's a baby parrot!" Shawn placed his index finger gently in front of the bird. "Hey, don't worry," he cooed. "I'm not going to hurt you. I just want to help. Otherwise, you're just food for some other animal with that wing."

The parrot stopped, cocked his head and climbed onto Shawn's finger. He sat still, looking up in expectation.

"That's the way," Shawn smiled softly. "I'm going to help you. I've fixed wings before." Shawn cupped his other hand around the bird and brought the tiny creature close to his face, where he could get a better look. "You see, it's your feathers – they're out of alignment." Shawn ran his finger along the wing and gently smoothed the feathers. The bird let out a plaintive cheep, and looked up at Shawn.

"Will you look at that?" Gannon said, smiling as he came up to them.

"You'll be flying in no time," Shawn reassured the chick. "Would you like to come with us? I promise I'll take care of you."

The bird cheeped once more, clasped Shawn's shirt in his beak and claws, and gradually climbed up Shawn's arm.

Kaela stroked the parrot's head. "He's so cute," she said softly. The bird leaned into her finger and half-closed his eyes.

Shawn carefully tucked the bird into his shirt pocket and declared, "His name is Peeper, and he wants to..."

The sound of metal crashing against metal interrupted Shawn's words, breaking the peace of the mountain. Kaela and Shawn reached for their weapons, while Gannon leapt up and drew his sword in a flash.

He turned back and whispered, "No! Stay here. Do not come out."

"GANNON!" Gavin yelled.

Kaela and Shawn obeyed their bodyguard and continued crouching behind the large rock.

Swords clanged and clattered, crashed and rattled in the distance as Gannon joined the fight. Then there was an ominous silence as Kaela gripped the hilt of her sword and held her breath, wondering if the twins were okay.

"Tell me where to find the red-haired girl or die, tree-scum," a husky voice demanded.

"We know nothing about any red-haired girl!" One of the brothers grunted.

"We be in search of a healer," the other said quickly. "One of the Tree People be terribly ill."

"I'll show you illness!" The voice rasped, and barked a short laugh. "See how you like the Rugu poison!"

One, two, three whistling sounds were heard, whirring through the air. Then nothing moved ... all was quiet.

Kaela and Shawn searched one another's eyes, unsure of what to do next. Then unfamiliar footsteps drew near, rattling the tall grass. Kaela and Shawn froze, barely daring to breathe.

"Come on out now," a deep, rumbling voice called. "Don't be afraid. We're here to take you to safety."

Kaela and Shawn looked at each other, wide-eyed.

"Do you really think you can hide from us?" The other man sneered hoarsely.

Two men reached the other side of the large rock where Kaela and Shawn cowered. The men stopped. The odor of their perspiration clouded the air while one man's heavy boot kicked stones down the mountainside.

"Your friends need you! If you don't want a taste of the Rugu poison," the husky-voiced man yelled, "you'd better come out now!"

The other one chuckled deep in his throat. "Oh, I see you now, little girl! You best come out. Don't worry – we won't hurt you."

Gripped with terror, Kaela hugged her knees to her chest, but didn't move.

There was a long pause, a rattling of grass and then the two figures stomped away over the hill. Kaela began to unwrap her fingers from her calves.

"Just you wait!" One of the men screamed through the fog, his raspy voice echoing around the mountain. Then all was silent once more.

Stillness filled the air, but Kaela and Shawn waited endless minutes more before crawling, snakelike, back to the burbling stream. Gavin and Gannon lay motionless, eyes staring unblinkingly at the sky. A four-inch-long dart was lodged in Gavin's arm and another poked from Gannon's neck. Their skin was as pale as paper.

Shawn leaned down, placing his ear to Gannon's nose.

"He's breathing," Shawn said with relief.

Kaela put her finger under Gavin's nose, and was overjoyed to discover that he, too, was still breathing. When she placed her palm on his forehead, a faint sound escaped his parted lips.

"Gavin is trying to say something," Kaela whispered.

A rattle escaped from Gavin's throat, "Oison ... okay ... hort. Go on ... go ..."

Shawn and Kaela bent close, listening intently to the garbled sounds.

"Oison ... oison ... go ..."

They looked at each other and simultaneously whispered, "Poison."

"Is it safe to remove the darts?" Kaela asked.

"Es," Gavin said.

"Shawn, you help Gannon. Extract it quickly and press the wound closed."

"Okay, but don't touch the needle!" Shawn ordered. "Whatever is on them has a paralyzing effect." Shawn pulled the one from Gavin's arm while Kaela carefully removed the one from Gavin's neck.

"It really isn't bleeding much," Kaela said, relieved.

But the poison had already moved through the twins' bloodstreams, and they remained paralyzed. Gavin's breathing quickened.

"Go ow, go ..." Gavin croaked.

"You want us to go on?" Kaela asked.

"Es ...es ..."

Shawn and Kaela looked at each other and Kaela stroked Gavin's face. "Are you sure?"

"Es - u ust urry efore ey eturn. O!" Gavin said.

"No, we can't leave you like this," Kaela said frantically. "You're in too much danger."

Gavin's face reddened as if he were mustering all of his strength.

"Ust ... o!!" He demanded.

Kaela and Shawn covered the two men with warm cloaks from their packs and gently closed the twins' paralyzed eyelids. As she ran, Kaela tasted the salt of tears pouring from her eyes. She prayed silently for the twins' survival.

Shawn and Kaela clambered higher and higher up the mountain. Kaela's heart beat hard against her chest, and she gasped for air while Shawn panted loudly. He was nearly invisible in the dense fog, though he walked just yards ahead of her. Kaela slowed, wondering if maybe they should turn around and get help for the twins.

When Shawn noticed she was lagging, he spun back and grabbed her hand, dragging her with him. "Come on. We've got to go. You heard Gavin. We've got to get out of here in case those men come back."

"Shawn, the twins need help. We don't even really know where the passageway is. If we hurry back now, I bet we'd have time for someone else to come back with us."

"And even more people on top of that to bring the twins to safety?" Shawn asked sarcastically. "Why don't we just put up a big neon sign: "Red-haired girl here!""

Kaela realized he was right, and her spirits fell.

"Look, Kaela," Shawn said, regretting his harsh words. "The twins wanted us to go on – and they understand this place a lot better than we do. Netri believed that we might have to make the journey on our own, and he believed we could find the way without the twins. They were here to protect us," Shawn said softly. "That's what they've done."

"But, it's just you and me," Kaela said, feeling young and vulnerable without the twins to protect them. "Can we do it by ourselves?"

Shawn shrugged. "Think about that little baby." He touched Kaela gently on the arm. "Do you remember that time your mom was reading to us?"

"She read to us so many times," Kaela said, smiling a little.

"Remember, you said, 'I wish that I could have a magic life. I wish magic would happen to me.' And your mom said, 'It's a wonderful thing to have a magic life, but it isn't easy.'"

The vague memory gradually surfaced in Kaela's mind, as if an inner fog had been blown aside.

"I remember," Kaela replied softly, "Then I said, 'No, it is easy. They can fly, and become invisible, and wonderful things happen.'"

"Yes," Shawn said, nodding. "And then your mother said, 'It isn't always like that. Sometimes it means having the courage to choose to fight for life and truth even when it's hard, even when everything in you wants to give up.'" Kaela felt something stir inside with the memory of her mother's words. She remembered the sound of her mother's voice, for just an instant.

"And I said, I still want a magic life." Kaela's heart beat steady and loud, sounding like a muffled drum in her ears. She felt a vague shift in the pit of her stomach, like buried courage and strength were taking root inside her, quietly urging her to continue. "The twins wanted us to rescue Eiren."

"Yes, they would want it this way, for sure."

Without another word, Kaela followed Shawn. Again and again their feet slipped on loose gravel, sending it cascading down the steep face of the mountain. The clattering sound echoed in the distance, making Kaela's heart pound with fear. What if Gulig's men heard the stones? She touched the hilt of her sword. She had to trust that she would know when to use it.

The higher they climbed, the more difficult it became. Even though the air was cool and damp, sweat poured from their brows and they breathed heavily in the thin air. Unable to hear the sound of water over her heavy breathing and pounding heart, Kaela caught up to Shawn and pulled him to a stop. She gasped, "Do you ... hear it ... the stream?"

Shawn hesitated, then nodded, "Yes ... but it's narrowing. It's not so loud."

Their companion, the creek, had turned into a little stream, tinkling along the rocks.

They continued on, and the incline of the mountain grew even steeper. Shawn slowed until he was proceeding so cautiously that he barely moved. Recognizing Shawn's anxiety about heights, Kaela said, "I'll take the lead. Just follow my back." Kaela climbed past her cousin, but soon discovered that she couldn't move much faster than he had. Every step demanded total concentration. The rocks were slippery with condensed fog and they had to claw their way up the cliff with their hands.

Kaela turned around and saw Shawn right on her heels. His face held a grim look of determination. When he noticed Kaela looking back at him, he gave her a wan smile.

Kaela pushed aside her disappointment over having lost the twins as guides and protectors and repeated to herself over and over – I choose a magic life. I choose a magic life. I choose a magic life.

She continued climbing up the steep mountain step-by-step-by-step, until finally they reached a ledge, which jutted out from a wall of rocks.

Kaela panted, "This must be it."

Shawn leaned against the rocks and breathed heavily. He nodded. "You feel around for an entry point there and I'll feel around to your left."

"The fog is just so thick – I can't find it ... wait ... this is it – the opening!" Kaela's heart beat hard with excitement.

"Okay," Shawn said, drawing a deep breath. "I'll light my lamp."

Though Shawn was only a few feet away, he was nearly invisible to Kaela and, for a minute, she felt utterly alone. She leaned against a tall rock outcropping to gather her strength. The perspiration from her earlier exertions dried on her skin and the damp air seeped through her clothes, chilling her to the bone. Still, it was a relief to catch her breath before they entered the cave. She turned to look out into the valley, but saw nothing. Not even a ray of sun broke through the mist.

Shawn rustled a few feet away as he prepared the lamp. She listened for other sounds. Were the Rugu soldiers on their trail? The little stream tinkled beside her like a series of tiny bells. The friendly sound brought her comfort in the foreign and dangerous place.

Shawn scraped a match against a boulder and Kaela saw a small flicker of light. She sighed with relief. But the next moment, Kaela heard a rushing rumble, which quickly grew to a roar as rocks cascaded down the mountainside, sliding right toward their small ledge.

"Take cover!!!" Kaela screamed, and dove headfirst beneath an overhanging rock shelf.

Chapter Nine · The Dark Cave

The sound of roaring and crashing grew further and further away, then stopped. But Kaela remained frozen, her arms tightly covering her head, too afraid to move. She waited and waited until the only sounds were the trickling stream and the breeze outside, which increased steadily into a strong wind. She mentally scanned each of her body parts, thankfully unharmed.

"Shawn?" She called softly. "Are you okay?"

Kaela looked for some sign of her cousin, but the murky air made it impossible to see. She ached to yell for Shawn, but she was terrified that any vibration would set off another avalanche, or attract the horrible Rugu soldiers. Kaela whispered loudly, "Shawn – where are you? Are you okay?"

There was no response. Panicked, Kaela called out, "Shawn, answer me!"

"I – I'm here, Kaela," Shawn replied. As he moved, Kaela was finally able to see him sitting up, just a few yards away.

"Are you okay?"

"Yeah, I think so. Something hit me in the arm, but it's just sore – not broken. My lamp is gone, though."

"You stay there." Kaela groped around for her lamp and miraculously found it to be in one piece. After hanging it from her belt, she stood and placed her hand against a large boulder to steady her balance. "I'll make sure it's safe to move, and see if I can find a way into the cave."

"Be careful," Shawn said, squeezing his sore arm gently.

Kaela patted her hands along the rocks, searching for an entrance into the cave. Her arm slid between some rocks, but she couldn't find an entry point big enough for her body to fit through. "I can't believe it. There's no way in."

The wind's intensity grew ever stronger, howling and crying mournfully. Kaela hugged herself against the chill.

"What do we do now?" She called, and received no answer. "Answer me, Shawn! How are we supposed to get in now?"

Kaela looked behind her. The fog that had cloaked Shawn was gone, banished by the wind's breath. The setting sun illuminated her cousin, who sat with his knees pressed to his chest and eyes tightly closed. The fog had hidden where they stood, but now their location was all too clearly exposed. Shawn huddled not three feet from the edge of a steep cliff – a very tall, steep cliff, which fell jaggedly into darkness. The wind howled again, and Shawn clutched his legs even more tightly.

"We have to get out of here ... please, Kaela," Shawn said, his voice muffled by his knees.

"I've already checked the rocks. There's no way into the cave," Kaela said woodenly. Come on, Shawn. She thought to herself. "You can do it..."

Caw, caw, caw! A large crow eyed Shawn and Kaela from his perch ten feet from where they stood. The remaining wisps of fog swirled around the crow as he clung to a branch that jutted from the side of a nearby cliff. Caw, caw, caw.

"Caw, yourself," Kaela grumbled.

Shawn cracked open his eyes and focused intently on the black silhouette of the bird.

"Shhh," Shawn said slowly. "I think he's trying to tell us something – I can't..."

Caw, caw, caw!

"What's he saying?" Kaela asked encouragingly.

"Shhh, I'm trying to understand." Shawn lifted his head momentarily, his eyes still tightly shut.

"Shawn, we need to do something. The men might come back."

"I can't get it," Shawn wailed. "My heart – it's still beating too hard – I can't hear anything else."

Caw, crckkk, caw crrrr, caw.

"What?" Shawn asked, straining to understand.

Caw, crrrr, crckkk.

"Wait," Shawn said. "I think he's trying to tell us about a way into the mountain."

"I don't know about this," Kaela said grumpily. "Remember the last crow? I don't think the crows are on our side."

Crash!!!

Fear shot up Kaela's spine and she froze. *Is someone coming?*

"We've got to hurry!" she whispered desperately.

"We have to trust the crow, except...." Shawn moaned involuntarily. His finger quivered as he pointed to a narrow ledge along the middle of a sheer cliff that led to an outcropping of rocks. "That's where he wants us to go."

Kaela stared hard at the ledge and imagined creeping across the narrow shelf with Shawn cowering behind her.

The clear sound of boots scrabbling over loose gravel approached them, but thick fog still clouded the mountain beneath them. *Was it a friend or a Rugu?*

"We can't let those Rugus get us," Kaela said, a sense of determination rising up inside her.

Caw, crrrr, caw!

Desperate for a solution, Kaela begged. "Please, Shawn...."

Shawn sat for a moment in stillness. "I'm not sure ... but I think he says he'll help us."

Crashing echoed in the valley as the footsteps drew closer and closer.

"Let's get out of here." Kaela's heart pounded against her chest as she approached the rocky ledge. She breathed deeply and tried to act calm so Shawn would not see her panic.

"Come on, Shawn. Let's do it."

Shawn crawled to Kaela and stood with quivering legs just behind her as the sun disappeared on the horizon leaving a bright orange glow.

"Look straight ahead," she soothed him. "Don't look down." Kaela flattened herself against the sheer wall of the cliff and dug her fingers into crevices in the cold stone. "See?" she said. "Just hold onto the mountain." Inching along the ledge, she willed her cousin to join her.

"I'm coming, Kaela." Shawn said without budging.

As the steps grew louder behind them, Kaela quickened her pace. Still, she kept her ear cocked for the sound of Shawn behind her. "You can do it," she whispered loudly. "There's only a little daylight left!"

Shawn mimicked his cousin, hugging the stone, but he slid his feet only a little at a time - far more tentatively than Kaela.

Caw, caw ... The crow's voice grew louder as Kaela approached the far side.

Eager for firm footing, Kaela focused her complete attention on the task at hand. She knew she couldn't afford one moment of doubt as she moved her fingers and toes from one crevice to another, until she sighed with relief upon reaching the stone outcropping. "I made it, Shawn. Come on - you can do it." She glanced in front of her, and her heart dropped. There was no visible entrance into the mountain. The crow perched on a root, cawing over the rushing noise of a waterfall.

"There's no opening, but there is a waterfall here!" Kaela called, unable to understand the bird. "Maybe I can go through the falls...." She stepped hesitantly towards the falling water.

"No ... don't leave me," Shawn pleaded from about two-thirds of the way across the ledge. At that moment, the ledge crumbled under his right foot. Desperately clinging with his fingertips to cracks in the rock face, Shawn tenuously balanced on his left foot while his right foot flailed about for solid ground.

Kaela swallowed her gasp-reflex, and ended up with a belly full of air.

"Don't worry!" she called to Shawn, "Just put your right foot a little further forward. That's it, there's the ledge. I'm right here with you."

"Hey - you there!" a man yelled.

Kaela looked past Shawn to where a hulk of a man approached them from the mist. In the blink of an eye she knew she didn't trust him.

"Ignore him, Shawn - just keep looking at me. You're okay."

Imitating a smile, the man said, "Don't be afraid, children. I'm here to help you."

"Shawn, just keep coming toward me," Kaela called, trying to keep the terror from her voice.

"Don't be silly," the man laughed. "Come here, boy. Give me your hand. We were sent to help you! C'mon now - You children shouldn't be here on your own. You'll never make it...." He finished softly.

Kaela flushed with anger at the obviousness of his trickery. Who did he think he was dealing with? She willed Shawn to move in her direction, but he stood, paralyzed, straddling air. "Please," Kaela begged, "Come on, Shawn."

"Here, boy, let me help you. Look how far down it is," the man said gently.

Shawn glanced down.

"No—" Kaela started to yell but caught herself, dropping her voice to a coaxing croak, "You're almost there." Kaela started along the ledge back toward her cousin but stopped, afraid it would collapse with her weight and there would be no way for Shawn to reach her.

Crrrrkkk, Crrrrkkkk. Caw, caw, caw.

"You could fall. Just look how far it is!" The man scowled and couldn't hide the harshness in his voice as he began to ease his huge body along the fragile ledge.

"Please, Shawn."

Finally Shawn shuddered, and inched his way toward Kaela once more. The last moments of daylight vanished.

"That's it ... c'mon now," Kaela encouraged as Shawn's body slid in her direction. "Almost there!"

"Come back here, you fools!" The man screamed. "You cannot escape the great Gulig! You're only making it worse for yourselves!" His body stretched wide, the fingertips of his right hand gripped a crack in the cliff, his left clung to an exposed root. When he shifted his weight to his right foot the ledge shattered, sending rocks and gravel cascading down the mountain. Shawn cringed, but did not look back. The man's body weight tore the root loose and he clung desperately with his fingertips to the side of the cliff. He swung himself back the way he came, retreating handhold by foothold until he stood on solid ground.

"Come here right now!" The man screamed. His voice, filled with both hatred and terror, chilled Kaela to the bone.

Shawn stared directly at Kaela and tensed his jaw with determination. One foot and then the other gingerly slid along the ridge until finally Kaela held Shawn's cold clenched fingers in her warm palms.

"I did it, I did it. I did it," he said faintly. At that moment the giant face of the moon began its rise on the horizon.

With no time to lose, Kaela released her cousin's hands. "Yes! Yes, yes," she said happily, turning to the waterfall and shoving her arm through the cascade, groping for an opening. Her entire arm easily moved through to open air on the other side. Without hesitation, she stuck her head into the cold water and then gasped as the frigid water soaked into her clothes.

Kaela pulled her head back, shivering uncontrollably and hugged herself for warmth.

"Do you think you can escape Gulig?" the soldier screamed. "You are delaying the inevitable! Come back here!"

"Thank you. Thank you," Shawn said to the crow. "You saved our lives."

"The beast is waiting for you!" The man roared.

"Shawn, it's really tight," Kaela said quietly, her teeth chattering.

"What?" Shawn asked.

"We'll have to squeeze through."

Determined, Kaela pushed Shawn while he wiggled his way through, and then she shoved the lamp after him. Next she entered, leading with her hands, scrunching her head and shoulders together as she squeezed herself into the narrow tube. For a moment Kaela panicked, certain she was stuck, but Shawn yanked on her arms and she squirmed with her feet and knees, exhaled, and finally dropped into a wide space, wet and muddy from the waterfall.

Kaela stood still for a moment, listening to the sound of their breath, which came in rapid, shallow gasps. The quiet of the cave was eerie, as if it held the deep secrets of the mountain. *Light*, Kaela realized.

"Let's see what we're dealing with, here," Kaela muttered to herself, patting her pockets for the tin. She found it and pulled out a match. "Shawn, can you get the lamp ready? We need some light. I have the matches."

"Sure, sure," he said, pulling up the glass chimney.

Kaela ran a wood match against rough stone and the tiny flame illuminated Shawn's enlarged pupils, which quickly contracted against the brightness of the match. She held the lit match against the wick, relieved when it easily caught fire, filling the cave with a soft light. She replaced the glass and held up the lantern to examine the opening. "Look ... this is tiny," she said, sighing with relief. "There's no way that Rugu guy can fit through. Where do we go now?" she asked, turning.

"I don't think we have a choice," Shawn said, pointing toward a dark chasm.

Holding the light up high, Kaela revealed a gaping black nothingness that interrupted the otherwise solid cave walls.

"Yeah, okay ..." Kaela took a deep breath. "Well, here we go."

The cave veered sharply to the left and then to right, making it impossible for the two to see very far ahead. At first they walked slowly, splashing through a narrow stream, but when the cave opened into a long straight cavern, they trotted and ran. The mere thought of enemy pursuit sparked their eagerness to widen the distance between themselves and the waterfall as much as possible.

After the exertions of the day, however, running quickly wore them down. Kaela stopped to catch her breath and Shawn joined her, leaning against the wall of the cave.

"That was so close," Kaela said, panting. "But we did it! I'm really proud of you, Shawn."

"Thanks," Shawn smiled slightly. "I'm sorry...."

Kaela gave her cousin an affectionate nudge on the arm. She wished she hadn't been so frustrated with him earlier. "No need to apologize. Hey, you know it kind of smells like dirty socks in here."

Shawn returned her friendly shove. "Well, if all we have to deal with is dirty socks, I'll take it. Boy, I sure hope this cave leads to where we're going."

"What do you mean?" Kaela stopped and looked at her cousin.

"Well, how do we know it even leads to the passageway into the castle? It could be a dead end."

"That's just great. Did you hear that guy yell something about a beast?"

"Yeah – he was probably just trying to scare us...." Shawn said without much conviction.

"That's all we need – to be stuck in here with the mysterious beast, or have to deal with that crazy thug of Gulig's," Kaela muttered.

They resumed walking in silence and, out of nowhere, Kaela screeched.

"Oh my God, what was that?" she cried. "Ooooh, it's a spider's web," she said, peeling the sticky strands from her hair. "Would you look and make sure there's not a spider there?"

"You just traversed a steep cliff and stood up to one of Gulig's soldiers, but you're afraid of a spider?"

"How would you like to have someone make a nest in your hair, and then hatch thousands of tiny babies without you even knowing it? Next thing you know they're burrowing into your brains."

"That would be cool!"

"Shawn!"

"Okay ... whatever." Shawn ran his hand over her hair. "All clear. But your scarf is gone."

"Oh well, it seems like the whole world already knows the red-haired girl is here, anyway," Kaela sighed.

They walked on until the cave narrowed and they were forced to crawl on their hands and knees. Just behind Kaela, pressed against the side of the cave, a bulge in Shawn's pocket squeaked.

"Wait!" Shawn said hearing the sound. "I forgot Peeper. Let me check on him."

Kaela and Shawn curled against the side of the cave wall with their knees bent close against their chests. Shawn reached into his pocket and pulled out the baby parrot, placing it in his palm while Kaela held up the lantern.

The bird puffed up his feathers and chirped cheerfully.

"Hey, you know what, Peeper?" Kaela realized as the stroked the chick. "You saved our lives. If we hadn't gone to rescue you, those Rugu guys would have gotten us for sure."

Peeper whistled.

"See. I knew helping Peeper was the right thing to do," Shawn responded proudly.

Peeper hopped onto Shawn's shoulder, and they resumed their difficult journey deeper and deeper into the mountain. They took turns holding up the lantern to see just a few feet into the darkness. Kaela kept hoping that the ceiling of the cave would lift, but more often found herself crawling on hands and knees or crouching awkwardly.

The fear of pursuit had left Kaela long before. Damp and bruised, back throbbing from being bent over for so long, Kaela sighed, "How much further do we have to go? It seems like we've been underground for days already."

"Let's go a little further and hope for a comfortable place to rest," Shawn said.

They were finally able to stand and move more quickly when they arrived at a vast open area. Kaela and Shawn couldn't even see the ceiling when they held the lamp high up over their heads.

Kaela waved the lamp and turned around in a circle. Light sparkled and danced around them, reflecting the lantern's glow.

"This is so beautiful," Kaela said, at once forgetting her weariness. "This must be the crystal cave."

Hundreds of stalactites hung above them, shaped like icicles. Some were long and thin, while others were wide with multiple spikes. Though they were all long and pointed, each one reflected the light in its own unique pattern. Stalagmites rose in towers just below the stalactites, glistening and glowing like castles in the lamplight.

Peeper whistled happily from Shawn's shoulder.

"They're formed from the mineral residue of evaporating water." Shawn ran his hand over a huge stalagmite and said, "I've read about them, but I didn't know they would be so huge."

"It's beyond beautiful," Kaela said, smiling. "Let's stop and rest. I love it here."

"Yeah, and I'm starving," Shawn added.

Kaela and Shawn stretched their achy backs and rubbed their hands together for warmth. Then Kaela sat up straight, certain she had heard a faint noise. "Shhh," she whispered, putting her finger to her lips. "Do you hear that? I think someone's following us."

"Nope," Shawn shook his head. "I don't hear anything."

"Do you think it could be – a beast?" Kaela suddenly remembered the man's words.

"Kaela, stop. Don't say that," Shawn answered nervously.

The light from their single lantern illuminated the closest parts of the cave, but left the rest as vast expanses of dark shadows. Kaela and Shawn removed their backpacks and sat down close to one another, leaning against the wall. Kaela listened again, but heard only silence. She relaxed a little and stretched out her legs, sighing as her body eased from the strain of the day.

Peeper crawled down Shawn's shirt with his beak and claws until he sat comfortably on Shawn's knee. "Well, Peeper, you must be starving, too."

Kaela and Shawn dug around in their packs and found chunks of cheese, apples and bread. Shawn crumpled small pieces of bread onto his knee for Peeper.

"Boy, cheese never tasted so good!" Kaela joked through a mouthful of food.

"I know. There's nothing like being hungry." Shawn tore off a piece of bread and stuffed it into his mouth. "Mmmm. This is good!"

Kaela sank her teeth into the apple. Sweet juice burst into her mouth.

Cheep! Cheep! Peeper cried, quivering with fear. *Cheep! Cheep!*

With the apple still lodged in her mouth, Kaela held up the lantern, and chomped down hard to stop herself from screaming. The apple fell with a thud to the ground.

A huge tiger crouched at the edge of their lamplight. His muscular body tensed, ready to pounce, blocking the direction they needed to go. He sat back and opened his jaws, filling the cavernous room with his furious roar.

"Peeper, get back in my pocket," Shawn whispered loudly.

Kaela grabbed Shawn's hand. "Come on," she urged. We've got to run."

"No, never!" Shawn pulled hard against Kaela's tugging. His voice quavered but his tone was firm and determined. "Move slowly! Otherwise he'll chase us for sure. Just follow my lead and stand up, ever so slowly."

Light from the lamp reflected off the tiger's glaring eyes. Overwhelmed by the cat's size and power, Kaela dropped her head. "He's ready to kill us!"

Shawn rose to his feet as slowly as he could manage. Kaela's knees quaked as she joined him, glancing again and again at the black and brown striped animal that glowered at them through narrowed green eyes. Even from a distance they could tell that he was of mammoth proportions - his body was at least ten feet long, his huge head the size of a bathroom sink.

The tiger sat back on his haunches, eyeing the humans. His stillness made them wonder if he might not hurt them, until the strength of his next roar slammed them against the cave wall.

Kaela's heart thumped so hard that she could hear the sound of it – *kaplunk, kaplunk, kaplunk* – drumming in her chest.

"Shawn, we have to get out of here!"

"Hold on." Shawn trembled and remained still.

The tiger snarled, baring teeth that could shred them to pieces.

"Come on, Shawn," Kaela begged.

"Don't do it," Shawn hissed. "We're going to creep out of here. Wave your arms wide and try to look huge."

The tiger slunk back and forth, his eyes glued to their every move.

"This is our chance," Shawn whispered. "Once we're out of sight, run like the wind."

The tiger shattered the quiet with another blood-curdling roar, but still he remained on his side of the cave. Their luck holding up, the boy and the red-haired girl backed up the way they came, until a turn in the tunnel blocked the tiger from their sight. Then they bolted as fast as they could.

When the cave branched in two, Kaela pointed. "Let's take ... this one..." she panted. "At least ... we can stand." They ran on and abruptly came to a dead end.

"Now, what?" Shawn asked, leaning over to rest his hands on his knees.

"I'm not sure." Kaela inhaled sharply. "I think, the tiger may be blocking our path ... on purpose. Maybe that's why they gave us the swords."

"You think we should go back that way?"

"Well, we can't very well go back where we came in. Gulig's men are sure to be waiting, and this is the only way we know to get into the mountain. This path turned out to be a dead end, so..." Leaning against the cave, Kaela closed her eyes and then said, "The tiger must be guarding the entrance to the castle."

Shawn nodded. "Tigers aren't naturally cave dwellers, so that would explain why he's here. But how will we get past him? I couldn't kill an animal just because it was in my way. It doesn't feel right."

"Me neither. Well ... maybe we could trick him somehow – distract him – get to the entrance. I don't know. He certainly wouldn't mind killing us," Kaela frowned, trying to figure out what to do. "Somehow we've got to get to that passageway, though."

Shawn agreed, "Okay, let's go back – but let's move slowly. He'll be waiting for us."

Kaela's blood pulsed in her throat as she followed Shawn down the narrow corridor they had come up only moments before. The volume of the tiger's roar increased with each step they took.

The two hesitated at the entrance to the cavern, hiding behind a curve in the wall. They took turns peeking around the edge of the wall to get another look at the enormous cat.

The tiger lifted his head and squinted his eyes, then paced back and forth once again, looking in their direction.

"I'm drawing my sword." Kaela whispered. "We have no choice." She pulled the sword from the sheath, and immediately it fell from her hands with a loud clang.

The tiger's fur stood straight up and he hunched, ready to pounce.

"What are you doing?" Shawn whispered furiously. "Are you trying to get us *killed?*"

"I'm sorry." Kaela frowned with confusion. She bent over and strained to pick up the sword, having to use both hands. "This is really strange. Here, you try."

Kaela placed the sword in Shawn's open palms, and he immediately bent over straining against the weight. "It's as heavy as a boulder," he said in wonder. "But why? There's something weird going on." Shawn looked between the sword and the great cat. "I'm sure he knows we're here. Why hasn't he attacked us already?"

"Move over. Let me see." Peering over Shawn, Kaela pointed at the tiger's neck. "Look. Is that a collar?"

"Yeah, and it's tethered to a chain. How could we be so dumb not to notice?" Shawn said.

"Do you see the jewels on the collar – that's totally weird."

Seeing the thick chain that anchored the tiger's collar to a hook on the side of the cave, Kaela and Shawn left the shelter of the cave wall and stared openly at the enormous cat.

"No wonder he's upset," Shawn said, shaking his head in pity. "Poor guy – he's being tortured. I think he's crying."

Again and again the animal's entire body twitched, as if the collar delivered excruciating jolts of pain. Each time, the tiger let out a huge roar of anger and despair.

Shawn's eyes glistened with tears. "Who would do such a thing?"

"I bet Gulig did it," Kaela said, despising the Rugu man more and more.

"Kaela, we have to help." Shawn handed the sword back to Kaela. "Here put this away. I'm going to crawl closer and see if there's some way to free him."

"No, Shawn, you're crazy!" Kaela argued. She quickly stuck the sword back in the sheath by her side and grabbed his hand. "That cat is furious. He'll rip your face off with those claws."

"I'm gonna try to talk to him." Shawn said, dragging Kaela toward the cat until she reluctantly released his hand.

"Shawn, stop!" Kaela pleaded, wanting to protect her cousin.

"I have to – I just have to. I can talk to him, remember? Let me have the lantern so I can see clearly."

Kaela watched as her cousin crawled, lantern in hand, to a distance outside the tiger's reach. The animal stared at Shawn, and howled once more. Kaela wondered at how her timid cousin, who couldn't even climb a rope in gym class, felt it was safe to approach an enraged tiger.

"Please, don't be afraid," Shawn said. "Don't worry; I'm not here to harm you. I want to help you," he continued in a gentle voice. "Shuuush, shuuush – don't worry. Everything's going to be okay. I'll take that collar off and set you free. Please ... let me release you. I can't bear to see you like this."

The tiger narrowed his eyes. This time when the collar jolted him he yowled.

Shawn closed his eyes to focus on the tiger's voice.

"I think he's trying to tell me something," Shawn whispered to Kaela as she came up behind him. "He's a prisoner," Shawn whispered. "He's Gulig's prisoner."

Shawn crawled a little closer. "I'm so sorry for what they did to you. Please don't be afraid of me. I promise not to hurt you."

The tiger moaned.

"I can't stand it anymore. Let me take it off."

The animal rested his head on his paws and watched. His eyes were filled with sadness as Shawn edged closer.

Shawn put down the lantern and took the bird out of his pocket.

"Peeper, I don't know what kind of a spell has been placed on the collar. You better stay over here, so nothing happens to you." Then he approached the tiger, very, very slowly.

Stunned by his bravery, Kaela followed her cousin deeper into the cave.

"Shawn, please, *please* be careful," she said quietly, crouching nearby.

The huge animal rolled heavily to his side, and Kaela studied his body. From a distance his fur had looked beautiful, but up close she could see that it was matted and his skin hung in loose folds from his body. Despite his tremendous size, his ribs nearly poked through his skin, and his sad eyes were dull and tired. His teeth and claws were undoubtedly long and dangerous, however. With each jolt from the collar, the tiger's muscles rippled with pain, but his roars of pain had quieted to yowls and moans.

Once Shawn came in reach of the tiger's neck, he waited for the latest jolt to pass. Shawn clasped the buckle tightly, working to release the fastener.

"Quick!" Kaela yelled. "It's gonna jolt him again."

Shawn didn't give up. As if in slow motion, Shawn released the buckle too late – the tiger's body jerked in a spasm of pain and suddenly became limp as Shawn fell to the ground with the collar still gripped tightly in his hands.

"Shawn," Kaela cried as she flew to his side and, without realizing it, knocked over the lantern. "Shawn, are you okay?"

Endless moments passed as shocks raced through his body, until the spasms passed and his hands fell open, finally dropping the deadly collar to the ground. The tiger remained in a lifeless heap on the side of the cave, and the puddle of fuel from the broken lamp burned in yellow flames.

Caressing Shawn's hands in hers, Kaela stared at the deep crimson marks the collar had made. She placed her ear next to her cousin's chest, listening for some sign of life. Shawn remained motionless, and so did his heart. No air flowed from his nose.

Kaela screamed "Somebody help me!" She leaned over and drew on her CPR training, learned just last year at summer camp, and began rhythmically pressing on Shawn's chest. Then she breathed deeply into his lungs. Shawn did not respond. She repeated the process, but his heart didn't start. Once more she pressed one hand atop the other on his chest, but – nothing happened, she did it again and again, but still nothing.

She sat back, not knowing what to do next. There has to be a way to *save Shawn*, she thought, Overcome with despair, tears poured from her eyes.

The tiger noiselessly crept to Shawn and nosed his lifeless body. The yellow flames on the cave floor burned to a soft blue. Soon they would be in total darkness.

"NO!" Kaela screamed, horrified. "DON'T HURT HIM!"

She leapt up to push the wild animal away, but something inside stopped Kaela. She stared, fascinated by the unbelievable sight of the tiger pressing his paw on Shawn's chest and then licking her cousin's face.

Uncertain what to do, Kaela watched as what appeared to be a huge diamond fell from the tiger's eye, sparkling as it dropped into Shawn's open mouth. The tiger stepped back. A final burst of flames from the lantern fuel was reflected in the tiger's eyes, and then complete and total darkness stole Kaela's sight.

Peeper hopped to Shawn and tangled his talons into the boy's hair. *Cheep, cheep, cheep,* the parrot chick cried.

Chapter Ten • Saving Shawn

Kaela bent her head, once again listening for the slightest flutter of life from Shawn's chest, and heard ... nothing. "Shawn, wake up!" she cried. "Wake up! You can't die, Shawn – please ... please." Her heart seemed to swallow itself with one horrible sob.

Peeper cheeped and Kaela felt the tiny bird pulling gently on Shawn's hair, scratching the boy's scalp with his talons.

Kaela sat in the pitch dark beside her lifeless cousin, held his ice-cold hand and whispered, "Shawn, you are the best friend anyone could ever have. Please don't go!"

Shawn suddenly gasped, sucking in a lungful of air.

"Oh my God, you're alive!" Kaela whispered hoarsely. The lump in her throat made it difficult to speak. "I can't believe you're alive ... Shawn, are you okay?"

Shawn took one labored breath after another, but did not speak. Kaela pressed her ear against Shawn's chest again and heard the irregular rhythm of his heart: *kaplunk, kaplunk ... plunk, plunk, plunk ... kaplunk.* Kaela stroked his hair and pleaded with him, her voice breaking as she spoke. "Shawn, can you hear me?" she cried. "Please ... wake up!"

Kaela tried putting her arms under Shawn to carry him, but she had no idea where to go in the pitch darkness of the cave. The situation was impossible. "Somebody help us!" Kaela shouted.

The only answer was a sound suspiciously similar to a growl.

Startled, Kaela's stomach lurched with fear. In the darkness she couldn't tell what was happening. Why was the tiger still with them?

Shawn had helped him, but he was still a starving animal. Would he eat them? What did the tiger want?

Kaela's heart pounded against her ribs as she crouched in the dark, blind and helpless. She placed her hand over her chest for comfort, and unconsciously clasped the butterfly pendant in her fist.

"I'm here to help you, girl," a deep voice rumbled.

Had a man joined them? Kaela remembered the horrible Rugu soldier trying to trick her at the cliff face. She patted Shawn's leg until she felt the dagger and she slowly pulled on the metal weapon.

"Put that away right now," the rumbling voice ordered, "You'll hurt us both with that thing."

Torn between fear and relief, Kaela hesitated. Trying to sound brave and strong, she deepened her voice "Who are you?" she called loudly. "Don't try anything, you hear me? We're armed."

"Stop your foolishness, girl," the voice called back with equal strength.

Kaela jumped at the fierce tone of the man's voice. What should she do? The tiger was somewhere in the cave, obviously starving, and yet the man didn't seem very friendly, either.

"Who are you?" She demanded. "Why should I trust you?"

"What choice do you have?" The voice grunted a few times, amused.

Defeated by her situation, Kaela realized the man was right. She could not get out on her own. "Alright," she conceded. "But if you do anything to hurt Shawn, so help me..." Her voice trailed off for a moment as she fought with her anger and fear. Then she remembered the tiger and said in a hushed voice, "Watch out! There's a tiger in here."

"You're afraid of a measly tiger?" the voice asked, rumbling.

"Of course I am! You should see this guy," Kaela whispered, noting that the man had come closer. "His teeth are as long as my arm."

"I wish I could light a lamp for you," the voice continued. "Girl, you're talking to the tiger. I am the hungry and ferocious tiger."

"What?" Kaela gasped as cold fear rushed over her.

"I can assure you that I never lie, girl. I am most definitely the tiger and you're right, I am tired and hungry - but I'm only ferocious when necessary. I will help you, but we must leave - now. Please follow the sound of my voice and reach out until you feel my fur. I'll carry the boy in my mouth."

"Whaa? Whoo? Wait – are you sure you're the tiger?"

"Yes, yes, yes, yes," Peeper squeaked in the darkness.

"I am quite sure. Now, hurry. There is no time to waste."

Kaela remembered the tiger's huge mouth and decided she didn't want to do anything that might offend his carnivorous side.

"You're sure you don't want to eat us?" Kaela asked, already groping toward him in the darkness.

"I have absolutely no desire to eat a couple of skinny children, especially children such as yourself and your friend, who just saved my life. Now, I am trying to help you both in return. Are you coming or not?" The tiger's voice rumbled unpleasantly.

"How will we get out?" Kaela asked, gripping fur in her fist.

"You must trust me." The tiger began to move slowly forward. "I can sniff my way out of the mountain. We must get this boy to the healers of Mount Sankaria before Gulig's soldiers come looking for us."

"Your nose can find the way?"

"Hold tight," the voice answered, ignoring her question. "I am going to pick up your companion now." The large muscles of his back and neck tightened as he lifted Shawn by his clothes.

Letting go of the pendant, Kaela reached out with her free hand until she felt Shawn's body hanging limply from the mouth of the tiger.

"Peeper, where are you?" Kaela called. "Are you okay?"

Peeper cheeped worriedly from the top of Shawn's head. Kaela grabbed the pendant again.

I'm here! I'm here! I'm here! Peeper whistled.

Kaela held out her other hand until Peeper crawled onto her finger and she placed him safely on her shoulder.

At first they moved slowly because Kaela held back, tugging on the tiger's fur and slowing their pace. Accustomed to relying on her vision, she tried to use her other senses by feeling for rocks through her suede boots and using her free hand to brush along the damp cave wall. She even listened for echoes created by their footsteps, to anticipate the twists and turns in their path. Finally, she realized she had to surrender to the tiger's superior smell and night vision. She responded to the subtlest shift in his movements, and the two became like one body with six legs. And Kaela allowed the tiger to pick up the pace.

The caves looped into a confusing maze with no center and no exit. On and on they ran, until Kaela felt like she was trapped in a nightmare from which she could not awaken. She could hardly remember why they ever entered this cold, hard place to begin with. She longed for the adventure to be over - for Shawn to be taken care of - for a warm meal, a hug from her father and the promise of sleep. But each time Kaela felt like giving up, certain that she couldn't take another step, she remembered Shawn's injured heart and ignored her own exhaustion.

Startled by a splashing sound behind them, adrenalin pumped through Kaela's veins.

"Tiger, stop! Please stop." she begged, gasping for air. "I hear something behind us." The tiger halted abruptly, and Kaela listened intently to the drip, drip, dripping of water and the panting of their breath. "Is it my imagination?"

"No, I hear it too," he rumbled.

They resumed their journey, now at a faster pace, until Kaela's rubbery legs threatened to collapse beneath her. Images filled her brain to form mirages in the wasteland of darkness. Shadowy shapes and forms appeared as they ran past, growing more and more clear. At first she didn't dare believe they were real. Could it be - could she see? Blinking a few times to clear her brain, Kaela's heart filled with joy.

"Yes!" She cried out as they approached the opening to the outside world. A half-circle of silvery light filled her vision, almost blinding her again.

Renewed, the tiger and Kaela separated and raced towards the opening until they were finally outdoors in the fresh air. Taking a deep breath, Kaela squinted at the huge moon smiling above them and fell to her knees in a mixture of gratitude and exhaustion.

The tiger carefully lay Shawn by the edge of a stream.

Kaela stood up long enough to throw her arms around the tiger's neck, leaning into him for support. "Thank you!" she said, near crying. Still panting, the tiger flinched and pulled away from her.

Confused by his response, Kaela withdrew and hugged herself. Then she noticed his neck glistening in the moonlight. It was his skin, burned and raw from the deadly collar. "I'm sorry," she sputtered "I didn't mean to hurt you. Your neck must burn terribly. I forgot what they did to you. You saved us. I thought we were going to die." She gasped for breath.

"Don't worry, child ... your touch is kind ... you mean no harm. Drink, drink some water. It will give you strength." The tiger lay down, exhausted.

Parched, Kaela turned to the stream and gulped water from her cupped hands. Kaela soaked up the moisture like a dried-out sponge. Peeper roused himself long enough to peck at the water a few times.

The giant cat soaked his paw and dripped water on Shawn's lips. "He still isn't able to drink," the tiger announced with concern.

Brushing Shawn's hair out of his eyes, Kaela searched her cousin's face for some sign of consciousness. "I'm afraid for him. Do you think he'll be okay?"

"Do not worry, Little One," The tiger rumbled, and Kaela realized that the soft growling noise he made was actually a chuffing sound. "We will find a way to take care of him. What is your name, child?"

"I'm Kaela ... and this is my cousin Shawn."

"And I am Kanu, King of the Wild Spaces."

Kaela bowed her head to honor the great cat.

Kanu closed his eyes and lowered his head, honoring her in return.

"Drink more, child. This stream carries the healing waters of Mount Sankaria, and it will renew us." The tiger sniffed the air and said, "I must leave you for a while. Can you watch over your cousin until I return?"

"Yes, Kanu." Kaela said, even though her eyes ached with fatigue.

Peeper let out a *cheep* and hopped to Shawn, snuggling against his neck, while Kaela sat huddled against the cold. She looked back and forth quickly, nervous she wouldn't be able to see her enemies in the darkness of night.

"Un-n-n-n-nh," Shawn moaned.

Kaela placed her hand on his chest, dismayed to discover that his heartbeat was still irregular and his body now burned with fever. He needed help, Kaela realized, unsure of what to do. She remembered when, as a child, she had burned and ached with fever, and the comfort that her mother's cool touch had brought her. Filled with tenderness, Kaela placed her hand on Shawn's brow. She imagined her palm to be a magnet, drawing the fever out like iron filings. A wave of fire shot into Kaela's palm and coursed through her body before penetrating the ground. Her hand jerked away.

"Whoa, what was that?" she said, frightened.

When she touched Shawn again, his skin felt cooler, but still his heart beat hard against her palm in an irregular rhythm.

"Are you okay, Shawn?" Kaela nudged him, but still there was no response. "I hope Kanu comes back soon. Please Shawn, wake up."

But now Shawn's face was as pale as the moon and he seemed far away and unreachable.

A large black silhouette appeared in the distance, a giant shadow against the night sky. Kaela pulled her dagger from its sheath, squinted to make out the shape in front of her and clutched the pendant in her other hand, trembling.

"Kanu, is that you?" She called.

Kanu's familiar form moved toward her and plopped a hunk of something strong-smelling beside her. "I've brought you some fresh meat," he said. "You need to eat."

"Raw meat?" she winced.

"Yes," Kanu said, licking his chops.

"Thank you, that is very kind of you." Kaela responded, not wanting to offend her new friend. "Uhm, well, I've actually never eaten raw meat. I mean, uhm, is it safe?" Kaela's stomach growled loudly as the blood-thick scent of meat reached her nostrils.

"Don't be foolish, child. Eat it quickly before it loses its life energy."

Kaela kneeled down and felt around with one hand for the meat. It filled her hand, and she squealed at the size of it. It was firm, but wet and squishy. She had expected it to be cold, like the hamburger she formed into patties with her father, but instead it felt warm - as warm as Shawn's forehead - like it was still alive.

"I am growing impatient," Kanu growled. "We must travel further tonight. This boy needs help."

"Okay, okay! But what is it? On second thought, never mind." Kaela preferred not to know. She lifted it to her mouth, bit off a little piece of meat and her belly accepted it, clamoring for more.

Kanu watched her intently and then said, "It is our custom to thank the animal that sacrificed its life for you. You can say it aloud or you can say it to yourself, but you must give thanks."

"Yes, sir." Kaela ate with more gusto.

Kanu's eyes glowed as he stared through Kaela.

"Oh – right. Now," Kaela said, abashed. She closed her eyes and felt the warmth in her belly from the food she had eaten. "Thank you for feeding me," she said softly. After being so deeply tired, she noticed how her body now tingled with life. She bowed her head, "Thank you, thank you for caring for me."

Kaela gazed at Shawn once again as she ate, hoping with every fiber of her being that he would rouse from unconsciousness. Finally, as she was licking her fingers, the cat stood.

He nosed Shawn, and said, "Your cousin still dwells deep in the ocean, Little One."

"What ocean, Kanu?" An odd bouncy rhythm thrummed against her fingers as she touched Shawn's chest and looked up into Kanu's glimmering green eyes.

"You do not know of the ocean?" Kanu cocked his head in surprise. "Dear child, when a tiger is at the end of one of its nine lives, we dive deep into the ocean of the Great Spirit. I believe Shawn is uncovering what lies on the ocean's floor so that he can move into the next life."

"Kanu, you are scaring me." Kaela stroked Shawn's hands, praying he would wake up. "When the waves are big, you can drown in the ocean."

"Do not be afraid, girl." Kanu's eyes softened as he explained, "Your ocean and Shawn's are filled with great kindness. Come. We will go to the finest healers in the land, and they will help him return to the shore of this world. Let's go – I want to put some distance between us and these wretched caves."

Kanu dipped his head over Shawn, while Kaela helped roll her cousin to one side. The muscles of the great cat's neck and back contracted as he strained to lift the boy once more, and Kaela drew on her last reserves to lift from underneath. The cat was so large no part of Shawn's body touched the ground as he hung limp from Kanu's mouth.

Stars blazed in the sky like leftover sparks from an elaborate Fourth of July celebration as the tiger and the girl walked into a valley. Peeper perched on Kaela's shoulder, worrying her earlobe with his soft beak. The path sloped downward into a vast meadow, perfumed with night-blooming wildflowers. An owl hooted just above them. The moist air caressed Kaela's face and the tall grass brushed against her hands while the evening breeze softly rocked the leaves of the trees and bushes around them.

As they walked beside the burbling stream, she looked at Kanu's bone-thin form and Shawn's limp body shadowed in the moonlight. Her face grew hot from the angry fire burning in her belly. She thought, Gulig *has to be stopped. Somehow, I have to stop him.*

They walked along quietly for a time, until Kanu gently placed Shawn in soft grass once again and panted. "I ... must ... rest ... for a ... moment, but ... I ... I promise to get your cousin ... to the ... healers."

Kaela patted the grass around Shawn and sat, murmuring close to his ear. "It's okay, Shawn. You're just finding your next life. You'll be okay. We're getting you help."

Kanu plopped down, heavy with fatigue, and rested his head on his paws, drawing air in noisily through his nose. Mewing loudly, he opened his eyes after a moment and rumbled.

Kaela clutched the pendant. "What is it, Kanu?"

"Long ago, when I was still a cub visiting the castle, there was a girl with hair the color of apricots who looked much like you. She was terribly ill, fighting for her life."

"Maybe it was my mother," Kaela mused, but then she grew excited, "Wait. I bet it *was* my mother!" Kaela bent her head down and whispered close to Shawn's ear, "I think Kanu knew my mother. She really was here. I bet they helped her ... they'll help you."

"Why yes, I think you are right," Kanu said sniffing the air. "Your scent is familiar. I remember she was lovely, and her heart was kind, like yours."

Kaela smiled shyly, flattered by the comparison to her mother. "Can I ask you something?" she asked.

"Of course, child. What do you want to know?"

"In the cave, I thought I saw something. It looked like a tear falling from your eye. Did that tear come from the ocean ... you know, the one inside?"

"Tigers rarely cry," Kanu said, answering but not answering. "When they do, it is only a single tear, for a great love."

"Is that what helped Shawn's heart start beating again?" Kaela asked.

"Perhaps, perhaps," Kanu said. "Or maybe it was all that pushing of yours."

Kanu softly closed his eyes, looking away from Kaela's gaze. Kaela sensed his shyness. She decided not to press him any further, but she knew what she saw. He shed one precious tear for Shawn.

She crawled to where Kanu lay in the grass, and wrapped her arms around his midsection. "Kanu, thank you. Thank you for everything."

"Oh Kaela," he said, nudging her gently. "Can't you see that gratitude moves both ways? If it were not for you two I would have died a terrible death in that cave, filled with darkness and pain. Thank you, dear girl. Thank *you*."

Kaela blushed. "It was all Shawn. He's the one with the pure heart."

"Child, there's more in your heart than you know."

A lilting melody drifting on the breeze reached Kaela's ears as the wind shifted direction, and she bolted upright. Blood coursed through Kaela's limbs as she stood and sprinted towards the sound, her heart pounding wildly with hope. The melody was that of her mother's lullaby. She heard the words of the song on the wind as she ran:

> *Sitting by the fire of your love*
> *I feel my walls burn away*
> *As the pain and darkness slip away*
> *I feel my night turn to day*
> *Oh love,*
> *You've been buried inside*
> *Oh love,*
> *I didn't know that you were mine,*
> *You were mine.*

Kaela realized the deep hope she'd carried within her, ever since she first saw the shell, lying pure and perfect on the locker-room floor. It was the hope that carried her through the caves, the desperate desire that allowed her to accept the trials that were laid before her. It was not a deep-seated wish for adventure and change. No – it was a single, soundless thought. *Is my mother here?*

Chapter Eleven · The Prisoners

Gulig ran his hand over the huge wooden table in front of him, frowning at the sight of his crooked features in the mirror-like finish. He experimented with different facial expressions, alternately frowning, knitting his eyebrows together in a scowl, and pursing his lips, until settling on a haughtily superior expression, created by jutting out his chin and narrowing his eyes. The diamond on his pinky finger sparkled with a fiery glow as he lifted a glass from the table and sank back into his fur-lined throne. He held up the crystal, wordlessly requesting a refill. His valet, Stennan, stood just behind him, prepared to meet Gulig's every need. Stennan carefully filled the sparkling glass from a decanter with a bright blue-green liquid. A bitter smell filled the room as the liquid *glug glug*-ged into the glass. Gulig drank deeply, delicately wiping the final drop from his lips.

"I am ready to hear General Taga's report." Gulig ordered, "Open the door."

A man dressed in the black pants and gray tunic of a Rugu soldier marched in, holding his helmet in his hands, and bowed low to Gulig. His right breast was decorated with multiple medals, which gleamed and glinted in the low light.

"At ease, General Taga," Gulig waved his hand. "What do you know of the red-haired girl?"

"She has been seen again and again in our world. We hid our men on the path up Mount Sankaria. We were able to poison and capture her bodyguards, and we did as you instructed and blocked off the usual entrance to the caves."

"So you are bringing her here, now?" Gulig asked pleasantly.

"I'm afraid not." The general gripped his hat in both hands. "The girl – somehow – she found – another entrance."

"So someone is following her?" Gulig tapped his fingers irritatedly on the table.

"No, Sire. The entrance could only be reached by traversing the steep face of a cliff."

"And no one followed her?" Gulig's tone grew more menacing.

"Yes, Sire. Forgive me, Sire – someone did pursue them," the general said hurriedly. "But the ledge broke off. It was not able to hold his weight."

"So you've been out-witted by a child?" Gulig glared, stilling his hands.

"No, no, Sire. I mean..." Unable to bear Gulig's expression, the general looked at the ground. "It was just dumb luck," he muttered. "But – we have good news, too."

The general looked up again with a flush on his cheeks.

Gulig leaned forward. "And what would that be?"

"We have located the girl. She – she is headed toward the Butterfly Women," the general said.

"She came out the other side of the caves?" Gulig cursed.

"Yes, sire. Apparently the tiger showed her the way out."

Gulig sat back, covering his astonishment with a stony faced look. "She tamed the tiger?" he said without expression.

"Yes, Sire. And now she is in the sacred land of the Butterfly Women, which makes things difficult...."

"Oh?" Gulig smirked. "And why is that?"

"That area has always been considered off-limits," the general said, beginning to suspect that his work was far from done.

Gulig sat up to his full height and once again assumed a haughty expression.

"General Taga, I have provided a generous – even royal – lifestyle for you and your family," Gulig began.

"Yes, Sire," the General agreed. "We do indeed live well in this land."

"And the other members of our tribe are treated generously," Gulig continued.

"Yes, Sire."

"Do you understand fully what it is I plan to accomplish here?" Gulig asked in a quiet voice. "It is time for the Rugus to assume their rightful place as lords of this land." Even though Gulig spoke softly, there was something ominous and threatening in his tone. "Do ... you ... understand ... that within hours ... I will be king ... and that I will make the rules?" Gulig spoke as though giving directions to a simpleton.

"Yes, Sire. Of course, Sire." The general bowed low. "And I am honored, Sire, to have a small part to play in this glorious undertaking." The general snapped his heels together and saluted.

"Then get me that girl," Gulig commanded. "And get her now!"

General Taga bowed over and over again as he backed out of the room. "Yes, Sire. As you wish, Sire!"

"Send in the prisoners," Gulig ordered as soon as the door closed behind Taga.

The servant opened one of the tall wooden doors, and two men identical in height and girth were shoved inside the room, closely followed by two guards. The wrists of the prisoners were bound behind their backs, and black hoods covered their faces.

"Remove the hoods. Let us see the liars' faces," Gulig sneered.

The guards yanked off the men's hoods and pushed them even closer to Gulig. The prisoners resisted, straining to keep distance between themselves and the Rugu leader.

"It looks like two of the tree-scum have decided to join us. You look alike, but then it is impossible to tell any of you apart. You people grow like weeds," Gulig snickered. "I understand you were accompanying the red-haired girl," he continued. "Apparently you are miserable failures, too weak to withstand the Rugu poison. Tell me her plans and I will have mercy on you."

Both of the young men looked away from Gulig with tight lips, refusing to respond. The guards pulled up on their arms, yanking painfully at their shoulders until the two were forced to kneel in front of Gulig.

"Sire, we have followed the usual procedures to make them talk. Perhaps we should take them to the dungeon for further questioning...."

one of the soldiers, a large man with a battered face, suggested hoarsely.

"Yes, that will be good," Gulig said waving his hand, losing interest. "I have more pressing matters to attend to. But ... one last thing, tree-huggers," he chuckled. "Turn their heads toward me," he commanded the guards.

The guards pulled the prisoners' heads back by their hair, forcing them to look up at Gulig.

"Scum, do you like my table?" he asked softly. "Is she familiar to you? Perhaps you have had a chance to see the amazing improvements that have been added to this castle ... wood floors, wood-paneled rooms, several new tables, beams. Who would have thought one could make so many improvements using just one tree?" Gulig laughed, watching the fury in his prisoners' eyes grow.

Gavin and Gannon recoiled as if they had been forcibly struck, and clenched their bound fists, fiercely closing their eyelids to avoid looking at the hideous leader of the Rugu Tribe.

"Take this filth from my chamber and throw them in the dungeon, where they belong," Gulig ordered. "Give me their headbands. I may have use for them later."

"Yes, Sire. As you wish, Sire," the guards chimed. The red and green headbands were torn from the prisoners' leaf-like hair and thrown on the table.

When the guards and prisoners had gone, Gulig turned to his servant, Stennan, and said, "I am so glad we listened to that young seer woman all those years ago."

Gulig did not notice the flash of pain that flickered across Stennan's otherwise dull eyes.

Chapter Twelve •
The Butterfly Women

Watching a flower grow
In a heart as cold as snow.
Melting ice
With the love it brings
I watch my winter
Turn to spring

As Kaela drew closer and heard the second verse of the familiar lullaby, she realized the clear voice, though beautiful, was not her mother's. The bursting energy that flooded her veins dried up and hardened like cement, slowing Kaela until she inched forward at a snail's pace. She hung her head, silently mourning her loss. A longing grew inside Kaela's heart - the longing to dive into the ocean that brought new life to Kanu again and again, and have it bring new life to her as well. At that moment, she felt that she could drown without fear.

Out of the darkness, two women appeared, glowing as though they held the light of the moon beneath their skin. Their long white dresses and cloaks flapped behind them in the now strong breeze. One had long gray hair, which sparkled silver, and the other had long blonde hair that streamed in waves behind her. The older woman's face was lined like that of a grandmother. She stood tall and lean, and ran to Kaela with the grace of a ballet dancer, her arms open wide.

"My cousin, Shawn..." Kaela cried, pointing behind her.

The younger woman smiled reassuringly at Kaela, but didn't stop as she ran toward Shawn and Kanu.

"My name is Janani and that is Ariala," the silver-haired woman said, wrapping Kaela in her arms.

"I'm Kaela, and this is Shawn, my cousin." Kaela melted into Janani's embrace. The woman radiated wisdom and welcoming like the ancient Grandmother Tree.

Janani stepped back and said, "We heard a cry for help. We are healers." The tenderness in her brown eyes reached deep inside, caressing Kaela's worn heart. She took Kaela's hand in hers and said, "Come, let's see about your cousin."

They hurried back to the field, where Ariala crouched, listening to Shawn's heart.

Janani caught sight of the tiger and yelled joyfully, "Kanu, my dear friend! Kanu!" She knelt down beside him and stroked his wounded body. "Kanu, what have they done to you? What happened?"

Kanu stared intently at Shawn. "This brave boy saved my life, removing a collar that Gulig placed on my neck – an instrument of torture that delivered excruciating jolts whenever anyone entered the cave where I was tethered. Fortunately, I had not yet gone mad from hunger and pain when these two arrived. They could have left me to suffer, but instead this boy removed the collar at his own expense. He is a very brave boy – a very brave boy, indeed."

Kaela sat beside Shawn with tears dripping down her cheeks. She shuddered, remembering the cruel scene in the cave. "It was horrible. Look at what the collar did to him." She turned Shawn's hand over. Huge fluid-filled blisters and bands of bright red flesh covered his palms and fingers, swelling them to nearly twice their normal size.

Ariala looked up and shook her head as she covered Shawn with her cloak. "This child has suffered a terrible injury. His body is still in shock, and his heartbeat is irregular. He has a fever, most likely because his body is working to heal the burns on his hands. His situation is dire. We must restore a steady rhythm to his heart before moving him."

Kaela fought to speak through the lump in her throat. "But - will he? Can you..."

"Kaela," Janani said, wiping Kaela's tears. "Would you like to help us heal Shawn's heart?"

"Really? You can teach me?" Kaela's heart flooded with hope.

"Yes, dear. We would be honored to have you assist us."

Ariala sat cross-legged in the soft grass and gently lifted Shawn's head so that it rested in her lap. Moonlight seemed to shine down from her eyes as she laid her palm on Shawn's chest.

Ariala pointed. "Kanu, please lay beside Shawn to warm his body. Janani and Kaela, sit along the other side of his body. Our warmth will protect Shawn from the chill of the evening.

Kanu softly chuffed as Janani removed her pack and pulled out a clear glass bottle filled with sparkling fluid. "Kaela, this is special water from the highest springs of Mount Sankaria. It is a gift from the Great Mother." She unscrewed the dropper from the bottle. "I want you to place a drop at a time on your cousin's mouth."

Kaela drew water into the dropper and carefully squeezed the bulb one drop at a time onto Shawn's lips, as instructed.

"That's perfect," Janani said, kneeling next to Kaela. "Now, while you do this I want you to hold onto the love in your heart."

Feeling safe to share her deepest secrets with the healers, Kaela said, "But I have so much sadness inside me."

"Sadness is a cloak that covers our heart, but it can never extinguish love." Janani smiled softly.

"But nothing's been the same since my mom died," Kaela tried to explain. "The prophecy says that I have a pure heart, but it feels like I have a deep dark hole instead."

"I know that feeling well, child. Each person we love is irreplaceable – a gift beyond measure. Please place another drop," Janani said, patting Kaela's arm.

Once again Kaela squeezed the bulb, moistening Shawn's dry lips. She carefully wiped a stray drop that dripped down the side of his chin.

"When we lose people we love, they leave a hole so vast and wide it seems that nothing will ever fill it."

Ariala looked into Kaela's eyes and for a moment Kaela knew that the beautiful woman understood the pain in her heart.

"In time you will discover that you carry something of your loved ones with you." Ariala continued. "You see, the way they loved you molds and shapes your life, and your soul. One day you will choose again to open your heart wide and free, Kaela."

"How do I do that?" Kaela asked.

Kanu's wide green eyes looked kindly at the young girl.

"Start small," Janani said, laying her hand gently on Kaela's arm. "Appreciate the love that exists within you."

Kaela's face fell. "I'm not sure I even know how to love anymore," she admitted softly.

"Listen to what you are saying," Janani said, concern shining bright in her eyes. "Please ... Shawn is ready for more of the healing water."

Kaela tenderly parted Shawn's lips with her index finger so that none of the healing water would be wasted. She stroked his face and, as she focused on caring for her cousin, she forgot about her own fear and anger. Her heart cracked open and love, like a tender shoot, grew inside her. A tear of kindness fell from her eye. Kaela looked up into Janani's, Ariala's and Kanu's loving eyes. She realized, "I do love Shawn, and my dad."

At that moment, Peeper chose to climb out of the nest he had made, which was hidden in Kaela's thick hair. The tiny bird chirped loudly from Kaela's shoulder.

"And Kanu," Kaela continued.

"You see!" Janani exclaimed. "Follow the thread. Like a mountain stream gathering drop after drop of melting snow, one day that love will grow into a mighty river."

Kaela carefully placed another drop on Shawn's lips. "I will," she said softly. "I'll do my best."

Janani looked at Ariala. Ariala nodded, closed her eyes and spread her hand wide on Shawn's chest. In a flash, her hand seemed to disappear inside of Shawn's body.

Kaela blinked, certain she was imagining things in the grey, black and silver silhouette illuminated only by the moon. She said in a hushed voice, "Ariala, your hand..." By the time the words were out of her mouth, Ariala's hand rested on top of Shawn's chest once again.

Ariala smiled and said, "Love goes deeper than skin, flesh or bone, Kaela. It is the great healer. Come. Listen to Shawn's heart."

Kaela placed her ear over Shawn's chest. She sat up and her cheeks were flushed with happiness. "His heartbeat is good!" Kaela cried. "It's working."

"Yes, dear. It's working." Janani smiled.

Ariala reached over and gently patted Peeper, who chirped against Kaela's neck. "And who is this?"

"Oh, that's Peeper – a little baby parrot that Shawn rescued. He had a hurt wing."

"Such a dear bird, and such a precious boy," Ariala said. "Kaela, the water will also help Shawn's hands."

Kaela nodded and carefully opened Shawn's hands. Heat radiated from his wounds. When the water made contact with his burns, a thread of steam rose and his skin noticeably cooled.

Shawn moaned and, for the first time since suffering his injury, he mumbled words.

"Kaela, Kaela..." he said.

"I'm here, Shawn." Kaela eagerly touched his forehead, but he didn't open his eyes.

"He still has some fever," Ariala said, frowning as she once again examined Shawn's hands. "Janani, did you bring the aloe?"

"Yes." Once again, Janani dug inside her pack and pulled out pieces of a thick-leaved plant. Carefully slicing the cutting in half lengthwise, she took one and then the other of Shawn's hands and gently rubbed Shawn's burns with the aloe gel, which oozed from the leaves.

"Janani, Kanu also has burns on his neck," Kaela said. "Can I rub some on him?"

"Certainly, dear." Janani turned to the tiger. "Let's see about your burns, Kanu."

Kaela drew the pendant from under her shirt and clasped it in one hand while she rubbed aloe with the other. Janani noted the sparkle of the pendant and smiled.

"I'll let you use your medicines on me just this once," Kanu said. He rolled onto his back showing his soft white fur, clearly enjoying the attention. "But don't go fussing over me too much. Just make sure the boy is okay."

"You're as proud as ever." Janani and Kaela rubbed the salve on Kanu's neck, Janani's falling tears mingling with the aloe juice. "Just look at what they did to you."

"Terrible things are happening all over our world." Kanu rolled back to his side and his eyes sparked with anger. "Gulig has no respect for life and destroys the natural balance." The tiger paused for a moment, wincing when Janani's gentle fingers passed over a particularly rough spot.

"I remember when my husband crowned you, 'The King of the Wild Spaces,'" Janani said. "He loved your visits. He was so proud to have you stay at the castle."

Ariala listened again to Shawn's heart and said, "The boy's heart is healed enough now to move him."

Just then Shawn moaned, "Kaela..." His eyelids fluttered open. With half-opened eyes he croaked, "I had the strangest dream. There was a tiger ... and I died."

"It was no dream," Kaela said, with tears dribbling down her cheeks. "Except you lived. You saved the tiger, Shawn. He's here – his name is Kanu. He's the one who led us out of the cave when the lamp went out."

Ariala's strong hands supported Shawn's back as he struggled to sit up. She held him against her shoulder.

"Where am I?" Shawn asked, still groggy.

"You are in the land of the Butterfly Tribe," Janani said, gently stroking Shawn's cheek. "We have beds and food a short distance away."

Kanu stood, arching his back in a deep stretch. "I will carry the boy."

"I - I can walk," Shawn said weakly.

"Kanu, no. You need your rest now," Janani scolded. "Shawn, Ariala and I will support you. It will be good for your heart and blood to walk a bit. It will help speed your healing. Let us help you up."

Janani and Ariala stood on either side of Shawn. As they bent over to help him up, their hair draped forward, revealing glowing markings on their necks. They carefully stood with Shawn between them.

Kaela stared at the likeness of a monarch butterfly, orange with black outlines and veins on Janani's neck, and the blue butterfly sparkling from Ariala's. The markings looked alive, more vibrant and real than any tattoo could be. "What is that, Janani ... on your neck?"

"That is my butterfly," Janani said. "Ariala and I belong to the Butterfly Tribe. We are born with a mark on the back of our necks - it looks like a birthmark. If we follow the ways of our ancestors and learn the healing arts, the mark grows until it becomes a complete butterfly."

"Can I see?" Shawn asked.

"Of course," Ariala replied, turning her neck towards Shawn.

"It is so beautiful." Shawn stared wide-eyed.

"Can I touch it?" Kaela asked.

Janani nodded.

"It feels just like regular skin." Kaela gently stroked Janani's neck.

Ariala held Shawn around the waist and said, "Let's test your legs, Shawn."

Shawn walked shakily between Janani and Ariala, mostly supported by their strong arms, as Kaela and Kanu walked behind.

"Are you okay, Shawn?" Kaela asked.

"Yes, thank you – all of you – for everything...."

As they walked further into the valley, peace filled Kaela, as if she was embraced by unseen magic. The smells of night jasmine and roses wafted towards her. The robes of the Butterfly Women billowed behind them in the gentle breeze and their marks emanated a warm glow.

These women are special – like angels in the night, Kaela thought.

Just in front of her, Shawn said softly, "Butterfly Women ... great healers...."

Chapter Thirteen • Marisa

The wind sang a whispering tree song as Kanu, Kaela, Shawn, Ariala and Janani walked down a winding path leading to a stone cottage with a thatched roof. Light poured from the windows on either side of the welcoming blue door and one window in the peak of the roof shone like a guiding light. All weapons and shoes were left at the door, and they soon made themselves at home. Janani and Ariala served their guests hearty soup and fresh bread from the hearth of a large fireplace that covered the length of one wall. Shawn curled up on a couch and Kanu stretched out on his side nearby, filling the floor of the small living room with his massive body. Kanu and Shawn drifted into much-needed sleep.

Kaela sat in a rocking chair and relished the comfort of her surroundings. Exhausted, but not yet ready for sleep, she stared into the dancing flames. The red and yellow fire crackled and spat, casting a warm glow over the pine floor, and shining from the copper pots hanging above the mantle. She knew that in the morning, she would leave this safe place; but for the moment she relaxed and enjoyed the comfort and safety of the Butterfly Women's cottage.

Janani touched Kaela gently on the arm. "I would like to take you down to the hot springs," she said. "You can get cleaned up there. The waters will refresh your spirit. You can leave your shoes here. I think your bare feet will enjoy the walk." She walked to an armoire in the corner and pulled down towels and nightclothes.

Kanu's ears perked up and the end of his tail twitched. "Be careful, Janani. I'm not sure that I trust Gulig to respect the sacredness of this land."

"Kanu, that is too horrible to even consider. The work of the Butterfly Women has been protected for countless generations."

"Many things have changed because of that man," Kanu said. "Please be careful."

"It is so good of you to look out for us," Janani said, kneeling briefly and stroking Kanu's soft fur. "Kaela, we should go now. It is already terribly late, but I am eager to speak with you, and the water will help you relax."

Kaela followed the Butterfly Woman down a white stone path behind the small house. The moon, still bright, lit their way as Kaela gazed up at the innumerable stars in the sky. The stillness of the night exaggerated the crunching of stones under their steps. The smooth, round stones of the path cooled and soothed Kaela's feet like a gentle foot rub. A short distance from the cottage a series of pools steamed in the moonlight.

"Be careful – the rocks can be a bit slippery. Here, give me your hand," Janani said as they reached one of the pools.

"Now, just step down here ... and step there ... here we are."

"This water's hot," Kaela exclaimed, stepping down into the water. "It's like a bath!"

"Yes, these are the healing hot springs. Water wells up here from deep underground – that is why it is a sacred place. Some pools are so hot that they can burn you, but this pool is just right."

Janani watched Kaela relax into the water, and then continued, "Kaela, I noticed you are wearing a butterfly pendant. I wear one just like it." Janani held an identical pendant above the water.

"Hey! It's the same as mine. Where did they come from?"

"Four pendants were made generations ago from the wings of a rare butterfly. The butterfly was the last of its kind, sadly, because all of the plants that his species lived on were destroyed. Just before the last one died, the tiny creature asked to have its wings preserved so that people would never forget its beauty. One pendant was lost to time, but three remain. When I married a human, my mother gave me one, and when my sons were born she gave one to each of them, so that we would all remember our butterfly hearts."

"But..." Kaela slowly realized the meaning of Janani's words. "My mom gave me this. Did she get it when she was here? Did you know her?"

A note of sadness entered Janani's voice as she held back tears. "Yes. I loved your mother like she was my own daughter."

Kaela gazed down at her pendant and, for the first time, knew for certain that her mother had gone through the hole in the sky. The pendant was living proof.

"You knew her? You really knew her?"

"Yes. She came to live with King Harrel and my boys in the castle – the whole family fell in love with her. Even though she struggled with illness, she always sparkled like a bright star. One of my boys must have given your mother his pendant. It was probably Arendore - he and your mother had a special connection."

"So he knew her? But why didn't he tell me?"

"I cannot speak for my son, but he is under terrible trials right now, Kaela. I'm sure it will be his great pleasure to tell you everything he remembers about your mother when the time is right."

"I miss her so much," Kaela said, lapsing into a short silence as she digested this new information. "Wait a minute - you're King Arendore's mother?" She blurted.

"Yes, Kaela," Janani replied.

"Then you are a queen. Why aren't you living in the castle? Why do you live in a tiny cottage way up here?"

"I was born a Butterfly Woman. When I married King Harrel from the House of Muraten, I chose a human life to share with him. After my husband's death, however, I returned to continue the work of my people. My heart shattered on the day he died." Janani grew quiet and a stream of tears fell from her eyes. "And now Gulig has my beloved son, Lorendale, under his thumb."

Tenderness welled in Kaela's heart. Eager to comfort the woman who had been so kind, she said, "Please, Janani, don't be sad. I'm going to stop Gulig. It's not right for him to hurt so many."

Laughing and crying in the same breath, Janani said, "Kaela, you truly are a remarkable girl."

Warmed by the hot springs - and by Janani's kind words - Kaela relaxed into stillness and savored the fullness in her heart.

"Now dear, I think it is time for us to get some rest." Janani emerged from the water and wrapped her long hair in a towel. She held out a towel for Kaela. "You must still get some sleep tonight. Come and towel off."

They entered the house, and Ariala smiled at them from a chair where she watched over Kanu and Shawn. Shawn's cheeks glowed with newfound health and a thick white quilt covered his skinny body like a soft cloud. Janani and Kaela both stopped and stroked Shawn's hair and then kneeled down to nuzzle Kanu's large head. He chuffed softly at the kindness in their touch.

A fire burned in the hearth of the bedroom, and a colorful quilt, sewn to look like a giant sun against a blue background, covered the turned-down bed.

"Come, dear, sit on the bed. I will comb out your beautiful red hair."

As Janani sat behind Kaela, gently working through the knots and snarls in Kaela's long hair, Ariala entered the room and whispered, "They are both doing well."

Kaela looked from Janani to Ariala, once again noticing their beauty and the way they lit up the room.

"Ariala, did you ever meet my mother?"

"Yes." Ariala sat in a chair in front of Kaela while Janani continued carefully combing Kaela's hair. "She was the first one I ever visited." As Ariala spoke, the timbre of her words resonated like a bow moving gently across the strings of a cello. "The first time I traveled to your world, I went with my mother to help Marisa." Ariala's inner light shone even more brightly as she continued, "I was only thirteen, like you."

"I read about you in her journal. She thought she had seen an angel!"

"What does that word – angel – mean to you, Kaela?"

Kaela blinked her eyes a few times, staring at the golden aura that surrounded Ariala. "Well, I'm not sure that anyone really knows what an angel is, but they are supposed to live in heaven, and they live forever. They deliver messages from God, I guess."

"It must be wonderful to be an angel. But we are mortal like you," Ariala explained. "Like all the Butterfly Tribe before us, one day Janani and I will leave our bodies behind forever. But while we have the gift of life, it is our blessing to help people know the kindness and love of the Great Spirit."

"You know what? I think you and Janani *are* angels. Maybe they just call you something else here."

Laughing, Ariala said, "And I'm quite sure you are one, as well."

As though a tuning fork had been struck, the joy in Ariala's laughter reverberated inside of Kaela's heart. Giggling, Kaela touched Ariala's hand. "Me, an angel? If only."

"Come get in bed," Janani said as she helped Kaela get under the covers. "That's it. Now let me tuck you in."

Kaela smiled as she snuggled in the soft sheets, and asked, "How do you travel again and again through the hole in the sky? It was pretty scary and hard for me."

Janani replied, "When we go through the hole in the sky, we leave our bodies behind."

"I don't understand."

"We leave our bodies at the bottom of the ocean and the turtles guard them for us. It is easier to travel without bodies, and that way we can be in a room full of people without making a big fuss," Janani said.

"I saw that. I saw three women's bodies at the bottom of the ocean when I first got here!" Kaela said, glad to have solved that one mystery.

"Yes, they must have been traveling to your world." Ariala paused and then said, "Kaela, you should sleep now."

"No, please. You don't know how long I've waited to hear about my mother."

Janani opened a drawer in the bedside table and pulled out a small book. "This is the diary that I kept while your mother was here. If you go to sleep now, I promise you can spend some time reading it in the morning. Does that sound good to you?"

"Janani," Kaela said firmly. "At dawn I'm going back to the caves – I'm going to rescue Eiren. But there's one thing. When I go, can Shawn stay here with you? He still needs to rest."

"Of course, sweet girl." Briefly holding the diary to her chest, Janani placed it in Kaela's eager hands, and said, "You are brave and you are a wonderful healer. Your mother would have been so proud of you."

Ariala and Janani leaned over, one at a time, to kiss Kaela on the cheek.

"We are going to check on Shawn and Kanu," Janani said, "and then

Ariala will sleep here in the room with you."

The women left. Kaela flipped to the first page and began reading.

9th Day of Dumanean

Last night, a loud neighing startled me out of a deep sleep. My heart pounded against my chest as I gazed out the window. Blanco, the white stallion, stood illuminated in the bright light of the full moon. He stared into my eyes, urging me to come to the castle courtyard.

I flew down the stairs and ran outside to find a girl, who lay slack against Blanco's mane. Though unconscious, one arm clutched a worn-out teddy bear, and the other hung loose by the side of the horse's neck. She had no hair on her head and her frail body was dressed in pink pajamas.

I put my wool shawl over her shoulders to protect her from the evening chill as our manservant carefully lifted the girl from the horse's back. "Ma'am, there's not much to this child," he said. "She's as light as a feather."

I instructed him to bring her to an upstairs bedroom and lay her down on the bed. Then I touched her face and whispered, "Hello, sweet one. Can you hear me?" There was no response. My heart broke to see how the illness had consumed her body.

Her skin was so pale that even the thin blue veins just under its surface were visible. In the dark she had appeared to be bald, but in the firelight I found that her hair was actually very fine and short – a beautiful red color like that of my boys. I gently stroked the silky spikes, gazing at her features, which were so much like my husband's that she truly could have been one of my children.

Usually I send the children to the healing waters of Mount Sankaria when they are ill, but I didn't dare move her from the bed. Her soul hung onto her body by the thinnest of threads. I stayed with her through the night, using all the healing wisdom I learned when I was a Butterfly Woman. I rubbed her hands and feet with oil of rose to open her heart, and myrrh to awaken her energy, and then I fed her water from Mount Sankaria, drop by drop. It's not as effective as drinking it straight from the source, but it will have to do.

Janani

12th Day of Dumanean

I have barely slept the last few days because I wanted to remain by the girl's side. We have been feeding her ancient ginseng root tea and broth made from high mountain vegetables to revive her energy and give her strength. Water is carried down from Mount Sankaria daily. We bathe her with it and make use of its healing energy in everything she drinks. The cook is fermenting fresh goat milk to soothe her weak stomach.

At first she woke just long enough to give me gentle, drowsy smiles. Finally her eyes opened wide, and she whispered, "Have I found the magic land?"

Tears sprang from my eyes as I answered, "Yes, yes you have. You are in Muratenland. What is your name, child?"

"My name is Marisa."

"That is a beautiful name. In our world, it means 'from the sea'. It is perfect for you, because you came to us as a gift from the hole in the sky over the ocean. How old are you, child?"

"I'm fifteen, but I might as well be a hundred. I need to know, please, is there hope for me?" she asked, pleading.

"My dear, you are terribly ill, but we have special medicines that might help you. There is definitely hope."

"There is definitely hope," she repeated, smiling, and then fell fast asleep.

Janani

23rd Day of Dumanean

Having the girl here is a bit like having my own children back again. My 16-year-old boys barely need me at all, in any case. My first born, Arendore, spends as much time as possible studying with his father, King Harrel. My wild child, Lorendale, has been traveling with our wise friend Netri, learning about the wonders of the Kingdom that his father rules.

I wanted so badly to have more children, but after Arendore and Lorendale were born I nearly bled to death. Thanks to the Great Spirit, my midwife was one of the Butterfly Women, and she was able to save my life. My womb dried up after that, so I have contented myself with raising my boys. This remarkable new child, who needs me so much, is a blessing I never dared hope for.

Marisa's fine hair glows like a halo around her head. Though she is weak, I feel the strength of her spirit. She is finally sitting up, propped against a large stack of pillows. We gave her a corner room in the palace so the summer breeze that wafts through the large windows will keep her cool and comfortable, and she can look out on the vast meadow in the front of our home.

It is my exquisite joy to have her here.

Janani

A miracle has occurred. One must never underestimate the human body's ability to heal.

Marisa has been with us such a short time, and already roses bloom in her cheeks. When I felt her neck and abdomen, the knots had grown smaller and softer. It is not just my imagination. It is true. She was just strong enough to dance around the room with me as the sun rose in the sky this morning, casting a rich orange glow on the clouds in the distance. It is truly the dawn of a new day.

Janani

15th Day of Rhianean

Something terrible happened while Arendore and Marisa were out walking today. The crazy woman, Tazena, who hears voices, ran directly up to Marisa's face. Pointing her gnarled finger at Marisa, she screamed, "It's the red-haired daughter. They'll come for what's owed to them. It's the beginning of the end. Beware the red-haired daughter!"

Arendore asked some of the servants to escort the poor woman home. Before they left, he saw Tazena's daughter, Zara, standing in the distance. Zara quietly walked up to her mother and took her hand, gently coaxing her to come along.

We are accustomed to the woman's madness, but I am afraid she frightened Marisa. Arendore said that she turned sheet white and buried her face in his shoulder. He sat with her afterward on a bench, his arm around her, until she stopped shaking, but she still has yet to speak.

Janani

18th Day of Rhianean

My heart burst with joy this morning when I saw Lorendale and Netri ride into the courtyard. I waved to them from the balcony. Lorendale ran upstairs and greeted me with a huge embrace, swinging me around as if I was a small child. What a man my boy has become!

I told him about Marisa. He was so eager to meet her that I immediately took him to her room. Lorendale regaled us both with tales of his many adventures. He was particularly taken with the Tree People, and told us of the boldness of a young Tree girl who insisted he dance with her. Then he told us joke after joke.

How wonderful it was to hear Marisa's unrestrained laughter.

I had my back to the door, but I suddenly realized someone was standing at the entrance when a hush fell over the room.

Lorendale said, "Arendore, come in, come in. I'm just telling everyone the latest jokes."

I turned around to see Arendore fuming. He slammed the door without a word.

Janani

18th Day of Rhianean

It is so frustrating to be a mother. No matter how hard I try to keep things fair for my children, someone always feels slighted. When my boys were little I remember having to use a string to prove that their pieces of cake were exactly equal.

This morning from my window, I heard Arendore and

Lorendale shouting at each other, behaving like ignorant fools. I desperately wanted to intervene, but their father insisted that they have to learn to sort out their own differences.

How could two people grown from the same egg, under the same stars, be so very different? Arendore is brilliant with adults. He sits in on many of his father's meetings with dignitaries, where he is applauded for his fine speech and intelligence. His youthful perspective is well appreciated. When he is in the company of girls his own age, he becomes terribly awkward. His feet trip over each other, and he blushes every time he speaks. Perhaps we let him spend too much time with his father and not enough time with children his own age.

Lorendale flits through social situations like a mosquito, flirting easily with every girl he meets until he has them all wrapped around his smallest finger. There is no one who can make dear Harrel laugh with more delight. Even when he was little, Lorendale loved to make people laugh.

This morning before the shouting match, I noticed Marisa sitting in the courtyard with Lorendale as I stood in my sitting room window. He entertained her with some poorly executed magic tricks and she giggled gleefully. Arendore found them together and blew up at his brother. Apparently, Marisa had promised to take a walk with Arendore and Lorendale had persuaded her to stay with him for a while longer.

I pray that Arendore's love for his brother is stronger than his jealousy.

Janani

23rd Day of Rhianean

Fear has a way of rooting inside even the wisest soul. Tazena's ravings about the red-haired daughter have been spreading among our people. I have known Tazena since she was a beautiful young girl. I can remember her standing next to me in the market and whispering to me, "One day you will marry Prince Harrel. He will be a much loved king one day."

I did not believe her, but her prediction came true.

When the King heard that I consulted Tazena from time to time, he asked me to stop. He warned me that she was a known liar, and that it was foolhardy to rely on her. Every year it seems that her mind grows more and more confused. Perhaps she has gone mad from seeing so many possible futures in her head.

Still, I am concerned for the woman, and for Marisa. I told my husband that predicting the future was the only way Tazena could make a living – her visions and fits prevent her from any other occupation. The King and I have made a point of providing for her.

Thank goodness her daughter, Zara, is finally old enough to help care for the woman.

I have asked Lorendale and Arendore to keep Marisa away from Tazena and her daughter, Zara. Marisa has enough to deal with right now without having to worry about the prophecy.

Janani

8th Day of Anaganean

Arendore and Lorendale have finally made peace with one another. Yesterday, Marisa wanted to go to the market and see some of the special things that our people create. She heard about the blown glass and hand-carved animal figurines. I gave her some coins and bid her to buy something for herself. Arendore was busy with his father, so Lorendale agreed to escort her.

When they arrived back in her room, Marisa told me an interesting story.

"Janani, something very strange happened in the market today," she said. "We passed a candy vendor, and I told Lorendale I wanted to buy a treat. He told me to stay at the candy stand while he went just across the way to purchase some new magic tricks."

"A dirty, blond girl with raggedy clothes appeared beside me after he left. She was younger than me, maybe twelve. She was wearing old clothes and stared at the candy with wide, hungry eyes. I could tell she didn't have any money, so I asked her if she would like something."

"I don't take handouts," she told me. "But I can tell you your future for a price."

"'Really? How can you tell my future?' I asked.

"I can. It's just the way it is," she said.

"I asked her name, and she told me it was Zara."

"Okay," I said, "I'll give you these two coins if you can tell me something true."

My heart beat hard against my chest and I was overcome with fear, terrified of what the seer girl had said to my beloved Marisa. I tried my best to pretend calmness. "What did the girl tell you, Marisa?"

"Janani, it was so strange!" The girl got real quiet and her eyes glazed over. It was like she was looking at something that no one else could see. As soon as the people around us saw me talking to Zara, and saw the look on her face, they became so quiet that the stillness was deafening.

Then she said, "I can see things coming. Could be difficult. I see the red-haired daughter," she told me in a slow voice.

"What do you mean by a red-haired daughter" I asked.

"You – maybe you'll have a baby, red-haired girl, or maybe it all goes dark. Not sure which one," she shrugged.

"I got very scared when she told me that, and the quiet of the people in the market was eerie."

"That's not a very good fortune telling!" I said loudly, to break the silence. I even felt a little angry with her. "Maybe I'll have a baby and maybe not? Anyone could tell me that!"

Just then, Lorendale noticed the crowd and he ran over to us saying, "Get out of here. What have you been telling Marisa?"

"Just the truth is all," Zara said.

"We told you and your mother to stay away." Lorendale tried to shoo her off.

"Soon as I get my money I'll go," she told him, standing firm.

Lorendale took me by the elbow, but I ran back and quickly gave her all the coins in my pocket. It seemed like Lorendale didn't much like her. *That girl frightened me.* "Who is she, Janani? What do you think it means?"

"Zara is the seer's daughter. I think she was telling you that your future isn't written in stone," I answered her cautiously. "Marisa, I want you to understand that we have the power to change our destiny."

Marisa looked relieved. "I liked the part that I might have a daughter. I really liked that part," she said with delight.

I told her that I really liked that part, too, and hugged her. Still, I never should have let her go to the market. It could have gone much worse.

Janani

Eager to read more, Kaela struggled against weariness – but her eyelids refused to remain open. She curled onto her side with the book cradled against her chest and dropped into a deep sleep.

Janani kissed Kaela's cheek and coaxed the diary from her hands when she returned, while Ariala wrapped herself in a blanket and settled into the comfortable armchair by the bed. Janani extinguished the lamps and returned to Shawn's bedside, but moments later the whole house awakened to the sound of crashing glass and metal clanking against metal.

"NO-O-O-O-O-O!" Janani's scream pierced the night.

Chapter Fourteen · Kanu's Ninth Life

Jolted awake with adrenalin streaming through her veins, Kaela bolted out of bed. Before she reached the bedroom entrance, Ariala, already there, yelled, "Kaela, you stay here! Do not move!" She slammed the door behind her.

Kaela scoured the room for a weapon, grabbed a fireplace poker and cracked open the door to find Kanu sprawled limply on the floor. Blood poured from his wound. Red blood dripped down Janani's and Ariala's arms as they frantically worked to save the giant tiger.

Splatters of red mixed with what looked like olive-green blood colored every surface. The comforter that once covered Shawn lay trampled on the floor, stained crimson, while Kaela's sword sat in a pool of blood on the floor. Kaela's eyes darted from the couch to the chair, from the floor to the walls, desperate to find her cousin. Horrified, Kaela released the poker, which fell to the floor with a crash. "Where's Shawn?" she cried. "What have they done with Shawn?"

"Kaela, Shawn has been kidnapped. You must remain calm. Please, hold Kanu's wound closed so that I can stitch it together," Janani said quietly.

Kaela sank to her knees next to the tiger. The warmth of his blood soaked into her nightgown and clung to her skin. Momentarily nauseated, she grasped the tiger's drenched, furry skin between her fingers, and the room tilted and spun, turning her stomach. Swallowing hard, Kaela bit her lip, willing herself to be brave.

"That's good, Kaela," Ariala said touching Kaela's arm.

Choking back tears, Kaela leaned close to Kanu's ear. "Please don't die," she begged, clutching her butterfly pendant. "Please don't die, Kanu."

The women cleaned the bloodied fur around the stitched wound. Kanu's limbs remained limp and unmoving. Then his thighs twitched, his feet jerked and the nerves in his legs began firing once again. The huge cat stretched, and rasped – "Now that's enough. I must go lie down on the cool earth. It will either renew my life or accept my spirit. I do not wish to die indoors."

Janani, Ariala and Kaela did their best to support Kanu's heavy weight as he struggled to stand. He growled at them to back away and lumbered towards the door, the strain in his walk revealing the intensity of his pain. Ariala opened the door, and the three generations of women stood outside, watching Kanu. His tail dragged in the dirt as he disappeared into the night.

"Will he be okay?" Kaela sobbed. "What about Shawn?"

Janani hugged Kaela, then looked her in the eyes. "I tried to protect Shawn, Kaela – I ... I broke the vow of a butterfly woman to do no harm, and I grabbed your sword. But Gulig's soldier ripped it from my hands and pushed me to the ground. The sword resisted his touch and dropped to the floor, but the soldier drew his own sword and stabbed Kanu before I could do anything – barely missing his heart."

Janani bowed her head. "Now we must pray for Kanu and hold him in our love. He is strong, and he is a survivor – he may not die. We must pray that he has one more of his nine lives remaining. I am sure it would delight him to live long enough to see Gulig banished forever."

Kaela, Ariala, and Janani all closed their eyes for a moment of silence and shared grief.

"Those were definitely Gulig's men who kidnapped Shawn," Janani continued, slowly. "When they threw the black cloak over his head, I heard one of them say, 'Remember, we have strict orders not to hurt the child. Gulig wants the girl for himself.'"

Kaela looked at Janani and Ariala, puzzled.

"Kaela, they came here looking for you," Janani said softly.

"And now they have Shawn, instead." Kaela whispered, despair and resolve hardening in the pit of her stomach. She prayed that Kanu still had one life left to live.

I am so terribly weak, Kanu thought, searching wearily for a resting place. *I smell blood seeping from my wounds and the scent of my essence leaves a path that follows me deeper and deeper into the forest. This must be the last of my nine lives.*

I find my spot under an ancient tree and crumple to the ground. The cool earth welcomes me, holding my broken body in her arms like a great mother.

I do not understand humans. Why do they take such pleasure in killing? They see my kind as vicious killers, but they do not understand. There is no question that I have killed again and again, but for food, and yes, when needed, for self-defense. When I take the life of another animal, I immediately eat the organs where the life energy lives. That animal becomes part of me. It lives on in me.

If only I had one life left, I would go rescue the boy. I owe him my life. But it is not to be. I am melting into the cool ground, damp with my own blood. I cling to my breath. I am floating down a river. The ocean calls to me – her voice is sweet...

Something rustles the nearby brush and I crack open my eyes for one last look at the world. A doe stands nearby, full of life and vitality. We stare at each other, knowing that I cannot run. The deer folds her knees and offers herself to me. With one quick bite to the neck, her pain is over. I bow my head in thanks – and then eat hungrily. The swiftness that once lived in her legs now courses through mine. I will find the child.

Janani and Ariala shortly returned indoors and began swabbing up blood from the floor and walls, but Kaela remained outside, lost in grief for her friends. Praying for Kanu's return, for some sign that he still lived, she strained to see the edge of the forest. At the same time, a fire began to burn in her belly. How could Gulig shed blood in this sacred place? Did he think he could kill the King of the Wild Spaces, kidnap children in the middle of the night, and get away with it? Kaela's anger momentarily overwhelmed her fear. It was time.

Rejoining the Butterfly Women, Kaela said with authority, "It is time for me to go to Gulig's castle. I need to find the Butterfly Breath and break the curse. I can't let his evil take over this land."

Tears gathered in Janani's eyes, but she nodded in silent agreement.

The mood was somber and few words were spoken. Janani and Ariala quickly gathered supplies to help Kaela on her journey. Kaela dressed in the suede clothes of the Tree People and the soft boots from Netri, both still filled with the smell of sweat and terror, of stone, steam and bark. Janani strapped Skyla's ruby-handled dagger and Kaela's small sword around Kaela's waist and calf. Ariala found the nuts from the Tree People, and Kaela tucked the bag under her belt. Ariala also gave Kaela a suede knapsack filled with food and warm clothes.

"Remember – when you carry the butterfly pendant, you can hear what your heart is telling you," Janani said, embracing Kaela tightly. She released Kaela and looked her deep in the eyes. "Our hearts are with you on your journey."

Ariala handed Kaela a canteen sewn out of thick, brown animal skin. "Kaela, this is the same water we used to heal Shawn's heart. All of the water on Mount Sankaria has healing properties, but this is the most pure." Ariala bent and tied the canteen to Kaela's waist. "One drop has the power to purify a large quantity of water," she explained. "You must be careful in Gulig's world – the food and drink he serves may be poisoned."

"I am ready to go," Kaela said, standing tall like a warrior. Clear in her mission, Kaela bathed in the love from Janani and Ariala as they each gave her one last long hug.

"The path is clear and wide to the caves, Kaela," Janani said. "You will find the way easily. I know that you have what you need to complete this mission. My heart is with you."

"Love is with you always," Ariala said firmly.

The drum of courage beating in Kaela's heart grew in intensity, strengthening her determination. Kaela breathed in the love that surrounded her and looked at both of their faces. "I am going to find a way to save Shawn and Eiren." Passion rose in Kaela's heart as she spoke, and her muscles twitched with restlessness. She needed to go now. "Gulig's evil must be stopped – I can't let him destroy this beautiful land. I promise I will do everything I can."

The two butterfly women stood on the doorstep as Kaela walked away. She turned around to give them one last look and then strode toward the caves in the dim light of dawn.

PART TWO
The Daughters

Chapter Fifteen · Gwenilda and Zarenda

Kaela walked swiftly to the caves, determined to rescue Shawn and Eiren from the Rugus. Roosters crowed in the distance as the sun rose in the sky. Bells tinkled from goats frolicking in a nearby pasture, and one, then two and finally an entire chorus of birds whistled their melodies – filling the skies with their songs – but Kaela barely noticed.

"Butterfly breath within her heart. Butterfly breath within her heart. Butterfly breath within her heart...." The mantra drummed in Kaela's thoughts, keeping time with her steps.

Seemingly out of nowhere, a large curly-haired dog bounded towards her. Its tail wagging in a flurry of excitement, the brown mutt knocked her over. He hovered over her, giving her big wet kisses.

"Oh, you're so cute," Kaela giggled, startled out of her reverie. "But where did you come from?"

Woof, woof!

"Oh, I remember you - you're the King's dog, Wooly." The dog growled a little and shook its head at her. She pushed it to one side and sat up. Within seconds, she saw Netri's familiar face bobbing towards her. His clothes were in mottled shades of greens and reds, and virtually disappeared into the landscape.

She flew to him with the dog by her side and kneeled down for a hug. "I just knew you would come!" Kaela cried.

"Of course," Netri began.

"Netri, they've kidnapped Shawn. I have to find him."

Netri took Kaela's hand and said. "I know - our spies have spotted

Shawn. For now, he is safe; but Gulig's soldiers will, no doubt, carry Shawn to their master, and Gulig has no love for children."

"Gulig's soldier came here to kidnap me. What will Gulig do to Shawn when he finds out his soldiers grabbed the wrong person?"

"I am sorry, Kaela – I cannot answer that for you. I have not walked in the footsteps of darkness, and do not know the twists and turns of a mind ruled by evil."

"What about Kanu and the twins?" Kaela asked, with a tremor of fear gripping her belly. "Is Kanu..."

Netri shook his head. "I am afraid I do not know how the King of the Wild Spaces fares. The twins are taken prisoner."

"Kanu, the twins, Shawn, Eiren." Kaela's face flushed with anger. "That guy has to be stopped!" She abruptly stood up, and said, "Netri, it's time."

Kaela resumed her brisk march and Netri trotted along beside her. The dog ran ahead, wagging his tail as he sniffed his way along the path.

"There is some time before we reach the caves. There are things I would like to share with you as we walk. Do you remember when King Arendore spoke of the Princess Gwenilda?"

Kaela thought for a moment and remembered King Arendore's story about the girl who died. "Yes, I think so – the one who died mysteriously?"

"Yes, that dear girl. As you know, the lifespan of my kind is very long. I actually had the good fortune of knowing Gwenilda – she was very dear to me."

"What was she like, Netri?"

"She was a beautiful red-haired girl like you. She was full of joy and loved to tease me, and she ran through the castle like a spring wind, but her story began before she was even born. I would like to share some things about her that may help you on your quest."

Kaela looked at Netri even as she continued walking down the path. "What things, Netri?"

"Well, to begin with – Gwenilda's mother, Queen Rhiana, came from the Butterfly Tribe."

"Like Janani?"

"Yes, Kaela, like Janani. Rhiana left the Butterfly Tribe to marry King

Muraten, who ruled all the southern lands of this peninsula. She tried and tried to have babies, but was unable to bear a child to term. She was completely heartbroken and became desperate for help. Rhiana sought the assistance of a seer named Zella."

"A seer, Netri? What's that?"

Netri frowned and continued, "A seer is someone who can see into the future. Rhiana hoped that the woman's fortune telling could help her change what was to come. Zella agreed to help the Queen have a healthy child, but on her own terms. Queen Rhiana had to promise that her first-born daughter would marry Prince Golan, the Rugu King's son. Zella told Rhiana in no uncertain terms that Rhiana would bring a curse on King Muraten's family if she did not keep this contract."

"I'm afraid the seer's intentions were less than pure," Netri shook his head. His face momentarily transformed, the lines deepening until he looked very old and tremendously sad. "From what I understand, the very day Queen Rhiana agreed to this promise, the seer sent a letter to King Grule, the Rugu King, informing him of Queen Rhiana's promise. King Grule said he would pay the seer her weight in gold when the contract was signed."

"When Gwenilda turned five, King Grule, ruler of the northern lands sent a marriage proposal to King Muraten. In exchange for peace between the kingdoms, he agreed that his son, Prince Golan, would marry Gwenilda. King Muraten was uncertain about the match, of course. The Rugus had been his family's mortal enemies for generations."

"To be sure that Rhiana did not let the promise be forgotten, Zella had a crow carry a gift to Rhiana. It was a purple crystal with the engraved words 'To Promises Fulfilled'. Afraid of bringing a curse on the King's family, the Queen realized that she had no choice but to fulfill her promise, and she encouraged her husband to agree to King Grule's proposal. The contract was signed soon after."

"A few weeks later the same crow arrived squawking and cawing, letting us know that the seer had been murdered and robbed, and that her four-year-old daughter, Zarenda, had no one to turn to. The crow family had tried to care for the child, but they found it too difficult to feed her. They came to the castle, asking for help with the little girl. One of the servants agreed to take her in."

Kaela tilted her head and asked, "A crow family tried to take care of the little girl?"

"Yes, her mother had a close relationship with the crows of the forest. Apparently, when her mother died, a crow family even built her a nest, but soon realized a human child was more than they could handle. In fact, to the children of the castle, little Zarenda was a terribly odd child. She loved nothing better than to stare into the crystal ball, the one possession she had of her mother's, and she was more adept at speaking to crows than to children her own age. She was prone to bouts of sadness and melancholy. Even as she grew older and fluent in human tongue, she often climbed into the trees to seek the company of crows. But Gwenilda adored the seer girl, despite her strangeness. They became almost like sisters."

"One day I walked in on the girls, when Zarenda was six and Gwenilda was seven. I found them leaning over something, whispering to one another. Zarenda's long blonde hair and Gwenilda's red hair completely covered the toy that engaged their attention. At that moment Zarenda said, 'Gwenny, I can see the boy you're going to marry.'"

"I fully expected to hear a description of Golan," Netri continued, "But instead Zarenda surprised me by describing a boy who lived far, far away with brown hair and brown eyes."

"Upon hearing those words, Gwenilda shook her head and said, 'No, Zarenda, Golan has green eyes.'"

"Zarenda was adamant about the vision in the crystal and insisted, 'No, Gwenny. I see another boy. You'll see – one day I'm going to be a princess too.'"

Netri shook his head remembering the scene. "Those two had no idea that they were playing with fire. I stepped out of the shadows, held out my hand and said, 'Let me keep that for you until you are older, Zarenda.' But she wouldn't hear of it. She clutched the ball to her chest and said, 'No! It's mine.'"

Netri walked a few moments in silence and then he softly said with a note of sadness in his voice, " And indeed, Gwenilda never married Golan."

"King Arendore talked about that," Kaela said slowly, remembering. "So Zarenda's prediction came true, right?"

"It did." Netri nodded and continued, "Gwenilda never married

King Grule's son, Golan. A bloody battle ensued and, although the Rugus fought ruthlessly, King Muraten's men defeated Grule and Golan. King Muraten then exiled the Rugus from this land, and the Queen's promise was broken."

"King Grule and Prince Golan swore that one day they would return to this land and claim not only a red-haired daughter born into the House of Muraten, but also their right to the throne."

"Golan married another and he soaked his son, Gulig, in the brine of hatred. By the time Gulig reached adulthood, he lusted after the throne and plotted his revenge, but no red-haired daughters had been born to the House of Muraten. One day, a spy brought word to Gulig about your mother's presence in the castle. The old wound ripped open and hatred flowed freely in his veins. He soon sailed to this land with only a handful of men and ran his ship aground, pretending to be a man without a country. He wormed his way into Lorendale's castle through lies and trickery."

Kaela thought for a moment. "Janani told me my mother was the daughter she never had. I guess Gulig decided that was good enough for him." After a pause, she asked softly, "Did you know my mom?"

"Yes, I had the good fortune of spending time with your mother when she was here," Netri said. "She was a remarkable girl. Like so many people who have looked death in the eye, she had a deep appreciation for life."

"I don't understand." Kaela stopped walking for a moment to fully understand the meaning of Netri's words.

"Even though each and every one of us will die one day, most people hide that knowledge buried in the closet of their awareness. But when someone faces a deep illness, it is like a shadow that follows wherever they go. The fortunate ones discover the hidden blessing. Moment by moment, gratitude for each and every breath awakens inside. Your mother was one of the fortunate ones who lived to appreciate her life."

"Did Janani heal her?"

"It seemed that way in the beginning," Netri explained. "At first your mother grew stronger. It was like a miracle, but then her illness returned with a vengeance."

"But how did she survive when she was so sick?"

"It was a gift, just as your life is a magic gift in this world."

Netri and Kaela resumed walking in silence for a few minutes. Then

Netri explained, "It was your mother's presence here that set the old prophecy in motion. I warned Janani again and again that Marisa needed to return to her world. There was no way she was strong enough to break the curse."

Kaela remembered the terrifying days when her mother was too weak even to get out of bed, and the terrible pain that gnawed at her heart, even today. *Could the pain in your heart actually get so bad that it kills you?* "Netri, what about Gwenilda? Did she really die of a broken heart, like Arendore said?"

As the steep face of the mountain drew near, Netri pulled a small leather-bound book from a pack he carried on his shoulder. "I promised Gwenilda that I would let her tell her own story. If you read the final pages of this diary, you will find the answers you seek. Read it when you can."

The diary was almost weightless in her hands. Kaela flipped through its pages, squinted at the cramped cursive handwriting, and asked, "How can I read this? It's so tiny."

"That was how Gwenilda kept her secrets. Do you see the ribbon at the back of the book?"

Kaela nodded.

"It's attached to a magnifying glass in a pouch at the back."

Kaela held the glass just above a paragraph towards the end of the diary. The letters immediately grew larger.

Please, keep the diary safe, the letters read.

"I will," Kaela said softly, holding it to her heart. "I'll put it with the nuts from the Tree People."

"And now we have arrived," Netri said, pointing to an opening between two large boulders that rested against the mountainside. "Remember – you must look carefully for the passageway. No doubt Gulig will have placed another beast to guard the entryway, but I can assure you that you have the tools and the heart to conquer anything that you might encounter."

"I am not afraid to fight."

"Wollan is eager to accompany you."

The dog yipped a few times and pushed his head under Kaela's hand.

"Oh! Wollan! That's your name." She dug her fingers into the dog's thick curls. "Thank you."

"Here is a small whistle whose sound is undetectable by the human ear," Netri said, handing Kaela a small brass whistle. "If you are separated, just blow on it and Wollan will find you."

"Aren't you coming with me?" Kaela asked, confused. She took the whistle from him and tucked it into the bag with the diary and the nuts.

"I'm afraid not, my dear," Netri said. "I have other duties ... with the King. And my old legs would just slow you down. Wollan will be a true friend and guardian to you – with him, you will have no need of me."

Kaela knew better than to argue. She leaned over and the old wizzen tenderly embraced the young girl.

"I know you will discover great things on this journey. Our entire way of life hinges on your recovering the baby," Netri said. And then, surprisingly, he knelt on one knee before Kaela. "In my eyes you are a princess," he said, bowing his head.

Wollan whined, looking up at her with his large brown eyes.

"Wait, Netri! One more thing, what is butterfly breath?" Kaela asked desperately, still not sure how she was to defeat Gulig.

"Do not worry," Netri assured her. "You will find it when the time is right. Search no further than your own heart."

After one final embrace, Kaela stepped into the dark opening of the cave while a crow cawed loudly from outside. Her new lamp, given to her by the Butterfly Women, illuminated water droplets falling in steady rivulets from the ceiling of the cave. Kaela and Wollan walked forward, their feet splashing in the narrow stream, which disappeared into endless dark depths. From within the darkness of the cavern, something screeched, and Kaela's heart lurched with uncertainty.

Chapter Sixteen • Followed

Woolen sniffed as they walked. Just the sight of the large dog loping ahead, checking each twist and turn of the tunnel, eased the churning fear in Kaela's belly. Then something rustled behind them, and every hair along Wollan's spine stood erect. She touched Wollan, motioning for him to stop. They held still and the noise disappeared. Walking ever so slowly, again Kaela heard the padding of another set of feet just behind her. Was it a Rugu soldier? Why was he staying so silent?

They stopped again. Wollan pressed his body against Kaela and growled at the unseen stranger.

"Thank you, Wollan. You'll protect me, won't you?" Kaela whispered.

They resumed walking and the footsteps returned. Kaela wrapped her hand around the pendant and asked, "Wollan, is that the beast?"

"It's hard to tell from this distance. It has the odor of a small animal."

As Kaela and Wollan moved deeper and deeper inside the mountain, Kaela jumped again and again, certain that whoever followed them was waiting to leap upon them at his first opportunity. Nervous sweat dripped from her armpits and forehead, and she grew ever more wary of the sound of trailing footsteps.

When she could no longer bear the suspense, Kaela quietly drew her sword.

"Wollan, if that's an animal we can scare it away," she whispered, "and I'm prepared to fight if it's Gulig's beast."

"Okay, let's just stop here for a while and eat something," she said loudly, putting her finger to her lips. Kaela motioned for Wollan to follow her, and then whispered, "I'll just stand here. See if you can sniff it out."

Wollan's sensitive nose snuffled for clues, caught the trail and pointed his entire body towards the beast. Kaela rounded a bend in the cave and cautiously approached the shadowed lump. It wasn't very big.

"Okay beast, prepare to fight!" she yelled. If this was Gulig's beast, she thought she could easily defeat it. "I'm not afraid of you."

A boy with black shaggy hair jumped up, sticking his arms straight in the air.

"Please, please, don't hurt me!" he said. "I didn't do anything. I was just following you 'cause I wanna help."

"Why should I trust you?" She held up the lamp and looked the boy up and down. "Wait a minute ... I recognize you. You're the boy who was with that crazy old woman."

His face turned beet-red and he balled up his fists. "Don't you talk that way about her! She isn't crazy."

"Oh yes, she is. She clawed at my leg like a maniac, almost broke my neck!" Kaela said, putting her hands on her hips.

"She is not crazy! She just sees things that you can't. Maybe if you saw what she sees, you would have jumped off a cliff long ago."

"Look, I'm too busy to argue with you..." Kaela said, turning. She wanted to be done with the boy.

"She isn't crazy," he said quietly. "She's my grandma. You just take back what you said. I mean it!"

"Oh!" Kaela blushed and turned back to the boy. "I'm sorry I insulted your grandmother."

The boy nodded.

"Well, if you're not trying to kill me, I'm just going to keep on. I've got things to do." Without a second thought, Kaela held up the lamp and said, "Come on, Wollan. Let's go." The dog trotted down the cave and Kaela took long strides after him.

"Wait! I am here to help you!" the boy yelled, running until he was even with her.

"You're just a kid," Kaela laughed. "How can you help?"

He grabbed her arm, forcing Kaela to look him in the eyes. "I can see the future."

Kaela stared back. "No way!" she gaped.

"Yup."

Kaela shook her head, still not believing him, and said, "I don't know what you want from me. Maybe you're hungry..." She stopped and dug down into her pack. "I've got some food in here." She pulled out a sandwich and handed it to him. Once again she resumed walking.

He eagerly tore off large hunks of the sandwich with his fingers. In between bites, he ran to keep up and insisted breathlessly, "I'm not going back ... I'm staying with you ... I told you. I can see things ... and I can help you. You'll see."

Wollan stopped running ahead and sniffed the air. He raced back to Kaela and woofed until she pulled another sandwich out for him and one for herself. Wollan gobbled his in a few bites.

"Okay, whatever," Kaela said, strangely relieved at the boy's presence, despite his age. She bit down on fresh bread that was spread with peanut butter and raspberries. "Mmm, this is good." She resumed a more leisurely pace with Wollan walking in between her and the boy. She looked at the strange child more carefully. His jet-black hair stuck out every which way and he had beautiful light-green eyes. He looked like he hadn't taken a bath for a very long time; but then, anyone who spent time in the caves ended up that way. His patched and ragged clothes were so short that his ankles and wrists looked extra long – the fabric so thin that it would soon shred into fine threads.

The boy stuck his hand in her direction and said, "Name's Zeke."

Kaela shook hands and said, "Pleased to meet you. I'm Kaela."

"Yeah, I know your name. And Wollan, too." Zeke scratched the dog behind its ears.

"How do you know my name?"

Zeke just stared at her as though she were an idiot.

"I already told you, I see things," he said a little impatiently.

Kaela blushed, focusing on her sandwich. As she licked peanut butter off her fingers, she said, "What about your mom and dad? Won't they be worried about you?"

"My mom died, and I never knew my dad. He didn't stick around."

Kaela's heart softened towards her new friend. "Gosh, I'm sorry, I..."

"It's okay. I mean, I never really knew either of them."

"That's sad...."

The boy interrupted Kaela, obviously eager to change the subject. "So you'll take me with you?"

"Uhm..." Kaela still felt reluctant to take responsibility for the boy. She frowned at him, trying to decide, when she noticed a familiar white kerchief tied around Zeke's neck. "What's that?" she asked, pointing.

"Just some old scarf I found in the cave."

"I think that was mine – it must have fallen off," Kaela said, thinking. "Wait a minute – that fell off a long time ago. How long have you been following me?"

"For a really long time. I hid at the mouth of the cave yesterday. When you came in, I followed you."

"But how did you know to wait for us at that entrance?"

"How come you can't understand me? I told you I see things – like the avalanche. I saw it before it happened. Why do you think the crow was at the other entrance to show you the way in?"

"You sent the crow?"

"Of course. That's Kalik, my friend. He stayed there to help you."

Wollan's tail wagged more vigorously, hearing this.

"Without the crow we wouldn't have known ... we would have been captured! Thank you, thank you," Kaela said gratefully, remembering the terrifying Rugu soldier that had followed them.

"See. I can help you."

"That's amazing." Kaela smiled, realizing he was right, and then noticed his goose-bumpy skin. "Hey I've got something for you." Eager now to help the boy, Kaela stopped again and pulled a spare sweater out of her pack. "Here. You must be freezing. Wear my extra sweater. There's no point in me carrying more than I have to."

Zeke pulled the wool sweater over his head. The sweater hung like a dress, coming almost to his knees, and he had to roll up the sleeves several times to find his hands. For the first time, he smiled at Kaela.

"This is really nice," he said, stroking the soft fabric. "It fits me perfectly."

"I'm glad you like it," she smiled back, and Wollan nudged her leg with the side of his head. "But there's no time to spare. If you want to come with me, we have to hurry. I have to find the baby before midnight, and my cousin was kidnapped ... oh wait, you probably know that already. What about Shawn? Have you seen Shawn?"

"Yeah, well ... kind of ..." Zeke hesitated and looked away, obviously wanting to hide something from Kaela.

"What? What did you see, Zeke?"

"It was a real scary man. I think it was Gulig. Shawn was with Gulig and he was threatening your cousin."

Kaela's heart lurched. "I have to go now." She turned and ran through the cave with Zeke bolting after her. Wollan quickened his pace and ran ahead, sniffing.

"Kaela!" Zeke yelled after her. "The future isn't set in stone. A person can do one little thing and it changes everything."

"I have to get there, get to Shawn."

"I know, I know, Kaela," Zeke said, panting. When he was finally even with Kaela, he pulled on her arm, slowing her down to a rapid walk. "Listen. Us rushing to find him – and me joining you changes everything. It creates a whole new set of pictures."

"So the future isn't already decided?" Kaela tried to understand Zeke's words as she walked briskly. Zeke trotted beside her to keep up.

"No. Everything we do kind of ripples ahead of us. That's the hardest part for me, because I see so many futures in my mind at once. Let's say you got too scared to come here, or you waited until you had breakfast, or you killed me ... it would all turn out different. Sometimes I think I'll go nuts 'cause I can't stop the visions."

"Is that what happened to your grandma?"

"Yeah. Well ... kind of. But I think it's something else, too." Zeke frowned. "Like maybe she knows secret stuff. When I ask about my mother, she just yells at me."

"That's sad, Zeke. But how do you and your grandma survive? How do you get money for food and stuff?"

"Well, when I was younger, people still came to my grandma to hear their futures. But after awhile, she got so she couldn't really focus. She'd yell at them about other people's futures, and even about the red-haired girl. So now I get hand-me-downs from other families, and sometimes Netri brings me stuff, and we get by."

Zeke paused. "But my gramma gets really mad if she finds stuff that's been given to me. She says we can't trust people. And ... sometimes ... if it's been really bad and I get sick of asking for help and, well ... sometimes I kind of steal or pick-pocket...."

Zeke avoided Kaela's searching gaze.

"It's okay," Kaela said. "I'm sure you don't mean anything bad by it." Kaela made sure to keep moving, even though she was fascinated by the boy's story.

"It's been kind of hard. None of the other kids would ever play with me. Sometimes they throw rocks at me and call me a Rugu. Pretty much my only friends are the crows." Zeke hung his head. "Maybe I look kinda like a Rugu? I know my mom was a seer like my grandma. I even asked my grandma once if I actually was Rugu, and she yelled at me."

"But why was she so upset?" Kaela was quiet for a moment, and then softly asked, "Zeke, what do you know about your father? Was he a Rugu?"

"What difference does it make?!" Zeke's face flushed red. "I don't know. And besides – what's so bad about the Rugus? It doesn't seem right to hate someone you don't even know!"

"I'm sorry, Zeke. I didn't mean anything by it." Kaela placed her arm around the boy's stiff shoulder and said warmly, "I'm really glad you're here." Wollan ran back, jumped up on Zeke, and licked the boy's face.

"It's okay, you guys. I'm okay. You don't know what it's like – people hating you for no reason. Anyway, I'm helping you so maybe my grandma will get better." Looking down at the ground, Zeke said quietly, "Besides ... I don't want to go crazy, either."

"That would be awful," Kaela nodded.

"You won't regret it. I've been seeing some of these Rugu guys in my head for as long as I can remember. Seems like it's time to go where they are."

"But can't you see your own future?"

"No more than anyone else," he shrugged. "Weird, huh?"

Kaela smiled at Zeke and realized her decision had already been made. She liked having his company and, since he was determined to come along, she said, "Okay, you can come with me. But now we have to hurry. Shawn's in trouble and we don't have much more time."

Zeke smiled broadly. "You won't regret it, Kaela. You'll see – I'll be a big help."

They walked deeper and deeper into the darkness, unsure of what they would encounter next. Again and again Wollan whined in front of them.

"What, Wollan? What's wrong?" Kaela clutched the pendant.

Woof, woof. "There's a bad smell, a terrible smell."

"I see something, Kaela. Really bad stuff – like a monster or something..." Zeke said, looking pale and shuddering slightly.

A chill shot through Kaela and she touched the hilt of her sword, knowing that soon she would need a weapon. She felt the dagger at her ankle and realized that Zeke also needed protection.

"Zeke, I want to loan you something. Queen Skyla gave this to Shawn, so I can't really give it to you," Kaela said as she bent down and unfastened the dagger from around her ankle. "I am sure she would want you to use it. I've already got a sword, so I don't need it. Here, let me put this on your ankle." Kaela pulled out the dagger and handed it to Zeke.

Zeke's mouth fell open as he stared at the ruby-handled dagger in his palm. "Really? You want me to use this?"

"Yes, Zeke. Do you think you can manage this weapon?"

Zeke waved it around in a figure eight a couple of times and stabbed at a pretend enemy. "Take that ... and that ... and that!" He cried. "I'm ready, Kaela."

"Okay," Kaela said. "But put it away for now."

They proceeded cautiously, holding up the lamp again and again to be sure nothing was in front of them. Now and then, Kaela caught the whiff of an odor that burned her nostrils.

When Wollan slowed and yelped, Kaela clasped the butterfly in her fist. "What is it, Wollan? Are we close?"

"He smells the monster," Zeke said, wide-eyed. "Now I really see it."

Woof. "It's just up ahead." *Woof, woof.* "He's horrible. He'll tear us all to pieces."

Kaela clutched the pendant tightly in her palm, drawing comfort from its familiar shape pressed against her skin.

"I want you two to wait here while I have a look." Kaela looked back and forth between Wollan and Zeke. "Zeke, be ready with the dagger."

The dog moved to follow her and she insisted, "Wollan, you stay back too!"

No. Wollan whined, *I promised Arendore I'd protect you.*

"Wollan, it's your job to listen to me. I mean it. You stay here – I'm going first."

Wollan's tail hung sadly between his legs, but he obeyed.

Kaela carried the lantern in her hand and slowly entered a huge area with a cathedral-like ceiling. Everywhere she looked, there were mineral formations reflecting the lamplight. She was back in the crystal cave. Only the sound of dripping water broke the eerie silence. An odor like a dead body that had been left to rot for days streamed into her nostrils.

Thump, THUMP, THUMP.

Kaela listened as, step-by-step, the unknown creature drew closer and closer to her. Kaela's eyes filled with tears and burned from the creature's stench. Her heart flooded with terror. Kaela pressed her body against the side of the cave, hoping to remain invisible, and then raced back to her companions.

"Hide with me behind this rock," she whispered. "We need a plan." She clutched her sword, and Zeke held the dagger in front of him. Kaela breathed through her sleeve, struggling against the smell, attempting to calm her pounding heart. "Sit close to me. Maybe the beast won't smell us."

The threesome peeked from behind the rock and gasped. Kaela quickly reached up and placed the lamp on top of the rock.

The hulk of a beast entered the cavern, stopped and shook his muscular body, rattling wiry fur that looked more like metal nails than hair. His massive body sat on tree trunk-sized legs, and his head jutted straight out from his shoulders. He glared at them with hooded eyes, bared his razor sharp teeth and dug at the ground with the long, sharp tusks that jutted from his lower jaw.

Kaela blinked, trying to clear her watering eyes.

The monster sniffed the cave and snorted, spewing thick snot from his snout.

"I'm pretty sure he can smell us," Zeke whispered. "Just look at his nose."

Slowly, the creature lumbered toward the cowering threesome, opened his huge mouth and roared. The tunnel walls and the boulder they hid behind shook with his voice.

"He's heading this way." Kaela grimaced and whispered, "Look how strong he is. I'm sure he can outrun us." Kaela thought for a moment more. "Maybe he's a prisoner, too. Maybe I can talk to him – I bet Shawn would. What do you think, Wollan?" Kaela clutched the pendant.

Woof, woof. "He's no prisoner! He's got only one thing on his mind – kill, kill invaders. We're on his turf."

"Okay," Kaela whispered, thinking furiously. "Here's the plan. I'll sneak around to the left. If I need to, I'll distract him, engage him in battle, and then you run to the right and through the opening. I'm sure the passage is down there. I'll circle around until I can join you. Okay?"

Zeke shook his head. "No, Kaela," he said. "That won't work. I'm not going until I know for sure you're safe. Without you, there's no need for us to even be here."

"Maybe," Kaela admitted. "But I'm also the red-haired girl." She smiled momentarily to herself, feeling a rush of warmth suffuse her body. "I'm going to take my chances." She stood and threw down her backpack. "As soon as you can, run towards the opening."

Kaela grabbed a small rock and threw it against a far wall. The beast looked back momentarily distracted by the sound. Kaela dashed into the cavern and hid behind a mineral formation while the beast was distracted.

The beast sniffed the air but did not move in her direction. Kaela ran further along the perimeter, where there was no place to hide – crouching in the shadows and moving as quickly and as silently as she could.

The beast caught her scent and whipped his head in her direction. He narrowed his bloodshot eyes and stared at Kaela with venomous rage. Yellow snot and steam spewed from his nostrils. He pawed the ground, opened his mouth and roared so loudly that Kaela wanted to cover her ears against the awful sound piercing her eardrums. The creature lowered his massive head until his tusks were even with Kaela's heart, and then he charged.

Chapter Seventeen • Kidnapped

Awakening to a surreal nightmare, Shawn felt his body jolt to the rhythmic drumming of horse hooves. Unable to move his bound hands, he strained to see through the darkness, but not even a glimmer of light permeated the hood tied around his neck. The rider clutched Shawn tightly at the waist, urging his horse to run faster. Not yet recovered from his ordeal, Shawn sagged against the man, struggling to find a shred of hope, knowing that every moment brought him closer to the inevitable meeting with Gulig.

Shawn lost all sense of time as he was carried further and further away from the Butterfly Women's cottage. But when the sound of the horses' hooves changed from a regular dull thud to a hollow clopping, he was aware that they had entered paved streets. Shortly thereafter, the horses stopped. People spoke in murmurs around Shawn, and strong arms easily lifted him from the saddle. Shawn's legs wobbled and collapsed as he tried to stand. Someone quickly caught him and pushed the dark hood that covered him just high enough to press a canteen of water to his lips. Shawn gulped the water eagerly, feeling the excess liquid dribbling down his chin.

Once again he was lifted onto a horse, and a man's muscular arm gripped Shawn around the belly. Was it the same horse or a different animal? Was it even the same arm? The clopping of hooves changed to thudding, and Shawn still didn't know if it was day or night.

When the horse clomped to a halt once again, unseen arms lifted Shawn and steadied him at the elbow as his rubbery legs threatened to buckle beneath him. The rope that tied Shawn's wrists was cut, and pain shot up and down his arms as his blood circulated freely once more. Then someone ripped the heavy hood from his head. Shawn's eyes contracted in the sudden light and he squinted through the glare, struggling to make sense of the scene in front of him.

Two muscular men stood to either side of Shawn with granite-faced expressions. He had to look at them twice before realizing that his eyes weren't playing tricks on him. The color of their skin was unlike anything Shawn had ever seen before – it was a dull shade of green.

A towering man with jet-black hair held Shawn's elbow in a vice like grip. Like the other men, he wore a steel-gray tunic, black pants, and heavy black boots. Strange green markings wound up and down the man's muscular arm like vines.

Emotionless, the man said in a flat voice, "Come on, you. Gulig's been waiting all night. We best not keep him a moment longer."

"Where am I?" Shawn asked through parched lips.

"Didn't you hear me?" the man looked at Shawn curiously. "I said I'm taking you to Gulig. Now, look smart and don't say anything stupid in front of him. He's been waiting for you all night; I don't think he's got much patience left."

Shawn's senses heightened to the danger around him in his body's desperate attempt to survive the impossible situation. He heard the restless pawing of a horse and a man cracking his knuckles, joint by joint. He smelled the acrid scent of the men's sweat and saw another man touching the shaft of his knife. Even though Shawn was puny, and a child, these men weren't taking any chances. His mind raced to find some means of escape, but it was impossible; any attempt would be foolish – doomed to failure.

Still, Shawn refused to give up. They stood by a vast building with towers rising into the air. Cast iron bars guarded the windows and hideous gargoyles positioned along the roof stared at him with bulging eyes and clenched fists. Shawn wracked his brains and realized that it was probably Lorendale's castle – a glimmer of hope rose within him. Trying to control his shaky voice, Shawn asked, "Sir, will you take me to see King Lorendale?"

"Lorendale is none of your affair," the man snarled. "The Great Gulig of the Rugu Tribe is all you need concern yourself with. Follow me."

When the rough supporting arm released his elbow, Shawn stumbled once again, but, as he followed the large man, steadiness returned to his quivering legs. Shawn and his guards entered the castle through a wooden side door and descended a stairway into a dark corridor. The pleasant aroma of baking bread wafted from a huge kitchen to their left, but an unfamiliar bitter smell burned Shawn's nostrils. His stomach churned with hunger and nausea.

Shawn and the large man plodded up a circular metal stairway. The guard's shoes reverberated on the iron steps, but Shawn's bare feet made no sound. His shoes remained behind in the Butterfly Women's cottage. On the main floor, they walked down a wide wooden hall that was covered with a soft purple carpet.

Thunderclouds filled the tall windows on the main floor, signaling an oncoming storm.

His guard's thick black eyebrows gathered together in a grim frown. "This man's royalty," he said in a hushed tone. "No smartin' off - you got it? Treat him in a dignified fashion."

"Yes, sir. I understand," Shawn said slowly.

They approached two massive wooden doors, and the man knocked briskly. With his very first knock, a deep voice penetrated the walls.

"Stennan, bring me the child," a haughty voice demanded. One of the doors creaked open.

Shoved from behind, Shawn staggered into the room, and the heavy door slammed shut. Shawn fell, cracking his knees against the hardwood floor. He groaned softly, overcome by the room's darkness. Long black curtains hung from the ceiling along one wall, blocking all sunlight. The only lights stood on either side of a large golden throne - lights that flickered, casting shadows in the hollows of a face that seemed to float, bodiless, above the throne.

"Well?" the haughty voice demanded again, and Shawn saw the man's lips move. "Come over here, girl! I've been waiting."

Shawn approached, confused. The man's eyes bore into him. Shawn's stomach lurched with fear and he reached for his inner strength, forcing himself to look back into the Rugu leader's eyes. Gulig's hard stare contained no trace of kindness or warmth, as if he saw nothing more than an inanimate object before him – one he would happily smash. Filled with dread, Shawn averted his eyes. Steeling himself once again, Shawn glanced at Gulig, but his heart fluttered with terror when Gulig moved his mouth in an imitation of a thin-lipped smile.

When Shawn drew near the throne, he noticed the deformity of Gulig's face. One of Gulig's eyes was set higher than the other, and his long nose bent to the left and then to the right. The man looked like an ogre. The same green tattoo-like markings displayed by the guard also covered Gulig's hands and forearms, but the Rugu leader's markings were far more elaborate. A terrible smell nearly overcame Shawn as he took another halting step toward the throne. He recognized it as the revolting stench he had smelled coming from the kitchen. Shawn pushed up his glasses and said a small prayer, thankful that he had somehow managed to keep them.

"Well, come here girl," Gulig sneered. "Let me get a look at you."

Shawn stumbled as one final push landed him at the head of the table.

"Don't worry – I'm not going to hurt you. Come closer."

Shawn inched towards Gulig until he stood within an arm's reach of the Rugu leader.

"Your hair is short for a girl's, isn't it, child?" Gulig's face stiffened, and his eyes flew wide. He grabbed Shawn's hair pulled him into the small pool of light. "This child doesn't even have red hair!" Gulig yelled, pulling Shawn's head back so he could stare into his face. "It's a boy!" Gulig snarled, yanking him closer, until they were nose to nose. "Did you think you could trick me, boy?" Gulig's voice was so quiet it formed an eerie whisper that traveled no further than their four ears.

Gulig's jaw tightened and he squinted as his muscular forearm bent Shawn's head back. As Gulig pushed, Shawn was forced to kneel before the great Rugu leader.

Shawn's voice quivered, wondering if Gulig would break his neck. "No, sir ... no ... I promise, I didn't do anything to trick you! A man grabbed me ... in the middle of the night and threw me ... on a horse ... No one asked ... I promise they didn't even ask ... ask who I was."

"Was there a red-haired-girl with you?" Gulig demanded, still gripping Shawn's hair.

Shawn hesitated. He didn't want to say anything that might harm Kaela.

"No, sir ... Uhm, I don't know ... Maybe she gave up...."

"Gave up?" Gulig sneered, his eyes boring into Shawn's brain. "Are you her brother?"

"No sir ... I-I-I'm her cousin," Shawn stammered.

"So, your cousin is a coward?" Gulig yelled.

Shawn's rage rose at the implied insult. "No!" he cried, "She is *not* a coward!"

"Then you are lying to me!" Gulig said, triumphantly.

"No, no! That's not it ... uh..."

Gulig stood up and, still clutching Shawn's hair, lifted the boy so his feet dangled just above the ground.

"Do not lie to me, boy!" Gulig yelled.

"Yes-s-s – sir," Shawn squeaked.

Finally, Gulig dropped Shawn and glared at his servant. "Stennan, clean up this filthy child. Now – get out of my sight." Gulig curled his lip at Shawn as though gazing at something loathsome.

Shawn resisted the desire to rub his sore head, and his body shook with fear and shock.

The servant, bowing low to the king, cautiously asked, "Uhm, excuse me, sire?"

"Stennan, I said I want you out of my sight."

"Yes sir. Of course, sire," Stennan said softly. "But, do you want the boy in the dungeon?"

"For now, keep him with the other bait. Later, you can dump him." Gulig pressed his fingertips together and said sarcastically, "Don't you worry, little *girl*. We'll find your red-haired friend. I have special plans for her – *very* special plans."

Chapter Eighteen • The Beast

The beast's tusks, its phlegm-filled nose and its glistening teeth filled Kaela's sight. Its massive body rushed forward to crush her, and she knew that her sword would be useless against its weight. She had to do something – the will to survive propelled her. Instinctively, she leapt to her left fractions of a second before the beast charged past her. The creature's thorny fur tore through the flesh of her right arm.

The monster ploughed into the cave wall with a thud, screeching with rage.

Kaela ignored the searing pain in her arm. She had to get away ... *immediately*. She backpedaled towards the center of the cave and ducked behind a stalagmite.

The creature wheeled around, snorting and sniffing with squinted eyes, then raised its nose and slowly lumbered in Kaela's direction.

Kaela held her breath, her heart pounding like a jackhammer against her chest. What would he do to her? She eased backwards into the shadows, but the monster was not fooled. The creature lowered its head and hurtled forward once again. This time, Kaela was ready with her sword. Just before it reached her, she sprang to the right and simultaneously swung her sword with both hands, aiming for the beast's head. Kaela's sword cracked against the beast's tusk, and the fragment flew through the air and crashed against the cave wall. The beast reared its head in shock and fury.

Blood and sweat flowed freely down her arm. She clung to the sword with both hands and sprinted to the right side of the cave with her eyes constantly focused on the beast. Kaela just had to distract him a few more seconds so Wollan and Zeke would be able to make a run for it.

The beast narrowed its bloodshot eyes, snorted short raging breaths and scraped the ground over and over, winding up for the kill. Kaela scooted sideways, trying to maintain a safe distance from the monster, but the beast pummeled towards her with his head low to the ground.

Kaela swung with every last ounce of energy towards the creature's head, but instead of making contact, the weapon flew from her slippery hands in an arc across the cave. Kaela gasped and then bolted in the direction of the secret entrance to Lorendale's castle as her sword clattered to the ground.

The beast turned and roared, then dug in his hoofs and plunged towards Kaela – but he was not alone. Wollan had leapt back into the cavern when he realized Kaela's sudden helplessness, reaching his peak speed at the moment the beast charged. He lunged at the creature's front leg and chomped down.

As though Wollan provided little more threat than an irritating fly, the creature kept his hypnotic eyes fixed on Kaela, and flicked his massive leg even as he continued barreling toward his prey.

"A-A-A-A-A-AH-H-H-H-H-H-H!" Zeke screamed as he, too, tore into the cavern and stabbed deep into the beast's back leg with the dagger. The beast screeched and shook his leg violently, and Zeke flew across the room, clutching the dagger tightly. Green blood streamed from the creature's leg as the monster roared.

Filled with rage, the creature resumed a full-out charge at Kaela, dragging Wollan behind him. Kaela frantically glanced along the cave wall for some place to hide, but all she could do was scoot along the edge.

The monster kept its hideous eyes locked on Kaela's quivering form. Slightly off-kilter from Wollan's weight, the monster wove relentlessly in her direction. Drawing on her last ounce of energy, Kaela dove to her left. The creature smashed into the cave wall once more. Its hooves slipped on the loose mineral fragments, and it fell with a thud on its side, shaking the overhanging stalactites with the weight of its fall.

"Watch out above!" Zeke screamed.

Kaela looked up and rolled away as a thin stalactite spun down and down with a *whooshing* sound as it sliced through the air. With a hideous crunch, the stone spike pierced the beast's body. Green blood gushed from his wound, and the bellow that escaped the creature's mouth boomed like a cry from the darkest bowels of hell.

No one moved. Only the *drip, drip, drip-*ping of water broke the deathly stillness.

Kaela scrambled to her feet and looked around. Where was Wollan? She could see him nowhere. She had to find him! Certain that Gulig's beast was dead Kaela leaned over its head, searching for her precious friend. With one last gasp the creature turned his head and scraped Kaela's arm from palm to elbow with its broken tusk.

Kaela screamed and jerked backward, clutching her blood-drenched arm.

The creature roared, shuddered and went limp as a cloud of foul-smelling gas erupted from his mouth.

Gasping for air in the putrid smoke, Kaela searched again for Wollan. Her sword was beyond retrieval, buried under the creature's massive body.

Still clutching the dagger – dripping with green, foul-smelling blood – Zeke grabbed the lantern and ran to the opening. "Come this way. Come on!" Zeke screamed as he ran.

Blood and snot covered Wollan's fur as he nudged Kaela from behind.

Kaela reeled around and cried, "Wollan! You're alive!"

Together, they bolted after Zeke's receding form.

Kaela ignored the exhaustion in her muscles and the searing pain in her arm. Determined to put distance between the terrifying creature and herself, Kaela robotically moved her legs one after the other, laboring to keep pace with Zeke and Wollan. It wasn't long, however, until her injury got the best of her. Trailing blood from her wounded arm, Kaela slowed to a weaving walk, stumbling like a drunk. A terrible thirst consumed her, and she opened her mouth to yell, but instead whispered.

"Wait – please wait," she called hoarsely, her throat tight and swollen. "I…"

Consumed by pain, Kaela fell to her knees, her forearm red with blood.

The light dimmed as the lantern vanished with Zeke into the darkness. Desperate for water, Kaela felt for the trickling stream she had splashed in earlier, and bent over to cup water in her hands, but her right arm refused to respond.

She awkwardly splashed water into her mouth with her left hand. Relief soaked her parched tongue and she sat back on her heels. A moment later, however, her thirst returned. Once again aching for water, Kaela leaned over to drink directly from the stream. Her knee slipped on the wet stone, and she fell face-first into the water.

"Move, move!" something inside Kaela screamed, but her right arm was dead weight and she was tired – so very tired. Kaela strained to turn her head to the side in a last desperate attempt to breathe, but the water trickled into her mouth and she choked. Exhausted and overwhelmed, Kaela tumbled into velvet blackness, drowning in the tiny stream.

⌒〜♪〜⌒

Wollan skidded to a halt and spun around, desperate to find Kaela. She was gone, left behind somewhere in the darkness. His paws barely touched the ground as he flew to her. Even as he ran, Zeke pounding on his heels, he howled, "*Owwwww, I'm coming … I'm coming.*"

The moment he found her, the loyal dog dug his feet in and tugged on Kaela's shirt until he pulled her from the creek. She remained limp and unconscious.

"Kaela!" Zeke screamed seeing her lifeless body. He kneeled down and gently shook her. Growing more and more desperate he coaxed, "Wake up, please wake up!" He placed his finger under her nose. There was nothing. She was dead.

Wollan whined, "*Don't give up! Please! Don't give up.*" He rested his head on her chest and yowled, "*I hear something – water.*"

"Okay, Wollan." Zeke pressed on Kaela's chest. Water shot from her mouth. She coughed and moaned.

Zeke sniffled with relief as he pulled the warm sweater over his head and covered her shivering body. Wollan whimpered and lay down next to Kaela to help warm her.

"This one cut is really bad," Zeke said, examining Kaela's arm. "His tusk dug down deep here. I'll have to tie something around the cuts to stop the bleeding." Zeke tore the sleeve from Kaela's injured arm and untied the dirty white scarf from around his neck. He swished the scarf in the creek, wrung it out, and gently wiped the blood from her arm. "The water ought to help; the Butterfly Women use it to heal." Zeke turned to the creek, cupped his hands, and dribbled some around Kaela's mouth.

Kaela whimpered. Then her eyelids shot open and she sat up, but she stared unseeing, lost in a dream world. She reached out blindly, flailing.

"Mother, where are you? Where are you?" Kaela cried.

"Kaela, it's us," Zeke said, shaking her arm. "Come on, Kaela. Everything's okay. You'll be okay."

Kaela screamed, ripping off the bandage as her face burned crimson with fever.

Wollan gazed at Kaela with his large brown eyes, willing her to regain consciousness.

Zeke soaked a scrap of cloth in the cool water of the stream and eased Kaela back into a prone position, gently cooling her forehead. Once again he wrapped the bandage around her arm.

"It's okay, Kaela," he whispered. "You're okay. Everything's okay."

Terrible visions unfurled in Zeke's mind. Gulig held a dagger to Shawn's throat, threatening. "I've waited long enough," Gulig snarled. "Do you hear me? First the baby, and then you will die."

"Kaela, please get better. Shawn and the baby need our help," Zeke begged.

Wollan moved his head, placed it on Kaela's lap and then leapt up, yipping. He pulled on the canteen and whined.

"What is this, Wollan?" Zeke said, helping Wollan remove the canteen from Kaela's belt."

"Yip, yip, yip!"

"Is this special?"

Wollan nodded his head and howled.

Zeke placed a few precious drops on Kaela's lip and a few more on her bandaged arm. A peaceful look spread across her face as she fell back into a deep, healing sleep.

"Look at that. Did she get this from the Butterfly Women?"

Wollan whined in agreement.

Kaela's head throbbed and her eyelids felt like lead, but she knew she needed to wake up. For some reason she had to wake up. Every muscle burned with exhaustion, but there was someone beside her, someone soft and warm who really cared. She shivered with cold and slowly forced her eyelids open.

The room in front of her spun and blurred as she squinted to see. Slowly, her eyes focused, and she was confronted with a young boy with shaggy black hair. She stared at the boy, confused. "Who are you?"

"I'm Zeke, Kaela. Remember? We fought the monster together."

Kaela frowned. "A monster?" She tried to sit up and the boy put his arm around her, supporting her weak body. A large loving dog panted beside her. "Where am I?"

"In the cave, Kaela. We're in the cave, on our way to rescue Shawn."

Memories floated into Kaela's brain. She was in a foreign world. Shawn was in danger. She was the red-haired girl. Then she remembered the terrible beast and pain gnawed at her arm. She unwound the part of the bandage that wrapped around her right arm. Her skin was covered in scabs and scratches. "Did you bandage me?"

"Yes, Kaela, I did. And Wollan helped, too."

Kaela blinked a few times, clearing her eyes, and shuddered at the realization that the beast had been so near. She remembered the dog's and the boy's valiant return to the cave, slowing down the beast and saving her life. These were her companions, her friends.

"Thank you. You saved my life. You both saved me."

Zeke flushed as the lamplight flickered across his face, "Well, of course ... you would have helped me." Unbuckling the dagger from his leg, Zeke said, "I think you'd better have this back now, Kaela."

The full memory of her fight with the beast shot through Kaela's mind and she hugged her friend. "Zeke, I don't know what I would have done..."

"It wasn't anything," he said, blushing proudly.

"I'm so grateful that you followed us," she smiled.

Zeke flushed again and replaced the dagger around Kaela's leg.

Kaela wrapped her arms around Wollan and said, "Thank you, dear loyal Wollan."

Her stomach growled and she realized she couldn't remember the last time she had eaten. "Zeke, do you have any food?"

"No, nothing ... we left the pack."

Wollan yipped and Kaela clutched the butterfly pendant. *"In your bag! Nuts, there's nuts!"*

Kaela felt around inside the leather bag at her waist and grabbed two limba nuts. She cracked them against each other and divided the nutmeat, remembering Clouda from the Tree Tribe. "Seems like this is a good time for some extra strength," she said, distributing pieces to her friends. They all drank from the stream, and energy coursed once again in Kaela's exhausted limbs.

"Listen, Kaela," Zeke began hesitantly. "I know it's soon, but I'm seeing terrible things about Shawn, and the baby. Can you walk now?"

"I'm not sure."

Wollan whined for Kaela to lean on him. Still wobbly, Kaela used the large dog and Zeke for support. "I think I can do it," she said. "Let's try." The more Kaela walked, the more confident she grew. "I'm okay," she said finally. "Let's try a little faster."

Zeke and Wollan trotted just in front of Kaela as she took long strides. One second Kaela was determined to proceed and the next a terrible anger erupted inside her until she was blind with rage.

"Hey, you two," she yelled. "Stop walking so fast. Don't you see that I can't keep up?"

Zeke whirled around and put his hands on his hips. "You told us to walk faster."

"Why would I do that? Wow, you're dumb," Kaela sneered.

"Hey, that's mean!" Zeke protested.

Wollan cocked his head, and gently placed his wet nose into Kaela's hand.

As rapidly as the anger flared, it vanished and Kaela was filled with a cool calm and remorse at her unkind words. "I don't know what got into me," Kaela apologized. "I'm so sorry, Zeke. I didn't mean that."

Wollan stepped away from Kaela, and the anger filled her once again. "I hate you!" The words flew out of her mouth. "I should never have brought you. Stupid baby. Who sends a kid to rescue a baby? What's wrong with these people?"

Wollan leaned against Kaela, and once again her anger disappeared.

Resting against the side of the cave, Kaela realized, "Something's really wrong with me. When you aren't touching me, Wollan, I feel like the only thing I'll ever feel is rage. You've got to stay close, please."

"Kaela, maybe that monster did something to you," Zeke said, worried. "Show me your arm."

Zeke peeled off Kaela's bandage and his eyes widened. "Kaela, this isn't good. Look at your arm…" They all stared as Zeke held up the lantern to look more closely at Kaela's arm. The cuts were almost healed, but two green stripes ran from the deep puncture in her palm towards her wrist, like two sprouts from a seed. Bitterness flavored her mouth, and Wollan gently licked her hand. "It's the mark of Gulig's people!" Zeke warned. "Maybe the monster infected you with their poison."

"Did you give me some of the water from the Butterfly Women?" Kaela asked, frightened.

"Yes, I did." Zeke nodded his head. "I'm sure that's what healed your arm, but I don't know why it didn't cure the poison."

"I don't know, either, Zeke. Wollan, you're just going to have to stay close to me." Kaela rested her hand on Wollan's curly brown fur. "I need you two more than ever, now," she sighed.

"It's okay, Kaela - don't worry. I see some really nice pictures in your future," Zeke said a little too cheerfully, looking down at the ground to hide the truth.

They walked as a group until they came to a place where the tunnel opened into a small circular room-like area. Kaela stopped and closed her eyes.

"Wait," she said quietly. "I feel something different in this room. It's like I can hear someone calling me. Zeke, hold up the lantern."

The light filled the area, but there was no sign of a door or entryway.

"It must be here somewhere. I hear a voice calling. Netri said it was small and hidden. Wollan, can you sniff around? Maybe … Zeke, can you use your seeing eye to find the opening?"

Kaela was careful to stay close to Wollan as he snuffled along the base of the cave. Zeke closed his eyes and then kneeled down to pat his hands along the wall. Wollan stopped and sniffed in one area, digging at loose rocks against the wall with his tail waggling back and forth behind him. He whined and his front legs scraped at a pile of rocks, sending gravel behind him.

"What is it?" Kaela asked, clutching the pendant as Zeke joined her.

Woof. "I smell something different here."

"Maybe it's the entrance. Let's clear these stones out of the way," Kaela said

Kaela and Zeke threw piles of fist-sized rocks away from the wall until they came to a boulder that reached to Kaela's waist.

Zeke put the lantern down and pressed his hand against the rock. "It's heavy, Kaela, but if we work together I bet we can roll it to one side. This side has a nice curve to it. I think it will roll."

They stood together to one side of the boulder and leaned down with outstretched arms, using their full body weight to press against the boulder. It rocked slightly and then fell back into its original spot.

"Come on. We can do it – we just need to keep pushing," Kaela said.

Kaela and Zeke took deep breaths and pressed hard against the boulder. It edged forward once more and they quickly moved their hands down a notch and leaned in with their shoulders, budging then rolling the boulder an inch further. They didn't give up until finally it turned over and they rolled it away from the wall.

Wollan sniffed the solid wall before them and yipped with excitement.

Zeke held up the lamp and Kaela felt around until she noticed a long thin crack running vertically along the wall. When she placed her open palm on one side of the crack the stone chilled her hand, but the other side of the crack was soft and smooth, like well-worn wood. She pried at the crack with her dagger. A small doorway – just large enough for a kid or a wizzen – slowly opened.

Kaela placed her hand on the edge of the door until it had opened all the way. Zeke held up the light. It was a small tunnel, but where did it lead? Was this the entrance to the castle?

Uncertain of what they would find on the other end, Wollan led the way with Kaela crawling just behind him, clutching some of his fur. Zeke wormed his way through behind them, but then stopped abruptly as they came to a dead end. Wollan pressed his nose against the wall and it creaked open. Zeke left the lantern behind and they inched into a small closet, which was lit only by the light that streamed in from the adjoining room. Kaela peeked into the room with Wollan at her side. Zeke peered past Kaela's elbow.

Lamps on either side of the bed illuminated an old man with gray stringy hair, who lay on an elegantly carved four-poster bed. His face was flaccid and colored a sickly green. Seeing Kaela, tears formed in his red-rimmed eyes.

"You heard me!" He whispered hoarsely. "I called and called, and you finally heard me. A Butterfly Girl has come for me." His voice caught in his throat. "Thank you, thank you," he sobbed, his body shaking.

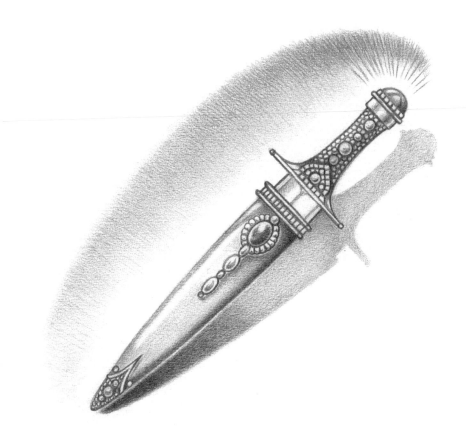

Chapter Nineteen • Anya

Stennan gripped Shawn's arm, bowing with every backwards step until he closed the door behind them, careful not to make a sound.

Relief flooded Shawn's veins. He barely noticed the servant's tight grip on his arm as he trotted to keep up with Stennan's long-legged stride. Though his heart still thumped rapidly against his chest, Shawn celebrated still being alive after having looked into the eyes of evil.

Retracing their steps down the circular staircase into the basement, the servant and the boy turned away from the kitchen and entered a bright room where a woman scrubbed laundry. The bitter smell that permeated the castle overwhelmed the inviting smell of soap and water.

"Hey, Nedra!" Stennan barked as they entered the room.

A round, gray-haired woman turned around scowling. "Get this boy cleaned up," Stennan ordered. "Gulig wants him locked away as soon as possible."

"Does it look to you like I don't have enough work to do?" the woman replied sharply.

"Gulig wants it done." Stennan looked at the woman very hard, and she backed down and hung her head.

"What's this boy supposed to wear?" she asked sulkily. "There're no clothes his size around here. You know how Gulig feels about children."

"You figure something out." Stennan said firmly, shoving Shawn toward the woman. "Watch over him while I get a little ganba."

"Whatever you say, Your Highness," Nedra grumbled under her breath.

After the door closed and locked behind Stennan, Nedra looked Shawn up and down and declared, "You look like you've been crawling around with pigs!"

A small form shifted in Shawn's inside chest pocket and crawled across his chest. It was Peeper, who had stowed away all this time.

"No, ma'am, no, I just..." Shawn mumbled with his eyes down. He scratched his chest and pushed the bird under his arm.

She motioned to a large metal tub overflowing with bubbles, and said, "I just finished some hand washing. You might as well jump in."

Shawn stood mute and didn't budge because of his embarrassment to be seen by a strange woman and his concern for the little bird under his arm. He wasn't sure what to do.

"Oh, I see. You're shy." Nedra shook her head and turned away. "Boys your age are always shy. Even with their mothers, who have seen them naked from the time they came out of the belly."

Shawn tore off his clothes, tucked Peeper under the pile, and leapt into the freezing water. His teeth chattered and he scrubbed his body as quickly as he could.

Still chatting, Nedra searched through a pile of laundry. "I don't know what you're supposed to wear. You're just a little thing. Don't know what I'm supposed to do with you. Everyone orders me around ... expects me to solve their problems. I guess this might work."

She glanced at Shawn, and then pointedly kept her face turned away as she dropped a large shirt atop his clothes and said, "This is the best I can do for you, and I don't have pants."

Shawn threw on the enormous shirt without bothering to dry himself, and tucked Peeper under his armpit. He yanked his old suede pants back on. By the time the woman turned back towards Shawn, his shirt sleeves were rolled up and over into a thick mass of fabric around his hands.

The door flew open, and Stennan stared at Shawn, clearly displeased. "What's that on his legs? He's still dirty."

"Well, give me your pants then and we'll use a rope to tie them to him," Nedra said, sarcasm dripping from her tongue. "I already told you that I don't have anything that will fit the boy."

Stennan glared at Nedra and grabbed Shawn's arm. "Come with me, boy."

They climbed up one flight of the circular metal staircase and Shawn's heart beat with fear, but then they continued up a second flight and Shawn audibly sighed with relief. The next floor up was a far cry from the luxurious quarters where Gulig had had an audience with him. The lighting was dim and the cold stone was harsh against Shawn's tired feet.

Shawn waited while Stennan unlocked the very first door, and he looked around. Dust collected in this far corner of the castle. The floor was worn and scuffed, and on either side of the door there were windows that had been plastered over.

Stennan pulled Shawn into a large limestone room that was carved into the mountain. A wooden cradle sat in the center of the room, and a cot with a crisply made bed sat against one wall. Faded murals of birds, clouds and sun must have once been a cheerful accent to the room, but now their worn, grayish colors offered a sad reminder that this room had been neglected for years. Forty feet above rays of sunlight poured through a large skylight illuminating the room. It was the only opening, other than the door.

The protesting cry of a child filled the room. A wrinkled woman with long, white, leaf-shaped hair leaned down in her chair, slowly rocking the cradle. Shawn quickly noticed that she wore the familiar suede clothes of the Tree Tribe.

"Stennan," she said, her voice quavering. "Oh, Stennan! I'm so glad to see you. I need help. Something is terrible wrong with Eiren. Please help me for a moment."

"No, Anya," Stennan answered sharply. "Gulig brought *you* here to care for the child. I'll have no part in it."

A smile crossed Shawn's face. They had joined him with the very people he needed to find. Stennan still had Shawn's arm in a vice like grip – but maybe, just maybe, there was some way to escape. Shawn watched and waited, hoping.

"Please, Stennan," Anya continued. "I just need you to lift him from the cradle so I can examine the boy. You know I'm just a weak old woman. We had a terrible time getting here, what with your friends grabbing us in the night. I don't want to drop the child."

Stennan looked over both shoulders, as though afraid that someone might be watching. Eiren let rip another babyish bellow.

"Well, all right – for just a moment." Stennan kept his grip on Shawn, then turned and locked the door from the inside. Only then did he release his hold on Shawn's arm. Stennan briskly walked over to the cradle, averting his eyes as he reached down and felt around for the baby's body. Still refusing to look at the child, Stennan lifted Eiren and dangled him by his armpits, keeping him at an arm's length.

"That's it, Stennan," the old woman coaxed. "Now please, hold him tenderly to your chest while I tend to his back."

The man drew the child closer, and his elbows jutted out awkwardly as he tried to avoid too much contact with the child. Eiren screamed in his ear.

The woman softly patted the child's back, and a tiny burp escaped the baby's lips. "Well, that is it," she said, smiling as Eiren closed his eyes, suddenly peaceful. "Thank you, Stennan."

Shawn looked away from Stennan to hide the broad smile on his face. He resisted the urge to laugh aloud at the woman's audacity.

Stennan soundlessly replaced the baby in his cradle.

The baby raised a hand, looking at Stennan, and a glimmer of light flashed across the servant's otherwise dull eyes. He hurried back to the door and let himself out. With a loud clank, the key turned in the lock, and Shawn was imprisoned.

When Stennan closed the door, she bent down and easily lifted the baby from his cradle.

"I can't believe you just did that," Shawn blurted. "Aren't you afraid?"

The woman giggled, emphasizing the deep laugh lines that crinkled around her pale blue eyes. "These Rugus be so fun to toy with. Oh! Forgive me – my name is Anya. And this is me grandnephew, Eiren."

"Hello Anya," Shawn said. He held Eiren's tiny hand for a moment and introduced himself, "Hi Eiren. I'm Shawn. Are you the one I've come to rescue?"

"Yes, Shawn," Anya said. "He is the one."

Peeper's head emerged from under Shawn's armpit. Shawn softly patted him and the tiny parrot climbed onto Shawn's shoulder.

"I see you brought us company," Anya said, peering at the bird with a friendly look.

"This is Peeper," Shawn said. "His wing was messed up when I found him, so I fixed it."

"It's a pleasure to meet you, wee Peeper." Reaching over, Anya softly petted Peeper's bright orange head. The baby parrot proudly puffed himself up. "Come sit with me, Shawn. Eiren hasn't had much rest this night." Anya said, placing the child once again into his crib. "Come, precious baby. Now it is time for you to get some sleep." She sat on the bed and patted the place next to her.

Shawn sat down on the bed and breathed a sigh of relief to finally have a soft place to sit. He looked into Anya's face. "They kidnapped you also?"

"Yes. It be a terrible, cowardly act." Anya's hands rose in anger, and then fluttered to her chest. "But at least they brought me to care for this precious child."

"I'm supposed to be with Kaela," Shawn offered. "But I also got kidnapped, and Gulig nearly killed me when he discovered I wasn't the red-haired girl."

"Oh, I bet that was something to see," Anya said, giggling. For a moment she looked like her young grandniece, Tressa. "Even in these stone walls, I've been hearing about the return of the red-haired girl."

"I'm really worried about her. She probably returned to the caves to get here and Gulig's beast is in there, too..." Shawn said, envisioning Kaela at the mercy of some large ape-like creature.

"Oh my, he is a dreadful, fierce monster." Anya grew solemn. "I hear they raise him on ganba root. Even his saliva is saturated with that terrible poison."

"Oh!" Shawn cried, realization finally dawning on him. "Is that what smells around here? Is that what turns everyone's arms green?"

"Yes," Anya said. "It is due to their abuse of the precious plant. It shouldn't be that way – shouldn't be that way at all." The elderly woman took Shawn's hand in hers and she looked him deeply in the eyes. "Each plant in this beautiful world holds special gifts. It is not the fault of the plant if it is used by humans in ways the Great Sprit never intended."

"So ganba isn't all that bad?" Shawn asked.

"No – not at all," Anya continued, shaking her head. "Ages ago it was used with great care and respect, and only in times of need. It was taboo to give the ganba to children. In the past, the Rugus only chewed the root before battles and special ceremonies."

"Then everything changed," Anya said sourly. "One of Gulig's ancestors, hungry for power, discovered a way to concentrate the ganba root, turning it into a potent elixir. He and his followers, who all drank the elixir, grew to be so powerful that they were able to overthrow the Rugu leader of the time. Then they were giving it to their wives, and even gave little bits of it to their children. The elixir made the children grow bigger and stronger than the other children. In time, the whole tribe used it. Now, when a child reaches thirteen years, they are given a large glass of ganba. It be a rite of passage. If they survive the drink, they be welcomed as full members of the tribe."

"Only thirteen? That's how old I am!" Shawn fell silent, wondering what happened to those who didn't survive. "So the Rugus all drink it? All the time?"

"Yes. It be a terrible thing. The tribe has been drinking the elixir for so long that they be afraid to live without it. After generations of abuse, they be completely dependent on the elixir for their strength. But the poison takes a terrible toll on the user – emotionally, physically and mentally – trust me, Shawn, the user pays a terrible price for the benefits."

"Like those markings?"

"Right!" Anya said. "Those hideous vines. When someone drinks ganba regularly, the plant grows inside of you. It starts as a wee vine in your arm or leg, but soon it takes over and the vine grows around and around your limbs and climbs toward your heart. Eventually the vines wrap again and again around a person's heart, until there be no feeling left in you for other human beings. Gulig – he drinks so much I don't think you could find his heart with an axe."

"What about Arendore's brother? Queen Skyla told us that he is drinking the ganba – is he okay?"

"Oh that be a terribly sad story. Lorendale started drinking the ganba in secret after Skyla left – after she broke his heart."

"Really? But Skyla is married to Arendore...."

"Long ago, it was Lorendale and Skyla. They were so young – probably too young, but so in love. Those two couldn't get enough of each other. When they got engaged, she came to live here. It was my job to chaperone them, and believe me – it wasn't easy."

"Gulig was already living here," Anya continued. "Lorendale took him in when he arrived by boat with a handful of servants. He claimed he be a man without a country, and hid his true identity. Soon after that, he became Lorendale's chief advisor. He helped Lorendale rebuild this region after a terrible fire."

"When Lorendale fell in love, Gulig be threatened by Skyla's presence. He was afraid that she would be having too strong an influence over Lorendale. At that time, one of the limba trees in this region had reached the end of her very long life. Though limba trees live for centuries, eventually even they die. That beautiful tree offered herself in service to Lorendale. It was all arranged, but on the night she was to be cut down, somehow Gulig's men 'accidentally' ringed the limba tree that was home to our family, instead."

"Lorendale had a soft heart and still thought the best of Gulig – he be sure it be a terrible accident. Skyla never trusted Gulig, though. She was furious and threatened to kill Gulig with that weapon of hers – the ruby-handled dagger. When Lorendale got between the two and spoke up for his advisor and friend, Skyla told him that she never wanted to see him again – and she never did. She wouldn't even speak to him. She left that night."

"It must have been pure agony for Lorendale to have his heart ripped in two. He was a naïve young man – the spoiled second son of a wealthy king. Thought the best of everyone. Gulig offered Lorendale the ganba elixir, and he began sipping that evil brew."

"Soon after, my people moved to a limba tree near King Arendore's castle. It took some time, but eventually Skyla and Arendore fell in love. I heard that news of their engagement nearly destroyed Lorendale, and he drowned himself in the ganba to forget his pain."

"But why did Lorendale trust Gulig? He's evil." Shawn asked.

"Yes. *Now* his corrupt nature is obvious – but at the time, Gulig was doing great things for this region. He carried so much responsibility. He built homes throughout the land, improving the castle. He built hundreds of homes from that one tree. He swore he did not realize that it be the wrong tree, and said it had been a terrible mistake."

"Most likely, Gulig and his servants arrived here with only a limited supply of ganba," Anya explained. "It takes time to cultivate the plants. Perhaps back then, Gulig still had something of a heart inside him."

"So then what happened?" Shawn probed.

Anya shrugged. "Lorendale became more and more dependent on the ganba, and after that it be simple for the Rugus to invade this land. Lorendale was ill prepared and betrayed – and easily conquered."

Chapter Twenty • Lorendale

The air in the room was dank and reeked with the sour smell of illness. Kaela looked around in the dim light, and with Wollan glued to her side, stepped towards the gray-haired man who moaned piteously from the bed. After endless hours walking on hard rock, her body welcomed the silk carpet's deep pile. She sank into a soft armchair by the bed.

"Hello, my name is Kaela," she said. "And this is Wollan and," Kaela motioned with her hand to Zeke to come forward, "... and, Zeke." Zeke tentatively took a few steps into the room.

The man tilted his head towards Zeke and his eyes closed in fear. "A ... *Rugu* boy ..." the man gasped. "You are spying on me!"

"No!" Kaela stood up, outraged by this remark. The man flinched and Kaela softened her tone. "Zeke is the bravest boy I know."

The man was so thin that the red velvet bedspread barely rose as he hoarsely whispered, "I'm sorry. Please ... don't leave me ... please ... I am ... Lorendale."

Stunned, Kaela gawked, searching to find some resemblance in the man to King Arendore. How could this be his twin? The man's face was deeply lined, and dark circles rimmed his eyes. A few streaks of red laced the sick man's hair, but that was where the similarity ended. Kaela eyes glistened with tears. "What has happened to you? Why is no one taking care of you?"

"Child, give me your hand," Lorendale said weakly. "Having you here ... I feel better.... You give me hope."

Kaela started to extend her right hand, but when she glimpsed her muddy, bloodstained arm and the new vines that sprouted under her skin, she quickly tucked her arm behind her back. Instead, she offered her left hand.

Lorendale's hand gripped her as if he never wanted her to go. "Thank you I ... I feel your healing power already." He smiled weakly.

Wollan stood and placed his head and paws on the bed right next to Lorendale. Kaela extended her hand and idly scratched the dog's rump. Seeing the dog, Lorendale responded joyfully, "Oh my! It is Frannie – my beloved Frannie."

Wollan whined. Kaela touched the pendant and translated Wollan's words for Lorendale. "Frannie was Wollan's mother."

Lorendale released Kaela's hand and weakly patted Wollan's head. Then he asked, "Could you ... could you do something for me?"

"Of course," Kaela answered with a soothing voice. "What do you need?"

Lorendale pointed with a trembling finger. "See that pitcher ... over there? I need a drink. I would feel so much better ... if I could just have a drink."

Kaela jumped up eager to help. "Why don't they keep it by the bed for you? It's not right for you to be so thirsty." She quickly took the few steps to the cupboard.

As soon as she popped the cork off the carafe of blue-green liquid, a bitter smell shot into Kaela's nose. Ice circulated in her veins, and the pain radiating from her injured arm vanished. Confused, Kaela paused, until rage exploded inside her and she whirled around, yelling, "This is ganba! How dare you trick me this way?"

Wollan's ears perked up, and he raced to Kaela's side.

"It's your own fault that you're so sick," Kaela said furiously. "This is why no one is taking care of you."

Tears gathered in the corners of Lorendale's eyes. "You are right. I am a failure. It's just the pain ... the unbearable pain. I will die without the elixir. You don't know what it is like!"

Wollan leaned into Kaela and his touch calmed her down. Kaela's heart broke, seeing the depth of agony on King Lorendale's face. "I'm so sorry. I never should have said such things to you. Still, you must give this up. You can't drink ganba anymore. Can't you see what it's doing to you?

It's *killing* you!"

Yip, yip, yip, woof! Wollan barked.

Still standing out of the way, Zeke said quietly, "The special water, Kaela. I saw it work. Give him some drops."

"Oh, of course!" Kaela said. "I have something that will help you." Kaela opened the leather water bag and dropped some of the pristine water into the bottle of bitter, blue-green liquid. Instantly, she inhaled a wonderful fragrance – the room filled with the smell of roses, gardenias, lilies and lavender.

Kaela sprinkled a few drops of the mixture into her palm and licked it, hoping the horrible vines would disappear from her own body. After pouring a drink for the King, Kaela returned to his side while Wollan diligently pressed his body to Kaela's leg. Zeke finally joined her and stood behind the armchair.

Kaela stood by the bed with Wollan at her feet, fluffed the pillows behind the King's head and helped prop him up. She tipped the glass against his mouth as he gulped the elixir. She smoothed the hair from his face and smiled kindly. The lines in his face softened and a spark of light glimmered from his eyes.

"Thank you, dear. I hoped – prayed – you would come."

Certain she could trust the man, Kaela said, "Lorendale, please – we desperately need your help. Gulig has kidnapped Arendore's baby. We need to find him. Please…"

"Arendore and Skyla have a child?" Lorendale frowned with confusion, retreating into himself

"Yes, yes, they have a child." Kaela said. "I know that you do not feel well, but we need to find the child. He is here in this castle somewhere…"

"Yes … I … think I heard they – they had a child, but … I'm sorry. I don't know." Lorendale shook his head.

"Do you have any idea? *Something* you could tell us?"

Lorendale closed his eyes and seemed to shrink into the bed.

"I'm sorry. I shouldn't push you." Kaela softly stroked his hand.

Seeing the pain on the man's face, Zeke joined Kaela by the bed, and Wollan sat on the floor between them. "Don't worry, sir," Zeke said. "We're going to help you."

"I am so sorry, dear children," he said softly. "Listen to me – look at me. Do not fall under sway of the ganba. It has addled my mind. The relief it brings lasts such a short time – and then the bitterness is everywhere."

"It's okay ... please don't worry," Kaela assured him. She leaned over to touch his cheek. "We'll get you help."

Wollan pressed his body against Kaela's leg and put his paws on the bed. He gently licked Lorendale's hand.

Lorendale dug his fingers into Wollan's thick fur, and a tear fell from his eye. He whispered, "You are a really good dog." Seeing the dog vigorously wag his tail, Lorendale's eyes brightened. "I have an idea. Perhaps, perhaps, he is in the old nursery." He quivered with excitement. "Yes, it is where Arendore and I spent our first years. The room is on the top floor of the original castle, at the end of the hall."

Zeke looked up at Kaela and they both smiled.

"Thank you, Lorendale! Thank you!" Kaela exclaimed, hope blooming within her. Then she looked over at Zeke and noticed a faraway look in his eyes. "Quick, Kaela, quick!" Zeke ordered suddenly. "Hide! You too, Wollan – someone's coming!" Then he dove under the bed.

Kaela and Wollan jumped up and Kaela returned the glass to the cupboard.

"Please, dear child ... don't leave me," Lorendale pleaded.

"Be strong, King Lorendale. I'll be back I promise, but please don't tell anyone we were here." Kaela and Wollan rolled under the bed.

A key turned with a "thunk" in the lock. The handle on the door turned.

Kaela crowded next to Zeke under the bed, and Wollan pressed against Kaela. She wrapped her arm around the dog, rested her head on his curly hair and peered out at the room.

"Kaela, pass me the water bag," Zeke hissed.

"Why?" Kaela started to question, but quickly realized there was no time for explanations and untied the bag from her waist. She shoved it behind her, trusting in Zeke's foresight, and the boy grabbed it from her.

A man's muscular body filled the doorway. His pale green eyes were like two dark holes, and the lines on his face were deeply drawn, like those of an angry mask. The two sides of his face seemed like a puzzle that had been put together in the wrong way. One eye sat high above the other, and his nose was drastically crooked. His ruffled white shirt and black pants were pressed to perfection, however. His purple cloak flowed behind him as he strode with a slight limp towards King Lorendale.

The air in the room seemed to change, becoming somehow heavier. Kaela's chest tightened like a vice around her lungs, making it difficult to breath. The unmistakable odor of ganba burned inside her nostrils once more.

"Your highness, King Lorendale," the man sneered, his voice full of contempt. "Hah! Look at you, now. I suppose you will be begging for more today. Well, I have decided it is finally time to give you a stronger dose."

Gulig popped the cork of the carafe and poured out a full glass, holding it up to the light.

Kaela and Wollan lay completely still, watching – hoping Gulig wouldn't notice the change in the ganba.

"Just look at that beautiful color," Gulig said. "The relief you long for will soon be here." The Rugu leader walked back towards the bed until his shiny black boots were so close to Kaela's face that the smell of shoe polish overwhelmed the bitter odor of ganba.

"Lorendale, here at last is the full glass you have longed for. Let me sit you up so you can enjoy it fully," Gulig said as the bed creaked. Lorendale moaned and then audibly gulped the liquid. The glass clanged as Gulig placed it on the bedside table.

Gulig sat down heavily in the armchair.

"Dear Lorendale," he said softly. "In truth, I could not have done this without you. It is through you that I have the power to take over Arendore's Kingdom. The crown that was promised to my family will, at last, be mine."

Lorendale's breath came in loud open-mouthed rattles.

Certain that Lorendale was unconscious and under the intoxicating spell of the ganba, Gulig's impenetrable mask fell away, and he whispered, "There is one thing I need to complete my plan." His face twisted with fear and loathing. "The girl – we have yet to capture the girl."

Kaela clung even more tightly to Wollan, afraid even to take a breath.

Lorendale whispered slowly, each word requiring its own breath. "You ... will ... never ... own ... her...."

Shocked to find Lorendale awake, Gulig's face immediately hardened again into its cruel mask.

"She will be mine," Gulig sneered. "A child could not stop me. My family has waited so patiently – for generations! But the time for waiting is over."

"The prophecy – the prophecy..." Lorendale reminded him, and laughed. Kaela realized that Lorendale enjoyed bringing pain and doubt to Gulig in the same way that Gulig savored destroying him.

"You superstitious fool," Gulig yawned, seemingly uncaring, and stretched his long legs under the bed. Caught offguard, Kaela and Wollan recoiled, but did not move fast enough. One foot rammed against Wollan as he scurried away.

"What?" Gulig reached his long arm under the bed. "What is under here?"

Wollan chomped down hard, and Gulig howled in pain. Kaela pulled the dagger from its sheath, and Gulig's face loomed large under the bed.

"How dare you, you mangy creature..." Then, catching sight of Kaela, Gulig grinned and said, "Oh, and yes! How delightful!"

Wollan snarled and bit down harder, tearing at Gulig's strong muscled arm. Gulig dragged Wollan towards him and pinched the top of the dog's nose, forcing him to release his bite in order to breathe. Then he trapped Wollan's head between his knees.

"You better let go of my dog!" Kaela yelled, propped up on one elbow, her legs still under the bed. She waved the dagger in her other fist.

"Oh dear. How frightening," Gulig laughed. "The precious red-haired girl has arrived unannounced. I knew you couldn't resist the bait." Green blood dripped off his hand, but he seemed not to feel his wound, and he grinned as he clasped Kaela's wrist. He bent her hand backwards until the dagger clattered to the floor – useless.

Still kneeling, Gulig admired the long knife. "Look at this – it's the famous ruby-handled dagger. This just keeps getting better and better." He tucked the dagger into his belt. "Now I can have my revenge with the very weapon that was used to betray my people."

Kaela screamed while he spoke. "You'll never win!"

Hiding in the shadows, Zeke waited for the perfect moment.

Wollan wiggled free of Gulig's knee and sunk his teeth into Gulig's thigh. With Gulig momentarily distracted by Wollan, Zeke lunged forward on his belly, his hand flicked out into Gulig's pocket and, like a frog's tongue, he recoiled into the background.

"My dear, I think you'd best call off your dog," Gulig demanded between clenched teeth. "I have no patience for ill-behaved beasts."

Lying on top of the dog, Gulig reached under the bed. He yanked Kaela's arm, pulling her toward him.

"Leave me alone, you creep," Kaela screamed. She scratched and then bit down hard on Gulig's arm. A disgusting, bitter flavor stung her tongue.

Gulig pushed Kaela's head away and struggled to drag her into the room. Kaela resisted with every fiber of her being, scratching, kicking and biting, but Gulig yanked hard and pulled her from under the bed. Wollan lunged for Gulig's face, and Gulig released Kaela to shove the dog aside. He stomped on Wollan with his heavy boot. Kaela pushed with all her might, but she was no match for Gulig. He grabbed her arm and stood upright, jerking Kaela along with him.

"So, here's the little savior of this land, hiding beneath the bed. Some hero!"

Kaela bent over and bit him again, then kicked him in the shins.

Gulig laughed. "You have no idea how long we have been waiting for you, generations. Come – let's not disturb our dear King."

Wollan squirmed under Gulig's foot, trying to stand. Gulig stepped back and kicked the dog violently in the neck.

Wollan yelped.

"You monster! Don't kick my dog!" Kaela screamed in rage, jerking against Gulig's grip.

Undeterred, Wollan wriggled free and leapt for Gulig's face, while Lorendale rolled to his side, trying to help the girl.

Grabbing the moment, Kaela punched Gulig's side.

"Guards!" Gulig roared, grasping Kaela arm.

Two muscular men dressed in black and gray military garb raced in. "Restrain this dog!"

Kaela kicked Gulig again and again.

One of the guards kneeled on Wollan and held the dog's mouth closed. The other pulled out a dart from his belt and asked, "Do you want me to poison him, sir?"

"No!" Kaela screamed, tugging against Gulig's grip. She tried to bite him again, but with Wollan fully restrained, Gulig held Kaela with her back against his chest and her legs above the ground. She continued kicking, but his wide stance made it impossible for her to make contact.

"I hate you, Gulig," Lorendale murmured weakly, "I hate you."

"Just tie it up!" Gulig said.

One of the guards quickly unbuckled his belt, whipped it off and bound Wollan's legs together.

"Take it to the prison," Gulig ordered. "And you know what to do if it gives you any trouble."

Gulig carried Kaela out of the King's room and into the wide hallway.

The two soldiers followed, one carrying Wollan upside-down by the legs while the other gripped the dog's muzzle in his hands.

"Wollan! WOLLAN! DON'T TAKE HIM!!" Kaela screamed, wiggling and worming her way out of Gulig's bear hug and biting him again in the arm.

Gulig twisted Kaela's arm behind her back and said with a painful jerk to her arm, "Don't worry dear. We're just putting him in a kennel in the basement where he belongs."

Kaela winced with pain. "I heard you!" she screamed "You're taking him to the prison."

"That's right dear, get mad. Get really mad," Gulig smirked. "We welcome your anger here. We will cultivate it so you will feel right at home." He turned her to face him with both of her arms firmly in his grip. A twisted smile crossed Gulig's lips as he caught sight of her right arm. "What have we here? How wonderful. You've been drinking the ganba."

"I'll never drink that stuff," Kaela spat.

Gulig firmly traced the green vines on Kaela's arm with his long green fingernail, scratching the tender wounds. "Well your body tells me differently. It looks as though you are becoming one of us."

Kaela jerked free from Gulig's grip. Her red hair flew around her face as she darted towards Wollan, screaming, "Don't take him away!"

Two more guards caught her and dragged her by her armpits back to Gulig.

"WOLLAN!" she screamed one more time, and then the dog was

carried out of view.

Gulig clutched her right arm. "Look at these beautiful vines, growing as we speak," he said. "Kaela, you do not understand fully, I'm afraid. You do not need to drink the elixir to grow the vine - the vine feeds on something that is already inside of you." He chuckled, observing the progress of the growth. "You're coming along nicely, child. In no time, you will be a daughter to me."

Terror tightened Kaela's stomach as images flashed in her mind of life with Gulig as a father. Horrified, Kaela gagged and retched, vomiting green bile all over Gulig's perfectly polished, black boots.

Chapter Twenty - One • The Crazy Seer

Chilled from the howling wind and aching for news of her child, Queen Skyla hugged a shawl tightly around her shoulders as she rocked back and forth in the nursery.

"Let me in! LET ME IN!" a woman screamed from outside the castle.

Queen Skyla ran downstairs just as her servant cracked the front door open.

"Let me in! You better let me in, you stupid..." The woman's voice faded to a dull mumble as her foot, wrapped in a torn-up shoe, wedged the door open and she pressed her hand against the edge of the door.

"Get out of here," the servant snarled as he pried one finger after another from the door. "Leave the Queen alone. She has no time to deal with you."

"Who is that at the door?" Queen Skyla asked.

"It's Tazena, the crazy seer," the servant spat.

"LET ME IN!" Tazena howled.

"Please ... I'll take care of this," Skyla said, firmly laying a hand on her servant's shoulder. "I'd like to hear what she has to say."

"Are you sure, my Queen?" The servant, in his surprise, lost hold of the door and Tazena rushed through the opening and fell to her knees, weeping on Queen Skyla's bare feet.

Skyla bent down and offered her hands to the old woman.

Appalled by the scene in front of him, the servant asked again, "You are sure, my Queen?"

"Please leave us," the Queen said firmly.

"Please, Your Highness – please hear me. You have to help me! Zeke's gone. Something terrible is going to happen if I don't find him. I should have told him – but I just couldn't do it. I promised I would, but I just couldn't tell him! You've got to understand – please, help me!"

"Come, sit with me." Skyla offered her hand to the woman and helped her rise to her feet. "You are Tazena the seer?"

"Yes, Your Highness. Tazena's the name."

Skyla escorted Tazena to a set of chairs at the far side of the elegant hall. "Please, Tazena, start at the beginning. Maybe there is something I can do for you."

Tazena shuffled alongside the queen. Her shoes looked like something she had found in the town dump. Her big toes stuck up through gaping holes and the soles flapped as she walked. Her dress was little more than a rag that she wore inside out, and her hair stuck out every which way, even though she had obviously tried to gather it into an orderly knot. Staring at her filthy hands, Tazena mumbled, "It is my grandbaby – Zeke. I never told him...."

"Never told him what?" Skyla interrupted.

"He's part Rugu." Tazena looked up for a moment, and then hung her head once more. "I didn't want them to take him."

"Yes, that would be terrible."

"His father never knew ... he never knew about his son."

"Then he does not know his father, either?"

"No, no ... I didn't want him to drink the ganba. Now he's gone – snuck out. It's that red-haired girl who did it – it's her fault he left."

"So your grandson left with Kaela, the red-haired girl?"

"Yes, it's her fault. I saw it. I can see him, too, you know – the father. I see things, all the time." A tear rolled down Tazena's cheek. "I don't want him to hate me."

"I'm sure he won't be hating you," the Queen said soothingly.

"He might ... could ... when he finds out that I promised his mother, Zara, promised her I'd tell the father." Tazena's tears fell in a steady stream, making tracks of clean skin down her soiled cheeks. "I should have found a way to stop her. Why didn't I stop her?"

"Tazena, I don't understand."

"It was years ago. My Zara ... my daughter ... it was before Gulig took over. He was helping Lorendale. Gulig wanted me to come to him ... he sent gifts."

"Gulig wanted you to tell him the future?" Skyla asked.

"Yes, yes, but I wouldn't go. When Zara saw the gifts, she ran to him, though. She told Gulig things ... things she never should have said."

"What kind of things, Tazena?" Skyla asked. "What did she tell Gulig?"

Tazena hesitated and shook her head. Her hands quivered.

"Please, Tazena, you must tell me!" Skyla demanded.

"Zara never had anything, living with me. Of course she told him! He paid her more gold than that poor girl had ever seen in her entire life...."

"What did she tell him?"

"I told her it was blood money! I did!" Tazena looked at Skyla imploringly.

"What did she say to Gulig?" Skyla snapped, growing impatient.

"It was when you and Lorendale first met – before you lived in the castle with him. My Zara ... she told him things."

"What things, Tazena?"

"It was wrong, she knew! She regretted it, but she fell in love."

"What did she tell Gulig?" Skyla asked even more firmly.

"That he had to find a way to separate you..." Tazena sniffed. "Told him your love was the one thing that could get in his way."

"What?" Skyla gasped. "Your daughter told Gulig to separate me from Lorendale?"

Tazena cowered and whimpered. "It was wrong, ma'am – it was wrong. She didn't realize! She fell in love with one of Gulig's men while she was there. And with every piece of information she told Gulig, the more gold dripped into her fingers. It was those Rugus – it's their fault...."

"But your daughter helped Gulig. She betrayed Lorendale – betrayed us."

Tazena hung her head. "She didn't know," she said. "She fell in love with one of Gulig's men, a Rugu. She wanted them to accept her – but then Gulig discovered her and threw her out. She died in childbirth. She didn't know what she was doing. I didn't keep my promise to her. I couldn't ... didn't want them taking him...." Tazena quieted as she sobbed, until she bolted up, crying, "No, no, don't!" A wild, far-off look came into her eyes, and then faded.

Shaking her head, Tazena sat back down and looked at the Queen.

"That Rugu man wants to hurt your son," Tazena said calmly.

"What do you mean, Tazena?" Skyla pleaded, terror gripping her heart. "Please, look carefully."

"It's the evil one," Tazena intoned. "He lied, and now he wants to hurt him."

"What?" Skyla jumped out of her chair. "What is he doing with my baby?" She paced in a small circle as she clenched and unclenched her fists.

"I should have killed that man when he chopped down our Grandmother Tree," Skyla muttered. "I could have stopped this. Please, Tazena..." the Queen breathed deeply, recovering her composure. "What do I do? How can I stop him?"

"I want you to help me ... you know..." Tazena implored, looking up at Skyla with tear-filled eyes. "Help me get there – to my Zeke. Please."

Chapter Twenty - Two • Ganba

As the stream of green vomit splashed across Gulig's boots, he roared, "Augh! Everyone here! Now!" Gulig looked down at his soiled boots. "This is an atrocity." A crowd of servants and soldiers from all over the castle fell prostrating to the ground, too terrified to move.

Still clutching Kaela, Gulig stared at his boots, then at the cowering mass of people. "Simpletons!! Idiots!! Pathetic weaklings!!! Clean up this mess! Move! Now!!! Clean up this mess at once!"

Kaela pulled free from Gulig, but two soldiers immediately grabbed her. She screamed, "I'll never be your daughter. Never, never!"

One of the soldiers covered her mouth, muffling her screams.

She bit down on a finger until she felt something crunch in her mouth. The soldier's hand flew off her mouth. He yelped, but continued to grip her arm with his other hand.

"Never, never, never..." Kaela yelled, writhing and fighting against the soldiers' grip.

Gulig whipped his head towards them, glaring. The soldier ignored his pain and stuck a handkerchief in Kaela's mouth.

The servants writhed like worms on their bellies to Gulig, wiping and polishing the fouled boots with their shirt cuffs.

After straightening his shirt and putting on a calm expression, Gulig said in a cloving voice, "Do not worry, dear. I'm sure you did not mean to do that. It is very common in the beginning to be ill from the ganba." He placed his arm around Kaela and gripped her shoulder tightly.

"Mmmm, mm, mm!"

Gulig pulled the cloth from her mouth.

She spat, and snarled, "Get your hands off me."

"I consider myself to be a very patient man," Gulig said, digging his fingers into her flesh. "But I have my limits. Are you ready to walk with me?"

"No! No! No!" Kaela screamed furiously and kicked Gulig.

Gulig turned towards her and clenched her shoulders in his long fingers. "This is getting tiresome. It is time for you to embrace your fate," he hissed, and then ordered a nearby guard. "Gag her until she's ready to be civilized."

A guard stuffed the rag back into Kaela's mouth and then threw her over his shoulder as he followed Gulig down the hall. She kicked and pummeled the guard until he threw her into a chair in Gulig's sitting room and held her arms down.

"Kaela, do you see the guards around you?" Gulig glared, and his cold green eyes bore into Kaela's. "Do you really think you can single-handedly fight us all? Are you ready to behave?"

Kaela realized Gulig's large and powerful hands could snap her bones into tiny pieces. She wished she still had the dagger or the knife. Instead, she gave Gulig a hard stare. Gulig nodded and the guard released his hold on her.

Gulig sat down in an ornate chair across from Kaela at the head of the huge wooden table.

Kaela looked around Gulig's vast sitting room, hoping for some sign of an ally, but instead sadness washed over her at the sight of dozens of tiger heads lining the walls, each staring through her with unseeing eyes. Their hides were draped over chairs and scattered on the floor as throw rugs.

A tiger fur warmed Kaela's legs as she perched on the chair, but could not warm her heart. Tears gathered in her eyes as she remembered Kanu, and wondered if he was still alive. She gathered some of the tiger skin in her arms, and brushed the bristled fur against her cheek, sniffing the faint musky tiger smell. Her heart ached for her friend.

"Kaela, I am happy to see that you have finally come to your senses," Gulig began.

Strength again trickled into her body with the memory of Kanu.

Holding back her tears, Kaela sat up tall and replied, "I'll never help you. Save your breath."

"Kaela, perhaps I am not making myself clear. You will listen to what I have to say, or that dog of yours is not long for this world," Gulig growled.

"Well, then speak..." she sighed, then fear stabbed her heart as she thought of Wollan and Shawn. "What have you done with my cousin?"

"My dear, I can assure you that your cousin is completely safe." Gulig drummed his fingers on the table and smirked, then continued, "Safe – for now. You will be reunited shortly. Perhaps my intentions have been unclear. I should not have been so rough with you earlier," Gulig said, smiling.

His smile chilled her heart.

"You will live very well here," he continued. "You will be a princess. Haven't you always wanted to be a princess? I have waited ever so patiently for you – I even came to this land to meet your mother, but it seems she was whisked away before I had the pleasure to make her acquaintance."

"So what?" Kaela asked, goading him.

"Ahh, Kaela, don't you know? Perhaps it is time for a history lesson. King Arendore seems to have forgotten the truth. I have a right to you, you know. A red-haired princess from the House of Muraten was promised to my father, the great Prince Golan."

"Everyone knows about that stupid empty promise," Kaela said, scowling. "Maybe you should just get over it."

The muscles in Gulig's jaw tensed as he continued, "They did not only break their promise. King Muraten threw us out of this land and destroyed all of the sacred ganba plants. Was that just? Was it right to rip us away from our homes?"

"Whatever," Kaela blurted, crossing her arms against her chest.

Gulig's eyes flashed with anger, and he rose, clenching his fists. Overcoming his rage, he sat back down. "I promised my father I would right this terrible wrong," he said sternly. "I must assume my rightful place as King over this land. I have been preparing for what is owed to us."

Gulig flipped over an ancient piece of parchment on which was drawn the picture of a beautiful red-haired girl. Underneath, in elegant script, it read:

We hope you enjoy this gift, a portrait of our beloved daughter, Gwenilda.

"I'm no princess." Kaela said, barely glancing at the painting. "I'm just a redheaded girl that looks like somebody else. I'm not even from here. This place isn't my home."

"You are home," Gulig sighed with impatience. "This is your home now. It is time for you to assume your destiny."

Gulig burst into laughter, showing his long green-tinged teeth. His crooked nose and his green skin made him ugly, but it was Gulig's eyes that truly terrified Kaela, filling her belly with wave after wave of horror – not a trace of light was reflected in his enlarged pupils.

His hand wrapped around a bottle of the blue-green elixir, which sat on the table. Gulig lifted the bottle to his face and swirled it around and around. Kaela was mesmerized as the liquid changed from blue to green and then back again. Gulig uncorked the bottle with a loud pop. He poured two glasses and reached over to pass one to Kaela.

"You must be terribly thirsty after your long trip," he said courteously. "Please, my dear, drink deeply. I promise it will make you feel so much better."

Kaela intended to turn away from the glass of ganba that Gulig placed before her, to reject the dreaded drink. But the sparkly blue-green color hypnotized her, and she felt a distant tug from the empty spaces in her heart.

"That's right, Kaela," Gulig said, nudging the glass closer to her. "Look deeply into the liquid. I have come here to help you, after all. I feel your longing – I feel your pain. The ganba will take away all of your suffering – you know this. You will feel nothing but relief – sweet, sweet relief. Your body is not weak like Lorendale's – you can handle the ganba. In fact, you will thrive on it."

Bile rose in Kaela's throat as the bitter smell wafted towards her. She fought once again against the queasiness in her stomach, but still the drink spoke to the pain in her heart, enticing her. Slowly extending her right hand, Kaela stroked the thick glass and tried to lift it. But caught off guard by its incredible weight, and still unsure of whether she wanted to drink, she almost dropped it. Gulig was ready, and he firmly placed his hand under Kaela's, his grip like a cold metal claw. She cringed at his hands' cool, hard touch.

He whispered, "Please, do not be afraid. I promise I will not abandon you."

Just holding the glass somehow eased the ache in Kaela's right arm where the green vines continued to grow and sprout new tendrils. She longed for the sensation of the blue-green liquid on her tongue. Somehow she already knew how the tingling drink would empower her, renewing her weak and exhausted muscles. Most of all she yearned for relief from the pain in her heart, for the ache of her loss to vanish, to disappear forever. And then she thought, *maybe if I only drink a little bit I will have the power to overcome Gulig.*

Gulig's face leered through the cut crystal of Kaela's glass, mirrored in hundreds of little blue green images. She peered at Gulig as he lifted his glass and eagerly drank the ganba. His shirt slipped down his arm, revealing a thick web of green hate-filled vines.

"Please, dear," Gulig coaxed, "If you are to be my princess, you must know the delight of the ganba."

He smiled and toasted, "To our future together."

Imagining King Lorendale lying on his bed, a voice within her screamed, *Stop. Stop! Don't listen to him.* A whirlwind of anger stormed inside of Kaela while her hands battled each other. The vine-covered hand struggled to bring the glass to her mouth while the other hand pushed the ganba away. Catching sight of the tiger skin behind Gulig's back, Kaela bolted upright, clutching the glass in both hands.

Kaela hurled the glass at Gulig, screaming, "This is for Kanu! Creep, I HATE YOU!"

Gulig ducked. The glass shattered against the wall, and tinkled as it fell to the ground. Kaela grabbed the heavy bottle from the table and heaved it onto the floor, the fine crystal crashing and clattering against the wood. Glass flew everywhere as large drops of ganba splashed her face.

"Guards, guards," Gulig hollered. "Stennan, get in here now! You stupid, stupid girl! Look at what you've done!"

Two huge soldiers grabbed Kaela's arms, and Gulig fell to his knees in front of the shattered bottle. He leaned over, dipping his hand into a small puddle on the floor and tenderly licking the ganba drops off his fingers.

Gulig leaped to his feet, his green-tinged skin dark with fury. He leaned over until his face was within inches of Kaela, and said, "You have no idea what you've done."

Kaela turned her head away, yanking against the guards.

"Look at me!" Gulig roared.

One of the guards grabbed Kaela by the hair and twisted her head to face Gulig.

"Do you have any idea how precious this drink is?" he continued, seething. "All of the ganba plants in this land were once destroyed, but when my people came back we brought seedlings. It takes years for the roots to fully mature. My people will die without this drink. Do you want the blood of my people on your hands?" His voice rose until he nearly screeched.

"You're the one hurting your people!" Kaela yelled back at him.

"You stupid girl. We will die without this drink. We must carefully measure and ration it for my people. Every drop gives someone life. You have wantonly destroyed an entire bottle. Sooner or later, a child will die because of you."

"No child needs that to live!" Kaela barked at him. "You destroy your children's lives by feeding it to them. That stuff is evil!"

"Stennan, get me another bottle of ganba, now!" Between clenched teeth Gulig ordered, "I've had enough of this child. Guards, take her to her room."

"Filthy pig!" Kaela screamed. "One more bottle for you is one less for the poor, weak child who will have none. Maybe one day that child will pity you – if you're lucky!" She spat in Gulig's face.

The guards dragged Kaela down the hall, screaming. "Let me go, you beasts! Let me go! Don't you touch my cousin!" Kaela screeched before Gulig's door slammed shut. One guard pulled open a door that lead to a winding staircase, dragging Kaela behind him; the other guard shoved her from behind until they reached a rough wooden door with a heavy iron handle at the top of the stairs.

Kaela envisioned iron shackles along the walls, whips and instruments of torture. But when the door creaked open, an altogether different living arrangement greeted her eyes.

The guards pushed her inside. "Gulig wants you to get cleaned up for tonight," one man said, "You better calm down before he sees you again. Don't try anything stupid." Without a second glance, the guards slammed the door behind them.

Kaela stood in a small round room in a tower of the castle. Even though she'd always dreamed of living in a tower room, this place offered her absolutely no comfort. She longed for the safety of her own blue bedroom at home.

A large red-haired doll sat on the bed, gawking at Kaela with unblinking blue eyes. Revolted by the sight of the thick green vines painted up and down its arms, Kaela snatched the doll, heaved it onto the floor, and the eyes fluttered closed as the doll lay prone.

Kaela searched the room for some means of escape. She ran to the only window and looked outside. She was high above the ground – it was too far to jump. There was no escape.

Outraged by her interaction with Gulig, Kaela paced the room and then kicked the doll. She threw a hairbrush and comb across the room, ripped the silk coverlet off the bed, and screamed, "I'll find a way!!!" But then exhaustion washed over her. She stood in the middle of the room and realized she was completely alone. There was no one to help her and nowhere she could go. Then, like a metal ball spinning down an endless dark hole, hope vanished. What more could Kaela do? Gulig had won.

Kaela sank to the floor. Wave after wave of sadness washed through her. Imprisoned in her grief, Kaela remembered her mother's illness – how she'd fought so hard for her life. But despite her struggles, no one could stop her death. Kaela couldn't save her mother – and she couldn't save herself. During that painful time, her father was often worn out by caring for her mother and frequently shuffled Kaela off to Shawn's house. Kaela had yearned for her parents' attention more than ever before, but found herself isolated and alone.

Long buried, painful memories continued to surface. After the funeral, endless streams of people dressed in black leaned down to hug her. Again and again they said, "I'm so sorry for your loss, I'm so sorry for your loss." *What a stupid thing to say*, Kaela had thought. She had lost things before – losing meant maybe you'd get it back. But her mother was gone forever.

Someone pounded on the door.

"Remember to get cleaned up," the man yelled. "Gulig is adopting you tonight. Be sure you're ready. He says to tell you that your dress is hanging in the closet. Whatever you do, don't keep him waiting."

The harsh sound of the man's voice reawakened the flame of rage in Kaela's belly, but her concern for Shawn's safety overrode her impulse to scream. Instead she said, "Okay, okay, I hear you."

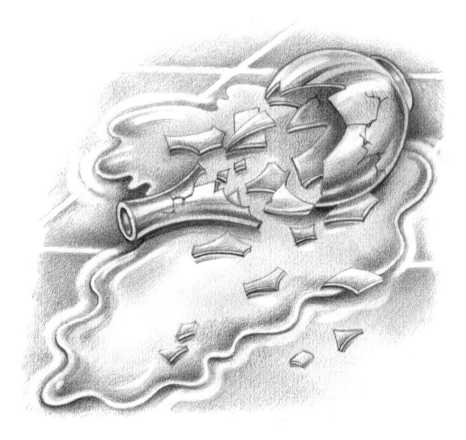

Chapter Twenty - Three · The Thief

Still safely hidden under the bed, Zeke listened to the uproar in the hallway. He slipped out from his hiding spot and cracked open the door to King Lorendale's bedroom, peering into the hallway. When he was certain that everyone was focused on Gulig and Kaela, Zeke crept out and, flattening himself along the edge of the hall, crept away silently, hiding in dark corners, behind marble statues and among the vines that curled and cascaded along the walls.

"Polish them till they shine!!" Gulig screamed.

An image of Shawn and the baby flashed through Zeke's mind as he flew to the end of the hall and up the metal stairs. His fingers turned the prize he had picked from Gulig's pocket over and over in his hand.

There was no guard in sight as Zeke fumbled with the stolen key ring, testing one key after another until one finally turned in the lock.

After slamming the door behind him, Zeke panted.

"Shawn, we have work to do."

Shawn and Anya stood up at the slamming door and the sudden words.

"Welcome, boy," Anya said casually, as if she had been expecting him. "Do you have a plan?"

"Yes, ma'am - you and the baby should stay here. Time is short," Zeke said, looking at Shawn. "Shawn, come with me - we have to help Kaela."

"Who are you? Why should I trust you?" Shawn frowned, crossing his arms against his chest.

"I came here with Kaela. I followed you both from the Grandmother

Tree. Gulig has Kaela – we need to rescue her." Zeke smiled and held up the keys. "I stole these. Gulig will not be happy when he finds out. We should move quickly."

"What about Anya and Eiren?" Shawn asked, still not convinced.

"Do not be worrying, Shawn," Anya soothed him. "We are safe here for now. I knew the Great Spirit would send help."

"Won't someone see us?" Shawn asked, remembering Gulig's threats.

"Don't worry Shawn; they're all busy because of Kaela. She's putting up quite a fight." The young boy grinned. "I think there's still time, but we've gotta go *now*."

Zeke grabbed Shawn's hand and yanked him out the door. They slammed the door behind them and scampered down the stairs. Peeper nestled under Shawn's shirt and clutched on for dear life as they raced down to the basement.

"Where ... where are we going?" Shawn asked breathlessly.

"I saw something. I think it's a good plan. We need to find the room where they store the drink," Zeke called, trying one door after another. Shawn shrugged, and joined him.

When they heard steps in the hall, they hid behind open doors and in the shadows. Shawn remembered where some of the doorways led, and steered them away from the kitchen and the laundry. They ran past the servants' living quarters, and they came to a heavy door with two sets of locks.

Zeke whispered, "I think this is it!"

Key after key failed to move in the lock. Zeke knitted his brow, even more determined, until finally one lock – then the other – turned. Zeke closed the door behind them, and an intense bitter smell overwhelmed the boys, forcing them to stop and calm their heaving stomachs.

"Shawn, it's time to be strong," Zeke said, breathing shallowly through his mouth to avoid the stench.

Shawn stared at the rows of large bottles with corks sticking out the top. "Listen, Zeke, what've you got in mind?"

"This is the drink that makes them strong – the ganba. And this is the water from the Butterfly Women. When we add a drop or two, it changes everything. I saw Kaela do it earlier."

Shawn quickly calculated the most efficient system, and instructed, "Okay then, I'm gonna take the corks out of this whole row. You run along behind me and add the drops. Then we'll do the next row."

At first Shawn and Zeke worked quietly and carefully but then, gripped with a sudden euphoria, giggles rose from their bellies like bubbles blown into the air. Delighted with their joy, Peeper tested his wings, discovered he could fly again, and fluttered wildly around the room, landing here and there on the edges of the bottles. Each time that Shawn or Zeke caught a glimpse of each other, their laughter erupted until they doubled over. Their stomachs ached with delight. Uncertain what evoked their continuous laughter, the boys gave into the feeling, and soon everything became hilarious. All the while they ran up and down the rows, uncorking and corking the bottles, and a beautiful fragrance perfumed the room as droplets of the healing water transformed the ganba.

Zeke's laughter stopped abruptly as he stared vacantly into space.

"What is it Zeke?" Shawn asked anxiously, wondering if the boy had gone into a fit.

The door rattled. "We're about to get caught," Zeke yelled, "Hide." The heavy door creaked as it flew open.

"What?" Shawn gasped as Zeke disappeared behind a row of bottels a few rows away from Shawn. Shawn mimicked Zeke, and fell to his knees.

"What's going on in here?" A man yelled. "Who's here?" The sound of heavy boots on the stone floor slowly made its way up and down the aisles between the huge bottles of ganba.

Curling against himself with his knees pressed to his chest, Shawn pushed the rim of his glasses up his nose while tightly closing his eyes.

A shadow fell across Shawn, and a deep familiar voice demanded, "How'd you get out? You better open your eyes and answer me."

Shawn opened his eyes to find Stennan's large, angry figure towering above him. Shawn mumbled, "Well, uhm, I just opened the door. It wasn't locked, and, uhm, I was hungry."

"This room is always kept locked. Don't lie to me, boy," Stennan growled.

"Well sir, it *was* unlocked," Shawn said, speaking with all the indignation he could muster.

"Stand up. Do you hear me? Stand up," the Rugu man ordered, and patted his hands up and down Shawn's shirt and pants.

Crouched alone in a corner, Zeke's heart thumped loudly against his chest. He looked at Peeper, whose head was pulled deeply into his breast.

"You trying to get me in trouble?" Stennan said, glaring at Shawn. "Sit there and don't move." A muffled sigh escaped Stennan's lips and he quickly popped open a bottle of ganba. With one move he hoisted it up and tilted the bottle over his mouth. Stennan's Adam's apple bopped up and down as he chugged the blue-green elixir. He shoved the bottle back in place and wiped his mouth with the back of his hand. "If Gulig finds out you were in here..." Stennan said shaking Shawn's shoulders. "Don't tell anyone about this drink. Do you understand me, boy?"

"Yes-s-s-s." Shawn tried to agree, but with Stennan shaking him, Shawn's teeth clacked together. It sounded like he was rolling down a bumpy hill as he spoke.

Zeke's legs had fallen asleep. Afraid he would topple over if he didn't increase his circulation, he slowly stretched his left leg. He rubbed the painful prickles, lost his balance, and fell with a crash into a row of bottles of ganba. Zeke had no choice. He leapt up and shot across the room.

"Stop!" Stennan yelled. "Stop where you are!" Stennan threw Shawn over his shoulder and bolted towards Zeke.

Blood rushed into Shawn's head as he bounced against Stennan's back.

Even carrying Shawn's weight, the Rugu's long stride easily outpaced Zeke's short legs.

"How did you get in here?" Stennan demanded, blocking the door. He stood Shawn beside Zeke and faced them both. "Which one of you opened this door?"

"Not me," Zeke looked up with wide eyes.

Shawn kept his eyes averted so as not to give anything away. After following Zeke on the wild mission, it startled Shawn to see how young and small Zeke actually was, especially compared with the large Rugu man. Shawn noticed something else as he glanced back and forth between Zeke and Stennan. Zeke looked so much like Stennan that it was easy to see what Zeke would look like as a grownup. Stennan and Zeke had the same pale green eyes and broad shoulders of all the Rugus, but they also had jet-black hair, the same eyebrow arch, and square faces. Even the way they stood was the same, with their feet slightly turned out.

"It must have been you." Stennan looked befuddled and mumbled to himself. "But how could a kid break in here?" He stared hard at Zeke and frowned. "I know what's going on here. You wanted to get a little extra ganba for yourself, didn't you? Who helped you? Which other Rugu is sneaking in here? Tell me the truth and you won't get in trouble."

"Uh, uhm, yes, sir. I mean, it was open." Zeke said, blushing and clutching the keys in his fist with his hand jammed in his pocket.

"Listen boy," Stennan noticeably softened, leaned over and clasped Zeke's shoulders. "I know what it's like to be hungry and have nothing. I've been in your shoes and if you're lucky Gulig will take you in like he did me. But if he finds out about this kind of thing, you'll end up in the dungeon."

"Yes, sir."

"You know the punishment for stealing the sacred drink, don't you?" Stennan said with a harsh note in his voice once again. Without any warning, Stennan swept Shawn and Zeke under each of his arms like two potato sacks. They bobbled up and down and glanced at one another, but didn't dare say a word.

Stennan mumbled something and spun around toward the back of the room. Then the Rugu put the boys down, clutching both of their wrists in one giant hand. He opened a cabinet lined with rows of crystal bottles, each filled with brilliantly colored blue-green elixir.

"Here boy, you carry this." Stennan shoved a bottle into Zeke's hands. "This is Gulig's special brew. You wouldn't want to anger him, would you?" Stennan said, glaring at Zeke.

These bottles of ganba had not been transformed, Shawn realized. Gulig's ganba remained potently infused with the slow but sure poison.

Zeke clutched the bottle of ganba in both hands as Stennan carried them out of the room, hoping that he wouldn't end up in the notorious Rugu prison. Shawn looked back, searching for Peeper, but the tiny parrot sat alone in a corner of the room, plaintively *cheep*ing as the key turned firmly in the lock.

At the end of the basement hall, Stennan grabbed the bottle of ganba from Zeke, tossed him out a side door like a bag of old garbage, and said, "I don't want to see you around here again. Understand?"

Zeke nodded and ran off.

After slamming the door, Stennan flew up the iron stairs with Shawn still clutched under his arm.

"What are you doing with that boy?" A sentry demanded as he walked towards Stennan. He lowered his voice and confided, "Someone's stolen Gulig's keys. He's infuriated. You heard anything?"

The sentry stared at Shawn's upside-down face. Shawn's heart beat hard against his chest. What would Stennan say? *Would he end up in prison after all?*

"How would I know about Gulig's keys?" Stennan replied evenly.

"Well, someone's in big trouble."

Stennan sighed, "I better get this ganba to Gulig. That should calm him down. I was just teaching this boy a lesson. Gulig didn't want him in the prison, but I thought I'd give him a little tour of the dungeon, just so he'd know where he'd be heading if he caused any trouble."

The guard nodded and chuckled. "Well, watch your step," he warned. "Gulig's in another of his moods."

Stennan unlocked the door and threw Shawn back inside the nursery with Anya and Eiren.

"Well, Shawn?" Anya asked.

"I guess we'll see. But for sure, Gulig's ganba hasn't been changed."

Zeke scurried to the nearby forest and sat against a rock, trying to calm himself, but his heart fluttered in his chest. He closed his eyes, grasping for a vision – for some clarity, an indication of how to proceed – but all he saw was the Rugu man's face imprinted in his mind.

PART THREE
To Promises Fulfilled

Chapter Twenty - Four • The Truth

Kaela paced back and forth in her tower prison, trying to release the rage that burned inside her belly. *Why is it so easy to feel angry? Is this what ganba does to you?* But she hadn't actually drunk any ganba. *What am I doing wrong? Am I becoming a Rugu?* She peered at her arm, dismayed to find the vines had inched even higher.

There had to be something she could do to counteract the poison. Kaela fumbled and tore at the ties that fastened the leather bag to her waist, remembering that Clouda had told her the nuts contained the strength of a tree. But the poison coursing through her veins made her hands tremble with fury. "This stupid thing!" Kaela yelled. "Why do they have to make it so hard!"

Kaela sat heavily on the bed and took a few deep breaths to calm down. She tried again to untie the bag. This time she moved more slowly and patiently, until the last knot finally untangled. She shook out the contents, spilling the special nuts, the whistle and the little book from Netri onto the bed. Kaela gripped two nuts in her fist, cracked the shells against each other and eagerly ate the bits of nutmeat.

Kaela ached for Wollan's company and longed to know the loyal dog was safe. She grabbed the silent whistle and blew hard against the metal tube. She knew that Wollan would respond if he could. Outside, the wind howled through the trees. She wrapped her hand tightly around the butterfly pendant and heard the faintest sound – as though someone was calling to her. She stuck her head out the window, listening carefully. Was it? Could it be? It seemed that Wollan's howl was carried to her by the wind. She clutched the pendant in her fist.

"Be brave, red-haired girl," she heard distantly. "Be brave. You are never alone." Kaela imagined Wollan's furry head on her lap. A tear fell from her eye and the love in her heart freed her for that moment from the rage that threatened to destroy her.

Behind the wooden screen that stood in one corner, Kaela found a metal tub filled with warm water and a silk nightgown hanging from a hook. Desperate to wash away her pain and grief, and the exertions of her long and exhausting journey, Kaela slipped out of her filthy clothes and sank into the water. It reminded her of her time with Janani, soaking in the hot springs behind the Butterfly Women's cottage.

Kaela thought of Ariala's words, "Love goes deeper than skin, flesh or bone, Kaela. It is the great healer." She thought of her love for Kanu and Shawn. Kaela examined her right arm and, for the moment, could see no sign of the vines growing.

Then she dried herself, pulled the silk nightgown over her head, and plopped down on the bed, tired but unable to sleep.

Remembering the diary, Kaela hurried to read about the red-haired girl from long, long ago. She held the magnifying glass over one of the final pages as the light outside from her small window dimmed, and read:

23ʳᵈ Day of Ogronnean (My Eighteenth Birthday)

The man I am contracted to marry, Golan, came to our home yesterday. I begged my dear friend Zarenda to accompany me to the meeting. I was so nervous that I really wanted her support. Even though she prefers to keep to herself, she agreed for my sake. I helped her prepare her hair and face, and dressed her in one of my favorite gowns.

Golan waited for us in the drawing room downstairs. I introduced Zarenda as my younger sister, and the moment we entered the room his eyes followed Zarenda's face. I don't know why I had never before noticed her to be a striking beauty.

A stack of presents sat by his feet and, although they were meant as gifts for me, each time he shook the contents he exclaimed, "I think this one is best suited for the beautiful Princess Zarenda."

He even said, "Perhaps I should marry you instead, Princess Zarenda."

He barely glanced in my direction the whole evening and, when he did, he had nothing but scorn for me. Even though he was handsome, I thought him to be the rudest person I had ever met. I realized there was no way we could be happily married if he thought so little of me.

I stormed out and raced to the stables, saddling my favorite mare. I rode away from the castle and into the dark night, my heart tormented. How could my mother do this to me? How could she promise me to such a horrible person?

    Gwenilda

3rd Day of Cutean

I don't even know how to begin to write about what took place this evening. Even now, my tears smear the ink as I write. I didn't think my situation could be any worse, but I was wrong. It's almost too awful for words.

My mother, father and Eirendale, my beloved brother, came into my room this evening, with Netri following close behind them. They looked so solemn that a jolt of fear erupted in my heart.

I sat on my bed with my brother beside me. My parents drew chairs close to the bed. My mother looked afraid and terribly sad, and my father gazed at my brother and me with great kindness. Netri stood by their side with his ever-changing face.

"There is something I must tell all of you," my mother hesitantly began, "It is something that I should have told you years ago, but I was too ashamed. Now, I hope it is not too late – you deserve to know. Before you grew in my belly, Gwenilda, I had been unable to bring a baby to term. Distraught, I went to the seer, Zella, for help. Zella was Zarenda's mother."

I assumed my father knew the story, but when I saw his eyebrows raise and the way he searched my mother's face to understand her words, I knew this story was new to him as well.

My mother continued, "Zella agreed to help me on one condition, that my first-born daughter would wed the Rugu

Prince."

"I don't understand," I said. "I thought that you and father didn't agree to the marriage until after I first met Golan – when I was a little girl."

"Yes, I made it seem that way. I never told either of you the truth – that I made this agreement before you were born."

"But..."

"Please, Gwenilda, let me finish," my mother said, near tears. "I hope to explain so you will understand why, and not hate me for it. First and foremost, I wanted a child; I wanted you so badly, darling. The seer told me she didn't believe a Butterfly Woman and a human could have healthy children, but said she'd try to intervene on my behalf. She didn't want her own daughter to marry the Rugu boy, saying that her daughter would be unfit for the royal life, so she promised to help me – if I agreed to the marriage. She promised there would be peace if you married Golan. Once I agreed to accept her help, she told me there would be a curse on this family if my daughter didn't marry Golan."

Eirendale and I looked at each other. I wondered what would happen to him. Would he be harmed if I didn't keep the contract?

I struggled to make sense of my mother's words and asked, "So, if I end the contract there would be a curse – even though Golan doesn't have a shred of love for me?"

I turned towards my beloved father, watching for his response. Sadness and anger passed across his face as he listened to my mother. Then, overcoming his anger, he wrapped his arm around my mother's shoulders. "Please, Gwenilda," he began quietly, "Sit and listen to what I have to say. Your mother is the kindest person I know. She would never want to hurt you. I see that she has carried the burden of this secret for many years." He looked at my mother and gently asked, "Did you think that I would be angry with you?"

Tears streamed down my mother's face "I don't know," she answered shyly. "At first I didn't know how to tell you. Then, as the years passed, I felt ashamed to have kept the secret from you *for so long."*

He kissed her on the forehead and continued, "Gwenilda, I pray that you will never feel the loss and longing that your mother faced after her first two babies died. I can assure you that your mother did what she did out of a deep and profound love. Gwenilda, my dearest, I am setting you free from your bond. You do not have to marry that Rugu boy. I do not blame you for your anger. Your mother and I have made a terrible mistake. Before your birth I knew that the Rugus were planning a war. I knew they lusted after our land. Your marriage contract only delayed the inevitable. It is time now. We will fight them."

Instead of relief flooding my veins when he released me from the contract, an even greater burden weighed on me – the knowledge that the safety of my people – and of my future children – rested on my shoulders. I knew that my father meant every word he said, but now the horrible decision was mine alone.

I have never told either of my parents about the yearning in my heart for the boy on the other side of the hole in the sky. Perhaps if they knew of the strength of this priceless love I hold so deeply in my heart, they would not leave this decision solely to me. Witnessing the abiding love my parents share, longing swelled in my heart to know such love in my own life – but I fear it is not meant to be.

"It is very difficult for me to tell you this, my Queen," Netri stepped forward and said, "but Zella lied to you. She did nothing to help you have a child. You were carrying a healthy baby when you went to see her."

My mother looked at him as though she could not comprehend his words. After a moment of quiet, she replied, "What ... what do you mean, Netri? Of course Zella helped me. I did as she said, and she helped change my future."

"No, my Queen. You already carried Gwenilda safely within your belly when you went to see her. I believe that Zella lied to you to protect her own daughter – Zarenda."

By this time all traces of daylight had vanished, and, except for the glimmer of a single candle, darkness filled the room. Then

I saw a glint of gold as someone slipped from the room. It was Zarenda. She had been hiding behind a chair and had heard every word of her mother's betrayal of my family, of the contract and of the curse. With their backs to the door, neither my mother nor my father noticed Zarenda's exit.

My mother frowned and said, "Whatever do you mean, Netri? How do you know?"

I watched Netri. His face, which usually melted and shifted from the face of a young being to that of a wise old man, became fixed to that of a young man. "I remember the day you went to see Zella." He added thoughtfully – "If I had known the purpose of your visit, I would have revealed to you what I saw."

"What did you see, Netri?" My mother asked anxiously.

"I saw Gwenilda's spirit, laughing and dancing around your head. She was so excited to know she would soon be playing in this world. She could hardly wait to smell the flowers and feel the wind upon her face."

"And what did you see with my first two children ... the ones who died?" my mother, the Queen asked.

"My Lady, your first two babies clung to the Great Sprit like children unwilling to attend their first day of school, too shy to play hide-and-seek. In His Wisdom, the Great Spirit decided it was not yet time for them to receive the gift of life."

"How could I not have noticed?" she wailed.

"I am afraid you were wrapped so tightly in grief that you left no chamber in your heart for the joy of possible new life to enter." Netri crossed to comfort my mother.

Tears streamed down my mother's face. "I am so very, very sorry, my dear Gwenilda."

Seeing the agony on my mother's face, I felt no anger or sadness, but only a strong desire to comfort her. I sobbed and wrapped her in my arms.

When I released my embrace, my mother's face brightened for a moment. "What of the contract?" my mother asked, turning to my father. "Zella lied, so the contract can't possibly be valid."

My father answered, "I am afraid that, whether Zella lied to you or not, the Rugus still hold the wedding contract; but in my eyes, Gwenilda, you are free to do as you choose."

I don't know why I said what I did, but I felt in my heart that it was the right choice. "Father, I know I do not owe anything, but one day I will be Queen of these lands. You have kept me by your side so that one day I can be a great Queen. I see the kindness and care you have for the people of this land. I must choose the well being of my people over my own happiness. I choose to fulfill the agreement. I will marry Golan, and we will have peace."

My father gazed at me with a look of love and respect in his eyes. "My beloved Gwenilda," he said, "you are truly a great leader."

My mother embraced me and I felt the wetness of her tears against my cheek. She rocked me in her arms, murmuring over and over, "My beautiful baby, my beautiful baby, I'm so sorry...."

Somehow, Diary, I must find the courage to face my destiny. I must someday rule these lands, and there is so much at stake. I cannot put my people in harm's way.

Gwenilda

5th Day of Cutean

The wedding is in two days and, as a gesture of peace, my entire family has traveled to the northern castle to meet the Rugus half way. I am so far from the hole in the sky that there is no way to ride off to see my beloved one last time. The Rugu men are camped outside the castle and have completely surrounded the perimeter, seeming more like sentries than welcomed guests.

The look on Netri's and my mother's faces frightened me when they arrived in my room this evening.

"What is it?" I asked, "What is wrong?"

"My dearest, I know that you wish to keep the wedding contract for the sake of your people," my mother replied. "But we have learned terrible things about the Rugu man who is to be your husband. It would be a tragedy for you to spend your life with him, and an even greater travesty to have him as ruler of this land."

"We cannot allow Golan any more sway over our land,"

Netri continued, resolute. "On the way to the wedding, his men committed numerous terrible atrocities in our kingdom. They stormed through villages – stealing and destroying everything in their path. Golan even kidnapped a young Tree Woman, the daughter of the Chief of the Tree People. After doing her terrible harm, Golan left her for dead under a pile of leaves. You see what kind of man he is? This wedding cannot take place."

"Won't there be a war?" I asked, trying to calm the thoughts in my brain.

"Yes, I am certain they will fight us for you," Netri answered. "We must sneak you out of the castle, although I am afraid that Prince Golan will not rest until he finds you."

"What about Mother's promise? And the contract?" I asked, still trying to weigh the possibilities.

"We must break our promises," my mother responded with conviction – "both to Zella and to King Grule. We have no choice."

"Our only chance to get you out of here safely is to trick the Rugus," my mother continued. "They are powerful warriors and we must, therefore, use the element of surprise. The Chief of the Tree People is nearly identical in height to you. After the harm that Golan did to his daughter, he is eager to fight the Rugus, and to help you escape. He has volunteered to dress up as the bride. He will wear your hair as a wig and cover himself with the traditional wedding garments, but he will carry something else with him. He plans to have a dagger by his side – to begin a war."

I closed my eyes as Netri collected the strands my mother carefully cut from my hair. As my hair fell away from my head, my neck showed bare – revealing the truth. The Butterfly mark appeared in clear view.

"Gwenilda," my mother gasped. "You have the butterfly on the back of your neck. But – you are human. How is this possible? Have you been going through the hole in the sky?"

"Yes, mother," I sighed. "Ever since I was a little girl, the ocean evoked a deep longing in my heart. It was as though something in the water called to me. One day the wind carried the scent of the ocean to my bedroom. The call was so strong that I rode my mare into the waves, and the turtles took me to the hole in the sky. I found myself on my hands and knees in another world, in a tiny dark chamber. Searching for light, I crawled out of the room into a larger room. A young man lay in his bed with his eyes closed. He moaned slightly as his breath slowly moved in and out of his body, making a loud rasping sound."

"When I gazed at him, love and kindness welled up in my heart. Kneeling by the side of his bed, I gently stroked his fingers and lay my hand on his forehead. His breathing returned to normal. I stayed with him a moment more and my heart opened, like a beautiful red rose. It was as if we shared one giant heart between us, a still pond to nourish both of our shores."

"That boy helped me discover my healing gifts – my Butterfly blood. From then on, I could no longer resist the call of the ocean. With every person I helped, the butterfly on my neck grew."

"But there is something else. I visited that young man again and again. At first he was very ill, but now he is healed. Every time I arrive in his room my heart explodes with joy. We are in love. He even asked me to marry him."

My mother stared at me, aghast.

"And you were going to go through with this marriage to Golan, regardless?" she asked quietly.

"Oh yes, Mother – but that's past, now. I can hardly wait for you to meet him. My beloved is kind and handsome – he has promised to provide for me. I would continue my healing work, and he is eager to have children...."

Tears dripped down my mother's cheeks as she said, "But ... don't you understand ... don't you know?"

"Know what, mother?"

"Once a Butterfly Woman marries a human, she is no longer able to travel between our worlds. Do you realize that marrying him means leaving us forever?"

"But..." I said desperately, unable to describe to her the fullness of my love, and yet terrified of leaving my family forever.

"Your father and I will never see you again – we will never

hold our grandchildren...." My mother began to cry, silently.

I looked down. Grief collected in my throat, making it difficult to speak. "I did not know," I whispered.

"You do not have to leave here. We will hide you from Golan and protect you from the Rugus. You must understand, Gwenilda, when you take your body with you to the other world, it is all too easy to forget from where you've come. Our world will become like a beautiful dream to you. It means giving up more than you know."

"No. I promise I will remember you," I cried, unable to give up my dream for a life of hiding and secrecy. "I will remember all of you."

Then I looked deeply into my mother's beautiful blue eyes and in that moment we both knew that my decision had already been made. We both knew that I would leave to be with my beloved.

Wrapping her arm around my shoulder, my mother wiped my tears as though I was a small child. "Of course you will, my darling," she comforted me. "Of course you will."

"Tell me the truth, Mother. What did the seer tell you? What will happen if I do not keep the contract?"

"Every time I see Zarenda I remember her mother's words to me: 'if your girl does not marry the Rugu prince, you will bring a curse on the King's family. It will be the beginning of the end. The curse will not be broken until King Grule's descendants secure a red-haired girl from the House of Muraten,'" Mother said.

"But she lied...."

"Yes, Gwenilda, she lied. But the Rugus are a vengeful tribe." Netri said with a look of sadness on his face. "I am quite certain they will not rest until the contract is fulfilled."

"But what about my brother? What about dear Eirendale? What if he has a girl-child?"

Netri said, "The Rugus will claim her...."

"Mother, how can I risk the lives of my brother's and my future children?" I asked desperately. "Isn't there some other way?"

"Only to not have children," my mother said, giving me a small smile. "Do not worry, darling. Love can overcome even the worst difficulty. Go and embrace your chance for happiness. My dear child, if you love this boy and he loves you, you will find absolute safety in the other world."

Netri looked deeply into me and I felt the ache in my heart – the painful tear ripping my heart in two, as though someone tore a hole in my heart.

Gwenilda

6th Day of Cutean

Zarenda asked for a moment alone with me. She told me that I had been like a sister to her, and then her voice softened until I strained to hear her words. "I am going to find a way to marry Golan."

I started to speak, but she placed her hand over my mouth and said, "Before you try to stop me, please listen."

I nodded and she continued, "I can fulfill the contract that your family has with King Grule. Golan thinks that I am your little sister. He told me that he is quite taken with me."

I cried, "No, Zarenda, don't be a fool. That man has no love for you. Haven't you heard about the poor Tree girl – what he did to her? Please, Zarenda, please. He will only break your heart."

Outraged by my statement, she said, "How can you be so selfish, Gwenilda? This is my chance for happiness. This is my chance...."

We argued back and forth and, after some time, I saw it would not be possible to dissuade her. I smiled, but the tears poured from my eyes as I said, "Please, dear Zarenda, if I cannot change your mind, then at least please take my dresses. You will be a truly beautiful princess."

Zarenda took the necklace from around her neck and removed a purple crystal from the chain. She placed the crystal in my palm, and said, "When I first arrived here, your mother had this made into a necklace for me. Before that my mother, Zella, gave it to your mother. I want you to have it. Let it remind you of our friendship."

I was deeply touched. Ever since we were tiny children, she had worn it around her neck – even when she slept.

We both wept and embraced. I am afraid for my beloved friend, but nothing can dissuade her from this course of action. I hope and pray that her future is bright and filled with love and joy, but ... I am afraid to even put this on paper.... I fear for her heart ... and her life.

Gwenilda.

7th Day of Cutean

My brother came in to say goodbye and I said, "Please, Eirendale, forgive me for this terrible burden."

He smiled sadly and said, "Don't worry, dear sister, the Great Spirit will see to it that I have many strong sons." My father entered the room weeping and hugged me goodbye. Then my mother and Netri held me in their arms. There was a gentle knock and Zarenda entered my room.

"My sister. I will miss you." She smiled with tears in her eyes.

"Remember a happy time, Gwenilda," Netri prompted me. "Your happiness will take you where you need to go. I have created a hidden opening for you through the back of your closet. It leads to the caves that will take you to the Butterfly Women. From there you will find easy passage to the hole in the sky."

This is my last entry. In a few minutes I will leave my home forever. My father asked me to keep my life in this world a secret – so that my daughters would never come back. My family is going to pretend I have died. They are even planning my funeral. The thought makes me weep buckets of tears. But he is right – the Rugus would never forget the contract – not after a million years. We all hope fervently that my brother never has a red-haired daughter of his own. Before I finally left, Netri held my hand and called me by my childhood nickname – Wyndy. I kissed his cheek, crying for all that I will lose.

I will ask him to keep my diary, and to keep it a secret, so that the girl who would one day bear the burden of this curse would know the truth of what took place.

This book is for your eyes alone, dear daughter. Please forgive me for placing you in this terrible situation. I know that you have a beautiful strong heart and will find a way to end the hatred and anger that are sure to result from my breaking the contract. One day I pray you will know true love in your life, and will understand why I have made this difficult decision.

I looked out my window for the last time tonight. The sun had already set, and on the horizon there was a bank of bright red clouds. The sky was a beautiful shade of blue – the perfect blue. Above the horizon I could see a sprinkling of golden stars.

Tonight I will go through the hole in the sky for the last time.

Wyndy

Kaela hugged the little diary to her chest, her eyes wide with realizations. Gwenilda went through the hole in the sky and never came back. Gwenilda was her great-grandmother.

Chapter Twenty - Five • Help

Billowing clouds covered the dark sky, masking all traces of moonlight, and the air was thick with electricity as thunder rumbled in the distance. Lightning flashed in the tiger's green eyes, illuminating his presence at the edge of the forest for only a fraction of a second. Cloaked in darkness, he remained undetected by the men who guarded the perimeter.

Kanu's wound had ripped open again and again on his arduous journey, forcing him to stop and gather his strength. But now he had Gulig's castle in his sight, and when he got up again, nothing would stop him. Human silhouettes darkened the windows. Kanu remained still and hidden, alert for the perfect moment to attack. He would wait for his opponent to reveal its soft underbelly. For now, Kanu conserved his energy.

The crying wind carried a vibration that perked Kanu's ears. Deep in the castle someone called over and over again, "Be brave red-haired girl. Be brave. I love you. Don't be afraid."

Seeing no sign of the red-haired girl, Kanu could only hope that the comforting words somehow reached Kaela's ears.

There was a gentle knock on the door and a key turned with a *thunk* in the lock.

Kaela woke with a start. How long had she been sleeping? The window revealed a pitch-dark sky. Kaela sat up and watched the door slowly open. She shuddered at the thought of another Rugu soldier, but she was prepared to do whatever she could to resist Gulig.

A woman peeked in, her face dark in the shadow of the doorway. "Can I come in? I brought you some food."

Kaela shook her head, but didn't say a word.

The door swung open and a broad shouldered Rugu woman entered, carrying a tray. "Why are you sitting in the dark? I'll just light this lamp for you."

The woman placed the tray on a table by the bed. Steam rose from a bowl, carrying a familiar friendly smell to Kaela's nose, and her stomach instantly responded with gurgles and growls. The woman struck a match and held it to the wick. The golden light illuminated the woman's haggard face and mousy-brown hair, streaked with gray, knotted in a bun at her neck. Dark circles under her eyes made her seem old and very tired. Kaela's heart softened to see the obvious fatigue on the woman's face.

"Stennan sent me here. He wants me to help you get dressed. Gulig will be calling for you soon. He has a grand ceremony planned for you. You're going to need some food."

Kaela turned away. The woman seemed nice enough, but she didn't trust the Rugus. They were probably trying to feed her ganba.

The woman sat down next to Kaela and touched her chin. "Don't be afraid. You're going to be a princess. You know how many girls wish they were in your shoes?" The woman motioned with her hand around the room. "Look at all the beautiful things Gulig's gathered for you."

Staring off into the distance, Kaela said, "I like the dad I've already got."

"Where is he? I don't see him here with you," the woman chided.

"He'd come rescue me in a minute if he could. Gulig is just adopting me so he can be King. Gulig doesn't care a hoot about me."

"Well, whatever Gulig wants he usually gets, so we may as well get started. My name's Nedra."

Kaela set her mouth in a firm line, refusing once again to have anything to do with the woman.

"Alright, then, have it your way. Maybe I'll make up a name for you if you won't give me one. Why don't you eat a bit of porridge while I get your dress?" She placed the bowl in Kaela's hands, but Kaela shook her head, refusing to eat, even though her stomach responded with a strong rumble.

Nedra giggled, "I guess your stomach has a mind of its own."

Kaela wrinkled her nose even as her belly roared loudly.

"I had this made special for you. I heard you were sick earlier."

The fierce hunger pangs in Kaela's stomach drove her to sniff the bowl. It was oatmeal with strawberries, and she could detect none of the bitter smell of ganba. She took a spoonful and nibbled a tiny morsel. She held it in her mouth and, once she was certain there was not ganba in it, she ate hungrily, relishing every bite.

Nedra walked to a wooden armoire in the corner. She discreetly looked back at Kaela, smiling. She pulled out a white silk dress that sparkled with silver threads woven into the fabric. "This looks like the one." The woman clucked. "Just look at this silk – and all that embroidery! Someone worked really hard on this dress."

"I don't care how pretty it is," Kaela grumped with her mouth full as Nedra returned to her side. "It's all just for show. I'll never be his daughter. Never."

Nedra took the now empty bowl from Kaela and said, "Well, why don't you stand up and take off that nightgown, I'll just put this over your head."

Kaela did as she was told, knowing it was pointless to resist. Nedra stood behind and slipped the dress over Kaela's back. "I just need to fasten the buttons." She divided Kaela's hair in halves and gently pushed the long strands over Kaela's shoulders.

Kaela expected Nedra's touch to be rough, but she was actually careful and tender.

"Now, let's see about your hair." Nedra went to the dresser and muttered, "Well, now where did it go?" She looked back at Kaela with a puzzled expression.

Kaela had been happy to make things difficult for the woman, but again noting the woman's stiff gait and obvious fatigue, Kaela pointed to a corner of the room and said, "It's over there on the floor."

The woman found the silver-handled brush on the floor and chuckled, "I wonder what it's doing down there? I guess someone dropped it." Then she stood behind Kaela and brushed her thick, red hair until it gleamed smooth.

"It's nice to have a young person in the castle," the woman chatted. "It's a rarity. You'll see – we'll all be doting on you now that you live here."

"Why aren't there any young people in the castle?"

"So now you'll talk to me?" Nedra teased.

Kaela nodded.

"Gulig likes things real quiet and controlled. He doesn't like the sound of laughter ... or crying. And he hates messiness."

"Well, then he picked the wrong daughter. I love to laugh, and I cry and I am totally messy."

Nedra turned Kaela around and stroked Kaela's cheek. "I think he's real lucky to have you."

Kaela smiled, shyly accepting Nedra's kindness, and then watched as a small tear fell from Nedra's eye. "Are you crying?"

"No, no, course not," the woman sniffed. "Don't you tell anyone about this!"

"Who would I tell? Come sit beside me here." Kaela sat down and patted the bed beside her. Nedra hesitated and then sat down with her hands clutched tightly in her lap. Kaela gently touched the woman's elbow. "Tell me. Why are you so sad?"

"It's just that I haven't seen my own boys for almost two years, now," Nedra sniffed. "Hadn't seen any children at all 'til that boy earlier."

"Which boy? What did he look like?" Kaela asked, thrilled that it might be Shawn.

"A skinny kid with glasses," Nedra said, surprised.

"It was Shawn. I can't believe you saw Shawn." Overcome with relief by news that Shawn was still alive, Kaela gave Nedra a brief hug. "Was he okay? Did he seem hurt or anything?"

Nedra's cheeks flushed, and small tears continued dripping down her cheeks. "He seemed fine to me. I let him take a bath in my washtub. He was a bit shy, but that was about it."

"Thank you! Thank you! Shawn is alive." Kaela wiped Nedra's tears with the hem of her skirt. "But Nedra, what about your kids? Why haven't you seen them? Where are they?"

"Well, they're big like me, so my husband enlisted them in the army. I wanted them to stay with me, but that's not the Rugu way. I guess I'm not much of a Rugu, though." The woman muttered, ashamed.

Kaela's ears perked up when she heard this, praying that she'd found a potential ally.

"Why do you say you're not much of a Rugu?" she asked.

"Well, I didn't want to give 'em the ganba," Nedra explained.

"Don't all the Rugus like ganba?" Kaela's excitement grew.

"I used to like it. Never knew there was any other way, you know? I grew up drinking it; but when my boys were in my belly, I lost the taste for it. I didn't tell my husband." Nedra stared down at her hands. "I knew he wouldn't approve. When they were born, their faces were just so open and innocent – I couldn't bear to give it to them. My husband kept lookin' at their arms, which were pure and pink as could be. He didn't know what was wrong, couldn't understand why they didn't have vines growin' in them."

"Gulig tried to tell me that Rugu children would die without the ganba." Kaela glanced at the vine markings wrapped around her right arm. She flushed, embarrassed that Nedra might think that she'd been drinking ganba.

"He's told us that myth, too," Nedra laughed without mirth, "But it's clearly not true. It's just the hate that dies is all – just the hate, and the taste for war."

"Where is your husband now?" Kaela probed.

"Oh, he left me long ago – for a real Rugu woman. He said I was no more than a big weakling. He found my boys playing with your kind – with weakling children. Oh, he was so mad. He grabbed me and scolded, 'You're not doin' your job, woman. You gotta fill these boys with hate; otherwise they'll never be able to kill the way they should.' He took 'em away from me and fed 'em more and more ganba and put 'em in the army where they'd get real discipline. It's the Rugu way. Gulig says we must be tough and make sacrifices. We're always preparing for war." Nedra fell silent for a moment, remembering.

"Even when I was getting the full dose of ganba, I couldn't stand all that hate…. I shouldn't be talkin' so much about myself," she said, shaking her head. "Gulig would be horribly angry if he knew I was talkin' to you like this."

Kaela took both of Nedra's hands in hers and gently squeezed them.

"I'm sorry," she said softly. "I don't want to get you into trouble, but I do want to thank you. I don't know why I never realized it. You're all just as much prisoners here as I am. Just because Gulig is mean, I thought you were all mean."

Sniffling against the tears, Nedra said proudly, "'Course not. Most Rugus are fine people – they only want what your people want. Lots of 'em are still mad about getting kicked out of Muratenland. That wasn't right. The ganba feeds their anger. Don't you forget it – they want a home and the means to take care of their families, same as you. They have a right to their homes. Fact is, there's lots of nice Rugus right in this castle. There are people backing you up, for sure. They're hoping you'll be fair...."

"What do you mean?" Kaela asked.

Nedra looked Kaela directly in the eyes, as if she was trying to discover something deep inside the girl. "They heard the prophecy – heard you might really be the one with a pure heart – you might be the one to treat us right." Nedra glanced at the window and said quietly, "People in the castle been whispering about you and Gulig."

"What?" Kaela asked, startled.

"Shhh. Someone could hear!" Nedra whispered. "I heard about you standing up to him and refusing to drink the ganba. It gives us strength to hear that. Gives us strength...."

Outside, the wind whistled through the trees and there was a faint sound, like metal clanking against stone.

Kaela and Nedra froze.

The color drained from Nedra's face and she held her index finger to her lips. "Shhhh, I best go." She rose and hurried to the door.

"Nedra," Kaela said quickly, before the woman could leave.

Nedra looked back at Kaela and put a finger to her lips. "Shhhhh ..."

Kaela mouthed the words, "Thank you."

A hint of a smile flitted across Nedra's face and she closed the door behind her.

Kaela thought about the woman's words. She had allies in the castle, but what did they want from her? How could she stop the adoption? Kaela stood up and the long silk dress rustled as she shuffled nervously back and forth across the small room. Thoughts about the adoption ricocheted in her mind like fistfuls of bouncing balls flung haphazardly in a small room.

She tried to breathe through her anxiety, but it was useless.

Kaela sat down and traced the throbbing vines from the dark spot where the beast had pierced her palm to the edge of the dress's elbow-length sleeves. How could she possibly have a pure heart if the vines were growing inside of her? Would they ever disappear?

Still barefoot, Kaela spied her dirty pants crumpled in a corner of the room beside her soft suede boots. She put the pants on under her dress for comfort and pulled on the boots for strength before she resumed walking back and forth. As she passed the mirror, Kaela caught a glimpse of her own face, and was momentarily startled. She looked surprisingly different from the Kaela she was used to seeing reflected back at her. Her blue eyes shone as though reflecting her own inner light, reminding her of the light she saw emanating from Ariala and Janani.

Kaela clutched the butterfly pendant in her fist. *Please show me the key – show me the butterfly breath!* She understood now that Gwenilda was her great-grandmother and that was why Kaela was the one who could break the curse, but she still didn't have the faintest idea how she would do it.

Chapter Twenty - Six - Into the Uknown

Finally free from the storeroom after a group of men arrived to collect jugs of ganba, Peeper flew up the stairs, searching for Shawn. There was no sign of his friend, so the parrot chick pumped his wings, eager to find an escape route. Three guards chased him with sticks as he flapped, batting at his tiny body. Desperate to escape, the bird's heart beat hard against his chest. When he saw a huge open doorway before him, he swooped through it and soared into the Grand Ballroom.

"You - you stupid bird! Get back here!" a guard yelled. "Oh! Ugh!" The man stopped, wiping bird droppings from his eye, and Peeper flew outdoors through an open window in the ballroom. Grumbling, the guard slammed the beveled glass panes closed and drew the heavy drapes.

Peeper coasted on the breeze, exhausted. It was dark and he was accustomed to sleeping when there was no light, but he didn't want to be alone, and he wasn't sure where to find a safe place to perch. Then he saw the dim outline of a crow sitting in a tree and spotted a boy sitting on the ground under the crow.

Cheep, cheep. Peeper nestled into Zeke's neck, relieved to find a friend. Zeke stroked the tiny bird and his mind catapulted into the future. A dreadful vision formed. A vision of life or death.

Tap, tap, tap.

Jarred by the sound, Kaela released the pendant from her hand, leaving behind the red impression of a butterfly in her palm.

Tap, tap, tap.

Kaela dreaded the arrival of Gulig's soldiers. She desperately hoped this wasn't someone who'd come to bring her to the adoption.

Tap, tap, tap.

No one entered the room. Kaela squeezed her eyes shut, hoping they would just go away.

Tap, tap, tap.

When none of Gulig's soldiers burst into the room, Kaela stood still and held her breath. She quickly realized the sound was not coming from the door.

Tap, tap, tap.

It was someone rapping on a window – but how? Kaela slowly opened one of the long windows and stuck her head outside. She shivered in the damp night air as a gust of cold wind whipped through her silk dress. Outside, thick clouds flew across the sky, masking the light of the moon. There was no one there.

She pulled closed the window frame and heard a muffled giggle. She leaned outside, looking both ways, then stifled a shriek of joy. The little Tree Girl, Tressa, and her brother, Mika, stood on tiptoes with their backs flat against the building, gracefully balanced on the ledge. They clutched the upper edge of the window and swung on it until they were able to scamper inside.

"How on earth did you get here?" Kaela asked.

"Well now, that's some kind of hello!" Tressa giggled as she twirled in circles around the room.

A tear fell down Kaela's cheek. "Oh Tressa, I'm sorry. I can't tell you how glad I am to see you here."

"I told you that you'd be needing my help," Mika said, scowling. "What is this place? What are you wearing, all silky and all – it doesn't look like you're in prison to me."

"Stop talking like that. Gulig is determined to adopt me. The whole thing is so twisted," Kaela grimaced.

Dancing around the room, Tressa pointed here and there, and said,

"Look at the dolly and all the pretty clothes. He be treating you like a princess. Maybe he really is wanting you to be his daughter."

"Sure he does." Kaela remembered her right arm and quickly hid it behind her back. "He wants to use me like he uses everyone else."

"What's going on with you?" Grabbing Kaela's right arm, Mika stared at the vines and then quickly dropped it. "So you're drinking the ganba and turning into a Greenblood!"

"I am *not* drinking ganba. I don't know why that stuff is growing in me. Would you just back off?"

"See, if you'd taken me with you, none of this would be happening to you." Mika stuck out his tongue.

"Shhh, silly," Tressa piped in. "Kaela, we've got a surprise for you."

Shaking off her irritation, Kaela asked, "What is it?"

"Come stand on the ledge. You'll be loving it," Tressa giggled and turned in a quick circle. Then she reached out her hand to Kaela.

Mika and Tressa helped Kaela as she boosted herself up and tentatively crouched on the stone ledge high above the ground.

"Lookie Mika. She's wearing the pants we gave her – she's got them under her fancy dress. This will be easy for her. Go on," Tressa instructed, "Stand up and reach out your arms. Now jump!"

"You want me to jump?" Kaela asked, frantic. The wind whipped against her body as she squinted to see in the darkness.

"I promise you'll love it. I won't be hurting you, Kaela," Tressa encouraged.

Kaela hesitated.

Mika said, "I told you she wouldn't do it."

Infuriated by Mika's put-down, Kaela ignored her fear and slowly stood, wobbling and using her extended arms for balance. She took a breath, closed her eyes and leapt into the unknown. For a timeless moment, Kaela flew in a free-fall as her dress ruffled in the cold air. Joy filled her heart. Before she could even think, she bounced in a soft bristly net. She looked around to discover that a nearby evergreen tree had bent deeply to catch her. The piney fragrance filled her nose. Delighted, Kaela rocked in the wind, reveling in her freedom.

Quickly joined by Tressa and Mika, Kaela lay across the branches, distributing her weight evenly so they wouldn't break. From this vantage point she was able to view the windows of the castle. "Have you seen any sign of Eiren and Shawn?" She asked.

"No. There's no sign of them, but we can get you out of here," Mika said.

"I'd love to leave with you – but Gulig told me that if I left, he'd kill Shawn."

"Look at that pretty room," Tressa pointed. "It looks like they're getting ready for a party."

Kaela's stomach lurched as she looked in the huge room, where servants cleaned and set up row after row of chairs underneath glowing chandeliers. "That's no party. They're getting ready for my adoption. Mika, Tressa," Kaela said softly. "Did you know Gulig captured your brothers? He has Gannon and Gavin."

Mika's face reddened. "I didn't know."

"If the soldiers discover I've escaped, Gulig will kill them – and Shawn, too. I can't risk that. I'm going to have to stand up to Gulig – not run away from him."

"I'll find a way to stop him!" Mika clenched his fists.

Kaela searched the castle windows again, hoping for a glimpse of her cousin, but Tressa and Mika were right. Shawn was nowhere to be found. Discouraged, Kaela lay down on the branch and drew comfort from the tree as she rocked in the breeze. Nothing in her wanted to return to her prison in the tower room, but what could she do? The movement of the branch suddenly reminded her of riding up and down in the ocean with the sea turtles, and she remembered Netri's advice. She sat back up and said, "Wait a minute, you guys. I just thought of something."

"What, Kaela? What? What?" Tressa asked, bouncing up and down.

"Netri told me that Gulig uses that which we fear most against us, and I'm most afraid he'll hurt Shawn. Gannon, Gavin and Shawn would want us to do everything we could possibly do to rescue Eiren."

Mika and Tressa nodded in agreement.

"I think we should try to rescue them."

"I'm ready!" Mika perked up, eager for action.

Kaela thought for a moment, formulating a plan, while Mika and Tressa kept their eyes glued on Kaela's face.

"Listen. When I was with Lorendale he said that Eiren was probably in one of the old rooms – one with a skylight. We need to get to the roof. Over there." Kaela pointed to the place where the castle met the mountainside. The roof was lower than her tower room, and if the tree bent over and they leapt from one of the highest branches they might be able to reach the roof.

"Skylight?" Tressa asked.

"I don't have time to explain." Kaela climbed from limb to limb until she was as close as possible to the roof. Mika and Tressa wordlessly followed her.

"The branches won't reach, but we can get there," Mika warned. "Your best chance is to jump up and down on that branch – the one closest to the roof. You have to trust the tree. You may have some problems wearing that ridiculous dress, Kaela, but if you catch yourself when you land, you can keep from falling off the roof."

Kaela crawled toward the trunk. She sat for a moment, gathered her hair into a knot and tucked her dress into the pants. She stood up and balanced against the trunk. "Okay, here I go." Kaela walked carefully along the branch that extended towards the roof. She held onto the branch above and focused on the place she aimed to land.

The branch had a bend in it like an elbow. She stood at the point and the tree moved its branch, along with her, in a large circle. When she was at the point closest to the roof she leapt off the branch. She stuck her chest out and used her arms for balance as her legs dropped towards the roof. She kept her eyes focused past the edge of the roof as she leapt.

Mika yelled, "Fly, Kaela, fly...."

Cold air caressed her cheeks as she crossed the chasm between the branch and the castle. She landed with soft knees and immediately balanced with her hands to keep from rolling off the pitch of the roof. The rough roof cut into her hands.. But she didn't wait to see if her body was okay – instinctively, she knew that she was able enough to do what needed to be done, and she raced ahead, hoping to find Shawn and Eiren.

She ran between two rows of skylights, but remembered that Lorendale said the nursery would be at the end of the castle. Mika and Tressa ran behind her. Light poured from the last skylight into the dark sky, and Kaela pointed down through it – overjoyed by what she saw. She motioned with her hand for all of them to get low to the ground and whispered.

"Look! It's Shawn – and that must be Eiren!"

Tressa pointed, trying to contain her excitement. "It's Eiren, and Auntie Anya, and Shawn."

"Look at that!" Mika said.

Kaela pounded on the skylight, but Shawn and Anya remained seated, engaged in conversation while the little baby slept.

"The glass is too thick. I'll have to get something heavy to break it – but then, how do we get them out?" Kaela asked.

"You be forgetting who we are, Kaela," Mika said sternly. "That distance is no problem for Tree People. I can hang from the edge and hold Tressa by the ankles. Shawn can tie the sheets together and Tressa will catch 'em. Before you know it, they'll all be climbing out of there."

"Of course, Mika! That's a perfect plan. Do you have a knife?"

"Course I do."

"Why don't you see if you can pry the glass at the edge? I'm going to find a big rock. We can use it to hammer on the knife and crack through the glass."

Kaela crawled into the darkness until the rooftop changed into the uneven soil and rocks of the mountainside. She felt for a large rock she could carry. Her heart beat hard against her chest with excitement. The tide had turned – everything was falling into place. She clawed at a large stone wedged in the cold, hard ground. This stone would crack the glass. They would free the prisoners. *She would win. She would defeat Gulig.*

Kaela was abruptly pushed to the ground with a thud. A heavy weight pinned her. As her vision cleared, she saw that a huge man sat on top of her. She inhaled, trying to regain her breath, and then screamed as loud as she could.

He slapped a hand over her mouth.

Rage rose in Kaela. Pinned on her stomach, she kicked and thrashed, desperate to escape and furious that her plan had been thwarted. She flailed her head, trying to free her mouth from the man behind her, fighting to scream again and warn her friends.

The man laughed with a phlegmy voice. "We've got a real tigress here."

"Look! There's more of 'em!" A second man yelled as he raced toward the roof.

Kaela tried to look and make sure her friends were okay, but the man was as heavy as a mountain. Still, the rage in her belly drove her to keep trying.

"They ran off ... took off like birds," the second man said, breathing heavily. "Looked like they flew right off the roof."

Yes! They're safe! Kaela thought.

"Give me a hand. This one's a wild thing." The first man flipped Kaela onto her back while the second stuffed a gag in her mouth. He tied her legs and arms.

"This net should tame her." The first man coughed and wiped his hand on Kaela's dress. A rough net encased Kaela's body and she was thrown over the first man's shoulder. The men scrambled down the hillside."

"How much you figure this one's worth?"

"Not much. She's wearin' the pants of tree scum. But it's the best we could do tonight, what with all the soldiers running around. Maybe she'll get us a couple of sips of ganba."

The first man grunted.

They scooted down a steep path a short distance from the castle until they arrived at a rough-hewn door built into the steep hillside. They rapped three times and a huge Rugu soldier cracked open the door. His bald head shone as he lifted his lantern and glared at the men. "What ya got there?"

"Caught another one trying to break into the castle."

"That slip of a thing doesn't look like much to me." The guard opened the door wide, and said, "Let's have a look. Come in."

The unbearable stench of fear filled Kaela's nose – it emanated through the smells of fetid sweat, filthy bodies, feces and old urine that filled the room. Still upside-down, Kaela's head throbbed as she looked down a long hall. Crowds of filthy prisoners were pressed against an unending row of metal-barred cells. Moans, screams and rattling metal filled the room as the inmates noticed the arrival of a new prisoner.

The soldier screamed, "Shut up or I'll throw you in solitary – you hear me?"

Then all was silent except for the wailing of a baby.

"All right, let's see what you got there," the soldier said, eyeing Kaela through the heavy net. "You'll be lucky to even get a taste of ganba from what I can see."

Kaela glared back at the warden as her captors stood her up. She wanted to leap at the warden and tackle him. How could he be heartless enough to keep a baby in prison? Her fingers clenched. She ached to rip the keys from him and free the suffering prisoners.

But Kaela struggled to contain her rage. She had to come up with a plan and she had to think with a calm mind. Her eyes darted around the room, hoping for some kind of solution. Then something caught her attention. Behind the men – in the shadows – she thought she saw a small animal ... something that had followed them inside. What did an animal want in this disgusting place?

The men tore off the net and unbound her legs and Kaela stood tall and proud. Her knotted red hair had come loose and flowed like a wild mane around her face. She struggled to speak through the gag, "Mmmm, mmmm, mm ..."

The three men narrowed their eyes, calculating her worth. Then their eyes all widened with recognition. One of her captors licked his lips and the other rubbed his hands together, while the guard flushed with excitement

"It's the red-haired girl! Gold – this one's worth gold," one of her captors said.

Kaela quickly realized – there just might be a way.

"She's mine!" The second one clutched Kaela's arm.

"Both of you stop," the warden barked. "This one's worth more than enough for all three of us."

"Mmmm, mmmm!" Kaela tried to speak.

The warden ordered, "Take off that gag."

"Yes, let's see what she has to say."

The wad of fabric was yanked from her mouth, and Kaela said haughtily, "Yes, it is I, the red-haired girl. Take me to Gulig, you filth."

The men laughed, but Kaela continued undeterred, "I am sure my future father would want to know how his men treat his daughter. Why don't you take me to him - so I can show him how you bound me like a common animal." She spat at the soldier's feet.

Behind the men, the little animal that snuck in behind them sat part way up. Kaela resisted staring. She remembered so many hours before when she had come on Zeke in the cave and thought he was some kind of animal. Now his clothes were nearly black with filth and his black hair stuck up around his head – but it was his green eyes that gave him away. It was Zeke. Kaela glared at the men and watched Zeke with her peripheral vision. Zeke had something in his hand and he was waving it at her. With a sudden insight, she realized it was a ring of keys. Zeke covered his mouth and she could see the light of a smile in his eyes, but Kaela couldn't afford to acknowledge Zeke for even a moment.

"You don't fool me, missy. We all know how well you and Gulig get along..." one of the bounty hunters sneered.

"How did you escape?" the warden asked sharply, looking into her eyes.

"Do you think I flew out of the tower room?" Kaela laughed. "I was simply out for some fresh air when..."

"Why should we believe you?" The warden continued to eye her suspiciously.

"Untie my arms and I'll show you."

The warden said, "Go ahead. Release her."

Kaela flashed her vine-covered right arm in front of their faces. "I may have resisted at first." She fought not to choke on her words as she continued, "But then I realized what Gulig was offering – *Supreme Power!* You see these vines? The ganba is growing in me even as we speak," Kaela scowled. "You ruined the special dress Gulig designed for me, and now you are making me late for my special day. Gulig will not be pleased to learn that you kept me from my adoption."

The greed on the men's faces turned to fear. The bounty hunters began visibly sweating as they backed out of the room. "It was a mistake, ma'am," one said. "There's no need for Gulig to..."

"Yes, we wouldn't want to bother our master, now would we..."

The first one mumbled to the other, "I heard she tamed a starving tiger...."

"And defeated the cave monster...."

"Maybe she *can* fly...."

They reeled around and bolted out the door.

Kaela stifled a smile. Somehow she needed to get the warden out of the prison so Zeke could do his work. "Will you return me to my room?" she asked haughtily. "Or should I just wander around and miss the adoption ceremony?"

"A soldier must never leave his post," the guard said woodenly, but there was a slight tremble in his voice.

"Do you understand that, after tonight, I can be your benefactor? What is a fine soldier like you doing guarding a prison? You should be leading troops, fighting battles – not babysitting a bunch of low-life scum." Kaela glanced furtively around the room, and whispered, "Take care of me and I will take care of you. There may even be gold, extra ganba – remember, I'm the rightful heir of this kingdom."

The warden's pupils dilated until his green eyes turned dark with greed. "Certainly, ma'am. I can take you through the underground passageway. We'll have you back in plenty of time for the adoption."

The warden pointed to his right motioning for Kaela to follow, then his head jerked in Zeke's direction. He scowled, "Did you see that? Some kind of animal got in here...."

Kaela's heart caught in her throat and she quickly ordered, "Who cares about another disgusting animal. This whole place is full of them. Take me to Gulig! Take me now!"

Far down the row of cells a dog barked.

"I'll take care of it," the man said quickly pulling something from his belt. He blew against a tube and a poison dart whistled through the air.

Chapter Twenty - Seven · The Adoption

The dim light of the warden's lantern barely illuminated the maze of foul-smelling passageways. The stench in the caves turned Kaela's stomach like the smell of a sewer – a very old, long-used sewer. The warden yanked on Kaela's arm, pulling her towards his reward. She was completely at his mercy.

Kaela's dress was filthy. Her right arm throbbed and she was sure that the vines were growing again. She yearned to run back and make sure Zeke was okay. What if the poison dart reached its mark and Zeke lay helpless on the prison floor?

Finally, they reached an iron ladder and the warden waved the lantern, indicating that Kaela should go first.

"After you, Miss," he said.

"Where does this lead?" Kaela asked, feeling wary.

"This takes you where you need to go. Don't you worry – I'll be right behind you."

Kaela had no choice. The metal was cold in her hands as she climbed, rung by rung, to the low-lying ceiling. With each step up she grew more and more nervous.

The man climbed just behind her and said, "Go on – press up on that cover there. It opens into the basement."

Kaela pushed hard on the metal plate and her head popped up into a hallway.

"Here she is!" a soldier yelled.

Immediately three soldiers pounced on her, and yanked her by the shoulders until she stood above ground.

At first Kaela resisted, but then she heard one of them yell, "The adoption! Gulig is waiting for her. He'll kill us all!"

Fear stabbed Kaela in the heart. Gulig told her that he would kill Shawn. "Take me to the ceremony now!" she screamed.

The warden pulled himself up after her and yelled as the soldiers and Kaela ran down the hall and up the iron stairs. "She's mine. The reward is mine!!!"

The warden's voice faded to nothing. They flew down a carpeted hallway, up another set of elegant stairs that led to the ballroom's grand entry on the second floor. The wind roared against the castle in the pitch-dark night, and hanging lights in the hall shuddered briefly as Kaela rushed past.

Kaela's worry for Shawn intensified with every step. Finally, the group reached a set of massive wooden doors, guarded by two stone-faced soldiers, who immediately threw the doors open when they saw who approached.

Kaela flew into the grand ballroom and yelled, "Stop! I'm here. Stop!"

There was a quiet rustling as every head in the crowd turned to face her, and then a dead silence followed.

At the front of the room, Gulig stood on a stage. Two guards to the side of the stage stopped in their tracks, gripping Shawn between them.

Shawn caught sight of Kaela and his eyes shone with tears.

Gulig's eyes bore into Kaela. He stood like an iron statue, clutching the ruby-handled dagger in his claw-like hands.

"What are you staring at?" he said quietly. "Bring me the boy."

The guards resumed dragging Shawn to their leader.

Kaela bolted down the aisle without a second glance at the rows of men and women, ignoring the gazes of those who didn't have the courage to stop an insane man from harming an innocent child. She dashed past rows of men and women who fed their children ganba - who fed their children anger and hate - her only thought that she must save Shawn.

"Stop!" Gulig screamed at her just as the guards presented Shawn to their master.

Kaela slid to a stop three rows from the front and stared up at Gulig with tears flowing down her face.

"Is this the type of daughter you will be to me?!" Gulig glared. "You disobeyed me and now there are consequences for your actions. Look at you! Just look how you come before me – I want to make you a princess, but you look like nothing more than a ruffian!"

"Please ... don't hurt him. I'm here, now. Please!"

Gulig crossed his arms across his chest and waited, all the while staring at Kaela. No one moved or spoke.

Stennan rose slightly from his seat in the front row, bowing as he stood with a baby clutched against his chest. "Sire, on this glorious day we are all grateful to know your mercy."

"Yes, yes, on this special day..." Gulig whispered ominously, still glaring at Kaela. "On this day I will have mercy for the sake of my future daughter!" Gulig roared with laughter and a flash of lightning brightened the room. Gulig waved Shawn away and said, "Go. Take your seat and enjoy the ceremony."

The guard took Shawn roughly by the arm and led him to a seat in the front row, next to Stennan. Kaela and Shawn locked eyes across the aisle, and a look of friendship and welcome passed between them, which warmed Kaela's heart and gave her courage. The baby lying against Stennan's shoulder in the front row lifted its head and opened its dark brown eyes. It was the baby from the tree-song – it was Eiren.

There has to be a way to stop this. There has to be a way to save Shawn, and the baby and – to save myself! Kaela thought wildly.

Torchlight illuminated the lines of soldiers, who stared straight ahead along both sides of the cathedral-like room. Each soldier stood in a wide stance, with a spear between his hands. Dark purple floor-to-ceiling curtains were edged with black sky – the only light in the room came from thousands of glimmering candles, mounted inside two rows of crystal chandeliers.

Kaela ached to run to Shawn, but she knew the guards would not allow it. Kaela was surprised to see Lorendale's frail body sitting just on the other side of Shawn, and an elderly Tree Woman sitting just beside him.

A guard pointed to a seat in the front row on the left side of the room. Kaela walked past rows of old military men, sat down in her chair, and looked again at Shawn and Eiren. Their smiles calmed her. Kaela glanced down at her soiled gown. It was filthy and ripped in places, and just underneath was the comforting sight of the pants from the Tree Tribe.

A purple cloak fastened with a thick gold chain fell from Gulig's broad shoulders. He wore the black and grey uniform of his soldiers, but his chest was covered with medals. Heavy gold chains, sparkling with rubies and diamonds, hung down Gulig's chest. In the distance, thunder roared, followed seconds later by lightning. Taking a long drink of ganba, Gulig began his speech, as lightinng flashed through cracks in the curtains like flashes from giant bulbs. He droned on about 'this glorious day', and 'destiny', and 'at last the day has come', obviously taking more pleasure in the occasion than anyone else in the room.

Kaela turned again and again toward Shawn, purposely ignoring Gulig until he snatched a parchment from the dais and said with satisfaction, "Here it is. The sacred promise made long ago: 'The House of Muraten promises to join with the Rugus by marrying their beloved Princess Gwenilda with Prince Golan of the Rugus. This is a sacred trust that shall not be broken.'"

Scanning the room, Gulig continued, "This sacred trust *was* broken by the House of Muraten. Today that promise will be restored. I, Gulig, rightful heir of the Rugus, will hereby adopt Kaela, of the House of Muraten, to be my daughter." A huge bolt of lightning emphasized his words and, within seconds, roaring thunder filled the room with a deafening boom. "This alliance will give me the right to assume the throne of the House of Muraten." He raised his fist to the air. "From this day forward, I will be King," he said triumphantly. "I will be the true King of the land." He paused briefly. "Does anyone have reason to object to this adoption?" he demanded, scouring the crowd with a deadly look.

Simultaneously, Lorendale and Shawn jumped to their feet and yelled, "I object!" Guards quickly tackled the two, muffling their protests.

"There are no objections!" Gulig boomed, his voice resounding through the hall. Again, thunder followed lightning in near unison.

"Bring the girl to me!" Gulig commanded, holding a large glass of ganba in the torchlight. His diamond ring glinted. "It is time for the girl to have the test of the ganba!"

Adrenalin surged into Kaela's muscles, urging her to run. Would she even survive a whole glass? Would someone - anyone - come to her rescue? What about Netri ... Arendore ... Janani? Surely they would not abandon her! Where were Mika and Tressa? What about the Rugus who didn't support Gulig?

Thunder cracked nearby, echoing loudly through the room. Kaela realized it was up to her, and so she resisted with every fiber of her being. She dug her feet strong and firm into the ground as the soldiers dragged her towards Gulig.

"NO!" she screamed, thrashing.

"My dear, of course you do not have to drink it," Gulig said, smiling. "I am sure that your cousin will not mind drinking it in your stead...."

Two soldiers pulled Shawn from his seat at a snap of Gulig's fingertips, and dragged him towards the dais.

"No! It will kill him!" Horrified, Kaela implored, "Stop! I'll do it."

"No, Kaela..." Shawn's yell was cut off as a soldier quickly covered his mouth.

Cackling, Gulig held the glass towards Kaela, clearly relishing her pain.

"Enjoy, my dear. Enjoy," he hissed.

Gulig held the glass up and Kaela turned her head away. Gulig grabbed her jaw and, forcing her lips open, he tipped the glass. Bitterness flowed over her tongue, and grizzly strength surged in the pit of her stomach, tingling in the muscles of her arms and legs. Coldness crept towards her right shoulder like a snake wrapping itself in tight coils around her arm. Ice circulated in Kaela's veins and moved inwards, the cool caress threatening to numb her heart. With renewed strength, Kaela grabbed the glass and tried to tip it away from her mouth.

Gulig yanked the glass, regaining control. "Kaela, are you resigned to passing the ganba on to your cousin?"

Hoping to find a shred of kindness in his cruel heart, Kaela pleaded. "No, please, I don't want to die."

"So, weakling, you don't want to die? You think that I should have mercy on you?" Gulig whirled around and grabbed a sword from the table behind him and waved it in front of Kaela's face. It was the gift from King Arendore that had been buried under the beast in the caves. "You did not show the guardian of the caves any mercy with this sword – did you?"

"No, I didn't kill him," Kaela shuddered. "I promise. He fell on it."

"Don't lie to me, girl, you are every inch a murderess. Now drink this. Either you will die ... or you will become one of us."

Images flashed in front of Kaela's eyes as she struggled to make the right decision. She remembered her mother's courage in the face of painful treatments – and even death. Janani's words, "Remember the love you have," flashed through her mind. Kaela looked longingly at Shawn and clung to her love for him, for her father, for the memory of her mother, even as the vines inched towards her heart.

"Do you really think you can defeat me, child?" Gulig hissed, grabbing Kaela's chin. He glared at the entire room.

"She thinks that she can resist!" he yelled to the rows of people that sat before them, whispering and murmuring to each other in dismay over Kaela's refusal to drink. As Gulig spoke, their whispers fell into an awkward shuffling, and then dead silence.

"I am more powerful than your feelings of love," he snarled, his voice carrying clearly through the room. "Think about it; think about the one question you never asked, the question you never *wanted* to ask. If those Butterfly Women of Mount Sankaria loved your mother so much, why didn't they save her? Why did they let her die?"

A jolt of searing pain shot through Kaela's heart as she fell to her knees. The vines beckoned, their tendrils thickening in her chest. They could take away her agony – make her pain disappear. She felt the hatred growing within her, filling her with cold strength.

"Oh Great Spirit," Anya prayed, her voice lifting above the murmur of the crowd. "Hold Kaela in your arms of grace, that she may know your love." Continuing in Tree-tongue, Anya sang, "Sheewaneeshanshay...."

Shawn jerked against the painful grip of the guards, struggling to free himself, to somehow help Kaela, but he was helpless against the brutal hands that pressed him into his seat. He turned to Anya.

"Love is with you always," Anya called. "Love is with you always."

Unexpectedly, the large Rugu man, Stennan, jumped up, clutching baby Eiren in his arms.

"STENNAN..." Gulig yelled. But he was interrupted by a group of Rugu generals who had discreetly moved to the front of the room, carrying jugs of ganba. One of them tapped Gulig on the shoulder, and whispered in his ear.

"How dare you interrupt these proceedings?" Gulig demanded.

"Sire, we must leave this place at once," the man said softly as the crowd strained to hear.

"I'm sure it can wait, General!"

"It is for your own protection, Sire!" The general continued adamantly, speaking loudly enough that the entire crowd could hear. "Terrible things have taken place."

A burst of hope shot through Kaela and she crouched slightly, ready for action.

"Look outside the window," the general cried desperately as Gulig motioned for his guards to remove him.

The line of soldiers yanked on the long drapes and threw open the windows.

The black night was illuminated by flashes of lightning, which revealed a white horse in the act of leaping and bounding around the courtyard. An army of horses surrounded the white one, bucking and kicking the men who tried to mount and subdue them. Whips cracked in the night, but the horses refused to be mastered. Just behind the horses, masses of weakling and Rugu women, young and old, chanted, "NO MORE! NO MORE! OUR SONS WON'T DIE FOR AN OLD MAN'S WAR." Hundreds of dogs of every shape and size barked and growled and tore at the men's heels, as one large, brown, wooly dog howled a battle cry. A cloud of crows dove and pecked at the soldiers below, blackening the sky, and a chorus of trees swayed and rocked in the background, while streams of freed prisoners joined the throngs of protesters.

Even without holding the Butterfly pendant, Kaela understood the meaning behind Wollan's cry. "Be brave, red-haired girl!" Wollan howled. "Be brave, red-haired girl!"

Clenching his teeth, Gulig turned towards the generals. "You have lost control!" he yelled. "Why aren't you out there, leading your men?"

"Our best weapon has been destroyed, sir," one of the generals said, quavering. "When we attempted to give the soldiers more ganba, look what we found." The generals simultaneously popped the jugs of ganba open, and fountains of light erupted from each bottle, infusing the room with a golden glow. "Sire, someone destroyed the ganba! There are only a few bottles that have not been altered. Arendore and his army are approaching the castle at this very moment! We must leave at once."

Wide-eyed with joy, Kaela realized she was free and started to bolt to Shawn, but a guard leapt from the side of the stage and grabbed her.

"Shawn, Grab the baby! Run... run!" Kaela screamed, fighting the soldier's grasp.

The crowd rose in panic, pushing and trampling to reach the exits. The sound of yelling and screaming echoed to a roar in the wooden room.

Gulig clutched his chest desperately. "Who has betrayed me?" he screamed. "Stennan, bring me the child! They will not risk the baby!! I warned them I would kill the baby if they did not surrender! Stennan, snap its neck or bring it here!"

The tiny child huddled against Stennan's chest. Handing the child to Shawn, Stennan said defiantly, "No, sir! I will not sacrifice this child. He is innocent."

"He is a weakling!" Gulig glared at Stennan, and reached for his ganba. A large crow swooped into the room and, when Gulig threw back his head, guzzling the remains of the bottle, the crow flapped his wings about the man, hovering over the bottle until he clutched the diamond from Gulig's ring in his claws. Gulig waved his hand and swatted at the crow, but the crow didn't let up until he yanked the diamond out of its setting.

Kaela struggled against the guard, hoping he would join the throng and bolt for the door. Despite her fear, Kaela's heart sang with joy. She recognized the delicious odor that spilled from the "tainted" ganba bottles, and realized what Zeke had done. "Run, Shawn, run!" Kaela yelled.

Shawn hesitated, not wanting to abandon his cousin.

Gulig grabbed Kaela's arm and tore her away from the guard.

"Shawn!" Kaela screamed. She kicked at Gulig, and he twisted her forearm until it was bent behind her back. He pushed the sharp point of a dagger between her ribs and hissed in her ear, "You are still the rightful heir." Pressing the cold metal harder into Kaela's side, Gulig ordered loudly, "You will come with us, girl. All you Rugus - come with me! We will use the escape passage through the mountain." Gulig looked up at the all-but-empty room, shocked to find that only his most loyal men remained. "Traitors!" Gulig screamed in fury.

"Shawn, run!" Kaela yelled, twisting in Gulig's grip. "Run! Go now!"

A bolt of lightning exploded in thunder. Kaela gasped as Gulig compressed her neck between his massive bicep and forearm. Searing pain shot into her back where the tip of the knife pierced her flesh.

Still Kaela yanked and bucked to free herself, "Go!" she commanded, choking.

Light flashed as a bolt of lightning hit the tree that stood just outside the tower - the tree that had been planted long ago by Queen Rhiana, as part of her promise to Zella. It flamed, a giant torch, and quickly ignited the wooden rooms on the outer perimeter of the castle. Plumes of smoke rose into the air as crimson and yellow flames hungrily consumed the wooden structure.

Chapter Twenty - Eight • The Fire

Eiren whimpered and coughed, and Shawn ripped open his shirt to tuck the infant's face inside the fabric. Deafened by the screams of the crowd and the roaring fire, Shawn ignored his own anxiety in the midst of chaos and soothed Eiren, cooing, "Don't worry. I promise I won't let anything happen to you." Tears poured from Shawn's eyes as he squinted to see through the haze and the crowds of Rugus pushing and shoving to flee outside. Having drunk thirstily from jugs of liquid sweetened and transformed by the waters of Mount Sankaria, the Rugus felt the vines that suffocated their hearts loosen and dissolve. Once their anger deteriorated, many of the Rugus were determined to get as far away from Gulig as they could go.

Shawn moved with the streaming crowd just behind Anya, while Lorendale clung to Shawn's shoulder for guidance. Shawn kept his eyes glued to Anya's back.

A cold nose touched his palm. Shawn glanced down to find a brown curly-haired dog, which yipped at him.

"*Follow me. Follow me.*" The dog wove his way in front of Anya.

"Come on, then," Tressa waved, slipping in front of Shawn. Shawn breathed a sigh of relief. He had friends to help him out of the chaos.

Shawn cradled Eiren against his chest with one arm and patted Lorendale's hand to reassure the ill man. Just in front of them, Tressa's leaf-shaped hair bounced as she led the way out of the castle. A sudden draft of air swirled the smoke, revealing that they stood two floors above the ground, on a skinny ledge above the grand entryway.

Tressa turned her head around towards Shawn, and coaxed, "Don't be afraid. Remember – just take one step at a time. Just be lookin' in front of you and you'll get there."

It was one thing to risk his own life, but now Shawn was responsible for Eiren, too. The added weight of responsibility terrified him further. What if he fell? But, what would happen to Eiren if they didn't cross?

A crow flew towards Shawn, cawing, and then landed on the end of the ledge where a stairway led down to the ground floor.

Knowing that a crow had led him to safety once before, Shawn kept his eyes on the black bird. He slid along the ledge, one foot after another until, at last, Shawn reached the marble staircase.

A voice creaked in Tree-tongue, *Creeaak...* "Do not be afraid..." *Creeaak, creeaak...* "The fire will not touch you. I am the Grandmother Tree.... I will not burn."

Shawn looked up at the massive beams that supported the entryway. Fire raged all around them and flames licked at the wood, but miraculously, the beams refused to burn. Shawn dashed down the marble stairway and out the door with Eiren safely cradled in his arms. Lit by the orange glow of the flames in the night sky, the crowd erupted with cheers when Shawn emerged from the castle, carrying Eiren safe in his arms.

A crowd of supporters lifted and carried Lorendale away from the inferno. Shawn, Anya and Tressa followed Wollan's weaving form through the crowds until, illuminated by the embers of the burnt castle, Shawn saw Queen Skyla with Gannon and Gavin by her side. Glistening tears streamed down her cheeks as the Queen ran to him with open arms. He uncovered the coughing baby and lifted Eiren towards Skyla.

Skyla held her baby to her chest and cooed, "Eiren, Mama be here. Mama be here." She looked up and spoke, choking on tears. "Thank you, thank you, thank you..." Then she turned to her Aunt Anya. "Auntie, oh Auntie - you're alive and well." They embraced with Eiren between them.

A smile of relief and joy spread across Shawn's face. They had saved the baby. *But what about Kaela? Where was Kaela?*

Gannon and Gavin, bruised and filthy from their time in prison, lifted Shawn and then Anya in a bear hug.

Gannon looked around. "Kaela ... where are Kaela and Mika?" He asked.

Shawn frowned. "Gulig took Kaela hostage. She insisted I save Eiren, but now that he's safe, I'm going back for her. As for Mika - I never saw him."

"Tressa," Skyla said sternly. "Your parents be worried sick about you and your brother. Where is he?"

"We tried to help," Tressa admitted breathlessly. "But then Kaela was taken prisoner. I leapt for the tree, and Mika and I got separated. Some soldiers chased him ... I don't know where he is."

A small, feathered form landed on Shawn's shoulder. *Cheep, cheep,* Pepper sang happily.

Shawn looked down at Wollan. He ruffled the dog's soft fur with his hand. "Come on," Shawn said eagerly. "Let's go find Kaela. I bet we'll find Mika in there, too. You can catch the trail."

Wollan yipped and took off running.

"Don't worry, Queen Skyla. We'll find him," Gavin yelled as he and his brother chased after Shawn.

"You're not going without your bodyguards!" Gannon cried eagerly.

Zeke was milling around in the crowd of freed prisoners, grinning from ear to ear, when he heard a familiar voice.

"Zeke, Zeke? Where are you, Zeke?"

"Gramma! I'm here," Zeke called, waving through the crowd. "I'm okay. Don't worry, Gramma."

Tazena fell to her knees in front of her grandson and sniffled. "Zeke, you know I didn't mean ... I thought it was for the best. I promise ... I never meant to hurt you."

"Gramma, what are you doing? Let me help you up." Zeke yelled to be heard above the crowd. "What is it? Tell me quick, Gramma. Kaela still needs my help."

Tazena wept, "Your mother wanted me to tell your father ... I never could ... please try to understand...."

"Understand what?"

"Your father is with Gulig. You met him - he's a Rugu."

"My father - I met my father?" Zeke cried, his head spinning. "I really am a Rugu?"

"Yes, Zeke." Tazena bowed her head, and wept. "He's gone, though. He went with Gulig."

"He's gone, gone, but why – why didn't you tell me?" Zeke screamed at her. "My father, I was with my father – he never knew – I never knew! Maybe he would have wanted me! I never knew him, and now he's gone...." Zeke wailed his loss to the night sky, his cries mingling with the roar of the crowd.

"I'm sorry..." Tazena cried. "I didn't want the Rugus taking you, making you one of them."

"I'm part Rugu and you can't change that, Gramma. I'm brave without the ganba – I helped Kaela defeat Gulig's monster." He stood tall, and said, "Why can't you see that when you hate the Rugus, you hate me too?"

Tazena sobbed as years of hatred battled her love for her grandson, and Zeke ran blindly back toward the blackened skeleton of the castle. Maybe he could still find his father. His father would love him for who he was – he *had* to.

Torn apart from the pain she'd caused, Tazena ran after her grandson. "Don't you see, Zeke?" she muttered through her tears. "It's me I hate, not you. It's the Rugu in me that I hate the most...."

Chapter Twenty - Nine · Butterfly Breath

Two Rugu soldiers carried torches high in the air, doing what they could to illuminate the narrow pass between two steep cliffs, but the smoke from the castle fire made it almost impossible to see. Gulig clutched Kaela's right wrist and dragged her behind him, all the while blathering under his breath. "Cowards! Turncoats! More ganba! We need more ganba!"

Kaela's lungs burned with exhaustion and smoke. She was furious with Gulig for holding her hostage and she tried resisting the Rugu leader, but the ganba still circulated in his veins, making him much too powerful. He yanked painfully on her arm until she had no choice but to keep up with his wild pace. They ran until Kaela's legs were too weak to take another step. In her heart she cried out, *help! Please help me!*

Gulig suddenly halted and faced his men. His face reflected the eerie red glow of the torches and his eyes were opened dangerously wide, like those of a madman. He glared at the crowd of Rugu soldiers who trailed him and screamed, "Where are we? Where are you taking me, you turncoats?"

Kaela realized in a flash that Gulig had lost his mind. She moved her arm slowly, hoping to catch her captor by surprise and free her arm.

He tightened his grip and cackled, "Hah! You're mine now – mine!"

Kaela looked from one soldier to another, desperate for help, hoping that one of them had drunk the purified ganba and understood that Gulig was a madman. But each soldier quickly averted his eyes from her searching glance. Maybe they knew he was mad – maybe they were ashamed of their leader. And yet, still they followed him. Kaela caught the eye of the Rugu man who brought up the rear. He had the same large body as the others, but Kaela remembered him. He was the man who had held Eiren – who had defied Gulig. There was something different in his eyes, also – a glimmer of kindness that shone, even through the darkness.

The man didn't look away from her pleading eyes. After a pause, he stepped forward. "Master," he said, "I'll help you with the girl."

"No! No – she's mine ... mine!" Gulig's eyes darted back and forth like those of a trapped animal.

Kaela's heart sunk.

"Sire," the man said softly. "I only mean to help. You should be free to lead..."

"Yes, yes, I must be free to lead. I am the great Gulig!!!" Miraculously, he released his grip on Kaela. Life returned to her vine-covered arm in painful prickles.

The group resumed dashing through the pass, and Kaela drew comfort from the gentle touch of the man's large hand on her healthy left arm.

The scene of the mob outside the ballroom window had warmed her heart, holding back the icy tide of the ganba. The baby was free, and Gulig would not be king – the knowledge that her mission had been a success filled Kaela with triumph. Wollan and Shawn were safe, and King Lorendale would be able to receive the help he needed. *But what of me?* Kaela wondered, frightened by the thought. With her silk dress in tatters, she was glad for her suede boots and the pants from the Tree People that she had slipped on underneath. When exhaustion overwhelmed Kaela and she slowed, the man said, "You must be tired. Come on. I'll carry you on my back. Don't worry. I won't let him take you on the boats."

Grateful for the man's protection, Kaela said, "Thank you. My name is Kaela."

"My name is Stennan."

When they finally emerged from the pass, Kaela blinked to accustom her eyes to the cool light, and slipped off Stennan's broad back. The moon shone down bright in the clear, smokeless air. Before her, fields of iridescent, blue-green flowers shimmered in the bright moonlight as far as the eye could see, surrounded by steep hills. The Rugu soldiers spread out, casting long dark shadows, until they encircled the immediate area. She hid behind Stennan's large body, hoping he would shield her from Gulig.

Gulig drew the dagger from his waist. A ruby caught the moonlight and sparked like fire. Gulig fell to his knees and frantically jabbed with the blade, then ripped up handfuls of ganba plants by the roots and screamed, "Dig! Everyone dig!! *Now*!! Bring all that you can carry to the ship."

"Sire, we have already loaded hundreds of plants into the holds of the ships." Stennan pleaded, "I have taken care of this. We are prepared. We must go quickly."

"No! Everyone dig now!!! We need *more*!!! We must never run out of ganba! Dig!!!"

Stennan whispered to Kaela, pointing away from Gulig, "Go, go over there. Duck down in the flowers. The darkness will hide you."

Relieved to be free of Gulig, Kaela hunkered down and discreetly backed away, keeping her eyes on the shadowy face of the fallen ruler. Then she squatted down in the waist-high flowers.

Touching Gulig on the shoulder, Stennan coaxed, "Sire, please, we will grow new ganba plants...."

Gulig whimpered, "I must show my father. I must show them – all of them – that I am a true Rugu. I need the ganba ... the power ... I am useless without it," he sobbed.

"Please, Sire, hand me the dagger. It is time to go," Stennan said quietly.

Gulig looked up and his features glowed red as his face reflected the light of a nearby torch. His hand trembled and he pointed the blade at Stennan. "You, of all people," he said coldly. "After I took you in as my own." Gulig's voice rose higher and louder in his excitement. "You were nothing but an orphan when I found you. And you betrayed me."

Stennan shook his head, whispering, "No, Sire – it is *you* who betrayed *me* – as you betrayed *all* your subjects. It was wrong – it *is wrong* to give ganba to children."

"What do you know, you ignorant fool." Gulig turned away from Stennan and squinted, scanning the field. "All of you – I want you on your knees. Dig!" When the soldiers hesitated, Gulig growled, "I said *now*!"

An eerie silence filled the air as the soldiers dropped to their knees and dug their fighting blades into the dense earth.

Kaela hid in the soft petals. Although it was dark, the flowers seemed to hold their own blue-green light. She breathed a sigh of relief to be away from Gulig and inhaled the fragrance of hundreds of ganba flowers. The smell was different than the elixer. Rather than turning her stomach, she felt renewed and strengthened by it. While the elixir had only strengthened her anger and her power, Kaela felt that the flowers strengthened her heart and soothed her fears. She picked a flower and brushed her face with the soft petals, each one edged in blue. In the flower's center, fine hair-like strands alternated blue and green, tipped with a gentle white glow.

As she gazed at the flower, something tiny landed in her hair. She grabbed the butterfly pendant in her left hand. Tickling her ear with its wing, a diminutive voice said, "Please. Please save us. We can only live on nectar from the ganba flowers. Don't let them destroy our homes again."

Kaela held a finger up to the creature, careful not to frighten the tiny being. She gently moved her finger towards her face to get a better look. A butterfly glimmered in the moonlight. Kaela stared, fascinated by the creature's iridescent turquoise wings, which looked so much like ganba flowers. The butterfly was about three inches long with a charcoal black body and hair-thin legs. Its antennae twitched as the wings gracefully moved up and down, caressing the air. Kaela compared the butterfly to the wings in her pendant. "Your wings are just like the ones in my pendant," she said. "Who are you?"

"I am a Bagan butterfly." The blue-green butterfly seemed to nod its head, and from the motion of the wings, Kaela sensed that the butterfly was softly smiling at her.

"Are you the same kind of butterfly as the one in my pendant? I thought you had all died!" Kaela exclaimed.

"Oh, yes I am – and no we didn't!" the butterfly answered. "Thanks to the Rugus, we survived. After the war between the House of Rugu and the House of Muraten, all the ganba flowers were destroyed so that no more elixir could be produced. Fortunately for us, the Rugus took ganba plants with them when they were exiled. Bagan caterpillars clung for their lives to the plants and grew into butterflies in the new land. When the Rugus returned here, we came with them. Please ... don't let Muraten's family destroy us again."

"I'll do whatever I can," Kaela promised as she continued watching, mesmerized by the butterfly's beautiful wings, which gently fluttered up and down. A sudden breeze blew across the acres of ganba flowers, and the flowers undulated, rippling like dark tide-water, while branches of the surrounding trees danced back and forth in the moonlight, rustling in the wind. But there was another sound that carried on the wind. Kaela blocked out all other sound to hear.... It was the sound of ocean waves crashing against the shore. Kaela remembered flowing under and above the surface of the water on the back of the turtle's broad shell.

It was as though the flowers, trees and ocean waves were all part of a great living being. Kaela closed her eyes and felt her breath slowly moving up and down with the rhythm of the butterfly's wings and the rhythm of the rustling trees. Up and down – in and out. Awake or asleep, happy or sad, her breath was moved by some unseen hand, up and down, like the wings of a butterfly softly stroking her heart.

"Don't stop digging!" Gulig screeched in the distance. "We must bring them all...." Kaela poked her head above the flowers to see Gulig crouched over, holding armfuls of ganba flowers to his chest.

"Remember, Kaela – remember?" the butterfly said. "Butterflies can mend a broken heart."

A buried memory from years before rose to the surface of her mind – sitting by her mother's side, Kaela had listened to the sound of breath in her mother's fragile body. The hospital room was strange, and alien – filled with scary beeping machines and nurses who bustled in and out just when you didn't want to be disturbed. With every long, tortured exhalation, Kaela held her breath until her mother inhaled once more. Kaela held her mother's hand tightly and, praying for help, she found herself breathing in rhythm with her mother's slow breath, trying to support her.

Then her mother had cracked open her eyes. "Kaela, I will always love you..." She whispered hoarsely. "Look," she said. "Feel her. She's here in the room ... my angel came back." Her mother's eyes drifted closed and a peaceful smile spread across her face. The sound of her breathing filled the room.

In that moment Kaela had looked over her shoulder. No one else was in the room, but she remembered she had felt something, as though someone had softly brushed the hair from her face. Later, she doubted that it really happened, and had forgotten the memory until now.

After a moment her mother spoke again, whispering so quietly that Kaela had to bend her head close to her mother's mouth. "Kaela, love is in your heart - hold onto it. I am with you."

Now Kaela's heart cracked open and a tear fell down her cheek. She realized that she still carried her mother's love in her heart. Even death could not rob her of that love - it would always be with her. Her mother's love was like the bright sun emerging over a silent sea - it burned the fog of grief from her heart. The love had never left her. It had always been with her.

The butterfly wings of breath moved up and down, and an ocean of kindness filled Kaela. It was the ocean of kindness her Kanu had told her about. Joy burst and expanded in her heart until she felt invisible cords of light and love connecting her to everyone and everything. All life was born from that ocean and yet contained the ocean at the same time. It was a great mystery - she filled herself with it; she felt it grow with every breath. It was the ocean that dwelt deep inside.

In the beauty of her heart, Kaela felt as though she were part of something sacred. She was connected to all life through her breath. She realized that deep inside everyone there was a pure heart. The realization seeped through her as she regained her self-awareness. A chord of love chimed within her. It was the 'Butterfly Breath'.

The roar of a tiger shattered the quiet air.

Is it Kanu? Kaela leapt up from the flowers and ran as though an invisible force lifted her above the whispering flowers.

"Help me!" Gulig screamed, "Someone help me!!!"

Kaela's heart beat wildly against her chest when she caught sight of Kanu, her beloved Kanu.

"Your time has come!" Kanu roared with the fierceness of a raging beast. Pouncing on Gulig, the giant tiger knocked him over, and the ruby-covered dagger flew out of Gulig's hand.

Mika bounded from the bushes and grabbed the dagger. His eyes flitted from Gulig to the weapon in his hand. His face contorted with anger.

"No, Kanu - No, Mika. Please! The hate stops here - we must end it." Kaela was already there, filled with the beauty of her breath, and love, and the sacredness of all life. Compassion filled her heart. Even though Gulig's heart was hidden away, buried in the ganba vines, he still carried the priceless spark of life within him.

Everything froze, as if time paused to interrupt the horror of the moment. All eyes turned to Kaela. In that moment, Kaela emanated the most powerful force of all – the power of love. Kaela wrapped her arms around Kanu's neck.

Kanu threw back his head and roared, releasing the rage and pent-up energy in his body, but he didn't kill Gulig. His love for the red-haired girl was greater than his fury for Gulig. He kept Gulig pinned to the ground, snarling menacingly.

At the same moment, Mika stepped backwards, his eyes wide with shock, looking as though something had punched him in the chest. His hand relaxed and the dagger dropped with a thud to the ground. Then he collapsed to his knees, confused, and began to cry.

"Kaela. That man is a monster. He deserves to die!"

Kaela kneeled next to Mika and said firmly, "He'll be stopped, but not by murder."

Mika shook his head. "Don't you see, Kaela? Gulig wouldn't hesitate to kill my people. He deserves to die."

"No, Mika. We can stop this. We're kids. Just because the adults hate each other doesn't mean that we have to. We can stop the anger ... the need for revenge. If we kill him, we're no different from him. We have to stop it."

Kaela looked in Mika's eyes, searching for the pure heart deep inside of him.

Slowly, something uncoiled inside of Mika. The burden of anger he carried on his shoulders was suddenly too heavy to bear. His heart longed to be free, longed to live in love. He listened to the still quiet voice inside and he nodded. "It's time to let the anger go."

"Yes, yes!" Kaela said, grinning. Impulsively she grabbed Mika and hugged him tight. Then he wrapped his arms around her and they leaned into each other. They stepped back and smiled shyly at one another.

The spell was broken, and the chords of anger that bound the people and animals of Muratenland in conflict dissolved. The love in Kaela's heart uncovered by the butterfly breath – was the key that unlocked the shackles of revenge. Kaela gave Gulig the most precious gift of all – his life – by including him in her love.

But Gulig clung to his manacles – what would he be without his anger? He wormed his way to Kaela and clutched her arm with his long, powerful fingers, pulling her to the ground.

"I owe you nothing," he sneered. "I am powerful, and you are nothing but a child! See how great my rage is!! It is the most powerful!!" In the setting moon he cast a long spider-like shadow.

The vine markings on Gulig's hands and Kaela's arm glowed together. He stared into her eyes. "You think you are free now, don't you?" he asked hysterically. "You think it is that easy! Well, chew on this, you arrogant child. Look at your arm. You think you are so different from me? Here is the truth – what I am lives in all of you," he cackled. "You're too late. The vines have made you my daughter."

"No," Kaela said softly, unafraid. "I'll never be your daughter." Before their eyes the vines on her arm wilted and faded.

"Why are you on their side?" Gulig asked, his voice rising like a child's. "You can still claim your right to the throne. I can offer you anything – you can have power, and no one will be able to hurt you. Surrender to the hate. Surrender to the power."

"Leave her alone." Kanu roared.

"No Gulig," Kaela said firmly. "I choose love." She looked at Kanu, and saw his love for her reflected in his eyes. Then she looked at the crowd of Rugu men, who stood a short distance away. They had all drunk the purified ganba and the vines around their hearts were slowly loosening. Their faces held a mixture of fear and awe as they gazed at her. Even though their swords were drawn, the soldiers did not move - except for the big Rugu man who had carried her to the fields. He walked toward her, smiling.

The light of dawn illuminated figures as they appeared at the edge of the mountain. Janani ran towards Kaela, followed by Shawn, Wollan, Gavin and Gannon. Behind the Rugu soldiers, Arendore, Netri, Leland and a group of Muraten soldiers rode up on horseback. When they leapt off their horses, Netri motioned for Arendore to wait.

Kaela looked again at Gulig. The cruel sneer that had played on his lips moments before had disappeared. Early morning light illuminated his face. In place of the powerful, frightening ruler she knew, there lay a weak and broken man. Kaela gazed on Gulig, and suddenly realized that she was not alone in her grief – she had never been alone. Now, as never before, her choice lay plain before her. Like Gulig, she could allow the pain of loss to harden her, and isolate her from the people she loved – or, like Janani, she could open her broken heart to the light, and allow herself to grow ever kinder.

Netri nodded to Arendore, and the soldiers of Muratenland began tying the Rugu men's hands and taking them to another part of the field.

Arendore extended his hand to Gulig.

"Stand up, Gulig," Arendore ordered. "You are through here. Even your own men do not want to follow you. You have broken countless laws that govern our land and committed atrocious acts. This time, we are locking you up for good. You are stripped of all rights to rule the Rugus. You cannot rule from a prison cell!"

Gulig stood straight, scowling, and sneered, "No prison can hold me. You have not seen the last of me, Arendore. You will get your due."

Arendore nodded to his soldiers and they chained Gulig's hands and feet and dragged him far across the field.

Behind all the others, Ariala approached Kaela, riding on the back of an old white horse.

As Ariala slid off Blanco's back, Kaela smiled and said, "It was you, Ariala. You helped my mother. You came to see my mother when she was dying. I didn't know what she meant when she said, 'She came back.' But now I know – it was you, wasn't it? You didn't abandon my mother ... or me."

"Love is there always," Ariala said, smiling. "Yes, I was there for your mother in the end. We Butterfly Women cannot control death, but we can help people know the Great Spirit's love is with them always." Ariala turned Kaela's hand over and tenderly pressed around her wound until she was able to pinch a thick, dark green splinter between her thumb and forefinger. Ariala pulled it from the center of Kaela's palm. "Look, the beast left a shard of himself in your hand," she said softly, "but now it is gone."

Kaela understood that her mother had left her with an eternal connection to love. It would always be with her. Even though she could turn her back on it, it would never be destroyed.

Unable to hold back a moment longer, Wollan and Shawn ran to Kaela. The dog slathered her with big wet kisses while Shawn hugged his best friend.

King Arendore and Netri joined the circle in the ganba field as the sky steadily brightened.

Kaela beamed. "Netri, I think I understand something, but I want to be sure. I'm related to Gwenilda, aren't I?"

"Yes, dear girl," Netri said, smiling; his clothes glowed iridescent blue-green. "Gwenilda was your great-grandmother."

"Gwenilda did not die?" King Arendore asked, clearly amazed.

"Gwenilda went to live on the other side of the hole in the sky and married the man that she loved. She made me promise not to tell anyone except for the girl destined to break the curse. That is why I gave Kaela her diary," Netri continued. "Your grandfather, her son, was safe from the curse. But when her granddaughter got sick, she knew she had to take a chance that the Butterfly Women could heal her."

"I'm sure it frightened her terribly to send her granddaughter to Muratenland, knowing first-hand about the contract with King Grule's family, but it must have been even more frightening to think of her granddaughter dying."

Kaela looked from Janani to Netri, wide-eyed, still trying to comprehend that she was actually related to someone so magical – a butterfly woman … and a princess!

"After your mother married your father, she was no longer able to travel between worlds," Janani explained. "Even if we had found a way to bring your mother back here, Gulig would have been waiting here for her, and she was far too weak to stand up to him."

Shawn listened, not quite understanding the conversation. Kaela and he had the same great-grandmother – but what did that mean, exactly?

"So does that mean that I have Butterfly blood, too?" Kaela asked, already sure that she knew the answer.

"Absolutely," Netri said. "It was the strength of that pure love that empowered you to stand up to Gulig. It enabled you to withstand the destructive power of the ganba elixir."

"Shawn, I need to tell you something," Kaela burst in with excitement. "Do you remember how my mother wrote about our great-grandmother, who told her about the hole in the sky?"

"Of course, Kaela," Shawn replied, pushing his glasses up the bridge of his nose.

"Well, she was actually Gwenilda, the princess," Kaela explained. "Gwenilda actually went through the hole in the sky and married our great-grandfather. Gwenilda was our great-grandmother. I read it in her diary."

"That is why you were the only ones who could break the curse," Netri added.

"So, I have Butterfly blood, too?" Shawn beamed.

"Oh, yes, of course! You can tell because of your special relationship with animals." Netri nodded happily. "Indeed, you are both great healers."

King Arendore smiled broadly, delighted to learn the truth. He bowed, first to Kaela and then to Shawn. "Princess Kaela and Prince Shawn," he said, his voice ringing. "I am honored to know you and welcome you as part of my family."

At that moment a bright orange sun burst over the horizon.

High in the sky a large crow pumped his wings, cawing with excitement. He clung to the fiery diamond ripped from Gulig's ring. He was headed home and the jewel that was promised to his ancestor, Krakaw, generations ago was his....

Chapter Thirty • Loose Ends

Pink and peach-colored clouds hugged the horizon while shafts of light broke through the clouds, casting a golden glow over the fields of ganba flowers.

Zeke stopped at the edge of the ganba field and inhaled sharply, struggling to catch his breath after the long hard walk through the mountain pass. His muscles clenched with fatigue, but he needed to find the Rugu man – needed to find his father. His eyes quickly swept the breadth of the ganba field. The feeling of celebration and victory that permeated the air somehow couldn't reach inside and touch his broken heart. He smiled wanly as he watched Kaela and Shawn run toward him.

Kaela gave him a big hug. "Zeke, you're ok!" she cried joyfully. "You changed the ganba, didn't you? And you released the prisoners. You saved the day!"

"Shawn helped, too," Zeke said, but that already seemed long ago, and now his heart was broken.

Shawn added, "It was so cool, Kaela. I wish you could have been there ... we couldn't stop laughing."

But Zeke barely smiled.

Kaela put her arm around Zeke's shoulders and asked, "What's wrong, Zeke?"

"I-I ... I need to find someone," Zeke said, but he could barely speak through the lump in his throat.

"Who?" Kaela asked, but the sadness in his eyes broke her heart. "Come on, we'll help."

Zeke shielded his eyes, squinting through the rising sun until he spotted a group of Rugu men. He tore off in their direction with Kaela and Shawn right behind him, until they found Arendore and his men dealing with the Rugu prisoners. Gulig stood to one side with his arms and legs in chains, and a pile of weapons lay in a heap on the ground.

Zeke discreetly stood in the background and searched face after face of the Rugu prisoners until his eyes locked onto the Rugu man from the storeroom. *Could it be him?* He wondered.

Seeing Stennan in chains, Kaela, still breathless from her run, said, "Please, King Arendore, you should thank that man rather than lock him up."

"What do you mean?" Arendore demanded.

"He saved Eiren. He stood up to Gulig." Shawn nodded vigorously.

"And he also helped me – he saved me from Gulig," Kaela said, her eyes pleading.

King Arendore bowed to Stennan. "Forgive me for making assumptions. Thank you. I am forever in your debt." Arendore turned to a guard and said, "Unlock him – he is free to go."

Zeke stared at Stennan, hoping for some sign – hoping to learn the truth.

Clenching his teeth as he glared at Stennan, Gulig seethed. "Go be with the weaklings. It is what you deserve. I remember your soft spot for weak women – she's dead now, you know," Gulig laughed and spat on the ground. "That seer was nothing but filth."

Fury flashed across Stennan's face. He opened his mouth, but then he shook his head, turned and drifted away. He sank down into the ganba flowers and laid his head on his knees.

Zeke discretely followed the Rugu man. He waited, then quietly approached him and whispered, "Excuse me, sir."

"What?" Stennan looked up, tears rolling down his cheeks.

"I just wanted to thank you. Thank you for not throwing me in the dungeon."

Stennan looked at the boy and said kindly, "A little boy like you shouldn't be on your own. You deserve better."

Zeke squatted down next to Stennan and they sat in silence for a time. Zeke gathered his courage and wondered, "Can I ask you something?"

"Well, I suppose…"

"I-I … I heard what Gulig said about the seer woman."

As though he had been dealt a painful blow, Stennan's eyes instantly filled with sadness.

Zeke lifted his hand and hesitated, too shy at first to touch the man. But then he brushed the back of Stennan's hand. "You loved her?"

"Yes, I did," Stennan said, nodding. Then, unexpectedly, he confided to the boy, "She was a beautiful woman. We even married in the Rugu way … but, we had to keep it secret – Gulig would never have allowed it. Being with her was the happiest time of my life."

Zeke blinked against the tears forming in his eyes. This man was talking about the mother he never knew.

Stennan looked off into the distance and he suddenly looked older and very tired. "But then something changed. We began fighting about everything, and then she made Gulig angry – she predicted he would be defeated … predicted he would be betrayed. And he kicked her out of the castle. I refused to go with her – I thought I owed Gulig so much. She divorced me." Stennan's voice choked as he struggled to continue. "Letting her go was the biggest mistake of my life."

The words touched Zeke's heart – giving him hope that the man would want to know he had a son with the woman he had loved so much. Zeke hesitated a moment more and said, "My grandmother refused to tell you – she didn't want her grandson to be a Rugu … didn't want me to drink the ganba."

Stennan narrowed his eyes, obviously confused by the boy's words. He looked at Zeke searchingly, as though digging for truth.

"Well, I…" Zeke's voice quivered and the lump in his throat made it almost impossible to speak. "I-I'm … your s-son. I'm Zeke."

Stennan blinked, his eyes widened with understanding and his face filled with surprise and wonder. He clasped Zeke's hand in his giant hands. "I have a son? I really have a boy?" The sad tears that had flowed freely in grief transformed to tears of joy.

Zeke's heart burst with joy as he nodded, and he smiled.

"Son, I never was a father," Stennan continued, "and I don't know much about it. But I promise to take care of you, now that we've found each other."

Head down, Zeke reached for his father and wrapped his arms around his waist, bursting into long-overdue tears.

"I promise I'll take care of you. I promise. Don't you worry." The remaining strands of the ganba vine wilted and disappeared from Stennan's body as he softly patted his son's back.

A light breeze cooled the air, spreading the fragrance of thousands of ganba flowers, while morning light illuminated groups of people connecting, reconnecting and sharing their experiences. Endless fields of shimmering blue-green flowers danced and waved in the wind. The King's men laid out blankets for a feast in the field before returning to King Arendore's and Queen Skyla's castle for a formal celebration. Wollan raced happily from Kaela to King Arendore and back, again and again.

Mika was reunited with Gannon and Gavin, his stern grandfather, Leland and other members of his family. They started to scold him, but were so relieved he was safe that they held him in their arms instead.

Gulig and his men were carried away to the dungeons of Muratenland. As Gulig's broken form slowly faded into the distance, the last traces of the ganba vine disappeared completely from Kaela's body. Kaela watched, feeling relieved, sad and joyful all at the same moment. She wondered whether Gulig would ever change.

The music of wind in the branches and murmuring voices filled the air.

"It's the red-haired girl ... she destroyed everything!!!!" Tazena screeched breaking the calm, seemingly appearing out of nowhere.

Kaela's heart lurched as she looked across the field where Tazena was standing not far from Zeke and Stennan. Tazena's stringy grey hair flew around her face as she shook her skinny arms at the sky.

"The end has come!!! It's all her fault!!!"

King Arendore motioned for his men to stay put as Kaela, Shawn, King Arendore, Janani, Ariala and Netri raced to soothe the poor woman.

Zeke bolted upright and grabbed his father's hand. "I have to help her ... my grandma needs me."

"Do you have any idea who I am? Do you know what he did to her ... did to my mother? You think I hate for no reason? Well now it's all gone. The red-haired girl did it ... destroyed everything!!!!" Tazena wailed.

Zeke slowly approached his grandmother and said softly, "It's okay,

Grandma – everything's okay. I'm not mad at you. I'm here with you. I still love you."

Janani walked quietly to Tazena's other side. King Arendore, Stennan, Shawn and Kaela waited in the background.

Tazena stared, wide-eyed and unseeing. "The Rugus hate you. You think you know the truth."

"Grandma, I'm here ... please. I won't leave you. I know you tried to protect me..." Zeke put his arm around her waist and said softly, "It's okay, Gramma. I'm here with you."

Tazena shuddered and her body suddenly went limp. Fortunately, Zeke and Janani were there to carefully lower her to the ground.

Janani whispered softly, "It's okay, Tazena. You are loved. No one wants to harm you."

The pain on Tazena's face broke Kaela's heart. She remembered helping the Butterfly Women when Shawn's heart was so damaged. *The special water, Tazena needed the special water.*

Ariala was already adding a few drops from a crystal bottle in her coat pocket to a tin cup from her backpack. Kaela took the cup in both hands and slowly approached the elderly woman. She squatted down and said softly. "I'm sorry if I harmed you. I never meant to, but I have something here – special medicine from the Butterfly Women. It will help you heal ... make you feel better...."

The old woman shook her head and shrank into herself.

Zeke touched her chin and said, "Please, Gramma ... the water will help you."

Tazena's hand shook as she reached out without looking at Kaela. She grasped the handle of the cup and tilted it against her mouth until a drop wet her lip. She waited a moment and the lines in her face noticeably softened. She sighed and drank every drop of the special water.

Janani stroked the woman's hair and said, "It might help to tell us the truth, Tazena. We are here to support you."

At first Tazena shook her head, then she slowly nodded and King Arendore, Shawn, Ariala, Netri and Stennan kneeled down in the ganba flowers, surrounding her.

Tazena looked off into the distance as she remembered. "I don't know ... never knew. My mother hid the whole story. My mother's mind was never right, but I did the best I could – I promise I did my best."

"My mother, Zarenda, ran off with Prince Golan when Muraten kicked the Rugus out of this land. She pretended to be Gwenilda's little sister. She thought she could fool him ... thought he would love her. She pretended she was from the House of Muraten ... pretended to be a princess, and they married. She thought she'd fool him and the Rugus would forget the contract. But Prince Golan was a cruel and violent man. They had a son together ... and me. My mama was afraid for her children – afraid he would hurt us. She knew she had to leave ... needed to protect her children, so she told him the truth – told him she was no princess; she told him she was a seer. She told him he was a fool – he had believed what he wanted to believe."

"He was furious – couldn't stand the sight of her – she had made a fool of him, so he agreed to let her go. Told her he would fake an accident – made her promise not to tell anyone she was going – he didn't want the shame. But he gave her a punishment – a punishment worse than death. He kept her son – Gulig. Then Golan placed my mother in a sailboat with me strapped to her chest."

"There was a terrible storm and she barely survived. It was the turtles that pulled our boat to land, and the crows led us to a home in the forest. My mother died young – died of a still-broken heart. Every day she ached for her son, but Golan kept him and raised him in the Rugu way."

"Gulig is your brother?" Kaela asked, stunned.

Zeke stared at his grandmother, trying to digest the information, then whispered, "Golan was your father."

"Never knew my brother, never knew Golan ... never wanted to," Tazena said, shaking her head. "Golan threw the crystal ball in the ocean – since then the future's been in our heads – can't get rid of it."

Stennan kneeled and bowed low. "Ma'am, you are Rugu royalty. I knew Golan had a wife and daughter. We were told they died in a terrible boating accident."

"I'm so sorry, Tazena. I misjudged you," Kaela said, humbled to hear of the terrible suffering Tazena's family had endured.

Shawn listened with his eyebrows knitted in a pensive frown. He pushed his glasses up his nose and said, "If you are Gulig's sister and he's in prison, that means you are the rightful heir to the Rugu throne."

Stennan nodded. "Yes, she would be. It is well known that Golan had no other children."

Tazena scowled and stared at the ground, "I don't want to be no Rugu leader...." Then she looked up at her grandson, her eyes soft with love and quickly swallowed any more derogatory words about the Rugus. "Here's what I'll do. I give up the throne. I just want to go to my little home in the woods. My grandson ... he's the one would be a good leader – he's kind and strong and brave."

Kaela stared open-mouthed as she realized what it all meant. "Zeke?"

King Arendore frowned and said, "Yes, according to Rugu law the throne is passed to the next of kin. You cannot rule from prison. Does that fit your knowledge, Netri?"

Netri's clothes glowed blue-green and he nearly disappeared in the tall ganba plants. His smiling face shifted and turned from old to young as he nodded happily. "Yes, indeed. Zeke is the rightful heir."

"My son is a prince," Stennan agreed, smiling proudly.

"I-I-I-I'm a prince!" Zeke said, wide-eyed. "But I don't know anything about being a prince..." Zeke gazed at his father. "But maybe my dad could help until I'm old enough. I think the Rugus like him."

Kaela suddenly remembered Nedra, the Rugu woman who had been so kind to her. "King Arendore, I want to ask you something that would make Zeke's work easier. I need to ask you something on behalf of the many Rugus that helped us."

"After everything you have done for us, I would be honored to fulfill your wishes," the king said, and bowed to Kaela.

"Well, I don't think it was right for the Rugus to be thrown out of this land ... to lose everything. There are some really nice Rugus – some really brave Rugus that stood up to Gulig." Kaela thought of Zeke and Stennan, and remembered Nedra and the crowds of Rugu women outside the window who stopped the adoption.

"Yes, King Arendore. It's true," Shawn agreed. "There were lots of Rugu women that helped prevent a war.

Netri beamed with the pure smile of an infant.

"I think you should return the lands that were taken away from the Rugus. They should be able to move back to their homeland," Kaela said.

Janani agreed, "Arendore, what Kaela is saying is very important. I always told your father that he needed to consider letting the Rugus return to their homelands."

King Arendore hesitated as he weighed the options in his mind. Then he decreed in a booming voice, "If the Rugus will swear off drinking ganba and agree to a peace treaty, their lands will hereby be returned."

The pieces of the puzzle all fell into place in Shawn's brain. "There is one more thing – I think I know how to break the curse, once and for all."

"I already broke it, Shawn," Kaela said.

"I know, but this will set it in stone." Shawn stood and said solemnly, "Kaela, descendent of Gwenilda, and Zeke, Supreme Leader of the Rugus – would you be willing to marry each other?"

Kaela and Zeke looked at each other, shocked by Shawn words.

"What!" Zeke sputtered.

"A girl would be lucky to have you, but maybe it's time to let that agreement go," Kaela said kindly.

"Then do you release each other from the contract?"

"You should marry whoever you want, Kaela," Zeke said, blushing.

"And you too, Zeke...."

Netri giggled, "So then...."

Shawn declared, "The contract is now null and void – both our families are free!"

King Arendore chuckled, "Shawn, you are wise, and clever, too. Kaela, we can never thank you enough. Your kindness and bravery will never be forgotten. I promise I will work with the Rugus to find a way to live in peace together."

"Thank you, King Arendore. Thank you," Kaela said.

At that moment, a butterfly landed on Kaela's arm, and another fluttered to Shawn's glasses. Two butterflies flew into King Arendore's beard, and then yet another landed on Zeke's finger. Even Tazena smiled when a butterfly lighted on her knee. The air filled with whirling and twirling blue-green butterflies. The butterflies danced in the sky and then landed en mass until everyone was covered in beautiful iridescent Bagan butterflies.

Kaela held a butterfly to her ear and giggled. "I'll talk to him," she said softly to the butterfly. "King Arendore? There's one more thing...."

"What is it, Kaela?"

"I made a promise to these butterflies – these are the Bagan Butterflies. Long ago, King Muraten destroyed the ganba fields when he chased the Rugus from this land. If it weren't for the Rugus, these butterflies would have become extinct. Please don't destroy the ganba fields again – the butterflies need the flowers to live."

"Yes, I promise to keep the flowers safe," King Arendore said. "The Bagan butterflies will be a symbol of a new era of peace. We will make these fields sacred."

Kaela had kept her promises and resolved the contract, and soon she and Shawn would ride with King Arendore to the family castle. There was to be a huge banquet and celebration, but first she wanted to see her special friend. She held a hand over her eyes in the bright sunlight, searching for Kanu. He was nearly invisible, sunning himself in the tall grass, covered over with ganba flowers. She trotted away from the crowd, eager to spend some time with the giant tiger.

"Can I sit with you for a few minutes?" Kaela asked, clasping the butterfly pendant in her hand.

"Of course, dear red-haired girl." Kanu sat up and chuffed softly. "It would be my honor to keep you company."

"How did you know Gulig would bring me here, Kanu?"

"Actually, a little bird told me – your little friend, Peeper. The seer boy saw a vision of life or death in the ganba field. Mika overheard and followed me here."

Kaela stroked the tiger's head and leaned against his body. He was still terribly thin, Kaela noticed, and was suddenly struck with worry. "Kanu, how many lives have you had?"

"Why do you ask?"

"I want you to live for a long, long time."

"I'm afraid I have lost count. But remember, dear red-haired girl, I will always be in your heart."

"I love you, Kanu," Kaela whispered in his ear.

"I love you too." Kanu blinked, and one tear – then another – dripped from his large green eyes.

"Kanu, you cried *two* tears...."

"Well, I have two great loves ... you and Shawn."

Shawn quietly joined them and sat down on the other side of Kanu with Peeper nestled against his neck. He said softly, "We did it, Kaela. We went through the hole in the sky! And look at everything that happened."

"Thank you for coming with me, Shawn."

"Thanks for bringing me...."

Kaela cuddled in Kanu's softness and relaxed to the sound of the tiger's breath.

The butterfly pendant pressed against her skin, warming her hand. The tree songs grew louder and louder, drowning out all other sounds until a distant voice seemed to call, tugging at her heart. *Someone needs to be healed*, Kaela realized. It was time – time to return, time to go through the hole in the sky once again. The aroma of sea air filled her nostrils and she opened her eyes to find the little wizzen, Netri, reaching out his hand.

Chapter Thirty - One • The Ocean

"Get off," Shawn grumbled, pushing against Kaela. "You're crushing me."

Illuminated only by the full moon, Kaela and Shawn untangled themselves and stared at one another.

"What?" Kaela asked.

Shawn looked around as he pushed his glasses up his nose. "Where are we?"

Completely befuddled, Kaela stood up and clicked on the light by her bed. "Shawn, what on earth is going on? I had the most amazing dream – it was about the pendant...." Kaela reached for the butterfly necklace, and felt soothed as she wrapped her hand around the familiar shape.

"Kaela, don't you remember?"

"I don't know. I mean, how could it be?" Kaela muttered, her mind a dizzy whirl of fleeting memories.

"Shawn, get down here!" Shawn's dad yelled.

"You can't leave yet. We've got to talk about this," Kaela said frantically.

Shawn's father called again, "Come on, Shawn. It's time to go."

"I'm sorry. We'll have to figure this out tomorrow," Shawn said, rushing out of the room.

Kaela watched him go, thinking slowly. Then she sat down on her bed to pull on her pajamas. With a start, she realized that she wasn't wearing socks anymore. Where had they gone? She kept an eye peeled on the floor. Her things were always disappearing in the mess.

Knock, knock, knock...

"Can I come in?" Her dad's voice called.

"Sure, Dad."

Her father eased the door open and frowned as he surveyed the room. "What's been going on here? I thought you guys were studying quietly – but it looks like you've been tearing your room upside down."

The dirty dishes from under Kaela's bed were in clear view, and a bunch of her clothes were strewn across the floor. She blinked her eyes and stared curiously at a small pile of confetti lying near her foot. Kaela wasn't sure what to say. Her room was always messy, but not *this* messy. "Uhm ... well..."

"Are you getting ready for bed already?" her dad asked. "It's still pretty early."

"I've had kind of a long day."

"Well, come on then, I'll tuck you in." Her father folded back the covers and helped Kaela get settled under the sheets.

"Your hair is damp," he said, looking at her strangely. "And you're acting a little odd. Do you think you're sick?" He placed his palm over her forehead then smoothed back her red hair. "You seem like you might be a little feverish."

"No. Actually, I feel great."

Her father sat back and looked kindly at Kaela. He hesitated a moment and said, "I need to talk to you. I spoke to your gym teacher this evening."

Memories of Stephanie, the gym teacher and the principal flashed through Kaela's mind. *How could I have forgotten?* "Dad, it wasn't my fault. It was Stephanie ... she was picking on Shawn. It wasn't fair...."

"Kaela, stop, please. You're not in trouble. Your teachers are worried about you. Can I see the letter from your principal?"

"What letter? Oh right ... that letter. It must be in my clothes from school." She threw off the covers, and then she remembered Netri.

Pointing at the spray of confetti on the floor, Kaela shook her head. "It kind of got ripped up."

"The letter somehow spontaneously ripped itself into tiny pieces?"

Shame washed over Kaela at the stern note in her father's voice. "Yeah, kind of..."

"Oh sweetie, I've been failing you...." Her father slumped forward a little, setting his head in his hands.

Kaela threw her arms around her father. "No, Dad, no. You're the best dad in the world."

"That's kind of you, Kaela, but I know I haven't really been here for you. I am so sorry." He was quiet for a moment, and then said, almost in a whisper, "I need to tell you something, Kaela ... it's what your mother would want."

Pulling the golden shell out of his pants pocket, her father continued, "Is this yours? It was on the kitchen table."

"Isn't it beautiful? I found it earlier today on the locker room floor." Kaela flushed, realizing how gross that sounded.

"It is beautiful. When I saw it, I remembered your mother laughing with her red hair blowing wildly in the breeze as she ran along the shore at our wedding. She loved the ocean so much. I wanted to remember that time – so I listened in the shell, hoping I could hear the waves. Even in this tiny shell, I heard it – I heard the waves crashing on the beach." He held the shell to his heart and then placed it in front of her mother's picture on the bedside table.

"I love that sound too," Kaela nodded with a smile.

"The shell reminded me that it was time to give you something – something very special."

Kaela's excitement quickly clouded over with panic, and she desperately hoped that her father wasn't planning on giving the butterfly necklace to her now. The necklace was hidden from view hanging around her neck. How could she explain everything to her father?

"Wait, Dad, before you go on. I have to tell you something." Kaela's words rushed through her. "I did something terrible. Please don't be mad at me. I've been in your office. I wanted to be near Mom. I borrowed the necklace."

A wave of sadness passed over her father's face. He looked down at his feet, withdrawing into himself. Once again she had disappointed him, Kaela thought sadly to herself.

"Kaela, you should have asked me first."

Shawn yanked off his shirt and threw it in the laundry basket.

Cheep, cheep!!

Feeling around in the soft cotton of his t-shirt, Shawn discovered a tiny parrot stowed away inside his breast pocket. Suddenly, the memory of riding on the turtle's back to the hole in the sky filled him. When he had turned around to wave one last time to the crowd of well-wishers, Peeper's plaintive cry had nearly broken Shawn's heart. Peeper must have flown to him and crawled into his shirt pocket.

Stroking his back-feathers, Shawn said, "It's you, Peeper. You're my magic bird, aren't you?" Shawn kissed the tiny bird on the beak. "I love you, Peeper." The bright orange and green parrot chirped with happiness.

"Dad, I'm so sorry. But why did you keep her stuff from me? I loved her, too," Kaela said, near tears.

Her father gazed at the picture of Marisa, Kaela's mother, the love of his life. "Kaela, it wasn't my idea. Your mother told me to lock it up. She said you were too young. She said you had already been through enough."

"I don't understand."

"I didn't understand either. She simply said you were too young. She wanted me to wait to show you, to give you her things. I did what she asked me to do."

Tears flooded Kaela's eyes as she pulled the necklace from under her pajama top. "Here it is. I'm so sorry...."

Her father touched the pendant tenderly and stared off into space. "Your mother wore this necklace for years, but then she locked it away. There was something about it that scared her. I think it reminded her too much of the illness she had when she was young, but I never really knew...."

Big wet tears continued to fall down her cheeks as Kaela clasped the pendant in her fist, relishing the comfort of the familiar shape in her hand. "Dad, do you know where Mom got this?"

"I can tell you the story, as much as I know."

"I'd like that...."

"You know your mother was terribly ill when she was fifteen?" Her father began.

"Yes, I read about it in the diary," Kaela nodded.

"Your mother was so sick that everyone felt sure that she was going to die. She had been in and out of the hospital, and finally they brought in a nurse to care for her in this very bedroom. I have never told anyone this, but I'm sure your mother would want you to know."

"I had known Marisa most of my life," he continued. "Your Uncle Mark and I were best friends growing up. Marisa and Mark were twins, but Marisa was a part of the popular crowd - everyone wanted to be around her. Your Uncle Mark and I loved science and chess and setting off rockets and gazing at the planets. Your mother and I never really got to know each other until she got sick. Mark and I took responsibility for helping with her schoolwork and entertaining her when she was stuck at home all day."

"My feeling for your mother gradually grew as I realized what an amazing person she was. I had always assumed that everyone in the popular crowd was snobbish and mean, but Marisa was truly a beautiful, kind human being. In my eyes, she grew ever more beautiful, even when she lost all of her hair and the illness nearly consumed her. I fell madly in love with her."

"One day I came to visit, and her parents told me that she was too sick for company. She had a high fever and was in and out of consciousness. I begged them to let me spend a few minutes with her, realizing that I had never told your mother how I felt about her, and that I might never get another chance. They finally relented, and I went up to see her in this very room. This was her room, you know, when she was a child."

Kaela nodded.

"When Grandma and Grandpa left us alone for a few minutes, I sat by the bed and held her hand. I told her how beautiful she was and I told her it wasn't her time yet. Then I said three times, 'I love you. I love you. I love you.'"

"I sat quietly with Marisa for a few minutes more, and then her mother ushered me out of the room. Mark went in next, and then the miracle happened - Marisa opened her eyes and smiled."

Stunned by her father's words, Kaela imagined what it would be like to have someone who you thought was gone to come back to life before your eyes.

"There was one more miracle, Kaela."

"What, Dad? Another miracle?"

"Your mother fell in love with me – a nerd of a boy. Of all her options, she picked me."

"Dad..." Kaela scolded playfully.

"Love is always a miracle," her father said softly.

Kaela fell silent for a moment, then asked, "What did it mean when Mom wrote, 'The fire saved me'!?"

"Well, some people thought that her high fever created a strong immune response that put her illness into remission."

Kaela realized sadly that her magical dream had probably been nothing more than a dream.

"When she woke up, she was clutching the pendant in the palm of her hand – it seemed to have appeared out of nowhere," her father continued. "Mark swore up and down that he hadn't given it to her, but to this day I'm sure he did. I think he wanted her to think it was magic."

Staring at the pendant, Kaela remembered the ganba field. She closed her eyes for a moment and clutched the butterfly in her palm. The feeling was still there, the quiet generation of her breath in tune with the fields and the ocean.

"What did Mom say about it?"

"You mother told us an incredible story of a dream she had while she was under the influence of the fever. She remembered crawling to her closet and going through some kind of hole in the sky, and then she found herself in another world. Marisa said she couldn't remember everything, but she vividly remembered a great Queen who had cared for her, and a tiger. She said a handsome prince gave her the pendant just before she returned. Her most favorite thing about the magic world was when a little seer girl told her that one day she might have a red-haired daughter."

"Your mother wanted you more than *anything*," her father said quietly, holding Kaela's shoulders tenderly in his hands. "She said the Queen couldn't heal her entirely, and that she knew she was going to die. Then she spoke of getting trapped in a castle in the other world – a castle on fire."

"Marisa told us she visited an ocean of light, and the Great Spirit spoke to her."

"What did he say?"

"This is what your mother told us. 'The Great Spirit said, you are so beautiful. It is not your time yet. I love you. I love you. I love you'."

"But, that's what *you* said to her." Taking it all in, Kaela tried to put the pieces together. "What do you think it means?"

"Honestly? I don't know." Her father shook his head slightly.

Placing her hand on top of her father's, Kaela said softly, "Dad, I was there ... I was in Muratenland."

"Kaela, did your mother tell you that word?" Her father's eyebrows shot up.

"No, I never heard it until I went there," Kaela said, wondering if he believed her.

"You mother used that name," he explained, searching her eyes with his own. "I looked up the root of the word, for its meaning. 'Murat' means 'wish come true'."

An inner strength grew in Kaela as she held the pendant in her hand.

"Dad, I think maybe it's time for you to wear this," she said softly. "I think that this butterfly can mend a broken heart." She took it from around her neck and handed the pendant to her father.

"Thank you, but...."

He held it up by the chain and they watched the butterfly change from green to blue and blue to green as the pendant spun slowly in the dimly lit room.

Then he looked deeply into his daughter's blue eyes, and for the first time in a long, long time Kaela felt like he was really seeing her.

"Look how much you've grown up – and without my help. Sweetheart, you're old enough now to keep it," he said, handing it back to her. "When I look at you, I see so much of your mother – you remind me of her every day. I know she'd want you to have it. I've been so foolish." He brushed the hair from her forehead and said, "I'm sorry, Kaela. I know I've let you down. I've just been so sad. I didn't know how to make it okay for you ... I missed her so...."

"I know, Dad, I know," Kaela said. "Me, too."

With tears gathering in the corners of his eyes, he said softly, "I know you do. But I still felt so responsible. I wished that if I said, 'I love you' enough that she would live, but in the end it didn't work...."

"You know what I think, Dad?"

"What?"

"I think we are always together in our hearts. Whenever I feel love, like right now, she's here." Holding her father's hand, Kaela collected his years of pain and heartbreak in her palm like dried seeds that, when planted, give birth to beautiful new flowers.

The vines guarding his broken heart dissolved from the love in his child's touch. The sadness that had kept him from living receded, and he was filled with wonder at the beauty of his little girl.

"Something inside of me died along with your mother," he said realizing the truth. "But now, I want to start living again – really living and being with you, being a real father to you."

As Kaela crawled more deeply under the covers, a newfound safety and comfort filled her heart. Her father kissed her on the cheek and said, "Kaela, there is one more gift I have to give you. When you were born, your great-grandmother asked us to keep this for you."

Curious, Kaela sat up again as her father pulled a small, light blue package tied with a red silk ribbon from his pocket. "Your mother said you would understand its meaning."

Kaela stared at her father. "Who did you say gave me this?" she asked slowly.

"Your great-grandmother."

"Did I ever get to meet her?" Kaela's heart beat with excitement as she remembered the diary. *Could it be Gwenilda?*

"Yes, she was still alive when you were a tiny baby," her father smiled.

"What was her name?" Kaela asked.

"We used to call her Nana Wendy. In fact – it was Nana who named you. She visited us just after you were born. When she saw your head of red curls, she said, "It's Kaela, beautiful Kaela."

"Why? What does my name mean?"

"Kaela, keeper of the key. She was right, you know." He smiled. "You have the key to my heart."

Speechless, Kaela took the delicate package from her father. *Nana Wendy really was the same Wyndy – the princess Gwenilda.* "I don't know what to say," Kaela said. "This is beyond special. But why are you giving this to me now, dad?"

"I asked Wendy when I should give it to you. She told me I would know when it was time. I think you should take a moment by yourself to open it." He walked quietly to the door and turned in the doorway. Just before leaving, he said, "Kaela, it's the strangest thing. Does it smell like the ocean in here, to you?"

"Yes, actually," Kaela giggled. "I smell it too." It was the smell of seaweed mixed with live fish and ocean water. The aroma brought back memories of riding turtles and watching stars on the beach. As her father closed the door, Kaela ran her hand through her thick, damp mane, and something clung to her finger. A slippery black squiggle stuck to her index finger. *Seaweed?* She wondered.

Holding the small package in her hands, Kaela touched the softness of the light blue package – the paper had been handled over and over so many times before being wrapped that the paper became supple and worn around the edges. Gently tugging on the ribbon, Kaela opened the package. A piece of purple crystal lay nestled inside. One end of the stone was set in silver, so that it could be hung on a chain. Stroking it with her index finger, Kaela noticed tiny words engraved in the stone. She leaned over and opened the drawer in her bedside stand, fumbling around until she found the magnifying glass that her father had given her.

She held the crystal to the light and magnified the writing. It read, "*To Promises Fulfilled.*" It was the present that Zarenda had given to Gwenilda, Kaela thought to herself, astonished. It had to be. It just *had* to be!

Staring deep inside the crystal, an image of Shawn grinning at Peeper, who perched on his index finger, danced inside. Then she saw her own face, smiling, happy – so much like the pictures of her mother.

Kaela realized that her loss would always be there – a place of tenderness that was sometimes painful and sometimes comforting. But now Kaela understood her choice. Her ache could awaken into compassion and kindness, or it could harden her to this world and all the people in it. She carefully placed the crystal by her mother's picture and caught sight of the golden shell, which seemed to glisten with a soft light of its own.

Holding the shell to her ear, the sound of the waves meeting the sand washed over her. Kaela was captivated by the sound, visualizing the waves rolling over and over and up and down. Clicking off the light by her bed, Kaela crawled under the covers and held the butterfly pendant in her fist, the memory of crashing waves still singing in her ears. The softness of the butterfly wings moving up and down in her breath moved her to tears.

Kaela cried freely, tears dripping down her cheeks. Down and down they dripped, meeting her lips. She licked her lips, and then licked again – sweetness tickled her tongue. These were not the bitter tears that had dampened her pillow over and over when her mother died. These were tears of happiness. These tears were of joy – the beautiful joy of opening her heart to life and love.

Kaela remembered Zeke's good-bye,

"*Don't be sad Kaela,*" he'd said. "*This isn't good-bye. This is just the end of the beginning.*"

A crow cawed noisily just outside her window and lifted, with thick wing beats, into the night sky.

The Beginning

Epilogue • Dreams

A tiny figured approached Lorendale's cottage high on Mount Sankaria. Lorendale waved his arms in greeting and as soon as the wizzen was at his gate he bowed his head and said, "Netri, welcome. It is an honor for you to come to my humble home."

Netri bowed in return and exclaimed, "It is beautiful here."

Lorendale smiled. "Yes, I am quite happy here."

"How is your heart these days?" Netri asked.

"It is mending. Skyla, Arendore and I have all made peace with one another. They make sure I have every comfort. They have been to visit many times. It was difficult, at first, to see them together, but over time I found I was happy for them – happy to meet their beautiful child ... my nephew."

"And how are you caring for yourself, Lorendale?"

"My mother dotes on me," he smiled. "Do you remember Nedra, the Rugu woman who began the women's uprising? I offered her land and a home anywhere she wanted. Well, for now she wanted to live on Mount Sankaria with her sons. She wanted a chance to heal any hurt she may have caused. She said she wouldn't know what to do sitting around all day like a princess, so she insisted on caring for me."

"She and her two sons live down the road from here," Lorendale gestured. "She cooks and cleans for me, and the boys have been helping me put in a garden. We all like to hike up to the streams of Mount Sankaria for the healing waters." He paused. "Forgive me. I'm being a terrible host. Would you like to come inside and have something to drink?"

"It is such a perfect day – I think I would prefer to just sit here on this bench," Netri answered, raising his face to the sun and closing his eyes. "I have something for you, Lorendale," he continued with a small sigh. "When Wollan was sniffing around the castle to see if anything precious remained, he found something I think you would like to have."

Netri opened his fist and dropped a metal object into Lorendale's palm, a silver chain and pendant, completely blackened by the fire.

"It is a miracle that it didn't melt. What is this, Netri?"

"Don't you remember? Your mother gave it to you when you were young. She had one for each of you boys."

Lorendale burrowed into the recesses of his memory and examined the pendant. "Yes, I remember now. She told us the story of the butterfly. She gave us each a pendant. I wore it when I was a child, but then I decided it was too feminine and stored it in a box with some of my other childhood treasures. Now, look – it is blackened from the fire. I have ruined it." Lorendale felt a great sadness come over him – here before him was another piece of his past, destroyed by negligence.

Netri took the necklace. "No, sir, you are wrong. It has been through a lot, but it is not ruined. It can still be polished." Netri rubbed it against his pant leg. He rubbed and rubbed and even used a little spit. Then he rubbed some more. "Look, Lorendale – it will still shine."

"That is amazing, Netri. I can even see a little of the wing in there," Lorendale smiled.

Netri gently touched Lorendale on the arm and said, "You are like this pendant, Lorendale. You have been through the fire, but your heart is not black to the core. Underneath all that soot, your heart is as beautiful and perfect as ever."

The two sat for a moment, basking in the sunlight.

"Do you remember what you used to dream?" Netri asked.

"It's been so long since I had dreams," Lorendale sighed. "Whatever they were, it is too late for them now."

"It's true that as the years pass, our dreams change," Netri said thoughtfully. "Think about what it is you most dearly want, Lorendale. Create some happiness for yourself. It takes great courage to dream when you think you have lost everything."

"I will try, Netri. I will try." Lorendale closed his eyes and smiled. "Do you think we will ever see the beautiful red-haired girl again?"

"Yes." Netri's eyes twinkled. "I think one day. One day she'll join us again ... one day."

Cast of Characters

Anya is an elderly woman of the Tree Tribe. She was kidnapped along with Prince Eiren, and is his nanny. She is Clouda's sister.

King Arendore is the current King of all Muratenland. He is the elder twin brother of Lorendale and is the son of King Harrel (who is deceased) and Janani.

Ariala is a Butterfly Woman who teaches Kaela about healing.

Blanco is an elderly white horse who takes people inland after they are carried to the shore by the sea turtles.

Butterfly Women are healers who are able to go through the hole in the sky. They visit people who are ill and help them know the love and kindness of the Great Sprit.

Clouda is an elder of the Tree Tribe and Chief Leland's wife. She is also the mother of Skyla.

Eiren is the baby boy of Queen Skyla and King Arendore.

Eirendale was Gwenilda's younger brother and the second child of Muraten and Rhiana. He inherited the throne after Muraten.

Golan was King Grule's son and heir to the Rugu throne. Gwenilda was promised in marriage to him. He was the beloved son of the Rugu king, but became a cruel and violent man.

Gwenilda was the first child of Muraten and Rhiana, and heir to the throne. She was promised in marriage to Prince Golan.

Gannon and Gavin are the eighteen-year-old identical twin grandsons of the Chief of the Tree Tribe and Clouda. They act as bodyguards and guides to Kaela and Shawn.

Grule was King of the Rugus at the time of King Muraten and Queen Rhiana.

Gulig is the son of Golan and the current leader of the Rugus, and is completely dependent on the ganba elixir. The ganba vines have grown thickly up his arms and legs, and has wrapped around his heart until he can no longer feel love.

King Harrel was Eirendale's son (Gwenilda's younger brother). He was king of Muratenland and is deceased. He was married to Janani.

Ms. Halsey is the gym teacher of Kaela and Shawn.

House of Muraten is the royal family of Muratenland.

House of Rugu is the ruling family of the Rugus. They once lived in the northern lands. King Muraten expelled them from the land and the entire region became Muratenland.

Janani is an elder Butterfly Woman. As a young woman she left her tribe to marry King Harrel and birthed twin sons, King Arendore and Lorendale. After the death of her husband she returned to the work of the Butterfly Women.

Jake Neuleaf is Kaela's father, and is still lost in grief since his wife's death two years earlier.

Mr. Jones is the principal of the school Kaela attends.

Kaela Neuleaf is a thirteen-year-old girl who goes through the hole in the sky to break an ancient curse in Muratenland.

Kalik is a crow, descended from Krakaw. He appears at critical moments in Kaela's journey.

Kanu is a huge tiger. He was crowned King of the Wild Spaces by King Harrel, and is captured and tortured by Gulig.

Krakaw was a crow and was a loyal friend to Zella, the seer. He was raised in the castle where he learned to read and write. He had a fondness for jewels and gold.

Leia is the sea turtle that Shawn rides to shore after going through the hole in the sky.

Limba Trees are called Grandmother by members of the Tree Tribe and have a symbiotic relationship with the Tree Tribe.

Lorendale is the twin brother of King Arendore. He has been manipulated and imprisoned by Gulig.

Malana is one of two giant sea turtles that take Kaela and Shawn from the ocean to the shore after they go through the hole in the sky and land in the ocean.

Marisa is deceased and was Kaela's mother and Shawn's aunt.

Mark is Shawn's father.

Mika is the brother of Tressa, Gavin and Gannon. He is eager to prove his bravery and accompany Kaela, but King Arendore refuses to allow him to go. He is the grandson of Leland and Clouda.

King Muraten married the Butterfly Woman, Rhiana and is the father of Gwenilda and Eirendale. He is famous for expelling the Rugus from the land after they committed terrible atrocities.

Nedra is a Rugu servant in Lorendale's castle.

Netri is a Wizzen (see Wizzen) who appears in Kaela's closet and takes Kaela and Shawn through the hole in the sky.

Peeper is small parrot. He has an injured wing and is rescued by Shawn.

Rhiana was the first Butterfly Woman to marry a human. She was married to King Muraten and gave birth to Gwenilda and Eirendale. In order to have children she made a pact with Zella, the seer, and brought a curse on her family.

Shawn is Kaela's thirteen-year-old cousin and best friend.

Queen Skyla is married to King Arendore and is the daughter of Leland and Clouda of the Tree Tribe.

Stennan is a towering Rugu who is Gulig's valet.

Stephanie Rickenbarker is the leader of the popular kids in school, and is a bully.

General Taga is the top Rugu general and the head of the Rugu army.

Tazena is Zarenda's daughter. She has endless visions of the future which overwhelm her mind. She is Zeke's grandmother.

Tiger is an orange striped cat and lives next door to Kaela.

Tree Tribe is tribe of agile, athletic people that have a symbiotic relationship with the Limba Trees.

Tressa is a nine-year-old member of the Tree Tribe who greets Kaela and Shawn when they reach the Limba Tree Forest.

Wizzens are tiny beings and can travel through the hole in the Sky and live for many generations compared to humans. Netri is a Wizzen who acts as a guide to Kaela and Shawn.

Wollan is the King's dog. He accompanies Kaela on part of her quest.

Zara is Tazena's deceased daughter and is Zeke's mother.

Tribe of Zaren is an ancient tribe of seers.

Zarenda was Zella's daughter, and is deceased.

Zeke is Tazena's grandson who can see the future.

Zella was a seer at the time of Queen Rhiana and King Muraten who manipulates Rhiana and puts a curse on the House of Muraten.

ACKNOWLEDGEMENTS

I could not have completed this book without the much needed love, support and guidance of so many friends old and new. First I would like to thank Rives McDow of Sea Turtle Publishing for believing in me and seeing deeply into my heart, and the heart of this story. I am deeply grateful to Catherine Clarke for being a mentor, coach and editor early in my journey.

Thank you to all the people who worked with Sea Turtle Publishing: Katherine Navarrette and Joan Swan for their beautiful illustrations, Elena Trevino for her design expertise, Sarah Norton, Margarita Wuellner and Tina Murphy, the wonderful editors who helped hone my story-telling skills, Molly Duncan for her amazing work with the website, theholeinthesky.net, Francis Mesina for his speedy work laying out the book, Gerry Greenberg, Margarida Muniz and Topaz Jan Abbott for their help with final timing and a special thank you to Tony Greco for giving of his time to critique the book cover.

Many friends have read and reread this book and encouraged me to continue through the many years. I am deeply honored to have Reesa Porter as a friend. I have actually lost count of the number of drafts and versions she has read of this book. Lee Kennedy, Gillian Ehrich, Joan Dana, Joanne Touchton, Jan Korr, Theresa Ugalde, Barbralu Cohen, Jennifer Ramey, Leslie Potter, Peter Walsh, Hildy Armour, Sarah Larrabee, Nancy Weinstein, Marie Catherine Toulet, Jessie Wyard, Flora Schiminovich,

Susan Gregory and Fran Meneley loved kernels of beauty in this story and I thank all of them for their kindness and support. I am grateful to Sam Hannaway for sharing her humor and playfulness and to Wyndham Hannaway for his helpfulness. Merrin Stein deserves a warm note of gratitude for reading a very early, very rough version.

Thank you to Tim Newberg who always supported my desire to write and to Barbara Rossman who has been a great help in my life. I am indebted to Marcia Roettinger, a wonderful friend and fellow writer, for sharing what she knows about the craft of writing, and to Marietta Moskin whose expertise and input was invaluable and helped change the course of my writing.

A giant thank you to Constance Peck and Kathy Scrimgeour for their belief in me. I also want to thank Adam Engle for his honest feedback. Ted and Sally Barrett Page shared many delightful hours writing and laughing, and helped encourage me through the years of writing. Merry Witty and Jody Shevins have been like butterfly women in my life by offering love and kindness at times of great need.

The loving support of Robin Lowry and Juliette Wells has meant so much to me. I also want to thank the other women of the "women's retreat"; Christina Albetta, Johanna Saldyt, Mary Siegler, Marie Simpson, Cheryl Griffin, Joan Cram and Mary Hendricks for listening to my story, and for not getting too mad when I was in a post-surgical stupor and almost set the cabin on fire. The Santa Barbara slumber party friends: Debbie Johnston, Ben Cochran, Susan Stiffelman, Sally Gallwey, Lucy Taylor and Carlos Crespo listened to me read aloud like a group of eager children. I couldn't have asked for a better audience.

I want to express a warm thank you to some of my best critics and greatest supporters: Jesse Ditkoff, Christopher Kupka, Ben Morrison, Heather Truesdale and Olivia Ostlund. Also I want to thank Francesca Navarette who loved my very first version and Ricardo Navarette for his help and support. Also I would like to express a note of appreciation to Jenni Tierney and her dear daughters Makenzie and Jessica for offering me so much warm encouragement.

I am very grateful to the people of Hawaii for sharing their beautiful islands with me. In special moments when I least expected it the Menahune have teased me and helped me on my journey. I am grateful to Brad Griffin for giving me a truly special place to write on the Big Island. I also really appreciate the welcoming environment of Logan's, Vick's and Amante Cafes in Boulder where so much of my writing has taken place.

Dear Leif Newberg deserves many hugs for being such a loving son and sharing so much joy with me. I would like to honor my brothers: Andy Mahler for his love of our beautiful planet, and Tony Mahler for being a kind "big brother" when we were little. I am forever grateful to my mother, Annemarie Mahler, for her unwavering love and inspiration.

Finally I want to express my deep and abiding gratitude to Prem Rawat for his kindness and true friendship. He has helped me discover so much beauty in my heart – a simple beauty beyond my most wonderful dreams.

Barbara A. Mahler was amazed when the wizzen Netri showed up in her life. Night after night he woke her up and told her stories about a land on the other side of the hole in the sky. She wrote down his tales and the result is her first full-length novel. In addition to writing Barbara practices Traditional Oriental Medicine. She divides her time between her homes in Boulder, Colorado and Malibu, California.

———

Kathryn Navarrette lives in the mountains above Boulder, Colorado, with her son Leif, daughter Francesca, dog Shadow and cat Starbuck. Her inspiration comes from being surrounded by nature, family and friends. You may contact her at navaboys@gmail.com.

———

Joan Swan draws much of the inspiration for her art from the beauty of nature and the cultures and folklore from around the world. She lives with her adorable dachshund, Schnitzel, whose portrait can be seen on her website, Swanillustration.com.